# BINDING
# SPELL

*Books by Elizabeth Arthur*

———

ISLAND SOJOURN

BEYOND THE MOUNTAIN

BAD GUYS

BINDING SPELL

# BINDING SPELL

## Elizabeth Arthur

A BANTAM TRADE PAPERBACK

BANTAM BOOKS
NEW YORK · TORONTO · LONDON · SYDNEY · AUCKLAND

This edition contains the complete text
of the original hardcover edition.
NOT ONE WORD HAS BEEN OMITTED.

BINDING SPELL

A Bantam Book / published by arrangement with
Doubleday

PRINTING HISTORY
Doubleday edition published September 1988
Bantam edition / April 1990
Title page illustration by Mikhail Ivenitsky

Library of Congress Cataloging-in-Publication Data

Arthur, Elizabeth, 1953–
    Binding spell / Elizabeth Arthur.—1st ed.
        p.   cm.
    ISBN 0-553-34805-1
    I. Title.
PS3551.R76B56    1988c
813′.54—dc20                                        89-39534
                                                          CIP

Published simultaneously in the United States and Canada

Bantam Books are published by Bantam Books, a division of Bantam Doubleday Dell Publishing Group, Inc. Its trademark, consisting of the words "Bantam Books" and the portrayal of a rooster, is Registered in U.S. Patent and Trademark Office and in other countries. Marca Registrada. Bantam Books, 666 Fifth Avenue, New York, New York 10103.

PRINTED IN THE UNITED STATES OF AMERICA

CWO     0  9  8  7  6  5  4  3  2  1

## Binding Spell

is dedicated to Bundy, whose gentle heart
knew the secret of absolute loyalty;
to Heidi, who dwells in the reaches of separation;
to Minimum, who could well be a gift of the Goddess;
and to Pittsburgh, whose boundless optimism
and indefatigable spirit
have revealed to me the realm of the possible.

*For everything created*
*In the bounds of earth and sky*
*Has such longing to be mated,*
*It must couple or must die.*

*—George John Whyte-Melville*
*from "Like to Like"*

# CASTING
# THE CIRCLE

# 1

RYLAND GUTHRIE had the perpetual feeling that he was getting gypped. He believed this had started in his childhood, when his mother, in a utopian and also somewhat chicken-hearted attempt to give her two sons equal treatment, had unfortunately ceased to discriminate between them, giving each of them precisely the same amount of food for dinner—she would weigh everything, peas, steak, rice, pieces of banana cream pie, on an old-fashioned baby scale that she had used to weigh the boys themselves, as infants— allowing each of them to stay up until exactly nine thirty-five, by the alarm clock, presenting to each of them the same gifts for Christmas: sweaters, books, toy airplanes. If it was a book, it would be the same book; one year both brothers received *The Tin Woodman of Oz*, although Ryland's brother, Peale, never really understood fantasies. Another year it was a Tom Swift, with its sickeningly competent hero. The sweaters came in different colors, and for a long time in different sizes, but they were precisely the same design, and each was accompanied by a note saying that the sweater could always be exchanged. As Ryland was almost four years older than his little brother Peale, the effect of all this equal treatment was to make him feel he was one of life's losers.

After all, wouldn't "equal treatment" suggest that Peale and Ryland be given the same amount of food, the same book, the same toy airplane, when they were the *same age*, something that could of course never happen, that the universe had made impossible

3

from the first, unfairly forcing Ryland to be four years older than his brother so that everything would always seem askew? Oh, he was big, he was old, no doubt about it, and though, as a child, he never complained aloud about this unequal distribution of years, he brooded about it all the same, carrying his big old body from place to place, arranging its absurd bulk on his bicycle—exactly the same color as his brother's bicycle, though a slightly different size—stuffing his huge aging cells into the window seat of the library, letting his large, elderly twelve-year-old form wander where it would. But despite his awareness that, regardless of all attempts that might be made to give him equal treatment, he would always, no matter what, be an also-ran, he still appreciated his mother's regard for the underdog, and in later years he could not help but look for the equivalent of the baby scale or the bedtime alarm clock in all his dealings with the world.

His job as the manager of Saguanay's Furniture Store, the finest store in Felicity, Indiana—one that in its high-gloss elegance seemed to embody much that Felicity was otherwise not—made this conceivable, since all the ledger sheets and invoice forms provided the illusion of exactitude in his relationship to *things*, but as for people . . . well. He knew his concern was foolish, but it seemed to him that if the world order was so unsporting as to force everyone to be different, the least that human beings could do was to *try* to erase the distinctions. But most people didn't. Not at all.

When he was married to April, for example, she had laughed at his desire for fairness. He had thought himself the model of the liberated man, doing half the cooking, half the cleaning, earning half the money, and though April seemed resistant at first to the idea of charts, he had posted schedules on the kitchen wall outlining the week's duties for each of them. One week he would take out the garbage, the next week she would do so, and the clothes shopping program was outlined as well, season by season and with allowable price limits decided in advance. This had seemed to him so impartial that he was amazed when she had, five years into the marriage, objected, explaining to him one day with preternatural calm that she wanted a divorce, that she planned to take their son

4

Clayton with her unless Ryland wanted to cut him in half, and that she was tired, so tired she couldn't quite say, of being mistrusted. Mistrusted? Ryland had asked her, amazed, and yes, mistrusted, she had answered. He acted as if she were an employee who might be cheating on company time.

Well, they had gotten the divorce, naturally, and Ryland knew he was partially to blame. But though he was making strenuous efforts these days to understand that his prerogatives and victories did not have to be exactly the same as other people's in order to have equal worth, he was certain that, no matter what, he would always be troubled by his own body. Oh, people might tell him that he was good-looking, even handsome, that he was, if anything, small-boned and elegant; and it was true, perhaps, that his face was a nice face, with sweet eyes and fine cheekbones, framed by red-brown hair. But to him, his body would always seem too big, too old, and intent on continually causing him discomfort. In fact, every twinge, prick, smart, throb, sore, ache, and kink that he felt, as he moved from place to place trapped in the confines of this born-too-soon body, he felt justified in attributing to the unsportsmanlike tendencies of the universe and, as a consequence of his deep suspicion, was certain that each of these throbs, smarts, and twinges was only the harbinger of far worse pains to come. He generally resisted buying medical books to trace each pain to its logical scientific conclusion, figuring he would know soon enough the nature of his incurable disease, but he could not help speculating—heart trouble, lung cancer, leukemia, kidney disease, gallstones; nothing was too big or too small to come within the sphere of his consideration. Right now, as he stood on the ground floor of Saguanay's, talking to a new customer about a couch, the pain was located in his left testicle; total excision would no doubt be required.

But in a world and a body that were so unreliable, at least he had this store. People shopped at Saguanay's from as far away as Indianapolis, people seeking Turkish rugs, or Italian music boxes, or French enamel work, or Scandinavian crystal, and the store's reputation was such that customers' voices were lowered when they entered. Then, to *keep* their voices down, Ryland had placed in the entryway a reproduction of an eighteenth-century desk, crafted of rare East Indian sandalwood with tulipwood banding, authentically correct in every detail, including ebony inlays, polished brass drawer pulls, an intricately pierced gallery—and a price tag of ten thousand dollars. Here was excellence, here was perfection, here was one place where Ryland did not feel gypped; moreover, given the fact that at any moment his body might go into complete systemic breakdown, he took some perverse comfort from the store's history: Saguanay's had originally been a funeral parlor.

The most public evidence of this origin still extant was a thermometer outside the courthouse. COURTESY OF SAGUANAY'S FUNERAL HOME, it read at the top, and it always showed exactly seventy-two degrees, as if it had absorbed the proper civilized attitudes of the funeral home's owner and founder and—when it broke—had broken on a day when the weather was absolutely perfect, so that for all time afterward it could take pride in registering, contrary to all conflicting evidence, that the weather was perfect then, too, whenever that was, whether a blizzard had entirely shut Felicity down or a heat wave was ruining all tempers. And at the bottom of the thermometer, just below the bulb of what was undoubtedly dried red dye but which looked more like blood, viewers were advised to PHONE 27 FOR AMBULANCE SERVICE. Now, that was really courtesy, to be willing to provide the phone number of your own chief competitor, though Ryland thought that probably, medical science being what it was, a kind of elaborate pretense, the risk to the funeral home's business had probably not been as great as all that. Besides, if anyone had had to rush out of his house and up the courthouse steps to find out the number of the ambulance service, the chances were excellent that by the time he said, "Hello, Central?" the victim would already have expired. And then— then Saguanay's Funeral Home would have come into its own.

And what a place that Saguanay's must have been!—more homelike, Ryland was sure, than any dead person might reasonably have expected, at least in its later days, when the slow evolution from funeral home to furniture store was already well advanced, when couches and chairs and humidors had slowly replaced lifeless bodies. Perhaps seventy years before, Mr. Thomas Saguanay, returning to Felicity after a trip away and thus able to see his main viewing parlor with fresh eyes, had noticed that, although it had one table and one couch, most of its chairs were of hard wood and there was little welcome in its aspect. So he had ordered in a brocade settee and two small walnut lamp stands and, soon, two wing chairs and a Louis XVI table. Then, with the passion of a convert, he had moved from the likely to the unlikely as he had accumulated quilt racks, washstands, sideboards, crowding the parlors where the bodies were displayed until it was practically impossible to walk into the rooms, and the bereaved, rather than concentrating on their dearly loved and lost, had begun—whether they wanted to or not—to study the elegant furniture. Some had liked this, others had not—what did one want a dining table for in a funeral home, they perhaps had sniffed suspiciously—and eventually the supply of bodies had begun to dwindle, even as wholesalers arrived at the door in ever-increasing numbers, carrying bolts of silk from China, Tibetan carpets, glass cases full of stuffed birds, solid brass long-necked geese, and umbrella stands made of elephants' feet.

Finally, Mr. Saguanay had given way to the inevitable and had stopped receiving corpses altogether, putting discreet price tags on his furnishings. Sometimes, though, even today, as Ryland studied his little kingdom, each gleaming and expensive object in its place, he liked to imagine a body still laid out in state here, perhaps reclining on a Scandinavian couch, perhaps lying less comfortably but higher up on the twelve-foot-long cherry table made in France. The body would provide the perfect accent, the finishing touch, to a place that Ryland thought with pride already had the atmosphere of an Egyptian tomb—quiet, ageless, reverent, with the suggestion somehow that the molecular structure of the universe had been fixed forever here. "That body?" he could imagine saying to an interested customer. "Oh, absolutely, guaranteed never to change a bit. An heirloom to pass down to your children."

At the moment, though, his customer was not interested in bodies, but rather in where bodies could be put. As Ryland shifted from foot to foot in the vain hope that the pain in his testicle—

which was like a delicate forefinger poking him in the region of his large intestine—would shift to some other, less emotionally sensitive area, a vain hope, since, even if the pain *did* shift, it would immediately occur to him that he couldn't really spare his, say, liver, either, he said, with some surprise, "You gave away your old couch?"

"When it wouldn't fit through the door of my new place," the man agreed.

"I see. And it was a Henredon?"

"I think so. It hardly matters now, though."

"No," said Ryland, though he thought it mattered a lot. "What matters now is choosing you another, Mr. . . . ?"

"Dr. Minot. Richard Minot. What about that one over there?"

Ryland glanced at the chosen couch, then back at this Dr. Minot. A tall, lean man, with a jutting chin and prominent cheekbones covered by firm, tough skin, he had the distinct aspect of the aggressively healthy, and the glowing, fanatical eyes. He might have been about the same age as Ryland himself, but since he had clearly spent most of his life to date running—the muscles that stuck out of his shorts testified to that as surely as did the shorts themselves, not the sort of garment men usually wore in Felicity, not even on a warm April day—he had apparently not had time to realize the dangers that lay all about him. He was one of those people whom Ryland, even at the best of times, resented—people who never had mysterious pains, who were never suddenly sleepy for no good reason, whose stomachs never gurgled exasperatingly after a simple meal of salad and meat—and in the present circumstances, with that finger poking Ryland unmercifully, Minot's insensitivity to atmosphere and his disrespect for fine furniture made his physical health unbearable.

Furthermore, he had with him one of the most beautiful women Ryland had ever seen, a red-haired woman with an absurdly classical body; her legs were long and tapered, her hips were neatly curved, her stomach was flat between them like a canvas, and her breasts were perfect and full. She was wearing baggy blue jeans and a loose cotton shirt that seemed designed to conceal her figure, but the various parts showed through in any case—announced themselves, in fact. The woman showed no desire to participate in the conversation, or in the selection of a couch, but instead had fixed her green eyes sardonically on a four-hundred-dollar lamp. This Richard Minot certainly didn't deserve a woman as attractive as that—if, indeed, they were actually together, which seemed a little hard to believe. Only the fact that the man was a local kept Ryland from actually being rude to him, and telling him that if all he cared about was the *size* of his couch, he should shop at a different store. But Minot must teach at Powell College, a small Methodist school that had been founded in 1898, some years before Saguanay's Furniture Store began its final transition from funeral home, and Powell was well regarded throughout the Midwest—though the inhabitants of Felicity did not always share the Midwest's high opinion of the college, whose students tended to be litterers and to pee on bushes when drunk, causing the death of cherished plants.

"That would probably fit through the door," said Ryland. "But would the chintz complement your other furnishings?"

"I don't have a lot of other furnishings just now. And I need a couch within the month."

"Ah," said Ryland. "You're expecting guests?"

"Not guests. Visiting professors. From Russia."

This piece of information was so surprising that Ryland lost track of his pain. Despite the presence of Saguanay's, Powell College, and even Felicity Pond—famous throughout the region as an apparently natural limestone quarry—the town, with its population of barely five thousand, was hardly a cultural center. And though Ryland was aware that from time to time Powell had guests from foreign parts of the United States, he could not remember any professors from abroad, and certainly not from Russia. Although Felicity was, no doubt, as broad-minded as any small town in eastern Indiana, it had to be said that Russia was not high on its list of favorite countries. Of course, the imported furniture in Saguanay's was about as close as most of the town's inhabitants had ever been to the world beyond Felicity, but that did not discourage strong convictions. Ryland's personal suspicion that he was getting gypped by life rather subsumed any fierce forms of patriotism. Still, so thoroughly bewildering was the idea of real living Russians in Felicity that when Ryland spoke again, it was rather idiotically.

"Oh, so they'll be sitting on the couch."

Minot's gravelly face softened into an expression of amusement, and the red-haired woman looked up at him. Hurrying to correct the impression that he was a moron, he said, "It's an awfully cheerful design, you know. Perhaps you'd like something more somber?"

This did not, of course, improve things.

"They're not moving in. Not even sleeping over. They'll just be in town for three days."

Now Ryland really wished he *could* be rude, but he had never practiced the art. And at the moment, out of the corner of his eye, he saw his brother Peale strolling down the street. Saguanay's large front window—in which sat, at the moment, an Italian writing desk with a chestnut burl top and a full lead lamp imported from Denmark—looked out onto High Street, Felicity's main thoroughfare, and down this thoroughfare almost every one of Felicity's leading citizens passed at least once a day. Generally, this brought Ryland pleasure, but the pleasure was rather muted in the case of Peale, not only because Ryland had never made his peace with his little brother—which Peale had never seemed to notice—but because Peale had, five months earlier, been elected the county sheriff in a landslide victory the likes of which the county had never before seen, and since taking office he had made it a practice to drop in on Ryland every morning, for professional advice and reassurance. While Ryland did his best to provide these things, it was always with less than his full attention, as just being in the same room with Peale made him feel old and bulky and in imminent danger of getting gypped again. Peale had always, he thought, been better-looking than he was—tall, but not too tall, with lots of sandy brown hair that, even cut short, looked pleasantly lush, with dark brown eyes that had a friendly shiftiness, and with the kind of masculine grace that accompanied charm of manner—and these days, that khaki uniform and the gleaming five-pointed star that rode on its chest gave an exaggerated gloss to his attractions. Two years before,

Peale had married, just at the time Ryland was divorcing, and his wife, Amanda, was as annoying as he was, perfect and organized and pretty. Suddenly, Ryland just couldn't stand seeing Peale today, and he came as close as he could to being rude when he said to Minot, "Do excuse me. I have to go now. One of my assistants will measure the couch for you," and, signaling discreetly to one of his saleswomen, he headed for the back of the store.

There he paused. Could he risk going into his office for a minute, or should he just bolt for the alley? He had an eleven o'clock appointment to visit a woman who wanted the entire downstairs of her house redecorated, and as it was twenty minutes to the hour now, it was hardly stretching it to say that he had to go. But he knew that if Peale managed to catch up with him, there would be no leaving until he had answered Peale's questions. On the whole, he thought it safer just to bolt. He remembered the order, anyway; the address was 102 East Walnut. Tucking his chin into his collarbone, and thrusting his hands into his pockets, he pushed open the fire door with his shoulder and then slunk down the alley to his car.

There he had a momentary doubt. East Walnut, after all, was on the far side of town, the side where the poorer people lived, but West Walnut was, in general, one of the nicer sections of Felicity, with large two-story Victorians. West Walnut, in fact, could afford him; East Walnut probably could not. Consequently, he turned the car west onto High Street, taking the corner at a dangerously high speed in the hope that he could race by the window of Saguanay's without being seen by his brother, and thereby nearly running down both the red-haired woman and Dr. Minot, who had just left the store. Ryland gave Minot an apologetic look and tried to imply that he was tearing away to keep an appointment as important in its own way as the international concord Minot was arranging with the Russians.

When he pulled up to 102 West Walnut, however, he felt this had all been a mistake. Although indubitably of the same period as the charming houses that surrounded it, this one had a dilapidated, disheveled appearance, not really unattractive—the trellis leaned gracefully away from the porch, the grass was already rather long— but suggesting a real lack of funds. While it was inarguably the house on this street whose downstairs was most in need of rede- corating, and while it was possible, Ryland supposed, that its owner had just recently acquired the property and was still at the initial stages of renovation, it seemed more likely, all things considered, that he had come to the wrong address. But as long as he was here, he might as well ring the bell—or, better, knock, since the doorbell was probably broken. With a firm *rat-tat* he struck the graying panels. Then he folded his arms and waited.

As he had driven over here, the pain had returned to accompany him. Now it was waiting, and he would have to go to a doctor about it, that much was clear, and was, moreover, annoying, because he genuinely detested doctors, thinking most of them inhuman mon- sters and the rest jovial charlatans. But when a pain got so persistent that it was impossible to think of anything else, then the time had come for action, because, really, not even dwelling on all those people in the world who were far worse off than he—people without any legs, for example, or people dying of terminal cancer—seemed to help a whole lot then. At least those people knew the extent of their own problems; the possibility of *anything* seemed to him far more frightening, in its shadowy insubstantiality, than the reality of whatever. As long as your disease could be anything under the sun, the size and shape of your future indignities knew no bounds at all. You might have to stop eating solid foods altogether at the same time that your hair was falling out from chemotherapy, and all this while they wheeled you around without any legs. He let out a sad little groan, then knocked at the door again. *Rat-tat-tat- tat-tat. Tat-tat!* he added for good measure.

As he did so, a very small dog peeked out around the corner of the porch. Its silky, feathery ears were thrust out to the sides in a way that seemed to signal both curiosity and alarm, and Ryland, who was fond of dogs, made a soft clucking noise with his tongue; he knew how to be both inviting and gentle. His own dog, Molly— a border collie he had acquired six years before, when his house's previous owners had left her locked in the kitchen for a week after they moved—had been so traumatized by her experience that she had been, ever since, a little mad. But this dog looked deeply sane, contented to be itself, contented to be sitting here on its porch. No doubt this was his client's dog. He would present it to her at their meeting.

# 2

WHEN SHE first heard the knocking on the door, Bailey was totally flustered. She was right in the midst of casting a spell to attract love, and she had created a circle of sacred space that she couldn't step out of until the end of the ritual—at least, not without attracting dire consequences, the nature of which she wasn't sure about. She hadn't been practicing the craft for long—this was just her second month as an aspiring witch—and right from the start she had found it surprisingly hard to remember the various rituals. She had taken to propping her witchcraft book, *The Spiral Dance*, on a metal stand and setting it right on the altar, along with the athame, the wand, the chalice, and the pentacle. The cauldron—not a real cauldron, unfortunately, just a big blue pottery bowl with hand-painted flowers decorating its rim—was *underneath* the altar, and she wasn't at all sure whether that was the ideal place for it. But then, she wasn't sure that having the book on the altar was completely ideal, either. Still, with these invocations so damned hard to remember, the book would just have to stay there.

In order to cast a circle, you had first to invoke some spirits. These spirits were called the Guardians of the Watchtowers of the East and also the South, and then the West and North, and though Bailey had *almost* memorized the first three invocations in the two months she had been reciting them, the fourth one, the one about the North, was really proving a killer.

"Hail, Guardians of the Watchtowers of the North," it ran. "Powers of Earth, Cornerstone of all Power / We invoke you and call you, Lady of the Outer Darkness / Black Bull of Midnight /North Star / Center of the Whirling Sky / Stone / Mountain /Fertile Field / Come! By the Earth that is her body, send forth your strength. Be here now!" Bailey had always been a terrific student, though she had never tried particularly hard in school—indeed, she was now convinced that the trouble with her brother had started when she was six years old and had come home from first grade with straight A + 's; Howell, struggling hard, had never managed to get better than a C in his life—and in this matter, she thought her difficulty must be caused by the North itself, the direction of the mysterious and the unseen.

In any case, once the circle was created, time was supposed to become "elastic," a "swirling pool" in which to dive and swim, and since she had never before been interrupted in the middle of a ritual, she had never had to confront time's obdurate persistence in quite this way before. And the thing that was pretty annoying about this interruption was that, although she had purified herself with salt water and banished all unfriendly beings, she hadn't even started on the real spell yet, which involved making an herbal charm, and for which she had purchased a square of red satin, a piece of blue ribbon, a copper ring, and small quantities of acacia flowers, myrtle, rose petals, jasmine, and lavender. She had had to go all the way to Indianapolis for the pentacle—and even there it had had to be special-ordered!—but these flowers she had been able to get right at home. About five miles outside of Felicity, near Felicity Pond Woods, lived an herbalist named Ada Esterhaczy. In her eighties, the woman was reputed by many to be a witch, a reputation that was unfortunately unearned, as Bailey could testify, since the last time she had been out there, she had invited Ada to a small get-together for some women who might be interested in forming a coven, and Ada had laughed at what she called "such fairy business."

Now, as the knocking came again, Bailey plucked her book from its stand. She seemed to remember that there *was* something you could do if you had to leave the circle before the ritual was completed and the cone of power grounded, but what chapter was it in, and how was it done? And who could that be at the door? For a moment, it crossed her mind to wonder whether this visitor might have arrived already in response to this spell she was working, but that didn't really seem too likely. Come on, come on, where was it? Ah. If she wanted to leave the circle before the end of the ritual, she could cut a doorway in it with her athame.

She picked up her athame—a knife in a leather sheath that Howell had given her the year she was so gung ho on Girl Scouts, and before they had had their definitive fight about Christianity—and slipped it from its sheath. Her book recommended a sword for an athame, pointing out its dramatic properties for outside rituals, but she didn't presently have the money to buy a sword, and besides, she liked this knife. It reminded her of the era of her childhood before she had become "that damned Bailey." Now, she stepped over to the invisible boundaries of the circle, raised her eyes toward heaven, and slashed the air twice with the knife. Then she flung her athame on the altar and ran to get the door, dashing her fingers through her tangled, curly brown hair and hoping she didn't look too peculiar; she was wearing riding boots, evidence of her job at Grey Rock teaching and training horses, and also, among other things, an Afghani shawl wrapped twice around her neck. Actually, some people might have thought she looked quite peculiar indeed, since the rest of her outfit was a one-piece yellow jumpsuit, a Turkish belt cinching it in place, an outfit that emphasized her spareness, the flat, straight lines of her hips and chest. The living room, with the paraphernalia of witchcraft strewn about, wouldn't contradict the impression given by her clothes; but then, whoever it was need never see the living room. She wrenched open the door, and "Yes?" she said, breathlessly.

She liked the man who was standing on her porch, looking gloomy and bureaucratic. He was about ten years older than Bailey, thirty years old, perhaps, though there was an air about him that bespoke a longer and more painful life than was easily explained by his years; still, he was rather attractive, with crinkly eyes and a sensitive mouth. His hair—brown hair, with touches of red in its depths—

was carefully arranged so as to conceal a budding bald spot, and though his body sagged at the moment in a disconsolate manner, his clothes, a pair of tan pants and a navy blue cotton sweater, had a simple confidence about them that Bailey couldn't help but admire. It was odd, however, that he held a small dog—its head nestled underneath the man's chin, its front paws resting on his forearm—since he didn't look like the kind of man who would peddle dogs door to door. The man gathered himself together and said, "Ah, I'm Ryland Guthrie, from Saguanay's. I've come to reassess your furnishing needs."

"To re-assess them?" said Bailey.

"Yes," said Ryland, more sadly than before. "I may have come to the wrong house."

"Oh," said Bailey, stalling for time. "The wrong house? Not at all, not at all." She had, of course, ordered no re-assessment of her furnishing needs—indeed, such as they were, her furnishings were still in need of an original assessment—but she had a sudden impulse to let him in and not tell him the truth. It was so refreshing to see a male face that didn't have a baseball cap perched above it, a cap advertising one of several similar brands of farm machinery or fertilizer; Joel, the man she was presently seeing, must have had at least thirty-five of them. And while it was clear to Bailey that this Ryland Guthrie could scarcely be a potential lover—he looked too nice for that, since she was inexorably drawn to thugs, misogynists, or cretins—at least he could be, for now, company. And then, there was the dog. So she added, "Was it *this* morning? I don't know where my head is!" At which Ryland looked slightly more pleased.

When he had stepped carefully over the threshold, Bailey shut the door behind him. She realized suddenly that now she would be forced to reveal the living room, where, at eleven o'clock in the morning, candles and incense were burning, and where her unsheathed athame lay on the altar—an old table she had salvaged from her parents' barn—in the midst of the salt and acacia flowers. But she led the way out of the entry hall and through the small pocket door into the living room, stopping only when they were fully inside it. Then, side by side, they contemplated the scene in silence, the dog—still in Ryland's arms—seeming as saddened as Ryland himself as it, too, stared, bemused, at the scene.

A horse trainer's salary was not sufficient to procure a whole lot of interior decoration, and ever since her parents had died the year before, Bailey had been saving to leave Felicity. So, in actual fact, not a single thing in the living room had been purchased or selected, but all of it had been scrounged, more or less gracefully from one farmer's barn or another, as a result of which a faint odor of cow had moved into the apartment with her, and it often seemed to Bailey, imaginative as she was about such things, that cow spirits were looming mournfully over the edge of the old truck seat that served as her couch, or trying to graze hopefully on the stem of the old standing brass floor lamp, black with age and lack of polishing, that rode over the shoulder of the truck seat like a large bird on a small perch. She swept gracefully and simultaneously into action and speech as she blew out the candles, brushed the salt onto the rug, and shoved the pentacle under the altar cloth.

"Looks like some kind of weird ritual, doesn't it? That's what I need some advice on. These candles, this chalice . . . I could really use some professional help."

Ryland seemed, Bailey thought, to agree with her, though at the moment he was at a loss for words. He kept shifting from foot to foot, opening his mouth as if to speak, and then closing it again, unused. He looked at her, and then down at his dog, and then up at the room again, and after a while Bailey wished he would get on with it; she couldn't spend the whole day watching him meditate. A week from Friday she was expecting seven women over for the celebration of the full moon—or not really the full moon, as the full moon fell this time on May 1, a Sunday, and since it would have been quite futile for her to try to get anyone in Felicity to come out for such an event on a Sunday, Bailey had settled for an *almost* full moon—and this afternoon she was planning to go out to the farm to ask Howell if she could have the old black cauldron, the one their father had taken to country fairs. The visit wouldn't be fun, but she really wanted the cauldron; she wanted to make just the right impression on the women when they came. It had been hard enough to find seven women in Felicity who were willing to try such a thing even once, and unless everything went perfectly next week—something that few of Bailey's plans could ever be accused of doing—she would have wasted all her work. As it was, she had been unable to come up with the requisite thirteen, and that after weeks and weeks of thinking; though Felicity had a population of five thousand, presumably only about a thousand of those were adult females, and Bailey was by now certain that 993 of those females would have advised her to see her physician—in Felicity, physicians were still thought to be the most appropriate people to approach when one was struck with mental illness—if she had suggested to them, as she had finally suggested to her expected seven, that they might be interested in witchcraft. There must be somewhere in the world she could go to escape these lead-headed Christians!

But now Ryland had broken into speech. "The budget?" he asked. "In round figures?"

"The budget?" said Bailey. "You mean the total? Well, whatever it takes, I guess."

She had expected this to be good news to her guest, and, indeed, he seemed to perk up now. He bent over to set the dog on the floor, and then began to walk slowly around the room, tapping a pen on a pad of paper and studying the walls and floor. As he walked, lifting his feet high as if to avoid yet-unpurchased furnishings—and also perhaps the little bits of clothing that lay on the floor here and there—he proceeded to probe her tastes: Did she want country estate? French provincial? English manor? Luxurious town house? Feminine, he assured her, was in again these days, if she wanted the feminine Romantic. For that, he could recommend, as a focus, a chair he had just gotten in, adapted from an original nineteenth-century design, a traditional eight-way hand-tied chair upholstered in mauve damask, with the gracious ornamentation typical of the period: braid tassels and button fan-pleating on the arms and wings. No? The country look? Ah. For that, he envisioned as a centerpiece a beautifully carved French armoire in the entryway. On the hearth, a wooden sleigh to hold the birch logs.

"And here, I think, a writing desk with a traditional library lamp in leather and brass. Green leather," said Ryland, apparently to himself.

Now that Ryland was happily occupied, Bailey could get acquainted with his dog. It wasn't a particularly pretty animal, at least not at first sight; its eyes were a tiny bit bulbous, and its tail had been unkindly chopped off. But it had an unwinking gaze, both friendly and curious, and it hadn't made a noise since it arrived.

"You want an egg? I have a nice fresh egg."

The dog came closer and licked her hand.

Bailey loved all animals, really much more than she loved any people. Dogs and horses were her special favorites, but she also had feelings for cows. When her parents had been killed in a car crash the past August, Bailey had long been sleeping in an outbuilding at the farm—she had moved to an abandoned chicken coop when she was a sophomore in high school—but she'd been visiting the main house, watching TV that night with Howell and his wife, Charlene. From the living room, where they sat, they had actually heard the thunderous crash and splinter of metal over the sound of the program, a TV movie, and Bailey, who had been weeping quietly over the way that the sculptor was so brave when he found out he was never going to be able to sculpt again, had not been able to shed a tear when she and her brother went outside to see the twisted wreckage of their parents' car, smoking upside down in a ditch, its headlights still on, and a lot of bewildered cows standing around in the twin beams, mooing and looking sympathetic. When she finally cried, she had cried for the cows, several of whom had been injured.

She had not been able to cry at the funeral, either, though everyone else had managed it. Great-aunts and -uncles, neighbors who had rarely even talked with Ezra and Eliza Bourne while they lived—all had wept decorously, some of them quite copiously, while Bailey had sat there, again dry-eyed. Only at the last minute, when they had left the church and gone to the cemetery, had she at last been able to summon up some tears. Although it was a rare occasion when Bailey didn't find something on TV to cry at (on film or in the theater, any display of human fortitude or compassion affected her greatly), when there was a choice, it was animals she felt for, animals she had no ambivalence about. When a volcano had erupted in Colombia several years earlier, and the resulting mudslide had wiped out a whole city, the pictures of the dazed survivors had left her relatively untouched, but when they had shown pictures of dogs and cows, completely covered with mud and unable to negotiate the slippery ground, their poor lost eyes looking out at the camera in desperate appeal, she had been haunted by them for weeks. Animals, she was convinced, had souls; humans she had never been so sure about.

And animals made her feel wanted, gave her a sense that she belonged—gave her *connectedness* to the world, in fact, which was what she had always been after. Certainly she had never belonged to her family or her family's hopes and values. Indeed, for as long as her memory reached back, she had wondered if she were a Martian. While Howell had, at an early age, trudged off after their father as he made his rounds in the barn, attaching the long sucking hoses to the cows' udders, washing down the concrete floor with powerful bursts of water, she, Bailey, had been watching from the woodshed, pretending that she was a spy. She had coerced other young girls from surrounding farms, and some of the young boys, too, to play these imaginary games with her, had persuaded them to take a rest from their normal pastimes—like hitting snakes with sticks—and to join her as she imagined she was a Confederate deserter, hiding out in a friendly hayrick.

One of her favorite games had been called Jail, and in this, she and her companion in illusion had alternately been jailer and jailed, and would simply sit for fifteen or twenty minutes, on either side of a carelessly rigged barrier of some kind—a ladder-back chair, a tarp attached to a beam—and imagine that the one had power over the other, that the other was unable to escape. Generally, the child who wasn't Bailey had prepared for this boring vigil by bringing a toy to play with, but Bailey herself, who far preferred the role of the jailed, would pass in the allotted time through all the stages of imprisonment, from incredulity, to depression, to anger, to acceptance, and as she, in imagination, was marched off to her execution, she would hold her head up proudly and say a few noble words on the scaffold while the other child watched her in alarm.

All this did not sit well with her parents. They liked a child who was alert, of course, but just alert enough to run a farm, and though they gave her her own little garden plot on her seventh birthday, and a tiny piglet on her eighth, she didn't take to the care of plants or animals in the way that they had planned. The garden plot she turned into a tiny corral for wild mustangs, and she would spend hours there building miniature, ramshackle fences and plotting ways to lure the mustangs into them from the canyons beyond so that she and the other outlaws could break them and use them in the robbing of trains. Realizing at some point that the poor mustangs, when caught, would resent the dry bare ground of the corral, she had carefully transplanted some moss so that they would have food to eat and green to rest their feet on, but away from the banks of the creek where she had dug it, the moss had quickly died in the sun—and when Bailey came out to discover this, she found all the poor mustangs dead too. So she dug a mass grave for the horses— her mother, watching from the kitchen window, apparently thought that she was finally preparing the ground for a potato bed, because she had called out at this juncture, "A little deeper. Roots like plenty of room"—and after shoveling the tiny horses sorrowfully into their grave, had wept on the fresh-turned earth.

Oh, and all that had just been the beginning of her unsuitability to her life. The pig, when he arrived, turned out to be so delightful that she would smuggle him food from her own plate at every meal, concealing it in her napkin, which she in turn thrust down into her pants, and then she would sit with him while he joyously consumed it, engaging him in long conversations. As he grew bigger, his ears— which were attached to the top of his head like floppy upside-down grain scoops—started to sway every time he moved, and he would sit on his haunches, his little trotters folded in, with a big smile across his face. Naturally enough, before he could be slaughtered, Bailey had released him into the woods. She missed him terribly but had never seen him again, though sometimes she still went looking.

Now here she was, twenty, still stuck in Felicity, casting probably pointless spells.

The little dog's tongue was tiny and agile and had gotten to work on her wrist and arm.

"You're a sweet one," she said. "A pretty sweet dog." At this, the dog leaped into her lap. It nestled itself in her arms, getting thoroughly comfortable and then thrusting its head up so that the silky top of its skull was pressed firmly to the bottom of her chin. She discovered that it was a female, and she kissed the top of its head, wondering when, if ever, Ryland would be done. Why, really, had she let him in?

At that moment, he looked up and nodded encouragingly and approvingly.

"You have very nice space here. Good light." he said.

"I do?"

"Absolutely. We can do a lot with this. Shall we go over some preliminary plans?"

"Why, all right," said Bailey, starting to feel a little bit guilty.

"Fine. I'm sorry, but I've forgotten your name?"

"It's Bailey. Bailey Bourne."

"Miss . . . Bourne, then. Shall we look at it?" Then, standing right in the middle of the circle of sacred space, he went over his initial furniture list, briefly but point by point, while she and the dog listened with polite interest. When he was finished, Bailey said, "Um, listen, I'd better tell you . . ."

"Don't bother," he said. "I think I can guess. It's really my fault anyway."

"If I ever have money . . ."

"That's nice of you to say. Well, here's your little dog, anyway."

"*My* dog?" asked Bailey. "Isn't that *your* dog?"

"No. My dog is much larger and insane."

"How weird," said Bailey. "Where did you get it?"

"It was sitting on the porch when I arrived."

The dog looked at her calmly, its head to one side.

"Do you want me to put it back there?"

"No, no, just leave it. Maybe it needs a home."

"Ah," said Ryland. "Well, thank you."

Bailey accompanied Ryland to the door and shook his hand in final apology. She watched him leave: on emerging into the outside world he seemed to slump around the shoulders slightly, and he shook his left leg with an odd little jerk, as if something had fallen down inside his pants. But as he went down the walk, he turned to wave, and Bailey waved back with vigor. Then she took a deep breath of the lovely April air and went inside with a sense of satisfaction at the unexpectedness of the encounter. In a little while she would have to ruin her mood by driving out to the farm to talk with Howell about the cauldron—she could never keep her temper around her brother anymore—but in the meantime she'd finish her spell to attract love, and play with the little dog. She thought she would name it, oh, maybe something like Chance.

"Hey, Chance. Here, Chance." The dog came running over. "Chance, do you want to live here with me?" At this, the dog jumped expectantly onto her knees, as if answering her question in the affirmative. And so she picked it up and held it while she lit the candles, and then, checking her book's chapter on the Cone of Power—"The universe is a fluid, everchanging energy pattern, not a collection of fixed and separate things. What affects one thing affects, in some way, all things"—she picked up her wand, held it above her, and began to chant aloud. The last words of the chant this time were "Spell, make it so," and Bailey felt a marvelous sense of warmth flow through her at the knowledge that she, Bailey Bourne, had just found a dog, and that now she was casting a spell. She felt, at this juncture, a wild sense of hope: "Spell, make it so! Make it so!"

# 3

HOWELL clasped his hands together in front of him and thanked God silently for lunch. For some reason, God had always looked to him a little like Kirk Douglas—cleft chin, square jaw, stern eyes—and now, as God acknowledged Howell's thanks, He put the tip of His finger into the dimple on His chin and, furthermore, seemed to wink. Howell pretended not to notice, as he bit into the grilled tuna and cheese sandwich Charlene had just set down, but he *had* noticed it, all the same, and he thought it was pretty undignified. Howell liked to have a little fun as much as the next man—he certainly wasn't self-righteous; still, all around Indiana these days farmers were getting letters that began, "Dear Borrower: As you well know, your loan is seriously delinquent," or, from the less polite banks in the state, notices that simply announced LIQUIDATION, and it seemed a strange time, to say the least, for God to be so filled with levity. Howell was not himself in danger, at least not from any bank, but he took the plight of his neighbors to heart, which was more than God seemed to do. Resolutely, he put the wink out of his mind and continued his discourse with Charlene.

"It just makes sense, that's all there is to it. That it's an international conspiracy of Bankers. CONSPIRACY, it's right there in the word. Just like on the open seas."

Charlene, who was at the best of times a woman of few words, and who at the moment had dropped down onto her knees in front of the stove to wipe its door, murmured only a sound that sounded like *uumph,* but she did it with an inquisitive intonation, and Howell was encouraged to continue. He had beside him on the table a pamphlet he had picked up from his church, a pamphlet entitled "Billions for the Bankers, Debts for the People," and now he con-sulted it again.

"Yes," he noted. "And it started with the Federal Reserve Sys-tem. They've got it so our government can't issue money, only this private corporation can issue money, and they charge our govern-ment usury—which the Bible forbids—until the government is *trillions* of dollars in debt."

"*Uumph,*" said Charlene resignedly, climbing back up onto her feet.

"*And* here's what's interesting,," said Howell. "They only *say* they can't just issue money, money without anything to back it up. But lots of governments have issued debt-free and interest-free money in the past, and those governments have been the most powerful on earth. Germany was one of them. In 1935 they pulled themselves right out of the Depression that way."

Here, Charlene surprised him. "But was that good?" she said. "I thought they were the Nazis." And this was so to the point that Howell was surprised he hadn't thought of it himself.

"Yes, that's true. But they didn't *have* to be the Nazis. Because Mandarin China was another one, it says."

"Oh," said Charlene, putting some water on for coffee. "Well, that was a long time ago."

It took Howell a minute to regain the thread of his thoughts after this strange disagreement. But, luckily, he hadn't lost his place, and now he read on to discover that the banks—or the international conspiracy behind them, which, though they didn't exactly say this, no doubt involved every Communist country in the world—wanted to put all the farmers and working men in the United States into debt so big they could never get out of it. The conspiracy was of such tremendous proportions that a whole lot of Americans had to be in on it, too, and those included all newspaper publishers, text-book writers, union leaders, TV newsmen, church ministers—church ministers?!—professors, and politicians. So-called economic experts wrote syndicated columns in hundreds of newspapers, craftily designed to prevent the people from learning the simple truth about their money system. Commentators on radio and TV, preachers, educators, and politicians blamed the workers and consumers for the increase in debts and the inflation of prices, when they *knew* that the cause was the debt-money system itself.

Why, this thing was big, bigger than most people suspected, and Howell felt lucky he'd even heard about it! Of course, he'd always known there was a conspiracy of some sort going on in the world; he just hadn't seen where to look for it.

Howell, in fact, had always felt aggrieved at the way They controlled things—and lately, with farms going under night and day, he had felt more aggrieved than ever. As a farmer, he was expected to understand so many things—nitrogen fixing, pre-emergent versus post-emergent fertilizers, methods for dealing with rootworm and cutworm—and on top of those, so many others, like banking and economics. Luckily, his father had been turned down for a loan in 1978, when he wanted to increase the size of his farm by two hundred acres—his health had been bad enough so that the bankers hadn't wanted to risk their money on a man who might drop dead any minute—otherwise Howell's farm would probably now be in danger, or even already foreclosed. But he now felt in danger of a different kind, danger from another direction. When his parents had died, it was discovered that they had somehow failed to make a will, and thus, under law, Howell and his sister had inherited the farm together. Though Howell had explained to Bailey he was sure their parents would have wanted him to have the whole farm anyway, since she had no interest in farming, all the ready cash had gone to pay the estate taxes, and all that was left was the land and the machines. Lately the bane of Howell's life was knowing he had to share them with his sister.

And here was the explanation, right in black and white, and simpler than just about anything. All that America needed in order to be prosperous again—and for Howell to get rid of the Bailey threat—was to cancel all debts as of this minute and restore the money to the people. It would seem nobody could argue with such a sensible idea—America had been *built* by the people, after all—but the trouble was that when some few patriotic people or organizations who knew the truth began to try to expose the bankers or any of their mad schemes, they were ridiculed and smeared as "right-wing extremists," "superpatriots," "ultra-rightists," "bigots," "racists," and even "anti-Semites." Any name was used that would cause them to shut up or at least stop other people from listening to the warning they were giving. Articles such as the one Howell was now reading were kept out of schools, libraries, and bookstores—all of them in on the CONSPIRACY.

Howell knew he should be getting on with his work; his combine needed some tinkering. Every day when he got up he made himself a schedule of things to do, and for today, Wednesday, April the twentieth, he'd put down "Work on combine." He was just about to put his pamphlet away—a slow reader, he had gotten used to its taking days for him to get through a piece that interested him—when some questions caught his eye, and he read them aloud to Charlene: "Is it possible that your grandchildren will own neither home nor car, but will live in 'government-owned' apartments and ride to work in 'government-owned' buses (both paying usury to the Bankers)? Will they be allowed to keep just enough of their earnings to buy a minimum of food and clothing while their Rulers wallow in luxury? In Asia and Eastern Europe this is called Communism; in America it is called Democracy."

Charlene had by now finished the coffee and set a cup in front of him. The twins, having devoured their lunch, had been playing quietly in the living room, but they now let out some quiet shrieks, as if to register their own protest at the fate of their future children, and Charlene paused for a moment, torn between her duties: should she answer Howell or go? Howell nodded at her to go—the questions were fairly rhetorical, anyway—then took a sip of his coffee, noting, as he peeked ahead to the end of the pamphlet, that the international financiers who seemed to have America almost completely within their grasp were afraid of only one thing—an Awakened Patriotic Citizenry, Armed with the Truth, and with a Trust in Almighty God for Deliverance. Here Kirk Douglas appeared again in Howell's head, this time looking suitably impressed; together they read the final words: "This pamphlet has given you the truth about this iniquitous system. What you do with it is in your hands, as in the hands of Divine Providence. The fear of man bringeth a snare: but whoso putteth his trust in the Lord shall be safe (Proverbs 29:25)."

This was a little confusing to Howell, as indeed were a lot of such messages. On the one hand, it seemed to be saying that you didn't have to do anything except believe in God and He would take care of the rest; on the other hand, there seemed to be a strong implication that you'd better take action yourself. Howell had always been more inclined to the latter belief; it seemed to him that if God hadn't wanted Man to take things into his own hands, He wouldn't have given him hands to begin with, and while many churches around here inclined in their Sunday preachings to the belief that faith was the only thing that mattered, Howell liked doing things, and he didn't see why he shouldn't. He always had goals and projects.

Of course, he wasn't saying that these goals and projects helped God in any way—that would be ridiculous—but they made Howell happy, made him feel he was worth something, and just having faith alone didn't. Thinking of this made him remember his combine and all the other pleasant little tasks with which he planned to fill his afternoon. Lunch finished, he went outside, and forgot all about the CONSPIRACY.

The air was soft this afternoon and the sky was utterly blue. While the smell of lilacs filled the air, it was just beginning to be planting time in Indiana; though they had now had almost six days of warm weather, not only was the frost still coming out of the ground after an unusually late winter, but there was always the chance there would be another frost before summer really arrived. So Howell, along with most of the other farmers, was waiting: waiting a week for the ground to dry out, waiting two weeks for planting to be safe, waiting, with a delightful expectancy, for the start of the new planting season.

Howell loved planting. He loved letting the seeds fall behind him like a meteor shower. He loved that first morning in May when the tiny green plants, thrusting their tips up through the soil and into the air, looked like a rash the earth had acquired overnight— a huge puzzling patch of green with which it had been beset. He loved the hot midsummer nights, when, lying in bed next to Charlene, the window open beside him, he would strain his ears in the perfect silence and literally listen to his crops grow. They made a strange, tiny, rustling noise, like insects tapping on a wall. And he loved the harvest, when the combine, charging down the fields like a personnel carrier, gathered in the army of golden stalks that had been, it thought, so victorious. What a satisfying grinding sound it made as the fields were bared and chopped and assembled! The whole process was a process of victory, of the transformation of matter.

Animals were not quite so simple, though in their own way also pleasing; they were universally wrong-headed and perverse, but Howell knew how to deal with them. They didn't know what they wanted, ever, so Howell helped them to find out. He felt they appreciated this help profoundly, and trusted their lives to his hands. Sometimes, to his surprise, he found himself regarding them with wonder, but this would always remind him of Bailey and her crazy theory about souls. When he watched a mother cow, for example, her flat bony face splotched with brown, her ears sticking out quizzically from the sides of her head like small paddles that had slid down from the top, carefully licking her calf all over, her tongue huge and rough and almost indescribably gentle, he would feel a catch of affection in his chest so enormous that it compared with nothing else in his experience—nothing he had felt toward another person, nothing he had felt about himself. But this was so clearly dangerous for him, both as a farmer and as a Christian, that he would resolutely turn away from the sight and address himself to an unpleasant task. Most of the time, he was able to maintain toward his animals the proper balance of concern and detachment that was his duty as a person, and if he sometimes slipped and lost himself in wonder, no one need know it but himself.

Out at the barn, he greeted the coon hounds, who were chained, as usual, to their stakes. They had been part of the farm now for six years, ever since the day Howell's father had brought them home, as pups, and had driven the stakes into the ground. Howell had been allowed to name the male, and he had chosen the nice, sensible name of Jake, but Bailey had gotten to name the female, and she had chosen the outlandish Samantha. No one, of course, except Bailey herself had ever called the dog this; they had shortened the name to the serviceable Sam and done their best to forgive Bailey's mistake. Sam dropped a litter of pups two times a year, and it was just about time now for her first. Howell loved the regularity of her production, and patted her on the head in approval. Now, while she strained at her chain and howled with joy, she seemed to be looking past him; Howell turned around to see, to his horror, Bailey's car turning into the driveway.

Immediately, Howell turned away and walked rapidly toward the silos. He had a vain hope that if he appeared to be occupied, Bailey would go away without bothering him. But Howell saw his nice afternoon vanishing in a cloud of car dust as Bailey drove straight across the barn lot and pulled to a stop beside him. Then she clambered out, looking at him with piercing directness, and said, "Hi, Howell." Though Howell tried not to look at her straight on, he couldn't help but see that her outfit today was as bizarre as always, a jumpsuit sort of thing with foreign-looking belts and shawls draped around it at all kinds of unlikely angles, and sneakers on top of bright purple socks. Why, she didn't look like a Midwesterner at all; she looked like one of those people who lived out in California or someplace—and to Howell, people who looked as if they lived somewhere far away were as untrustworthy as people who actually *did* live far away. Or almost so. There were no two ways about it: from the moment she was born, those intense, skeptical eyes alarmingly large in her face, that short brown hair, already curlier than hair should ever be, plastered to the soft spot on her skull—from that moment to this, with hardly a moment's respite, Bailey had been a trial to him. It seemed to Howell incredible, really, that she should be a Bourne at all, and he felt quite certain that if L'Hommedieu Bourne, the great-grandfather whom he had always been proud to resemble—a very dark and smoky portrait of the old man, which hung in the upstairs hallway of the house, seemed to suggest that he and Howell shared a determined stockiness of shoulder and chest, a resoluteness of chin and nose—if L'Homme-dieu Bourne were still alive, he would simply deny the relation. Bailey was so emotional, so disrespectful. She was just an embarrassment all around.

"Hello, Bailey," he said in response. "What brings you out to the farm?" He tried to fill this brief question with all his conviction that it could be nothing good and that she should leave as soon as possible, but she had gone immediately over to Sam and was down on her knees, scratching the hound behind the ears, shaking her paw, and making soothing remarks that Howell couldn't hear, since Sam hadn't yet stopped howling. When she did, Bailey got to her feet and said, staring straight at him in that way she had, "Howell, they need more exercise. They're going to go crazy on this chain."

This was the beginning of an old argument between them, and one Howell particularly disliked. In his opinion, coon hounds should get exercise only when they were hunting coons, and should otherwise be storing *up* energy, but Bailey, of course, with her crazy ideas, thought they had energy and to spare. Howell, determined not to get sucked into a discussion with Bailey, who almost always got the better of him somehow in argumentation, said merely, "Maybe. But that's not what you came about."

"No. I came about Daddy's cauldron."

"His cauldron?"

"His *doughnut-making* pot. You know. The big iron one, with legs?"

"Of course I know it, when you put it that way. It has bran in it, Bailey, for the horses."

Though Howell could not imagine what Bailey wanted the cauldron for, it was clear that she had designs on it. Their father had taken the pot to county fairs when he was younger, making doughnuts in the huge vat of simmering oil, and selling the resulting still-hot circles when they floated, triumphant, to the top. Though it was years since he had done this—his health had not been good for quite a long time even before his death—thinking about it now made Howell sorrowful for all those days which could never come back. Though the cauldron had for years been relegated to one of the horse sheds, and Howell had probably not thought of it once in all that time, Bailey's mention of it now made it acquire great value. At the very next fair he would use it himself. Charlene and the twins could help him.

"Well, I'd like it," she said firmly. "I've got a use for it in town."

"I've got a use for it myself," replied Howell.

"When was the last time you even *looked* at it, Howell?"

"It's not a matter of looking at it, is it?"

"What is it a matter of, then?"

"It's a matter of knowing where it is."

"You'll still know where it is—you can even come *visit* it."

"What do you want it for, anyway?"

"What business is that of yours? Oh, *forget* it, just *forget* it."

And to Howell's great astonishment, she jumped in the car and kicked up more dust. Howell, dumfounded and angry, watched her drive up to the house; she and Charlene, unluckily, were friends. Well, goll-darn her for ruining his day! Goll-darn that Bailey anyway. She would have ruined it less if she had defied him. And then to go visit his wife . . . it was all becoming too much. What was he going to do now? Oh, she'd always been a thorn in his side; but when their parents were alive he'd put up with it better, largely because he had been able to express his feelings about her to them, not directly, of course, but by dropping small remarks like "That Bailey!" When aimed at the right ears, ears that felt the same way he did, those two words spoke volumes. Now there was no one to whom he could speak that way except Charlene, and Charlene didn't feel the same way he did. She had told him a number of times, in fact, that Bailey would never have the farm sold out from under them just so that she could have her share—as if that was the point at all. The point was that she *could*. The point was that she could any time.

In general, the driving of heavy machinery gave Howell some relief from feelings of anger or aggravation, and it occurred to him now that he might climb on his combine and dispel, that way, some of his resentment. As Bailey disappeared into the house, he strode over to his machine shed and checked the gas in the combine; then he mounted it and slammed the cab door behind him. Turning on the engine, he was delighted to feel the vibrations washing through him, the vast and ponderous power of the machine, and he backed it up, then sent it forward and into the nearest unfenced field. This was probably not the best idea he had ever had, since the ground was still damp from the rains, but he thought he could just barely get away with it if he stuck quite close to the edge.

He drove down the east side of the field as fast as the engine could take him, and in his mind sent Bailey up the field the other way, in her little foreign red car. Entirely by accident, she came too close to the combine as she passed it, and he couldn't help impaling the car whole on one of the prongs at the combine's front, which sliced neatly through the car's engine, and then through the fire wall, and finally through Bailey herself, who sat in the driver's seat and was carried along, like an apple on a stick, before Howell sensed that this wasn't entirely working. Maybe it would have been better if he had actually been harvesting, but since there was no resistance, and no delightful grinding noise in the bowels of the machine as something got chewed up and spat out, the whole exercise left him feeling worse. If heavy machinery wouldn't relieve your feelings, what would? He turned the engine off and sat in the cab, gripping the wheel with his hands. What did she want the cauldron for, anyway? She'd probably turned into a witch!

After he had settled the combine back in the machine shed, he wondered what he could do next. He didn't feel like working on the engine now, and he certainly couldn't go to the house; he decided to go down to Rosie's Café for a slice of pie and a chat. This was a treat he allowed himself maybe three times a week, and though he'd been in there just yesterday, he felt that going there again today would show Charlene how he really felt. Besides, he might pick up some business; farming being what it was today, he'd been running a small truck on the side for three or four years now, and though he didn't get a lot of business, occasionally someone at the café would know about a moving job he could handle. The last job he had had—moving a professor at the college—that had been a reference from Billy Bob Watson, who did maintenance there at Powell. The move had taken an unexpected twist when the professor—his name was Dr. Minot—had *given* Howell a couch when it wouldn't fit through the door of his new apartment.

Howell still hadn't decided just how he felt about the couch. It was a comfortable couch, and Charlene liked it, but that someone would just give it away? Why, it indicated a lack of respect for your own belongings if you just let them go without a fight. That was why he hadn't wanted to part with the cauldron—because he respected it; it was his. Somehow, the Bankers and that international CONSPIRACY they had cooked up tied into just this point; stealing things and giving them away were both equally bad. They both meant, after all, that you hadn't worked for what you had, because if you'd worked, you'd want to hang on, you'd want to hold everything close. Oh, you could give Christmas presents, of course, and baked goods, and perform charitable acts like giving old clothes to tornado victims and the like, but that was different, because you'd get the same things back when you needed them in turn. But with anything else—couches or money—it seemed that the givers hadn't had to work very hard for what they were so willing to part with. Probably they were the usurers to begin with—the ones who were in on the plot.

Rosie's Café was almost full when Howell parked his pickup truck beside it. He had managed to work off a little more steam in the drive over, and when he pushed his way through the heavy glass door and saw all the friendly faces turn toward him —most of them framed by duck-billed caps advertising various brands of farm machinery—he felt much of his remaining upset vanish.

"How's it hanging, Howell?" said Billy Bob Watson.

"Got that drier working yet?" asked Mitch Ketchum, and while everyone in the room shifted his buttocks slightly to imply a willingness to make room for Howell, only Billy Bob and Mitch really moved, clutching their coffee cups and staring at the table as they wiggled sideways, chairs and all, so that Howell could pull up between them. From behind the counter, which she was swabbing with a wet cloth, Rosie caught his eye and said, "What'll it be?"

Howell asked for a cup of coffee and a slab of cherry pie, and while they waited for the order to be delivered, the three of them sat in silence for a while, adjusting to the table's new constituency. There was some discussion of tractors, a desultory attempt to work up interest in the new baseball season, and finally a return to the topic that had, apparently, been under discussion before Howell's arrival.

"You heard about those Russians coming to Felicity?" Mitch said.

When Howell looked blank, Billy Bob explained, as the expert on Powell College's affairs, "They got Russians coming up to the college next month. It's this new initiate the President wants."

"What new initiate?"

"Exchanging, like, art and science."

"Just two," said Art Johnson from the next table. "Two professors in . . . something. It don't sound real dangerous."

"Dangerous? They're only professors," said Mitch. And while the others, with a feeling of self-satisfaction, sat around appearing to agree, Howell felt troubled: Russians in Felicity? Why, that wasn't right, not at all. And if American professors were part of the conSPIRACY, how much more so must Russian professors be?

And *why* were they coming? There seemed to be no reason. On this one, the President must be wrong. And as Rosie arrived with Howell's coffee and hot cherry pie, the comforting aroma wafting up toward him from his plate mixed with the aggravated feeling he had about these Russians. Maybe he should *do* something—about the banks, and Bailey, and these Reds. But what could he do? He forked up the first delicious mouthful of pie and gazed at the parking lot outside, where the new sheriff, Peale Guthrie, was pulling up next to the café.

# 4

PEALE turned off the engine of his red Corvette—a holdover from his college days. He noted glumly that Rosie's was packed, and although he had come down here hoping for just such an eventuality—it was pretty pointless trying to probe the mood of the town if the town was all somewhere else for the day—still, confronted with the actuality of it, he didn't relish facing the whole crowd. Before he'd been elected sheriff, five months earlier, he would never even have imagined such a feeling, but in the last five months his life had changed, and not, he felt, for the better. Growing up in a world that was steeped in uneasiness, he had always felt himself to be almost indecently happy, indelicately normal, possessed of a kind of incurable good fortune that always made everything work out for him. From the time that he was a tiny child, in fact, he had been blessed with sheer luck in matters great and small. As a toddler he had wandered out into traffic only during inexplicable lulls, when all the cars that should normally have been passing had been diverted or delayed, and a balloon of quiet hung over the street like an exclamation point; when he reached up to explore the pot handle that stuck so invitingly out above him, it happened that his mother had accidentally turned the electric range all the way past High to Off again, so that the "boiling" water had been cold and refreshing, a nice unexpected shower as it poured down over his head; when everyone else in his class came down with the flu or the measles, he was bouncing along to school, as healthy as ever, to spend a happy day with his favorite teacher.

Later on, when other boys his age were breaking out in pimples, or tripping over their own legs, or even lying awake at night in agony as their bones grew with spurts of pain, he was scooting effortlessly through adolescence, no pimples, no growing pains, his sunny disposition and his reliable kindness to friends the only things that made up, in their opinion, for his perfect good looks and his indestructible charm. His first girlfriend had approached him when, at six, he was standing on the playground looking cheerfully out on an impromptu game of tag; she had yellow curls and bright blue eyes, and she had said, in a high and slightly wavering voice, "Peale, I love you." The same thing, more or less, had happened a hundred times since. And when Peale had finally, two years before, decided that the girl had come along with whom he wanted to live happily ever after, there had been no hitches at all in the pleasant and fairly rapid progress from courtship to marriage; Amanda was now his wife.

But it was funny; since he had married, his life had started to seem a little *finished*. Although he had never exactly assumed that getting married would introduce excitement, even exhilaration, into a life that was already so sane, so happily ordered, he imagined that it would somehow shake things up a bit, would whet, perhaps, undiscovered appetites. He understood, from books, television, movies, and most of all from the testimony of his friends and relatives, that love was supposed to heat you up, to make you fume sometimes, make you at other times delirious, and the fact of the matter was that Amanda made him just nothing at all. A tallish brunette with soft hair that fell to her shoulders and there ended in a blunt line that would rearrange itself perfectly after it had been upset, she was quite gorgeous, in the opinion of all, and spoke in a low, soft voice. She had graduated from Powell College three years behind Peale, majoring in library science, and she'd planned, before he asked her to marry him, to return to her home after graduating. But she had shifted her aims quite effortlessly when he had proposed to her one night after a movie, and she was now working full time in the Felicity Public Library and waiting for a baby to come along. Not that they were actually *trying* to have a baby just yet—Peale felt, he didn't quite know why, that at twenty-seven he was still too young, though of course by now most of his friends had two or even three children—but she seemed to have put herself into a kind of trance until such an event should overtake her. She liked to bind books, and she enjoyed going to auctions. She was less trouble than her pet cat.

No, Amanda was perfect, there was no doubt about it, and yet something kept nagging at Peale's mind; when he was away from her, he rarely thought about her at all. While they were dating, the same thing had happened, but then he had had a calendar on which he kept track of all their dates, and being the conscientious person that he was, he had held to a regular schedule. For four years after his own graduation from Powell, he had worked as an assistant manager in an agrichemicals business and had kept a date book for his appointments. There, as often as not, he had found an entry that read "Call Amanda," or "Pick up Amanda," and he had always felt a mild surprise on seeing her name written out in dark blue ink. "Amanda?" he would think for a fraction of an instant, and then "Oh, of course, Amanda": he would remember his bride-to-be, later his bride. Now, with no date book and no reliable method of reminders, he would often find himself walking up the flagstone path to their front door before he recalled that she would be there waiting for him, and he would just have time to rearrange his expression so that he didn't look startled when Amanda opened the door.

There were times, though, when he had no trouble at all re-membering her existence, when his memory was supplemented by her soothing, perfumed presence. He enjoyed eating with her, as she would chew rather loudly for someone who was usually so quiet and he felt that she took a true relish in her food, for all that she was genuinely slender. He liked that; it was unusual in his expe-rience for women to chew hard, and it would stimulate him to chew hard as well. Then, of course, it made him happy when they went out together, since he could tell that everyone they met thought them a perfect couple; he felt orderly with her, supported by a bastion of approval. Finally, there were the times in bed together. He could not help but feel that there was a surgical precision to the way they fit together, that her body had been designed to be linked to his own.

Well, naturally, there was nothing there to concern him—or whatever was, was awfully vague. No, what had him really worried—what was terribly strange and disheartening—was his sense that he should never have run for sheriff, that he hadn't the foggiest idea what a sheriff should do. He had been swept into office in the last election—the youngest sheriff ever elected in Rock County— by a consortium of people that cut across all barriers in their enthusiasm for him, for Peale Guthrie. All the Powell professors and staff had voted for him as a testimony to their own good taste in choosing a townie as a student to begin with, and all the townspeople had voted for him also, since he came from one of Felicity's oldest families. Even the farmers had decided to vote for him. They just liked him. It was really very simple.

And somehow, in the excitement of running for office just a few years after his graduation from college, in the thrill of seeing his face on posters all over town and hearing his name on everybody's lips, he had forgotten that when the election was over, he would have to be a real sheriff. He had run for office in the belief that it would be something like being president of his senior class in high school; it had been Amanda, actually, who had suggested it to him when he tired of agrichemicals. His only obvious qualification for the job was that he was an excellent marksman and had been a founder of the Felicity Gun Club, but around here, being sheriff didn't really *involve* shooting, though his skill won him points from his men. When he had decided to run for sheriff, he had actually thought, if he had thought about it at all, that it would involve a round of functions to attend, ribbon cuttings and the like; public relations, that was what he'd imagined. Making everybody feel good.

Instead, it was much more grim and demanding, and it dealt most unremittingly with crime. As a sheriff in the state of Indiana, his official duties were to maintain a jail and to serve warrants, as well as to take prisoners to and from court and to protect them for the duration of their trials. He went to the scenes of accidents to provide assistance and to fill out accident reports; he issued gun permits, served subpoenas, and filed tax warrants when they were called for. He had no fewer than twelve men working under him, most of them far more qualified for their jobs than he was, since he had been elected but they had been appointed and had had to attend the police academy first.

All of this was bad enough—but the crimes themselves were terrible. Why, this week alone the aggravated burglaries reported to his department amounted to thousands of dollars, and the things that had been stolen were hardly crucial items—stereos, bikes, grills, and cameras. Since there was really not a lot of through-town traffic in Felicity—it was hardly on a major route from somewhere to somewhere else—the chances were good that these things had been stolen by people he met every day.

And there had been a car "egged," a garage window damaged with a pellet gun, a mailbox uprooted, a tent reported damaged with a knife, three evergreen shrubs removed from behind a restaurant, a leather wheel cover taken off a pickup's spare. In fact, vehicles had had a rough time in general this week: a school bus rear window had been broken with a rock, two rear tires of the Union 76 Station wrecker had been damaged with beer bottles, a mail truck had been stolen and left with both fenders bashed, four lug nuts had been removed from the wheel of a parked car. All of this had happened in his home town of Felicity, and all of it had happened in just one week. And this had been, amazingly enough, a good week! Since he had taken office there had been two suicides, and those he hadn't known whether he would get through. Around here, people committed suicide with shotguns, and the resultant mess could hardly be described; both times, Peale had gotten sick afterward, though he had managed not to get sick at the scene.

And being around the jail—that, too, made Peale uneasy. He hated to see the men locked up in cells. Most of them landed there to begin with because of things they did while they were drunk, and once they sobered up they were always chagrined and often frankly disbelieving. As a young college student, Peale himself had gotten drunk once and accidentally taken down the lamppost in front of his mother's house, and on another occasion he had charged down High Street singing "Hoosier Madness" at three A.M. But even drunk, he had never beat up a woman or broken a chair over a friend's pugnacious head, and he felt totally out of his depth with men who could, and the occasional woman as well.

Still, he—Peale Guthrie—was now the chief defender of Law and Order in Rock County, and all the people he had grown up with, all the people he had grown up knowing, were looking to him and his sunny disposition to take charge of their general welfare. And his major reaction to this unspoken request was to look back over his shoulder for help; anyone was invited. "Who, me?" might have summed up his feelings in two words, and "Why me?" would have worked just as well. How was *he* supposed to know how to uphold Law and maintain Order when his own personal existence had always been ordered without him? He'd had a guardian angel standing at his shoulder, and though this guardian angel had not, he thought, gone away, it certainly wasn't powerful enough to take the whole county under its wings. Thank God for his brother Ryland—Ryland should have been the sheriff. To be a sheriff, a measure of gloominess and suspicion was evidently absolutely essential, and Ryland's grim view of things, his pessimism and cynicism, had become invaluable to Peale in lieu of a natural inclination to doubt.

Now, on top of his general worries, he had a specific worry, too. At first, when he had gotten the call from Maggie Esterhaczy, a counselor at Powell College who was in partial charge of the coming event, he had reacted with disbelief to the news that two professors from Russia would be visiting Felicity soon. He had tried to laugh her out of it when she had suggested that he provide security for these two foreign professors; what on earth, he had asked, could happen in Felicity? Security was for people in big cities. But then, after she had pointed out in frighteningly clear language that terrorism was taking its toll everywhere these days, that the Soviet Union was in high disfavor among average Americans at the moment, and, finally, that the citizens of Felicity were xenophobic in the extreme, Peale had stopped chuckling and had started to see the unpleasant possibilities. Between the shotgun suicides and the several gory accidents he had been called to, he was not as naïve as he had been just a brief five months before, and after a surprisingly short time for thought, he found "providing security" for these two foreign professors an ominously sound idea. The only problem was that Peale had no idea what that would involve.

Right now, he was going out to test the waters, to see how things sat in the town. Rosie's Café was an excellent place to do this, since both farmers from the surrounding environs and the hard core of Felicity's workmen came here, and Peale knew a lot of them from summer jobs, when he had put up fencing or stacked feed. By now, the same men had probably begun to wonder what he was doing, sitting in the front seat of his car, and reluctantly he supposed he'd better get out and do what he had come for. He straightened his star, adjusted his hat, and got out to stride for Rosie's doors.

Before he was even fully over the threshold, many voices were raised in greeting.

"Hey, Peale, over here!"

"Peale, sit yourself down."

"It's the sheriff, boys. Hide the drugs."

Peale gave a general acknowledgment to everyone in the room— "What are you all doing, lazing around here on a working day?"— and then a specific greeting to men at two of the tables.

"Hey, John, I understand there's a blonde in your life these days." (This to a man who'd just acquired a palomino horse.)

"Phil, you sure do look a little seedy." (This to a farmer who'd fallen into his own silo and had escaped, luckily, unhurt.)

Then, when he had put the general population of the café at ease, he went up to two of the men who he knew had real troubles: Mitch Ketchum, who'd just gotten a notice of liquidation on his farm, and Murray Anderson, the artificial inseminator.

"Awfully sorry to hear about your farm, Mitch," he said to the first. "Anything I can do, you just let me know."

And Murray Anderson had just been dumped by the first woman

43

he'd ever been serious about; they'd been engaged to be married in June when she'd decided to fall in love with someone else.

"Murray, bad luck about Bonnie. Tough to get through," he said, to which Murray replied, only a slight bitterness in his voice, "Oh, well, Peale, you know my work comes first anyway."

Considering that his work consisted of sticking his arm up to the shoulder in a cow's vagina about four thousand times a year, this was perhaps a rather sad comment on Murray's life, but Peale, clapping him on that same shoulder, said, "That's the attitude, Murray. When it's right, it'll happen."

Peale decided to sit down at the table with Mitch, which also held Billy Bob Watson. When Peale had been a student at Powell, he had acquired a healthy respect for Billy Bob, who was famous for trying to run students down with the large tractor-mowers he rode on. Since Peale had become sheriff, he had not, fortunately, had to arrest Billy Bob for anything, but no doubt it was only a matter of time, because Billy Bob loved to get drunk. The third man at the table, Howell Bourne, Peale had met only once, but he thought there'd been some trouble about the family inheritance, though he wasn't sure just what it was. These three should be a fairly representative sample of the local population; smiling genially, Peale tried to encourage them to talk.

"Hey, fellows, mind if I join you?"

"Hell, no. Pull on up," said Billy Bob.

Once he had settled himself in a chair, the conversation in the café resumed. From the table next to him, Peale heard someone saying, "Yes, pigs is smart. In pigs you learn something every day," and another man responding, "They's a lot like people. Only they probably don't want to admit it!" He ordered coffee—which, since he had become sheriff, Rosie insisted on providing him free of charge—and then said, "So what's the news? Anything going on?" An odd silence greeted this remark. And once the silence was broken, by dint of a good deal of supplication on Peale's part, cleverly disguised as repartee, he wished that he had simply left well enough alone rather than confirming his own fears. Because these friends and neighbors, far from peace-loving at the best of times, seemed to view the coming of these two Russian professors—which they already, naturally, were aware of—as a nasty incursion on Felicity's sovereignty, and a mighty suspicious event.

"We should just blow those Russians off the face of the earth. This disarmament stuff is crazy," said Billy Bob, and while the others didn't seem inclined to agree with this view, at least not right away, Mitch said judiciously, "You may be right there, Billy Bob. World peace would be the best thing, of course, but if we can't have that, let's totally destroy them."

"But what about this here nuclear winter they're talking about?" asked a man from an adjoining table. "They're not sure you could grow crops, after, I mean."

"Yeah?" said Billy Bob, surprised, and when Peale added his voice to the other "Yeah," Billy looked as if he'd gotten something to chew on. Peale pointed out that of course these Russian professors wouldn't have anything to do with international policies; they would just be folks, like everyone else. This was met with a dubious silence that Peale found quite disheartening.

He left Rosie's about ten minutes later to pay a visit to Ryland. That morning when he went by Saguanay's he'd had the feeling that Ryland had been purposely avoiding him, but he couldn't imagine why that might be, so he'd put it out of his mind. Now, as he tried hard not to speed while he traversed the two or three miles from Rosie's to the center of town—with his Corvette and his hat and his shining badge, he could certainly have gotten away with it—he wondered why he'd never appreciated Ryland before, with his clear-headed hunger for disaster.

He found Ryland on the floor of Saguanay's, talking intently to a customer. Just the other day, Ryland had let Peale in on a little trade secret of successful sales, and ever since, Peale had been on the lookout to catch Ryland using this technique. If the customer had cast her eye on a piece of furniture that was top of the line, the most expensive in its category, the salesperson would say, "Oh, yes, madam, you're very discriminating. Frederick Cooper makes the finest lamps available. They're head and shoulders above the rest. As you can see, these imitations by Top Lights look quite a lot like the Cooper to the undiscerning. But from sockets to shades, they're far less fine." If, on the other hand, the customer had first become interested in a second-string product—at Saguanay's, this meant it was still rather good—the salesperson would say, "*What* a good eye you have for workmanship! Although these are only *half the price* of the Henredon couches, they are made with precisely the same attention to detail, from the wood of the frame to the button covers of the arm protectors. You're simply not paying for the name." There was something about this technique—and its seemingly universal effectiveness— that fascinated Peale; although he didn't give a hoot about furniture, he had recently become so terribly aware that whether something was good or bad could all depend on how you looked at it. Because when it came to making decisions these days—even those requiring only the simplest distinctions—he found himself sidestepping, shuffling, fencing, parrying—engaged in high equivocation.

But as he sidled casually toward Ryland and the customer— hoping to catch them in the act—he heard the customer, a woman in her fifties, saying something, instead, about pain: "Oh, then you really should go see Ada; she's marvelous with pain."

"But herbs, Mrs. Hyde?" said Ryland. "What can *they* do?"

"Oh, you'd be surprised. And she's a masseuse."

"A masseuse?" Ryland looked embarrassed.

"Shiatsu. Energy flow. Pressure points."

When the two of them noticed Peale approaching, the woman smiled pleasantly in his direction, and Ryland turned to him with a resigned look of inquiry. Peale felt a rush of love. Golly, it really amazed him that he had never *appreciated* this brother of his before, had never seen his sterling soul. What a superb talent it was to be able to anticipate every disastrous eventuality. Why, it was almost like a game—Universal Catastrophe—in which every decision led to dire misfortune.

"Hi, Peale," said Ryland, and Peale plunged right in as the woman politely drifted away.

"Listen, I really need your help."

"Another stolen cow? Another woman walking naked to the store?"

"There are *Russians* coming here—to Felicity."

"Yes," said Ryland, who apparently knew already. "But I don't see why that should upset you."

"I have to protect them. Make them feel secure. And I have no idea how to do that. I'm meeting tomorrow with this Maggie Esterhaczy woman up at Powell. What should I tell her I can do?"

"How hard could it be to protect two professors?"

"Well, what? Armored cars? Bulletproof vests?"

Ryland shifted from one leg to the other, sighing a little as he did so. "I know this isn't as important as the international intrigue that you have to avert, Peale, but I've got a terrible pain in my groin. To tell you the truth, I'm going to see Dr. Ludgar about it in the morning, and I expect he'll probably have me hospitalized. But since Felicity doesn't have any armored cars, and bulletproof vests are a little uncomfortable, I suggest you simply assign the Russians a bodyguard. Someone nice. A kind of tour guide."

Of course! That was it! A bodyguard, a tour guide. It sounded sensible and perfect. Peale couldn't imagine why he hadn't thought of it first, and for a moment he felt quite jaunty. Oh, he'd get this sheriff business licked; he'd learn how to exercise volition! For the moment, the strange and disheartening feeling vanished. Worry was a thing of the past.

# 5

WATCHING his brother leave, Ryland sighed. Life was certainly upsetting. The pain in his testicle had been getting steadily worse, and though he had just made an appointment with Dr. Ludgar for the morning, he had no faith that an appointment would lead to results. Why should it? It never had before. To make matters worse, he had just gotten a phone call from an irate woman who lived at 102 East Walnut. Mrs. Lucas Mindell had wanted to know why he had missed his appointment that morning when she had canceled her tennis lesson *just* to meet him in her home at the time *he* had suggested, and she had told him that it would certainly behoove him to show up when she scheduled him again. Now Peale appeared to be bordering on a complete breakdown just because the visiting professors who were due at the college in five weeks happened to be citizens of the Soviet Union. Ryland could see already—it was all too plain—that although *he* hadn't run for sheriff and *he* hadn't been interested in the job, it was *he* who was going to end up doing it, and not getting any credit, either. Oh, although he'd hold out for a while, he had no doubt that by the time the Russians actually arrived he would be drawn inexorably into the plans for their disposition; he would probably have to entertain them in his home.

But the fourth thing was really the worst of all, the note that had arrived from April. According to the terms of the divorce, Clayton was supposed to come stay with him two weekends out of every month, all the longer school holidays, and a month of every summer

48

as well, but lately April had been trying to fudge on this, to keep Clayton home in Richmond. That was where she lived now, working at a printer's specializing in revolutionary pamphlets; people from all over the Midwest could count on Green Apples Press to set and duplicate on cheap paper whatever ravings other presses were too sensible to engage with. April had occasionally passed on to him some of the more outlandish productions of her company, and you really had to see them to believe them. You certainly couldn't dream them up. One, called "Enter the Sword," was subtitled "The Real Reason Why Communism Will Soon Swallow up America," and the text included such meditations as *"The sword of communism is going to mercilessly slaughter your descendants before your eyes, forcing you to watch. They are going to ravish your sacred wives and virgin daughters all the way down to infant girls, in grossly perverted ways you can not even conceive of, if you have a halfway clean mind."* The reason this was going to happen, according to the author of the prediction, was that the average American family spent seventy-two dollars a month on carbonated beverages, and this money, spent "for a beverage consumed solely for pleasure which destroys and poisons our body which is the Temple of the Lord," should instead be spent to spread the Gospel throughout the world; then the Sword of Communism would stay where it belonged, which was in countries that had already been "painted red."

Now, while Ryland was not a political person, this sort of thing was bothersome for a number of reasons that he couldn't put his finger on, but that all had to do with brain pollution. Clayton was now five and was only just learning to read on his own, and though his favorite to-be-read-from books were still, reassuringly, Edward Lear's *Book of Nonsense* and the Pooh volumes, the last time Ryland had been to Richmond to pick him up, he had found his son on the floor painstakingly trying to put together the phonemes in one of these raving treatises. Of course he had not been succeeding, but the implications were still disturbing. Worse still, when Ryland had confronted April with this, she had laughed and said there "was a lot of good in some of those things," making him wonder if she had lost her mind, or if she had ever had one to begin with. Now, she

wanted to keep Clayton for the weekend so that she could take him
to Indianapolis, and this was one of Ryland's weekends. Ryland had
already tried to call her to tell her "No way, forget it, April," but
he hadn't yet gotten through.

Lately, Ryland had been more and more bothered that he had
not argued about custody after the divorce. He had been so confused
then—that was the truth of it—that he hadn't really known *what*
he'd wanted; he'd been certain only of what he *didn't* want, which
was to end up feeling gypped. At the time, he had somehow figured
that it would be unfair for him to have to take care of Clayton all
by himself and for April to get off scot-free, but he sensed now that
this had really gypped himself; he wanted Clayton with him all the
time. Why, even when April and Ryland had still been married,
Ryland had actually done more than half of the child care, for once
ignoring the charts on the kitchen wall in favor of his own incli-
nations. He had loved giving Clayton his bath, for example, and
would climb right into the tub with him each evening, where they
would soap each other's backs and sing happy songs together. If
April didn't watch it, he was going to reopen the custody issue. In
fact, even if she *did* watch it, he might just do that anyway.

With that thought, Ryland felt marginally better, but his improved mood was fleeting—through the front window he saw Mrs.
Wickenden approaching for her monthly visit. These visits never
resulted in sales, but merely in genteel covetousness, but Ryland
braced his shoulders bravely and strode forward to meet her at the
door. The wife of a retired Presbyterian minister, she was an elderly
and goodhearted woman who, since she was less deaf than her
husband, thought she wasn't deaf at all, and who had, on a long
ago visit to Turkey—where her husband had been sent for a brief
time in relation to his ministerial duties—acquired a lust for Turkish
rugs that bordered on the demented. She had about four in her
home, but now that she and her husband were living on a pension,
it would probably be impossible for her ever to get any more, and
that made her longing more painful. Ryland loved rugs himself and
had a nice private collection in his home, but for sheer desire, Mrs.

Wickenden beat anyone he knew, and he found this perpetually draining.

"Mrs. Wickenden," he said in feigned delight. "How nice of you to drop by." And then, for the next hour or so, he took down one after another of the Turkish rugs, wrestling them from their hanging display board and letting them fall with a susurrous thump to the floor, where Mrs. Wickenden, on her knees, would straighten them out, smooth them down, and look at them from every angle.

"Oh, the coral," she said. "Look at that nap. Oh, the green, just like Nature's First Color." Luckily it was, eventually, closing time, and Mrs. Wickenden, assuring Ryland that she would think seriously about his selection, gave it one last lustful look and then minced away, leaving Ryland feeling exhausted and guilty—and still, alas, in testicular pain.

The next morning, bright and early, he was sitting in Dr. Ludgar's waiting room. He had arrived for his nine o'clock appointment five minutes early, as he always did for all appointments, only to find that there were no fewer than nine people in the waiting room ahead of him, and more arriving every minute. *Whoosh-bang* went the door and *whoosh-bang* again, and a mountainous woman dressed all in brown appeared, followed by a mountainous child with a white moon face. Now the room—which had been designed to hold about fifteen—was completely full; it might have been a party, Ryland thought bitterly, with the piped music playing vehemently in the background and most of the future patients chatting happily with one another or, if small enough, crawling on the floor between the table legs. He had been to Dr. Ludgar only once before, and then had been pleasantly surprised by the speed with which he'd been processed, imagining that Ludgar differed from the mass of his fellow physicians in that he knew what an appointment really meant and, furthermore, had a timepiece.

But nothing of the kind, as it turned out. The receptionist, a deceptively sweet-looking gray-haired woman, glanced up for a moment from the papers behind which she had barricaded herself;

Ryland flashed her a meaningful look, but she only smiled politely and returned to her papers. From long experience, Ryland knew that there was absolutely no point in going over to ask her how much longer he would have to wait. She would say to him, as to a naughty child, "The doctor's a little backed up this morning. But it won't be much longer now," and then smile at him pityingly, implying that it must be terrible to be a man with so little patience.

Ryland was certain that the entire process through which doctors forced you to go before you finally got to see them had been carefully calculated, worked out for a fee, by some genuises in a think tank. In a large, deeply carpeted room high above Chicago, sitting with their shoes off and their feet in tubs of sand to stimulate their creativity, they had grappled with the problem: "How can we completely remove the patient's sense of identity, strip him, as it were, of his will power, before he gets into the doctor's presence?" First brooding individually, then speaking tentatively into the void, they had gradually perfected the concept of which this was the first step. By setting up an appointment at least forty-five minutes before he had any hope at all of seeing you, the doctor asserted his superior position and your impotence. Often, Ryland had plotted to deduct the cost of his wait from the doctor's bill, charging $20 an hour for his own time and appending it to the doctor's statement, but somehow he had never been able to bring himself to do it, perhaps because such a move would imply that one could actually be compensated for the indignity and the misery of being kept waiting.

There was no doubt that the making of too many appointments, however, was just the thin end of the wedge; doctors no doubt made back-to-back appointments not only for the obvious brainwashing function, but because they wanted to make as much money as possible, and because, Ryland was willing to admit, they had too many patients. But why did they have too many patients? Because the AMA made sure that there was an artificial scarcity of doctors, made sure that only so many—far too few—would be admitted every year to medical school.

The wait would not have been so bad if you'd gotten value for your money. Value for your money would, in Ryland's opinion, have been a doctor who came fully into the room, knew your name, listened carefully to your symptoms, explained to you what they could mean, explained to you what steps you could take yourself to help, and explained what steps he, the doctor, might be able to take at that point. It would be even more desirable if the doctor actually knew something about human health, which most of them certainly did not. They knew pills and surgery, and that was it. Health was a mysterious state that landed on some people, sometimes, for reasons doctors certainly did not understand.

What happened, of course, by the time you got to see the doctor was entirely different from this ideal. Just as your fury had reached a peak in the waiting room, a nurse would come to the door, folder in hand, and "Mr. Guthrie," she would say, "please come in." Not "The doctor will see you now," because of course the doctor wouldn't; all that had happened was that you, in accordance with the plan of the sand-footed geniuses, had moved up from the outer circle of waiters to the inner circle of waiters. Still, you couldn't help but feel that things were looking up, that some progress was being made—though at that point you were still quite determined to tell the doctor, when you saw him, exactly what you thought about the way you'd been kept waiting. You knew, however, that it couldn't be *too* much longer now, so your fury began to ebb. The nurse would choose one of several identical cells, usually windowless, always without anywhere to sit except the examining table, which was covered with thin paper that crinkled nastily every time you moved, and then she would say, "Well. And what did you want to see the doctor about today?"

Here you would be faced with a choice. What you wanted to see the doctor about was that you were afraid you had some deadly disease, that you were tired of being sick all the time, that you wanted some advice on how to get healthy and a diagnosis of what was wrong. You wanted, in a word, a nice long talk with a health expert about health, followed by a leisurely physical examination. You didn't want to say this to the nurse, though; she had been cut from the same cloth as the receptionist and was interested only in protecting her doctor from unruly patients. If you said that you had a pain in what you thought was your prostate but might of course just be your urethra—here Ryland noticed that, annoyingly enough, his pain had entirely disappeared since he had been sitting in Ludgar's waiting room—she would write "Bladder infection?" down on your chart, tell you to go in the bathroom and pee in a cup, and then come back and remove all your clothes.

This was where the final stage in the brainwashing began. Somehow, you would find yourself doing as she said, peeing in a cup, then returning to take off all your clothes and climb under a paper sheet on top of the paper blanket. You would sit there, stark naked, all alone, in a windowless cubicle without any pictures on the walls, any reading material, or any comfortable place to sit or lie down, and with any number of ominous-looking instruments and repugnant substances on the small available counter space. All the fury you had felt at being kept waiting so long would have ebbed, and now you would be numb, chilly, and frightened. Ten minutes might pass, fifteen—who could tell in this place which was not really a place, this time which was not really time?—and you would start hoping that the nurse would drop by for a little chat, or that some stray animal might wander into the room. By the time the door finally opened and the doctor entered, you would be inarticulate with gratitude at the sight of another human face, and when the doctor asked, "Well, how are you today?" you would, like anyone trying to be polite to a much-desired visitor, say graciously, "Oh, fine, and how are you?" and the doctor would say, "Well, I feel pretty good, all things considered"—you yourself undoubtedly being one of those things that troubled his precarious health—and you would feel ashamed and eager to please.

All this, naturally, left you putty in the doctor's hands. "So," he would now say, peering at the chart. "Maybe a bladder infection, eh? Well, couldn't find any sign of it in your urine, but just to be on the safe side, better take some tetracycline. Hate to have that infection work its way back to your kidneys." He would then scribble something on a prescription pad, hand it to you, poke you once in the naked abdomen, say, "And how's the job going? You look pretty healthy to me," and slip out the door, in one liquid maneuver, brushing some dust from his chest and leaving you, suddenly, completely panic-stricken at the thought of the damage that even at that very moment your kidneys might be suffering, damage that, in all your worries, you hadn't even considered until then.

At this, Ryland suddenly got to his feet. The office was so stuffy, the music so irritating, and his pain, in abeyance for a time, had returned with a vicious poke. There must be some alternative to this, some other place to go; it just wasn't fair that he was so unhealthy and had to deal with doctors, *too*. He knew, vaguely, that there were other sorts of doctors than those licensed by the AMA—chiropractors, osteopaths, kinesiologists—but he had never really given them much thought. Of course, there was that herbalist Mrs. Hyde had told him about, but she did massage, and anyway—herbs?

Ryland had by now made his way to the receptionist's desk, with the intention of telling her that he would wait outside until the doctor saw fit to see him; he would be scathingly sarcastic and would put her for once in her place. But before he could open his mouth, she got to her feet, disappeared around the corner of the glass partition that separated her from the common run of humanity, and then reappeared in the waiting room proper, clearing her throat for attention. This attention was immediate and complete, though slightly marred by the music, which was now tinkling a lugubrious rendition of "Lineman for the County," and by the mountainous child with the white moon face who was banging a small headless horse repetitively on the carpet.

"I'm sorry to have to tell you," the receptionist said, "that Dr. Ludgar has just been called away on an extreme emergency. I'm afraid we're going to have to reschedule all appointments." This was not met with an outraged roar of anger, as Ryland would have thought only natural, but with an attentive look of silent absorption on the part of all concerned. Ryland himself experienced a strange feeling of relief at the news that he would not have to proceed through all the humiliating stages of the program that he had recently reviewed in his mind and, moreover, was almost glad to have an excuse to unload Dr. Ludgar for good. An emergency! Of course it was an emergency. The only time doctors ever paid the slightest attention to you was when you were dying at their feet.

He had had enough of them; that was all there was to it. He'd been pushed a little too far. And in the aftermath of this exhilarating recognition, as he pointedly left the office without rescheduling anything, he thought he might actually go see this herbalist, this Ada Esterhaczy who lived near the Pond.

An hour later he stood on her doorstep, in an almost pugnacious frame of mind. He had called Mrs. Hyde to ask her for directions, but it had still been surprisingly difficult for him to find this place, though it was only five miles out of town. To get here, he had had to drive around the west end of Felicity Pond—on a difficult and sometimes dangerous road that had been cut into the cliff—and then take a winding narrow road farther west, looking for a well-hidden driveway. So well hidden was this driveway that the first time, Ryland had gone by it, driving on for at least five more miles before he stopped and went back. The country here west of the Pond was as uncharacteristic of Felicity in general as the Pond was of the Midwest; it was rolling and hilly, with densely treed woods and little streams that cut small valleys. When, on retracing his route, Ryland discovered the entrance to the driveway, he could hardly believe it led to a house, so virgin was the woodscape around it. But after driving for several hundred yeards along a steep and potholed driveway, he came upon a clearing of enormous dimensions, in the center of which was a farmhouse. Back behind the initial clearing, a nicely kept lawn through which the flower beds had been woven, there was another, even bigger clearing—this was a pasture, fenced and with barns, the whole again surrounded by trees. In the pasture two dogs were playing; they barked at him loudly as he walked. As far as Ryland could tell, the woods that lay around the pasture must stretch uninterrupted all the way back to the Pond, southeast of the house. But the unusual character of the place did not win him; it made him more antagonistic, in fact. He pounded hard on the door, then waited for an answer to his knock.

"Come in," a voice called from what seemed quite a distance, and Ryland pushed open the door. He had only a moment to notice that the room he was in—a living room that apparently doubled as a consulting room, since part of it had been arranged behind a carved wooden screen—had a strongly European flavor to it, with its ornately carved furniture, its thick-leafed plants, its copper jars set near the fireplace, and the lace doilies that decorated its tables, when the floor creaked in another room, and a door connecting them opened.

Out came a woman about five feet tall, with a tiny bone structure to match. She wore a floor-length dressing gown, but she had no slippers, and her bare feet slapped firmly on the floor. Her hair, abundant and almost pure white—the streak of yellow that ran down from her part on the left side gave her an oddly punk look, as if she had put it there herself—was tied up on the top of her head in a great rope that circled the crown. Some wisps of it had escaped to curl around her cheeks, which seemed to be rouged, because there were two unexpected red spots dabbed there in the middle of white skin. Although that skin was quite wrinkled, the woman's lips were still smooth and pinkish, and the eyes were dark and fierce with life; they fairly exploded, crackled, sizzled. The outfit she was wearing—the white cotton robe marked with eyelets and ribbons, hand-sewn—looked a little too demure for this fierce, vibrant presence whose size simply emphasized its strength.

"Good day," she said. "I was still in bed. Now tell me what you have come for."

But for a moment, Ryland couldn't speak. The pain in his groin had temporarily disappeared; from the minute that small figure had walked into the room, placing its two bare feet firmly on the oak floorboards, Ryland had felt immeasurably better, and the strangeness of this confused him.

"Ada?" he asked. "Ada Esterhaczy?"

"Yes, of course," she said. She looked at him appraisingly and then added, "We will have some sherry, I think." She turned to a sideboard where a crystal decanter sat and poured out two hefty glassfuls.

By the time Ada handed him his sherry, Ryland felt slightly more self-possessed. While Ada settled herself in a chair and prepared to entertain him, Ryland managed also to take a seat and to sip at the sherry he'd been given.

"So," Ada said. "I have not seen you before. You look like a nice young man."

"Oh, well," said Ryland, abashed again. "Ryland Guthrie. I manage Saguanay's."

"Ah, yes, that marvelous furniture store. You have some quite good things there. Ah, you should have seen, though, the Esterhaczy collection. All lost, of course, in the wars."

"The copper . . ." said Ryland, pointing.

"Oh, yes, those, of course. And a few of the pretty baskets."

"So you're from . . . ?"

"Hungary, yes. Oh, many, many places. But Hungary first of all. And you, I can see that Felicity is your home. You have traveled far only in the mind."

"Oh, not so far, even in my mind. I've always been something of a pessimist."

"A pessimist! Oh, no, that is *not* good! To be happy; this is everything in life."

"But how do you manage it?" Ryland found himself asking.

"As you manage everything else. You *practice* happiness; you, what is it, you *encourage* it. You must think of it as an art. Of course, health is vital, the health must come first, but after . . . well, we all do love ourselves before anybody else in the world, and it is pure silliness to say otherwise. So let us take our own lives by the hand and be artists. Let us paint our lives as we wish them."

Ryland took another sip of his sherry. It tasted hot in his mouth. To paint his life as he wished it; to get well; to be happy—how could this be possible? Never had he heard another human being admit aloud that she loved herself more than anybody else in the world, and the frankness of this disclosure was so breathtaking that Ryland felt emboldened to say, "Yes, but what do you do if you are always sick?"

Ada gave him a keen look, and thought for a moment before answering. "You are not, of course, always sick. It merely seems that way to you now. So let us start with the problem as it is at this time. Where is the pain? Does it move?"

And Ryland, who had dreaded this moment, the moment when he had to admit that he had a pain in his testicle, and admit it to a woman at that, found himself saying quite naturally, even eagerly, "In my testicle. My left one. Can you help me?"

Ada smiled as if, of all the pains that one might have, a pain in the testicle, and only the *left* testicle, at that, was certainly the least of the littles, a mere bibelot in the category of pain, and Ryland felt a wave of relief sweep through him so profound that it felt as if he had been filled with hot liquid, which was now being drained, leaving him slim and clean. He had waited all his life to meet a doctor like this one, a doctor who was not scared of pain and death, and who could face down all the enemies of happiness as if they were so many contemptible little villeins, and she, the ruler of the keep.

# 6

A D A had woken up slowly that morning, luxuriating in her bed. Although the town of Felicity, like other contrary towns in Indiana, had decided years before to scorn the idea of Daylight Saving Time—unimaginative muffins, these people could not seem to take pleasure in the simplest flights of fancy, and insisted that if it was time at all, it had always to be the same—Ada herself changed her clock in the summer and lived on what she called Ada Time. On Ada Time it was eleven o'clock in the morning, and not only did Ada take enormous pleasure in lying in bed so much later than the Felicity townspeople would have considered healthy or respectable, she also loved the idea that the time *she* was now on was that of the Atlantic Ocean, that of the waves which rolled toward Europe, and as she lay there watching the bright light of a sunny morning seeping around the edges of her window shades and smelling the pleasant nutty smell of trees in the sunshine, she wondered whether it might not be a good idea to set her clocks even farther ahead, so that instead of sharing time with the rolling ocean she would share it with the ports of France, with the Isles of Wight and Man.

Oh, how she had ended up *here* of all places she could still hardly conceive. As a girl in Hungary she had often dreamed of seeing the world; in imagination, she had roamed the globe, from stem to stern. She had, she remembered, followed the news about the polar explorers with great interest, learning all the strange names by heart so that she could roll them on her tongue like candies—Peary,

Cook, Amundsen, Scott, Shackleton. She could see them all still, their bodies swathed in wool and fur, a little figure following them around in a specially made Eskimo suit; but she had never, even in school, encountered *Indiana*. Of course, when she had married Tibor—she was only seventeen at the time, and he a handsome young balloonist in the Austro-Hungarian Army—she had not even known that she was going to travel, since only after the war had he resigned his active commission to join the Hungarian consular service, which had taken them all over the world. And when, after the Second World War, he had been forced to retire by the Communists who had taken power in Hungary, he and she had both become Americans, and fervent, committed ones at that. Still, being a fervent American and living in Felicity were two different things, and when a great-uncle, who had emigrated to Felicity fifty years earlier, died and left them his house, it had been against Ada's vigorous protests that they had moved here at all. Tibor had hoped that he could get a job teaching European history at the college, and indeed had been lucky enough to do so. But then he had died, ten years before, and Ada had just kept on. She had made her own happiness, of course, and when her darling redheaded granddaughter had arrived the year before things had certainly changed for the better. But lately, in spite of Maggie's presence—well, lately she had been rather *bored*.

Oh, that drive across the Midwest! That had been grim. The rolls of hay that looked like Yule logs were all right, and the cows that peered mournfully at her from beyond their wire fences, even the clothes flapping from the clotheslines—the garments hung according to size and kind—but the landscape itself, all squares and lines, with roads that intersected only like T's—that had been upsetting to someone who had lived in Egypt, in the Alps, and in the Carpathians. When they crossed into Indiana, they'd seen a sign that read THE PEOPLE OF INDIANA WELCOME YOU, a friendly thought, perhaps, but one that seemed a little indiscriminate, and then, once in Indiana, all those signs—Wilson Agricultural Chemicals Farm Market, Kentab Health Products, Kentab Goat Chow, Wilson Aluminum Drainage Culverts—well, goat chow and drainage culverts

were two things that had never before been brought to her attention, and she was sorry to know they existed. The sheer number
of welding shops they'd passed had seemed ominous, as if whatever
was wrong here in Indiana was simply *welded* together. Just before
they pulled into Felicity, she had seen a sign in someone's front
yard that said INCLINE YOUR HEART UNTO THE LORD GOD, THE
FEAR OF THE LORD PROLONGETH THE DAYS, and in Felicity itself
a large sign in front of the courthouse that read WELCOME TO
FELICITY. JAYCEES WELCOME YOU. LIONS CLUB INTERNATIONAL
WELCOMES YOU. OPTIMISTS INTERNATIONAL WELCOMES YOU.

All this had been rather alarming, and Ada had closed her eyes
in despair by the time they got to the quarry road and the stillness
of Felicity Pond. But then the dangerous curves of the road, the
stark density of the woods, these things had lifted her spirits; and
though, given the nature of the last three hundred miles, she still
half expected that their house would be square, set in a square
field, with a flat line of driveway leading directly up to it, and
perhaps a small billboard nearby that read THE FAMILY THAT PRAYS
TOGETHER STAYS TOGETHER, instead she found herself in this marvelous woody kingdom planted with trees from Europe by the old
uncle who had moved here so many years before. And she had
been happy here, yes, happy, much of the time. But lately? Well,
yes, yes, a little *bored*.

It was at this point that she heard the car drive up and attended
to the sound with interest. She scrambled out of bed, slipped on
her dressing gown, and put a tiny bit of rouge on her cheeks—just
a tiny bit—looking at her wrinkled face in disgust. The things that
time did to you were certainly grotesque, and while she had, perhaps, never been beautiful, as a young woman she'd had many an
admirer; she'd had, well, a certain something. And when she went
out to find that her patient today was a man, and a handsome young
man at that, she was glad that she'd taken time to put on the rouge
and glad that this man had come. The truth of it was, she just
adored men, she always had, and they still seemed to like her, too.
She even noticed, when she was getting the sherry that she offered
to all her patients—*she* had had a glass of wine a day from the time

she was twelve years old and it had certainly not done *her* any harm—that he seemed to be quite abashed in her presence. But she was too old now to take pleasure in her effect on men—well, at eighty-seven, she was, anyway, *almost* too old—so she set herself to the task, now, of putting this poor boy at ease. He couldn't have anything too terribly wrong with him. Probably all he needed was a woman.

"Of course I can help you," she said in response to his question. "But first, we must do a physical examination. Not of your testicle, of course," she said to reassure him, because she knew from long experience that men, the darlings, were very shy creatures, "but of the body tone. I must feel your health through my fingers." And she urged him to the hard-backed chair behind her wooden consulting screen. Then, as she put her fingers on the top of his head and began to locate the energy blockages that had gotten him all tangled up, she started to make soothing conversation.

"So," she said as she moved her fingers ever so lightly in small concentric circles on Ryland's scalp, "you manage that marvelous furniture store. And do you have any family?"

"I have a son."

"A son. How lovely. I adore little boys."

"And a brother. He's just been elected sheriff."

"Oho! You must be proud."

"Not really," said Ryland. "Not really. I . . . ahh, that feels really good."

"Yes, it is good. You will see. Now just trust my hands; that's right."

Ada moved her hands down to Ryland's neck, urging his muscles to let go. All disease, of course, came from the same source, an imbalance of energy in the body, and Western medicine was so *very* pitiful, with its emphasis on cure rather than maintenance. Western medicine divided the human anatomy into categories and regarded each malfunctioning part as separate from the whole, but in holistic medicine things were just the opposite, and the illness was not really important. Ada did not like to brag, but there had never been a patient she hadn't helped, except perhaps that one woman who had come to her after years of treatment for cancer. Just days away from death, she had looked like the bird with the snake. There was nothing Ada could do; the woman was already staring into darkness. But this young man, with his tiny prostate infection, he was healthy enough under all this tension—but what a knot he had made of his neck! They could hold a conference in the biggest lump there! All the Western doctors in the world.

"I have a granddaughter," she said conversationally. "My darling little Maggie."

"Oh?"

"Yes, she is a counselor at the college. But a very wonderful girl."

"Um."

"She has her peculiar ideas, of course. This theory that the whole world is going to end at any moment is such a fine example of the idealism of youth!"

"She thinks the whole world is going to end?"

"Oh, yes, she studies the Doomsday Clock. Still, I am lucky to have her."

Yes, Maggie was really such a darling, the youngest and most beloved of her grandchildren. Indeed, the only one of her descendants who was worth a peanut shell, in Ada's opinion, and Ada had seen much of life and character in her time. With her brain and her looks, she should certainly be doing something more valuable than working as a counselor at that second-rate college where all the male students seemed to dress like Mohawk Indians, but ever since Maggie had decided to come here to Felicity to live with her grandmother, Ada had taken a whole new joy in having borne two children. Ilonka was now in Chicago, and Peter in California somewhere, and really, they had always lacked something vital, a sparkle, a fire, a glow. Oh, they had been dutiful enough for a while, and treated Ada with all the respect she deserved, but, though she hadn't actually known it at the time, that wasn't quite what she wanted.

And bearing them to begin with had been such a nightmare— those long months of dragging herself around like a cow with a wounded belly, those endless hours in the hospital in pain, those utter fools of doctors. Well, *pouf,* she had certainly been glad to get it over with and move on to other things, and glad too when she had discovered that little cap she had put inside her vagina. So she had had a life, a fine life, and with her talent she could have been many things, a doctor, a dress designer, an actress. So often had they moved, though, she and Tibor, that she had never really had the chance to pursue these careers, and had had to settle for her children. What would have been truly interesting, however, would have been if they'd ever put up a fight. Instead they'd been like dough in her hands, like these muscles turning limp under her fingers.

Then, when they had grown up, Ilonka's husband had managed to impregnate her just once, with a young woman who was now, apparently, sterile, and while Peter had had two children, Maggie's brother was living as a catamite. Well, Ada made no comment about the homosexuality—actually, though she rather liked her only grandson, so polite, so refined, so sensitive, it was better anyway that *those* genes die out; and though she felt sure she could help the sterility if she could only once get her hands on the grand-daughter who suffered it, that granddaughter laughed her medicine off—the more fool she.

The truth of it was, Ada wished that Maggie would have a child. A little daughter who looked just like Ada, and who could take, maybe, Ada's name. For the last ten years, ever since Tibor died so rudely, leaving her alone here in Felicity, she had devoted herself to her patients and her doggies, and had been quite content to do so. The children and the grandchildren visited from time to time, and she was always happy to have them, but happy to have them leave as well, to tear the sheets from their beds. Now, at this late date, having spent a whole lifetime feeling that she had no need for genetic immortality, that although she had had children she had not *needed* to have children, because she, Ada Esterhaczy, was what evolution had been striving for all along, now she felt rather different; how nice it would be to raise Maggie's child. The fact that Maggie did not yet have a child, or a man capable of inducing one—she certainly was not going to count Richard Minot, that man

Maggie went around with, run, run, run—this struck her as a problem to which she should devote herself. Perhaps she could somehow help out. After all, if she were unlucky, she might live for just another ten years, and though she certainly hoped for a round one hundred, either way there was little time to lose. It didn't matter whether Maggie had the child in wedlock or out of it—good God, everybody was very modern these days, and Ada had certainly always been modern with the best of them!—what mattered was that she just get pregnant. Whether she wanted to or not.

"Oh, that feels wonderful," Ryland murmured as she moved on down to his shoulders. This was more like it. What a project it would make! It would certainly relieve her boredom.

"Oh, God," he added as she pressed on his breastbone. A very sensuous young man.

And now she regarded the top of his head with an interest entirely new. A sensuous young man, essentially healthy, already proven fertile; maybe this Ryland would do for her Maggie, to quicken Maggie's little egg? Certainly at the moment his sperm was probably not in the greatest shape, sluggish and enervated as it no doubt was, by the strain of his probable prostate infection, but once she got him into tiptop shape, what then? Would he do as the father? The little bald spot on his head was a pity, and the generally sorrowful air—but Maggie had a magnificent head of hair, and Ada wanted a girl, in any case. What a wonderful idea! She would make Maggie teas, passion teas to stimulate her hormones. And she would introduce her to this Ryland soon, as soon as he felt a bit better. Oh, life was truly marvelous, so full of the unexpected. And just this morning she had felt bored!

She finished the treatment a half hour later and encouraged Ryland to rise. This was difficult for him, as he had finally fallen asleep under her fingers, and his cheeks were flushed bright red. What a difference it made to free up that energy, to let it connect to itself. And how really handsome this young man would be if only he didn't look so sad. Parsley, cornsilk, saw palmetto berries, buchu leaves, cayenne, kelp, pumpkin seeds; these would help his enraged prostate, but he must help himself, too.

"You are fine," she said aloud. "A very healthy specimen. The pain is, I think, a tiny little infection, and it will be taken care of by the herbs I give you. You must also take a whole body tonic, which will help make your blood strong and masculine. But mostly, you must free up your energy so that your body can cure itself. For the time being, a daily treatment would help you very much. And anyway, pessimism, that is the heart of it. Remember, you must feel *happy.*"

And then, as she marched off into the kitchen to mix the tonic and the medicine, pinching and pounding and grinding with the pestle in her little mortar, throwing in a touch of peppermint to make the mixture smell sweet and some camomile for good measure, she saw her doggies playing in the field, their tails held high like jet streams. After she said goodbye to Ryland—and found out when he would come again—she would go visit her dogs, and take a walk. Maybe barefoot, it was such a fine day.

When Ada went out to the dogs, both came rushing up to meet her. Oh, these doggies, how she loved them, and how they simply adored *her.* When they were together, they could unfortunately whip each other into such a frenzy of excitement at the prospect of seeing her again—it had been so long, twelve whole hours, how were they to survive it?—that their paws simply would not stay on the ground but would spring off into the air. Raga was small, a white terrier-cross with ears that were usually cocked intelligently—*he* could not do her much damage—but Boonskie was big, a big hound with a small brain and gorgeous brown eyes. When *he* jumped, he would land on her chest and almost knock her to the ground.

"Boonskie," she said in her most disapproving tone as he began to fly through the air in ecstasy, "I have on, as you see, my best white housedress. Do not, please, muddy it now." And with a twist of the forepaws, he managed at this to swerve apologetically to the side so that he hit her only below the knees and got just the smallest paw print on her robe.

"What a wonderful boy!" she added then. "And you, Raga, *what* a fine fellow!"

She had loved dogs since childhood, when they spent summers in the vineyard and the peasants had all had little pups. But with all her travels, until she moved here, she had never been able to keep her own. Boonskie, the darling, had been born in her house, the son of another of her dogs; when the time came for her to have her puppies, Rathskeller had woken Ada by crawling directly under Ada's bed, which she must have decided was the only appropriate place to have her babies in safety, and she had actually heaved the bed up, with Ada on it, in her efforts to get underneath. If Ada had not intervened, Rathskeller would undoubtedly have managed to kill every one of her babies as it tried to make its entrance into the world, but by dint of a great deal of hauling and scolding, she had gotten the bitch into the closet. There, Rathskeller had lain, panting crazily, her tongue lolling out of one side of her mouth like something she had spilled, and Ada had watched in fascination as her puppies started to come. As the first neatly wrapped cellophane package was delivered between her legs, Rathskeller had scrubbed it firmly with her tongue, stickily, as if she were eating cobwebs. Then she had watched, bemused, and Ada, delighted, as it swam drunkenly toward the teats. That first package, a muddy brown color with fur slicked down as wet and glossy as a seal's, a snout like a little sucking machine—that tiny package had turned out to be Boonskie, her marvelous big brown boy.

Of course, Ada had not known at first that he was to be Boonskie, since for weeks he had hardly moved. For at least ten days the puppies had simply lain around in little curls of questionmarks, sometimes stirring themselves into a feeding frenzy, and the rest of the time fast asleep. But as soon as they progressed from the stage at which they swam around randomly on their stomachs, with their legs outstretched to the side like flippers, to the stage at which they wanted rather badly to see what was just over *there*, Boonskie had led the way for his litter mates to follow by standing up first on his legs. They were hardly sturdy legs, not then, but as he wobbled around, thrusting himself forward in great ambitious surges, and then landing flat on his face as his legs collapsed beneath him, Ada had seen in his great determination the pathos of all life— because poor Boonskie was scared of everything, right from the first time on his legs. When, at the grocer's one day, Ada had bought a little blue ball with a bell inside and brought it home to give to the litter, Boonskie had been the only one to go near it, barking in warning as he approached. Then, ever so tentatively, he had thrust out one paw to touch it, and when it had rolled away from him, bell ringing, he had fled back to Ada, ears flying, yelping in terror as he landed on her lap. There he had quivered for a while, regaining his strength and his purpose, then trying again until he had mastered the ball completely, until it was just a piece of rubber.

As he grew older, other things had scared him; everything had scared him, in fact. A scrap of paper blowing across the yard, a piece of furniture that had been moved, the knocking sound of a patient arriving; all had alarmed him to his core. He was aghast at the horrific sight of a bag of groceries on the kitchen floor; dismayed when a bee buzzed near his hindquarters, which forced him to turn in panicked circles; quite undone by the disquieting appearance of a concrete hippo-shaped doorstop. Oh, Boonskie was so brave, the way he kept trying to be tough in spite of the appalling dangers of life; when he got big enough to go outside by himself and play in the yard, he would run back to the house to see her every few minutes, when his own boldness surprised or frightened him.

Even now, of course, he was hardly a confident animal, for all that he put on a show. Sometimes when a stranger appeared at the house, he would start to howl, head thrown back toward the sky, and while he howled his hackles might be up, but his tail would be wagging like crazy. It was always his hope that this new menace, whatever it was, would turn out to be, after all, a friend, and just to allow for all the possibilities, he wagged, he howled, and he tried to look big. When he saw Ada or Maggie, his whole body crashed from side to side like a thrashing fish, and his ears would cup up and back like aerodynamic leaves. Sometimes, when he was particularly excited, his tail would spin in a perfect circle, as if he were gearing up for a takeoff. His tail was wagging that way now.

"Are you my best boy?" she inquired fondly. "Are you my best, most marvelous boy?" She really couldn't deny him anything, and when, one morning, Raga had appeared at the house, a small white bundle of fur huddling by the woodpile, and Boonskie had—after an initial period of consternation—decided that this little dog was her special present to him, she had had, naturally, to keep Raga also, for Boonskie to have to play with. And that was despite the fact that once Raga had come to live with them Boonskie had had nothing like the same interest in her, Ada, that he had once had, but gave a lot of his attention to his sidekick and protégé, who followed him around like a shadow. One big, one small, one dark, one white, one long-haired, one short-haired, they could be found together always, side by side, flowing from place to place in their perpetual quest for new smells. Boonskie was seven now, and had some gray hairs, which made Ada feel somewhat worried.

"Oh, Boonskie, darling, you would not leave me? You would leave me, at least, a son?" But how could he do that? Raga was a male. And anyway, not a hound. Well, she was going to breed Maggie; why not Boonskie, too? Find a nice hound bitch for him to mate with? What a good idea! Oh, she had always been smart!

"Would you like that, darling?" she said.

Boonskie, after staring at her for a moment with adoring eyes, dashed off to get a rag to bring her as a present; on the way back, he smartly broke its neck, like the clever dog that he was. Yes, he was clever, but Maggie was even cleverer—she would not be so easy to persuade. Herbs, however, were difficult to argue with; Ada headed for the house again, to make tea.

Since she had never before had to stimulate the hormones of passion, in a woman at least, as part of her herbal practice, she had to think a little before she decided just what would be best to include. Siberian ginseng, of course, was vital; much as she hated the Russians—oh, what she had suffered, or at least imagined suffering, at their hands when they came into Hungary after the First World War, bringing with them their oh so precious Commune—

she had long ago bowed to the truth that the best ginseng in the world came from those barbarian steppes. And kelp, of course, to stimulate the thyroid, which controlled the rest of the glands. Then gentian root and ginger root, to stimulate circulation of the blood, and finally traces of comfrey root, passion flower, squaw vine, sweet woodruff, witch hazel, licorice root, blessed thistle, cayenne, Dong Quai, and saw palmetto berries. What a ghastly concoction it sounded like, and how fouly it smelled; when she had pounded and mixed and brewed, she discovered that it tasted rather repulsive also, though of course she had only a sip, lest it excite in her desires inappropriate to her present way of life. Funny, though, how it rather grew on you, and what could it really hurt? She poured herself a nice big mug and went out to drink it on the stoop.

# 7

MEANWHILE, drinking not tea but coffee, Maggie was feeling a little tense. She and Richard Minot were about to meet with Sheriff Guthrie in order to talk about security arrangements for the visiting professors, and Minot had arrived before the sheriff, which left her, once more, alone with him. He'd come striding into the conference room, his aggressive jaw thrust in front of him, his Velcro-fastened sneakers squeaking on the wooden floor; at the sight of him, Maggie felt that queer combination of lust and revulsion she'd had since the first time they met. The mixture of sensations was clearly physical, but her revulsion was also theoretical; Minot claimed to be a Democrat and insisted he wanted world peace, but he believed in, of all things, capital punishment, and life sentences for second offenders.

Ever since he arrived, the autumn before, he had been trying to maneuver Maggie into bed, and although, on the one hand, she was tempted—she hadn't had a relationship since leaving Normal, Illinois, after all, and he was one of the few people she could even talk to in Felicity—she had resisted, in the end, with very little effort. Something about Minot frightened her. She could just imagine lying in bed with him, getting all slithery with sweat, and then, in the throes of physical passion, confessing to him some small crime. In her imagination, Minot would hop out of bed, take a nice hot shower with lots of suds, scrub himself down vigorously with a towel—and then sentence her to life imprisonment. This was not seductive, not at all. She maintained a deep reserve. But right now, he was trying to put the moves on her again. It was the bane of her life that she was beautiful.

"Forget it, Minot, you're not getting anywhere."

"You went with me to Saguanay's, helped me pick out my couch . . ."

"I went to the store, that's all. I had nothing better to do."

"They delivered it this morning," he said suggestively.

"All right, Minot, all right. I should never have gone with you, I can see that now. Could we talk about something else?"

"So what shall we talk about? Retributivism again?"

"Good God, no. Why don't we just drink our coffee?"

"You don't want to talk about these Russians and world peace?"

"Let's just wait for the sheriff."

"All right."

"All right." Maggie stomped to the window, still sipping her coffee; she pretended to be looking for Peale Guthrie.

It made Maggie feel good to be so thoroughly cantankerous; to her, it was a political statement. She had been six years old in 1962, the year of the Cuban missile crisis, and although up to that time, as she recalled, she had enjoyed being alive, seeing it as a real opportunity of sorts, with a happily limitless aspect, when those missiles had started steaming across the Atlantic, all that had changed forever. A frenzy of air raid drills had possessed the Chicago elementary school where Maggie was a tiny scholar, and she had spent what seemed like hours at a time sitting not *at* her desk—a sweet little wooden control tower with a top that was hinged at the back—but *under* it, peeking out from beneath her shielding palms at the large hot water radiators that sat ominously below the huge old windows; Miss Russel had informed her charges, perhaps unwisely, that RADIATION, which was deadly, would come in through the windows when the war started; that made Maggie think that the radiators themselves would somehow be responsible. Sometimes they hadn't just sat beneath their desks, holding their heads in their hands to protect their faces from flying glass, but instead had trundled in single file through the halls and down to the basement of the monolithic brick building, where a yellow sign indicated that they were now in an AIR RAID SHELTER—at other times known as the lunch room. Since sometimes they ate there, and sometimes they simply crouched there among huge boxes of food, Maggie had acquired early, along with her fear of the deadly radiators, a sense that eating had to be accomplished as quickly as possible, because the food might at any moment be needed as a barrier against incoming bombs.

Well, naturally, given all this, she had drawn the logical conclusion. There was absolutely no point in thinking about, planning for, or taking into account the future, and she had immediately thrown herself into the task of becoming an underachiever. Her parents' constant unhappiness and their subsequent divorce might, she admitted now, have had something to do with her own uncertainty about the future, but if it had, she had not been aware of it at the time; she'd been aware only of the bombs. Since she knew she would die young, it clearly didn't matter if she didn't accomplish anything meaningful in her life, and actually it was almost her *duty* to take a stand against the attempt. Those who allowed themselves to be sucked into the grim cosmic joke that was the history of the earth were simply weak, lily-livered ninnies, and while they would all think it fine if a terminally ill cancer patient decided to use his last weeks in taking a trip around the world, visiting the Louvre one day, seeing the Acropolis by moonlight a few days later, then moving on to Egypt and the Pyramids, perhaps ending with a safari in Kenya, they were completely incapable of applying the same methods to *their* existences, which were certainly just as terminal.

But Maggie could, Maggie did, or at least Maggie *tried;* she had done her best in her life to date to accomplish absolutely nothing. Of course, she had graduated from the University of Chicago with a degree in psychology, and had gone on, while she was waiting for the End, to get her master's degree as well—but when the End had not come by that time, she had stopped, refusing a doctorate. She had felt confident that this would prevent her from getting a job of any kind, and when she had discovered, to her amazement, that an experimental clinic in Normal, Illinois, had wanted to hire her anyway, she had worked there just long enough to be offered an assistant directorship, at which point she had hastily quit. Every year that had passed, bringing her nearer to thirty, she had had to adjust her expectations of when the human race would extinguish itself, and every year had gotten a little more peeved at the exasperatingly long time it was taking. She had replaced underachievement—at which she was clearly a failure—with fractiousness, as a political stance, against the confusion of it all.

But even there, things were getting out of hand, she thought as she turned to glower at Minot. After almost a lifetime of peaceful indifference to the future, she was suddenly discovering in herself a capacity for enthusiasm, a fascination with events to come, that was embarrassingly uncontrollable and utterly unexpected. Because she had always been entirely cynical about the future, which was, in her opinion, probably not going to get here at all, and if it did arrive would endure only for a very short time—even while she had counseled people to let go of their commitment to pain, she had always done it with a secret edge of irony, because she didn't believe they'd actually have the time—it had never occurred to her that it was even possible to really look forward to anything. Since she had moved to Felicity the year before, in an ongoing attempt to sabotage the continuity of her own life, and with a sense that it was time, in any case, to plunge into the turgid heart of the xenophobic Midwest, she had heroically resisted all of Ada's attempts to instill in her a sense of hope.

But then she'd had the misfortune to see this movie, this movie about nuclear war. Oh, why on earth she had settled herself down in front of the television that night she really couldn't imagine; she generally watched very little TV, preferring to read instead. But there she'd been, lying comfortably on the couch, when this show had just begun. It was called *Threads*, an innocent enough title and certainly one that had tricked Maggie into watching until she got hooked; this movie, a British film, had supposed that only 250 megatons had fallen on Great Britain, and furthermore, that there had been time in advance for some evacuation of the cities. It had, in fact, in every way, given earth the benefit of the doubt. As a result, some people had been left alive after the war was over, and it was the vision of those people, still alive, that had ruined Maggie forever. As long as she had assumed that everyone was going to die in a nuclear war—everyone, that is, except perhaps some children in South America somewhere who would know, too young, the grave responsibility that had been thrust on them of rebuilding civilization, but who would face it bravely anyway, their clean-cut, polished faces shining as they emerged from the forest where they had stayed safely hidden until the fallout washed itself away and who were now heavily into the business of husbanding chickens and goats as they set about to garner all the undamaged books they could find, and to study engineering, astronomy, geology, pharmacology—as long as Maggie had assumed that everyone but these brave young people would die in the first wave of the war, she had simply accepted that extermination as a fact, a grim but impartial disaster.

So why had she had to see that damned movie, which showed people *after* the war? Actually, to call those ambulatory bipeds people was stretching the meaning of the word beyond reason, since, although they were not dead, they were certainly not people either. They scrabbled to harvest grain, after the killing nuclear winter, on a planet that, with its protective ozone layer burned away, was exposed to the burning and blinding ultraviolet rays of the sun. Their eyes swathed in bandages, their skin bedaubed with cancers, they stumbled about, impelled by hunger, and by hunger only. They had no feelings, no feelings at all, and their lack of love, of charity, of generosity, of hope, was almost minor compared with their lack of grief, of fear, of hatred, of anger. *They had no feelings;* they were entirely indifferent to what went on around them. And so they lost, in one short generation, much of their ability to use language, because without any feelings they had little worth communicating, and what words remained to them—perhaps five hundred—were shortened and twisted, changed beyond all recognition, so that they sounded like the random noises made in a house at night.

Well, this was truly appalling. Extinction was not a nice thought, certainly, but there was a simplicity, a clarity about it, that had always braced Maggie up. It wasn't that if *she* had to die, everyone else might as well die too and keep her company, like the Egyptian pharoahs who had all their wives and servants slaughtered along with them. But it had seemed to her that one of the things that made the certainty of her death in a nuclear holocaust a little less painful was that everyone, after all, was going to have to do it, and that would be it—all gone.

Instead, it was at least possible that this would happen instead, that it would be all just messy, that human beings—human beings exactly like herself—would be reduced to an existence of mewing and grunting, with no clever young scientists discovering a way to patch the world up again in their garages, with no whiz kids in senior high school reinventing electricity and medical science. No, even that scrub-faced band from South America wouldn't exist, wouldn't have a chance to circumnavigate the globe, collecting all the remaining treasures of the world, all of its great books, and bringing them back to their forest home. That would have been wonderful, but acceptable also would have been a clean sweep, a total tragedy. What was *not* acceptable, totally not acceptable, were these creatures in human form stumbling around the earth, living short—very short—and unhealthy—very unhealthy—lives completely devoid of meaning. If civilization ever got rebuilt, it would be unimaginably far in the future, after the pitiful remnants of Homo sapiens had died out and given some other intelligent species a chance to develop. Or rather, given some intelligent species a chance to develop for the first time, since the definition of intelligence was an ability to adapt in order to survive, and any species that let loose a nuclear war upon the world had clearly failed this crucial test.

And where did all this leave Maggie? In a pickle, that was where. Thirty-two years passed in mournful anticipation of the End had been predicated on the assumption that the End would be the End, and instead it might be just a horror. Actually, living in Felicity made it possible—even probable—that Maggie would be one of those who lived through the initial blasts, and therefore, if she didn't die of acute radiation sickness, she would join the ranks of the Stumblers. Well, she didn't plan to be a Stumbler, not if she could help it, and without being able to stop herself, she had determined to do something about it. She had been happy, of course, about the recent American visit of the General Secretary of the USSR, and glad when he and the President had signed the European arms reduction treaty. But that had been only the merest beginning, and she still felt she had to do her part. So, not only had she started picking up peace pamphlets wherever she came across them—there was actually a group in Felicity associated with an organization called Beyond War and she was thinking about attending its next meeting, on the following Saturday—but she had also volunteered to help organize the visit of these two professors from the Soviet Union. Worse than that, she would wake up every morning champing at the bit, eager to get started on something with meaning. Her elegant solution to impending doom—a passive resistance to hope—had become, recently, frayed around the edges, and she didn't like some of the consequences. For one thing, it had her working with Richard Minot—who at least had stopped leering at her now.

"Seriously," he said, "why are you really worried? What do you think could happen?"

"The Russians could be murdered. That's what could happen. And the Doomsday Clock could advance another minute."

"I don't think . . ." Minot was beginning when Sheriff Guthrie walked pleasantly into the room. The sheriff seemed awfully young to have the fate of the earth in his hands, and a good deal too handsome as well—but when Minot, clearly assuming that, as the chief defender of Law and Order in Rock County, Peale would be a natural retributivist, asked him for his opinion on whether or not people should be punished just because they deserved it, the sheriff disappointed Minot and delighted Maggie by saying, "But who decides if they deserve it?"

"Society," said Minot.

"Society!" said Maggie. "Society blows up the world!"

When Maggie got home after work that day, she felt happily tired and relieved. Neurotic as her fears no doubt were—Felicity, after all, was a peaceful town, not the sort of place where assassinations happened—she felt that she had done her bit to prevent an international incident, and that she could sleep more soundly that night. And as she drove up the driveway to Ada's house, to see Boonskie and Raga rushing out to meet her, she felt once again, as she always did here, that she was somehow, now, actually safe. Ever since she'd been ten years old, farmed out by her parents to the country for the summer, she had felt this way about the place in Pond Woods, that it was somewhere she couldn't be threatened. Her parents, involved in an acrimonious divorce, had not even come to visit her that first summer, and after a few weeks it had hardly mattered. At that time, Maggie had been just Ada's height, and as she had stood beside her in the kitchen, watching her crush herbs together in her marble mortar from Hungary, she had felt very proud to be an Esterhaczy; she still felt, really, the same way. The dogs leaped on her legs as she emerged from the car, and she was shouting, "Down, down!" when Ada came out to stand on the doorstep and wave at her. Maggie waved back. The dogs dropped down, looking shamefaced and eager to please.

"Good boys," she said. "Are you my furries? My little furry friends?" They wagged their tails to assert that they were, and then loped beside her to the house.

"Give me a kiss, you brat," said Ada. Maggie hugged her instead.

"Oh, my beautiful Maggie," Ada added. "Come in. We will talk while we eat." She marched Maggie in through the kitchen door, where soup simmered on the stove and a large salad sat on the table. She handed Maggie two bowls, took off her apron, and sat down.

"So what did you do today?" Ada asked presently. "Are you still counseling that hoodlum with the hair?"

"No, he's left school. It was a Mohawk, like the Iroquois."

"He was an Indian? Fine. Goodbye."

"He wasn't an Indian. He just wanted to be one."

"I'd like to be a bird, but I don't wear wings. And Doomsday? How are we doing with Doomsday? I checked and the clock hasn't moved for a month."

"Where did you check that?"

"Oh, I'm not an absolute bumpkin. Here, eat your soup. You look a little peaked."

"I do not look peaked."

"It's because you have no man."

"Please let's not talk about that again."

"Why not? You know something more interesting to say? A beautiful, talented girl, an Esterhaczy, she sits around talking to hoodlums? What you need is a man, and a baby to follow. Then you will have more color."

"I'll bet I would," said Maggie. "What is this?"

"A baby gives one such focus."

"As I recall, you hated them yourself. What about that wonderful little rubber cap?"

"Yes, yes, but that was later. I already had two. Well, let us talk of something else."

Maggie smiled to herself as she finished her soup and salad and got up to put on some water. Ada had always felt that one set of rules applied to her and one set applied to everyone else, and though she had always taken great pleasure in mourning aloud about how much she might have accomplished if only she had not had children and been dragged from place to place all over the globe, she seemed unembarrassed by her lack of consistency in suggesting now that Maggie have a child. She knew perfectly well, of course, that Maggie intended never to have children—good God, who, believing the things she believed and knowing the things she knew, could possibly justify bringing a child into the world? It would be an utterly immoral act—and she knew as well that Maggie had once been pregnant and had hated every single minute of it. As a teenager, when other girls had happily imagined their future families, Maggie had been so pessimistic about the earth's future that she had simply reminded those girls they'd be lucky if they got to subject the little creatures to their birth traumas before the world went up in a puff of smoke; she had always found those same girls' reasons for having children the most profoundly selfish justifications she had ever heard. They wanted to have children, they told her, because they wanted someone who would look like them, or who would love them unquestioningly, or who would do all the things they had never gotten to do. What they wanted, in fact, was to foist consciousness—which had never struck Maggie as such a great gift—onto beings who had never asked for it, and who would suffer from it for most of their lives. Oh, Maggie was well out of it, from what she had seen in her work. Everyone hated their parents, after all.

"Are you making tea?" Ada asked as the water started to hiss. "I have a new blend you should try, a very good tea. And I've decided to make Boonskie a father."

"Male dogs eat their babies."

"Oh, piffle, they do not. *One* might have, once—you are so catastrophic."

"So breed him. It's a great idea."

"Yes. Here is the nice new tea."

"Aren't you having any?"

"It's a little too strong for me. But you will find it tempting, I believe. A perfect little pickup."

"A pickup is a stranger you meet in a bar."

"Marvelous!" said Ada. "What a language!" And then, smiling sweetly, she spooned some tea in a pot; Maggie regarded her with faint suspicion.

# SWORD
# MEDITATION

# 8

BAILEY wished that Joel would *leave* so that she could go get the herbs she still needed. She was glad that it was a clear and sunny day, since tonight—Friday, April 29—she would, she hoped, be starting a coven. It would be nice if the moon could be clearly viewed, even if it *was* two days from the full. Though she had already cleaned the house and gotten everything all ready—she had even baked brownies, as a refreshment, and bought a bottle of red wine for the section of the meeting her book called "Cakes and Wine"—she needed a few herbs to create a charm for eloquence to help her in her public address. She knew that all the women who were coming to her house tonight—with the possible exception of Charlene, whom Bailey had talked to a little over the last few months—could not possibly know what witchcraft was, much less how to go about doing it; her first task would be to get rid of their prejudices, which were probably weird and deep-set. Old hags cackling on broomsticks, horrible Satanists performing unspeakable rites—these were the images she had to dispel, and she was scared she wouldn't be able to do it. She tended, when she was serious about something, not to get tongue-tied, exactly, but to get so intense that she scared people off—she really didn't know why. So she was going to take Chance and make a run out to Ada's, if only Joel would get lost. He showed no sign of getting lost, though, as he complained to her, as usual, in that rather grating voice of his.

"So what does my wife do next? She tells me I'm going to have to buy her a new car! Not just any car, you understand; a *new* car, something I've never in my life even smelled the inside of, much less driven around in the streets."

"Oh?" said Bailey, sounding sympathetic in spite of herself.

"Well, I don't know, I told her, I don't know. You think I could find one for under nine hundred dollars? So she said she could take me to court."

"Listen, Joel, I've got things to do."

"Yeah, that's OK, I don't mind."

"I mean, I've got things to do *alone*."

"Oh." He looked slightly hurt.

There was not really anything wrong with Joel except that he was kind of a creep; Bailey didn't know why it was that she always got involved with such men. They tended to be fun in bed, but since she had long ago proven to her own satisfaction that that was not enough to get on with, why did she keep it up? Well, she had hopes. They generally lasted about ten days. Somewhere out there, Bailey thought, there must be a man one could love, but she sure never seemed to run into him, and had just about given up trying. Her spell to attract love had so far not produced any results, and while she hadn't really expected it to, she was still slightly disappointed.

"Goodbye," she said, impulsively kissing him.

"Oh, all right. I'll see you on Sunday."

The minute he was gone, Bailey felt vastly relieved; Chance seemed to be relieved, too. After only a week of having Chance for a companion, Bailey already adored her—she was attentive and intelligent to an extraordinary degree, unlike any other dog Bailey had known. She had a habit of stretching herself out on the floor so that her soft underside was pressed flat against the boards and her two short hind legs stuck out straight behind her, looking rather like the handles of an old-fashioned washboard; in this position she would await events, and spring to meet them when they came. She would follow Bailey from room to room, from house to car, and from car to stables, for all the world as if she had been doing this for years, and whenever Bailey settled down long enough to permit it, she would curl up next to her side with her shoulders tucked into Bailey's armpit and her head resting on Bailey's chest. There, after regarding her new person with a direct, almost speculative stare, she would fall asleep for as long as possible. Outside, she was vigorous, and capable of running flat out so fast that she could catch up with dogs much bigger than herself; when she was feeling especially playful she would leap into the air and pounce on imaginary objects precisely like a cat or a rabbit—or a fox—the arc of her body leaving the earth and meeting the earth again, having traced a semicircle in the air. Bailey loved to carry her from place to place; just holding Chance in her arms seemed to bring her a sense of calm and hope, as if the dog's body, small as it was, radiated elemental energy.

Now, Chance followed Bailey into the bedroom, where she changed her clothes for the evening. She put on a pair of pants from Afghanistan, gray wool pants with hundreds of tucks at the waist, and a matching gray wool vest. She hoped this outfit made her look somber and respectable, and she approved a red shirt to go with it. Then she checked her book to see what herbs she needed—fenel, hazel, mandrake, and valerian—and wrote them down on a slip of paper, tucking it into her vest. She scooped Chance up and took her to the car, then started out toward Ada's.

At the corner of Walnut, she put on her brakes and noticed that they were in need of grinding. Her money situation being what it was, maybe she should fix them herself, but she'd never been good with the physical world, and she didn't know whether she could manage it. If only she *had* been good, everything might have been different, but since she'd grown up on a farm, in a family whose definitions of excellence and whose expectations of behavior revolved entirely around the contest with matter, she hadn't had a chance of winning their approval.

She was happy to arrive at the Esterhaczy house; it always cheered her vastly to see Ada. Kneeling, her feet tucked behind her, Ada was attacking the weeds next to the granite front stoop, attacking them with a trowel, first ramming the trowel into the dirt to loosen their roots, then hitting them several times over the head—probably to kill their spirit—and finally pulling them up, shaking their roots furiously so that sprays of dirt flew in all directions. She waved at Bailey over her shoulder, a wave that looked more like the brandishing of a weapon, and then she stopped and got to her feet while Bailey parked next to the trellis. Here, her trouble with the brakes continued—she had to punch them four times before they would properly engage. As she emerged from the car, holding Chance in her arms, Boonskie and Raga came rushing up to meet her, Boonskie as usual barking furiously and at the same time wagging his tail so hard that it whipped his hindquarters violently from side to side, and Raga flattening himself on the ground in an ecstasy of humility, and then leaping riotously at her legs. They were both overjoyed when they noticed that she had brought them another dog to play with, and after deducing from the slight wiggle in her hindquarters that indeed Chance wanted to get down—she had never made a sound in Bailey's hearing, not a bark, not a growl, nothing louder than a pant—Bailey yelled, "Back off, guys!" and then set Chance down in the cleared space, where she wagged her stump of a tail until it practically buzzed. Then she ran a short distance and folded her front legs under her; her rump she left in the air, her tail wagging on top of it. The other dogs didn't need to be asked twice, and they joyfully bounded away.

"Hello, hello," called Ada cheerfully. "I have been wanting to see you for a week."

"To see me?"

"Yes, you. You, my little pumpkin. I see that you have a new dog. But she's too small, and anyway not a hound. I need a hound. Do you know some?"

"You want *another* dog?"

"Not to keep. Just to rent. I will need her female apparatus."

"Her *what*?"

"Her apparatus. Her private parts. Boonskie wishes to have pups. Don't you, darling?" she called to the dog. Boonskie, on whose huge ear Chance was now chewing, looked as if this was news to him.

Boonskie was one of Bailey's all-time favorite dogs, or had been, before she got Chance. She had seen a picture once in the *Pure-Bred Gazette* of a dog called a Rhodesian Ridgeback, and Boonskie could have passed anywhere for a Rhodes if only he had had the ridge. He had a broad, noble forehead, and a long, wide nose with dark coloring all around the snout. His eyes were large and brown, and they were rimmed with eyelashes that were thick and black; the eyelids themselves looked as if they were made up with eyeliner, because the dark line all around them stood out in marked and elegant contrast to the biscuity color of his fur—if the eyes had been a human male's, women would have swooned over them regularly. His ears, another of his good features, were as mobile and expressive as ears ever could be, large and well proportioned, not houndlike—most hounds had long and droopy ears like Sam's—but just the perfect length and width, and capable of infinite mood and expression. His body was large and muscular—he must weigh over eighty pounds—but there was a leanness to his ribcage and a sleekness to his lines when he stood, attentive, with his legs thrust slightly back, in classic canine attention.

What made him such a special dog, however—and Bailey had to admit that, crazy as Ada might be about him, calling him "her darling boy," "her handsome man," and so on, this was a dog that justified such excess, which anyway Bailey, too, indulged in—what made him so special was not his good looks, but their combination with his clownish nature. There was a basic silliness about him that manifested itself in everything from the way he wagged his tail—so that his whole body whipped around as if his tail were wagging him—to the way he panted, his long pink tongue framed in a perfectly lunatic grin; the combination of the panting sound and the excessive curve of the lips certainly allowed him to laugh. And when he raced, roaring, after something that would, the next minute, send him fleeing in terror, or when he, with obviously no sense at all of the incongruity of the endeavor, tried to climb into your lap and curl up there, struggling to get first one enormous haunch and then another situated comfortably, and always surprised when it seemed impossible to accomplish both at once—a position quite bone-crushing to the recipient of his affection, who, nevertheless, could hardly bear to push him off, since his total contentment was signaled both by his thumping tail and the grinning pant of his laugh—well it was just elegant comedy, and anybody in the world would have to love it.

"He does, does he?" Bailey asked.

"Yes, yes. He doesn't know it yet. Come in and we will think on this together."

Bailey followed Ada into the kitchen, where Ada put water on for tea. Sam, she thought, might be the perfect mate.

"My brother has a bitch hound," she said.

"Your brother the lunatic? I met him once, remember?"

"I know. At the farmers' market."

"Yes. Is the hound a lunatic, too?"

"No. She's a little depressed, though."

"And her name?"

"It's Samantha. Sam for short."

"Sam! I have always liked Sams!"

Ada poured tea, and also procured an order slip. She shoved the mug of tea and the order slip simultaneously under Bailey's nose, and while Bailey carefully wrote down the herbs she needed, Ada kept talking, telling Bailey about some past Sams.

"There was an Englishman in Egypt; he would tell the children stories. And a Canadian priest with a small lisp. He later married; well, the lisp was very sexy! Sam will be perfect, I am sure."

As usual at Ada's, things had moved rather quickly, from beginning to end, with no in-between, and as Bailey sipped the tea, she thought about her brother; he wouldn't rent Sam to *her*. When Bailey explained this to Ada, suggesting she contact him directly, Ada, a natural conspirator, agreed. Then she began to select the herbs Bailey needed, from the vast collection of green glass Mason jars in her pantry, and said, "They are for your witchcraft?"

"Yes, for the meeting tonight."

"Tell me, what does all that have to say about conception?"

"But if you're interested, why not come over?"

"No, no. It is just fertility I wish to know of. What are the rites, the practices, and so on?"

"Well, I'm not sure. I'd have to look them up. I know a spell to be friends with your womb."

"Aha!"

"But that's more for cramps, irregular bleeding, and so on."

"Oh. Cramps have nothing to do with this. And anyway," said Ada, carrying the herbs back into the kitchen, "it would be someone else's womb. Mine no longer has much pep."

"Yeah," said Bailey. "But I really don't think . . . I mean, do you think dogs need the help?"

"We all need the help," said Ada grimly. "It is sad but true. But never mind."

"Call Howell tonight. He'll be home then, I know. Because Charlene is coming over to my place."

Back in her apartment, Bailey lit some candles and did a quick meditation on her athame; she had better get her mind off dogs and their virtues, and onto the subject at hand. In her book, the meditation was called a Sword Meditation, and it was supposed to remind you of your own power—to influence others, with the strength of your mind; to be responsible in the way you used it. The power of the sword was that of discrimination—of making choices and carrying them out—and Bailey liked the meditation; it was still so new to her, the thought that she might be able to *change* things. When she had discovered this book on witchcraft, in the library three months earlier, she had felt as if it explained everything. Everything was connected, everything was important, everything was part of something else. She and her dogs really *were* equals, part of one great living thing; there was nothing beyond what she was a part of.

Then, meditation concluded, she assembled her materials on the altar, and began to raise power to make her charm. With her mortar and pestle she ground the herbs while visualizing herself being eloquent.

And eloquence was needed, she had no question about that. It was hard to explain witchcraft. Why, even the women who had agreed to come tonight probably still believed the lies that had been spread about it during the great burnings, when the Christian persecutors in England and Europe, determined to eradicate all pagan religions from the world, had claimed that witchcraft was evil. And while most people today probably didn't believe that anyone who had ever been executed as a witch had actually been *able* to make a neighbor's cow go dry, or to turn someone into a beast, they certainly still believed that witches had *wanted* to do these things, and would have, if they only could. Although "the devil" was an entirely Christian invention, unknown to the old religion of the Goddess, Christianity had picked "devil worship" as its rallying call, since pictures of the devil in Christian art were based upon distorted impressions of the Horned God himself. Naturally, witches worshipped the Horned God, but to claim that he was the devil, and was evil, was about like non-Christians saying that Christians worship *Jesus*—this in an appalled tone of self-righteous indignation— and that Jesus, as everyone knew, recommended that small babies be boiled at least an hour before being salted and eaten.

But the medieval Christians had been fanatical and ruthless, just like the fundamentalists today. Determined to kill both the flesh and the spirit of witchcraft, they had put at least a million witches to death in sixteenth-century Europe, and in the centuries that followed at least four million more had been killed. When Bailey first read about this, she found it incredible that such a large campaign of genocide went totally untalked about, was hardly mentioned in history texts. Some estimates put the number of witches executed in Europe at nine million, more than the number of Jews killed during the Holocaust, and there was no doubt that the persecuted had been mostly women; in some villages every female alive was murdered, and the deaths had often been horrible. In the end, witchcraft had gone deeply underground. There was nothing else it could do.

Bailey gathered her herbs and spread them on the cloth, adding a dime and twisting the top over them. Tying the cloth shut with one silver thread, she breathed on it to charge it with air. Then she passed it through the candle flame to charge it with fire, sprinkled a few drops of water on it to charge it with water, and finally dipped it into the salt to charge it with earth. As she tied it again with thread and held it close to her breast, shutting her eyes and charging it with all the energy she could summon, she had a vision of something like an army, gathered, listening raptly to her words. She would teach these people, she would lead them, she would open up her heart; she would stir them to see that they were all one. She would not scare them, she would not freak them out. Or she hoped she wouldn't. But she probably would.

At eight o'clock there was a knock on the door, and Bailey ran to answer it. The moon was just rising behind the big oak tree to the east of the house, and it could be seen through the large front windows; it looked like an explosion of light below the horizon, dusky, diffused by the sky. It was lovely, she was lovely, the Goddess of the Moon, and Bailey paused for a moment to watch her before she opened the door. She didn't know why she was attaching such significance to the coming occasion, but in some concrete way it seemed her last chance to make peace with Felicity, to find something of value here. She felt a moment of breathless excitement, and then she opened the door to discover Janet, Phyllis, and Thea, who formed a phalanx on the old gray boards of the porch and looked as if they shared a secret. It seemed bad luck that they were the first to arrive; they were the wives of some of Howell's friends, and although they had all, at one time or another, expressed in Bailey's hearing intense dissatisfaction with their lives as they were presently living them and had, furthermore, ridiculed their "goody-Goddy" relations, they were not very positive people, taken all around, and Bailey was almost sorry she had asked them.

But "Come in," she said. "Glad you could make it."

"We wouldn't have missed it," said Thea.

Bailey settled them all in the living room, with wine, and then went to bring in some brownies. Strictly speaking, the refreshments were supposed to be pulled out a good deal later in the evening, after the talk and the ceremony, and the earthing of the power, but now was when they were clearly needed, whatever her book suggested. Happily, the rest of the guests arrived shortly, but separately and more manageably than the phalanx. Charlene—who had told Howell that she was going to be playing Bingo tonight—had obviously gotten dressed up for the occasion; she'd a circle pin on her collar. Pearl Watkins, from the grocery, came next, and then Linda and Jane, who both rode at Grey Rock. Bailey introduced everyone to everyone else.

She felt nervous now, extremely nervous, in spite of her charms for eloquence, and she drank a glass of wine herself while she lit the candles. Then, while everyone sat stiffly around her living room, surreptitiously studying first the altar and then their own hands, Bailey pulled down the front shades. Suddenly, for no reason, her motives seemed unclear to her. She couldn't remember why she was doing this. She finished the wine, then sat down cross-legged in front of the altar. She tugged at the buttons on her vest.

"Well, hmm, witchcraft," she started off at last. "It began a really long time ago. And what it does, you see, is worship the energy of connection, the way that everything is tied together. I mean, witchcraft believes that all energy is one, and that energy can be, like, stored and directed. Thoughts can affect things, and feelings can move through space. Every life has an impact on every other. And desire, in a way, holds the universe together—through gravity and atomic attraction. The most amazing thing is the way modern physics upholds this, which witches knew thirty thousand years ago."

The spell for eloquence seemed to be working; so far, her audience looked interested.

"Thirty thousand years?" asked Jane.

"That's a long time," said Linda. "How do they know it?"

"Well, cave paintings, and stuff like that. When the great ice sheets covered Europe, and people hunted reindeer to survive, that's when it started, according to the legends. The weapons they had were very primitive. So in order to be successful hunters they had to somehow get in touch with the spirit of the herds; they had to understand the animals they hunted. Shamans dressed in horns and skins to increase their feelings for the deer—this became the Horned God, consort of the Goddess. Gradually, witchcraft developed as a religion that worshipped all the natural cycles, of birth and death, of the seasons, of the sun and the moon."

"So what are the rules?" asked Janet, a little sourly.

"There are no rules. It's all inside us."

"I don't get it," said Phyllis. "Who's the boss?"

"Yeah, I thought it was all to do with Satan," added Thea. "I don't get all this stuff about reindeer."

Almost half an hour later, Bailey felt pretty exhausted and terribly discouraged, too. Although Linda and Jane and Pearl all appeared to be sympathetic, and Charlene at least neutral, the other three had formed a unified front. They had made it eminently clear that what *they* were interested in was not this newfangled interpretation of witchcraft, but the good old nitty-gritty kind, where you hexed people, and turned them into trees, or maybe stuck pins in their feet. Bailey explained that, while there might be occasions where you had to hex a person for the good of the world—a rapist, a sniper on a rooftop—you never ever could do it for purely selfish reasons; that would be totally irresponsible. Then Bailey emphasized again that witchcraft was a religion that essentially worshipped the earth, and Janet and Thea found that quite hilarious. As if they didn't spend enough of their time cleaning it up off the kitchen floor, now they were supposed to worship it, and when Bailey clarified that she wasn't talking about *dirt*, there was still no positive response. There seemed to be a triple consensus that what with tornadoes, floods, droughts, blizzards, and pig shit, the earth wasn't all it was cracked up to be, anyway, and they wanted something that would take them away from all that—maybe a kind of movie actor in the sky. Indeed, the transformation of the broom from an implement of labor into a vehicle that would make possible a formal introduction to this guy seemed to be the only part of witchcraft lore they liked, and when Bailey explained that, as far as she could tell, brooms had absolutely nothing to do with being a witch, they began to lose interest fast.

"So you mean I can't turn Billy Bob into a frog?" said Phyllis ironically. "Not even for a little while?"

"Don't worry, he looks like a frog already," said Thea. "Just use your imagination."

"Witchcraft respects *all* living things."

"Not Mitch," said Janet, and laughed.

When Bailey, in desperation, told them about the dimensions of the slaughter—of *women*, she emphasized—in the Middle Ages, that didn't help at all, not even a tiny bit.

"We can identify with those millions who were killed," she said. "Can't we? They were people just like us." But Thea and Janet and Phyllis appeared to have no desire to identify with even one murdered witch, much less nine million of them, and this unfortunate turn of phrase basically brought proceedings to a halt. Each of the three suddenly seemed to remember that she had a child, or a dog, or an irate husband waiting at home, so with three mumbled variations on "So nice . . . we really must get together again," Phyllis, Thea, and Janet gathered whatever they had come with, and headed posthaste for the door.

The others followed, but Charlene surprised Bailey by being the last to leave, and by touching her on the shoulder as she did so.

"It's nice," she said. "Better than Church of God." She paused for a moment and studied the floor. "Are you going to that auction tomorrow?"

"What auction?"

"The Widau place. The whole thing's going up. And there's a cauldron for sale, appears like."

"Why, Charlene, thanks for telling me."

"Your brother really loves you. You know that, don't you? He's just scared."

Bailey supposed that was true, but it didn't seem to mean much. She waved to Charlene from the door. Well, that was that; there wouldn't be a coven. Once again, Bailey was all alone. And while, on the one hand, she felt a certain sadness, on the other she felt a real relief. She was used to being alone, by now, and though she had, all her life, sought connection with other human beings, she had never really found it, so she could hardly be devastated by its continuing to elude her. And the air tonight—the air was so sweet— and the moon, though not full, looked so. She sat down on the porch steps, took Chance in her arms, then held her face up to the light.

# 9

HOWELL was feeling rather at loose ends, with Charlene gone
for the evening. He wasn't expecting her home for hours—she had
gone to the Methodist church to play Bingo—and he had already
put the children to bed, so he was, at least practically, all alone.
He had decided to spend the evening reading, but he'd had a little
trouble settling down and had just gone out again to check on the
animals, though he knew they had all been fed and cared for. Now
he was heading again for the living room, where he had left his
mystery, *Vanishing Act.* It was lying on Richard Minot's couch, a
couch that—despite his continuing suspicion of the motives that
had allowed him to acquire it—he had gradually taken to sitting
on, as he found it unusually comfortable. Turning on the goose-
necked lamp that stood beside it, he settled himself back against
the cushions and picked up his book, anticipating an hour or two
of pleasure.

Howell loved mysteries, he always had; they were his main window on the world. In mysteries things always looked very complicated and then turned out to be so simple, and that was how Howell
thought the world must be, too, if you could only find the people
responsible. In mysteries, of course, the person behind the scenes
was always just a murderer, leaving a trail of blood wherever he
went, while in life the responsible ones were part of conspiracies,
like those international Bankers. But instead of figuring out the
clues of the world, and guessing the way They managed it, Howell

enjoyed something a little more manageable to take his mind off
the really big questions: the questions about Bailey and whether
she would rob him, the questions about those Russians.

Howell had been born in 1960, and his earliest memories were
of the Cold War. That was a time that had spread its cloud of
suspicion over Felicity as surely as it had over larger and more
cosmopolitan centers, and it had shadowed indelibly the lighting
of Howell's brain, all that talk of the terrible Red Menace. Why,
red was a color that he still couldn't abide; that was why he owned
John Deere tractors. And though Howell knew that some people
these days thought the Russians were just like everyone else, he
could not think that this was anything but absurd, and that so were
the people who believed it. If the Russians were like Indiana farmers, they would live in Indiana, it seemed to him, and their living
not in Indiana but in a country six thousand miles away seemed
pretty suspicious, in and of itself. Add to that the fact that they
wore not baseball caps, but those square fur fortresses on top of
their heads, and also that they were never seen in photographs
without heavy overcoats on, overcoats that would make farming
impossible, and that might, additionally, conceal almost anything
within their folds, and finally, that they were *Reds*—well, you'd
have to be a fool to trust one. Bailey did, of course—or would, he
was sure; she drove that little red car, didn't she?—but that just
proved his point, since no one could trust her either. About the
only thing Howell found sympathetic about the Russians was the
way they didn't like to smile at the cameras. Neither did he, come
to that, and he never once had.

But that was a small point compared with how different they were
from him, and though it wouldn't have mattered much if they hadn't
had any power, it was extremely irritating to know that someone
so different from you yourself had just as much power in the world—
or more. Because Howell was smart enough to realize that his own
power as an American citizen was pretty limited when you came
right down to it—look what was happening to the farms—but the
Russians, from what he had read, seemed to act not like a bunch

of individual people, but like a big block of people, all connected in their minds by hypnotism or something. He imagined them all getting up in the morning at the same time, moving toward their eggs and bacon like automatons, and then all popping out of their houses on the dot of eight, all the doors of all the houses popping open at the same time, *bang, bang, bang.* Then they would all climb into their cars, tiny foreign cars, and—perfectly in line—move out into the traffic. If they lived in the country, they couldn't work on farms, it seemed to him; they must work on enormous chunks of land like those agribusinesses, all harvesting on the same day, like a bunch of bees collecting honey. The whole thing was rather like synchronized swimming when you thought about it, and he didn't know a single other American who approved of the way that synchronized swimming had been allowed into the Olympics. Only, in Russia it was *everyone* who was synchronized, not just some women swimmers, and that was what made it so dangerous, that was what made it so sick. Communism was like when your *brain* was taken out and pickled and then put back, because if your brain wasn't pickled, then why on earth would you want to be just like everyone else? God had put you here on earth to be you, and if He had wanted you to be like everyone else, He would have attached you all at the elbow to begin with, like a bunch of paper dolls. And it wasn't just Howell who thought so. All his decent neighbors thought the same.

So now two of these bees, these *units,* were on their way to Felicity. And while it seemed a God-given opportunity for Howell to do something fine and American, he just couldn't figure out what he could do. He certainly couldn't, well, kill them. He didn't even want to hurt them, really; he just wanted to do something daring and clever that would result in a lot of good for a lot of people like him, and would make him a sort of hero. The obvious thing that *needed* to be done, of course, was to stop all these bank foreclosures; but even if the Russians were in on the CONSPIRACY, these two particular ones might not be. On the other hand—and here Howell stretched out his feet and put them up on the couch, resettling the cushions behind him—on the other hand, what if they were? What if that was why they were coming? This thing was big, so big it was slippery. Were they coming to, maybe, check up on it?

Howell always thought slowly and steadily, and better when he was relaxed, so he turned now to the first page of his book and settled in for a nice long read. At first, he paid only the careful, ethical attention that the printed word was always due, but then, as he turned the pages one by one, thoughtfully licking his thumb each time he placed it in the upper right-hand corner, he noticed that something was going on; God seemed to be giving him a message. Because this wasn't a murder mystery at all, it was a kidnapping mystery, and it was so clever, so unbelievably clever, that he certainly couldn't have thought of it himself. In this story, a car full of children disappeared somewhere between the north and south end of a quarry road. It was seen entering by at least three independent eyewitnesses, and it was never seen to emerge. Naturally, it was at first believed that the car had crashed through the fence on the east side of the road and sunk without a trace in the water, but a close examination of the fence showed that this couldn't be true, and as for the other side of the road, it was a very steep hillside, riddled with trees, up which a car could hardly have driven. Everyone thought it was magic; where could the car have gone to?

Well, where this car had gone to was inside another car! Or a truck, rather, which had pulled up in front of it and forced it to drive up a ramp. Then the truck had collapsed the ramp, crashed the rear doors shut, and driven right out on the road, and straight through the middle of town. It said in the story that this was an old bootlegging trick, only instead of liquor this time, they had hidden human beings. When you found out how it was done, it was absolutely obvious. But before, you knew it was just impossible, something that couldn't be done. And Howell, as he set the book down in his lap and gazed steadily at his feet, figured that if it had had *him* stumped, why it would stump anyone at all. It was simply and clearly an answer to his prayers, a direct sign from the Almighty. Because Felicity Pond Road was exactly like the road described in the story, and he himself had a truck, and it would be no trouble at all to kidnap those Russian bumblebees. Not only would it be no trouble, but it was certainly now his duty, because God would never have sent him this story if He hadn't meant him to use it. One day, when they were out driving around Felicity Pond, he would lie in wait, force their car into his truck, and drive them off the face of the earth. Or not off the face of the earth—just to somewhere nearby—but it would *seem* that they had disappeared. It would *seem* that it was magic. And then, when everyone had had a chance to get used to the idea, he would call the police and tell them he had them, the units, and that he wanted—what?

Well, that he wanted just to expose a CONSPIRACY, not to gain a personal revenge. Why, the whole point of this was to show what a real American was like, and a real Christian, also; the whole point of this was to right a wrong. And the wrong was the way that this international CONSPIRACY of Bankers was defrauding everyone of their land, and also, on a bigger scale, the existence of the con- SPIRACY itself. Why, it meant that good citizens—deliberately con- fused by brainwashing propaganda—had to stand by and watch helplessly while politicians gave their food, goods, and money to Banker-controlled foreign governments, under the guise of "better relations" and "easing tensions." And they couldn't keep anything for themselves. The tragic absurdity of this hopeless position was such that for a moment Howell felt poleaxed by it, and he took his feet down off Minot's couch and placed them on the floor in front of him. Once he had the Russians, then, what would he do with them? He clasped his hands and inquired of God.

It took a minute for God to appear, and when He did He looked mussed. His hair, generally very neatly combed—so neatly combed that it seemed to be painted on His head—looked this time as if it had been caught in a wind and then gotten damp from a rain. Moreover, He appeared to be breathing heavily, and His cheeks were flushed and glistening, all of which did not, somehow, inspire confidence—but Howell asked his question anyway. What, he asked, should he do with the Russians? Should he demand some kind of ransom? And if so, who should he demand it from? He settled down to wait.

He thought of these little sessions with God as he thought of going to the store. Sometimes you had to stand in line for a while, but you could usually bring home what you'd gone for, so he was patient while God caught His breath and furrowed His forehead in thought. Then He said, in that "I've got you covered" voice of His: "Ask for all the farm mortgages held in Rock County. You can burn them, then let the men go." And as God faded slightly, and then some more, and finally vanished with a hollow *pop*, Howell sat straight up in his seat and stared out the window in pleasure. The perfect seemliness of this suggestion fortified him like a good meal. It would be ticklish, it would be touchy, but he thought he had found Their soft spot.

Howell was suddenly jerked from his thoughts by the ringing of the phone in the kitchen. Since Charlene was well known to hate the phone—and never to answer when it rang—only at night, when Howell was inside, did people even try to call them. As Howell himself loved the phone, on which he often tried to convert his listeners—he found it easier to marshal his arguments like that, when people weren't staring at him—it was with pleasant anticipation that he marched off to the kitchen, where he picked up the receiver.

"Howell Bourne speaking."

"Yes, yes. This is Ada Esterhaczy calling."

"Who?"

"We met by your sister Bailey."

"We did?"

"Merely in a manner of speaking. We met as we bought tomatoes."

At first, Howell could not think who this was, but now he managed to remember. His sister had introduced her once at the farmers' market, where Mrs. Esterhaczy had, he now recalled, been buying several flats of tomatoes, and where he had, at first, had trouble understanding what she said; she had a strong European accent.

"You're the one from Hungary?" he asked.

"That is right. Actually, I have lived many places."

"Yes, Mrs. Esterhaczy, I remember. And now you live out in Pond Woods."

"So. You have a hound dog, do you not?"

"I have two dogs, a male and a female."

"It is the bitch I speak of. I would like to rent her. You understand? Rent her apparatus."

"What?"

"Puppies. My dog must have puppies. So I need to find Boonskie a mate."

"You have a male dog?"

"How else would it happen?"

"I see. Yes, I understand."

After further discussion, Howell had it pinned down, and it sounded like a very nice deal. Mrs. Esterhaczy wanted to get Sam as soon as she went into heat, and to keep her until six weeks after the pups were born. Then Howell would get Sam and all but one of the pups back. Mrs. Esterhaczy would pay him eighty dollars. Since Mrs. Esterhaczy would have all the feeding and upkeep for the four months that Sam would be gone, and Howell would get the bulk of the litter, good coon hounds that he could sell off, he agreed to the plan, then got directions to the house; he would bring Sam by in about four weeks. He hung up, just slightly disappointed that he hadn't had the chance to try to proselytize.

He no longer felt like reading, so Howell went to check up on the twins. Their room was at the front of the house, a funny little room with eight sides and two long windows that opened out onto the roof of the porch and that had, therefore, to be kept closed at all times lest the children wander out and kill themselves. Charlene had papered the room with a flowered print in gay pinks and greens— the green like the green of early spring, the pink a nice soft rose. Some of the lines were not quite straight, and in one part the glue was drying out, but Howell thought she'd done a very good job, and the children seemed to like it, too.

Right now, they were asleep, lying in their separate beds. Daisy had her thumb lying damply near her mouth and Darell was com-

pletely entwined with his covers. They were so solid, so indisput-
able, so alive, that it seemed incredible that they had ever not
been, and that for a while it had seemed they never would be. It
had taken Charlene almost two years to get pregnant, and while
Howell had accepted this is a fact of life and had not been unduly
disappointed—his only experience with new family members up
to that time had been the arrival of his difficult sister, and if she
was any gauge of what was possible, he couldn't help but have his
doubts about babies—when Charlene had reported that she was
going to have twins, he'd been almost incoherent with excitement.

He thought it was the tornado that had done it. The evening that
the twins had been conceived, a tornado had struck behind the
house while he and Charlene were making love, and while it had,
without a doubt, done some damage—it had blown in all the windows on the west side of the house, and had sliced the protruding
chimney neatly off at the roofline—it had also done this wonderful
thing, which was to bring the twins into being. When the wind had
started picking up, Howell had already been inside Charlene, and
though he had glanced, somewhat distracted, out the window to
see if they should go down to the basement, it hadn't really been
tornado weather, so he had kept on with what he was doing. When
the tornado actually came into sight, it was too late to stop and go
elsewhere. He was on the final arc of his thrust, his whole being
reduced to a tiny glow of light, when this spiral of darkness swept
perilously close and grabbed the chimney in its hand. And Howell,
defying danger, laying himself open to death, marched right up to
the cannon's mouth, thrust once more, and came. The windows
shattered, the spiral rushed away; Howell's reward had been his
children.

Ever since, Howell had been rather fond of tornadoes; he felt
they brought out the best in him. He was also, of course, rather
fond of his children, though they didn't look very much like him.
Daisy, as she lay with her thumb so carefully available, lest she
wake up and need it suddenly, looked a bit like Bailey, and Darell
looked more like Charlene. It was unusual for Howell to be in their
room at night, and it struck him as he saw them sleeping that he

liked them like this, quiet and silent, perfectly comprehensible. Normally, they were intransigent, unpredictable, with their reasoning minds. Now, as he bent over to touch Daisy's head, she opened her eyes and stared at him.

"Hello, daughter. How are you sleeping?" he asked, despite the obvious truth that she was no longer asleep.

"Can I have a glass of water?" she asked, and at her voice Darell woke up, too, and thrust his legs, which were wrapped in the sheets, rigidly down toward the footboard. On discovering that he was trussed like a mummy, he panicked and kicked and yelped. Howell stood there foolishly, wondering why it was that he was so good with plants and animals but could feel so helpless around children.

"Darell, calm down. Unwrap them slowly. I'm going to get Daisy some water." But when he came back with the cup—a plastic one that glowed in the dark, and both Daisy and Darell loved it—Darell, who always had trouble waking up, was still fighting with the tangled sheets. And now he started to cry, but when Howell said, as he handed Daisy the cup, "Darell, be a man. Stop thrashing around," Darell just cried harder than ever. Tentatively, Howell bent down to try to hold Darell's legs in place long enough for him to unwrap them. He was delighted just then to hear the truck in the driveway. Charlene had come home early. His plan quickly changed; he would hold the legs down until Charlene got up here to help him.

Daisy, meanwhile, was drinking the water in tiny little sips. Why? Was it because she wasn't really thirsty? Or did she want to annoy him? Or what? If she'd been a young calf, he would have known what she was doing. With people, it was just so much more puzzling.

Now Charlene's steps sounded on the stairs and she came deliberately into the room. She seemed to absorb the situation at a glance, as she told Daisy to drink up, but to drink only *half* the cup, and then she said, "Darell. Lie still," which he did, right away.

Howell then watched his wife take the bedding entirely off the bed, shake it out, and tuck it in again under the end of the mattress, and it amazed him that this simple task—as simple as any physical task one could confront on a farm—had been somehow completely beyond him. Darell pulled the sheet up around his chin, and turned over on his side, and Daisy held the cup up to be taken; Charlene set it down on the bureau.

"There," she said. "By the time it fades, you be right asleep."

"OK, Mommy," Daisy said.

"Good night, Mommy," said Darell.

Back downstairs, Howell gathered his wits. "Why are you back so early?"

"No reason," said Charlene. "I just got tired. I wasn't winning anything, anyway."

"Oh," said Howell. "Well, that's too bad. Shall we have a nice cup of Ovaltine? While you were away, I had an idea. In fact . . . well, let's sit down here." And, adopting his lecturing tone, he told her all about it.

Quite sensibly, she asked, "What'll you do with them? You can't very well bring them here." And while, in general, Howell had no very high opinion of his wife's intellectual capabilities—not that she was stupid, not at all, but she just wasn't interested in the kind of large issue that Howell found so compelling: the world situation, politics, economics, theology, the history of mankind—this time, he had to admit, she had hit on a troublesome question. He'd have to take those Russians *somewhere* while the Bankers admitted to the world that they were involved in the most gigantic fraud and swindle in the history of mankind, and though that clearly couldn't take forever, it would take a few days. So, as Charlene set about making them the Ovaltine, Howell remained on the couch in the living room, where he waited for inspiration. Who did he know with a house in the woods? With a house that was out of the way? And someone, most important, who they'd never suspect? Who, preferably, disliked Russians?

The truth of it was, he didn't know anyone. Not who met *all* those requirements. But . . . but . . . well, he might know *about* someone; here God seemed to intervene again. Mrs. Esterhaczy was Hungarian. Hadn't they had a revolution? Where the Russians brought tanks into Hungary? And Pond Woods, where she lived, it was the back of the beyond. Why, she might be just the perfect person. They wouldn't suspect her, not in a decade; she was old, after all, and a woman. Her call tonight; it must have been providential. Yes, yes, God was surely leading him. All he had to do was ask her, and everything would be set. Never in his life had Howell felt so confident.

Bringing the Ovaltine, Charlene returned. "We going to the Widau auction tomorrow?"

"Of course," said Howell. "We never miss an auction." And he took a sip of his drink. But auctions—who cared about auctions? Good God! *He* was going to raffle off some Russians!

# 10

THE NEXT MORNING, Saturday, saw Peale up bright and early, in deference to Amanda's love of auctions. The ad in the paper listing the goods to be sold had emphasized the splendid basket collection old Mrs. Widau had acquired through the years, and since Amanda liked baskets even more than she liked books, the ad had sealed his fate. Now as she got her bidding number, standing with a small crowd of other serious buyers while her name and address were properly entered, Peale noticed that his deputy Alf Stilton was coming toward him, and he ducked behind a quilt hung on a clothesline. The other day Alf Stilton and Tommy Widau— great-nephew of the woman who had just died and thus part inheritor of whatever outrageous sum Amanda paid today for baskets—had been in on an arrest together, and Tommy had apparently muscled Alf out of the way so that he could pop the perp one "right in the gourd," thus preventing Alf himself from doing so. Ever since, the two men had been feuding, and though this happened all the time, at the moment Peale simply didn't want to be reminded of it; the auction itself was trial enough.

Although Peale's childhood had been a sunny one, occasionally small clouds had floated over his horizon, and auction Saturdays were one of them. Peale's mother had held that it was her duty, as the only remaining representative of one of Felicity's oldest families, to show up at community functions such as auctions, and while Ryland had adapted fairly well to the long days spent in the hot sun—he must have felt it was better to be present when the equivalent of gifts was being distributed to all and sundry—Peale, who had never had much interest in *things*, quickly got thirsty, and itched. Often he would end up spending most of the afternoon sitting on a pile of linens atop an old bedframe, and though some of the more atypical citizens would occasionally pull old chairs up alongside him and share with him their auction desires and dreams, most of the people who attended such events were fanatically secretive and silent. They engaged, in fact, in cartilaginous rivalries; they thrived on competition.

Peale, a little boy who had never had to fight for anything, was vaguely horrified by the way his mother and all her friends and neighbors, in perfect silence and with the air of wrestlers about to go to the mat, had assessed the tables and the glassware. He had gathered that they *enjoyed* this, this bloody jousting, these pitched battles, in much the same way that his men now enjoyed their feuds, but it all dismayed Peale. Once, when Peale had been about twelve, Catherine Lee and Janice Smock—women in their sixties who had been friends from childhood—had found themselves bidding for the same framed photograph, of a school reunion at which both had appeared. As the bidding shot up right through the roof, the friendship had ended forever; and when Janice, the successful buyer, had triumphantly carried her prize away, she had found herself unable to look happily at the image of her lifelong friend, and had ended up mutilating the photo by cutting out Catherine's face. And in Peale's own family a generation-long feud had begun at an auction, when old Roland Guthrie, his father's grandfather, had bought an entire quarter-section of land right out from under the nose of his first cousin. The first cousin, Whittlemore Guthrie, had thought his rival was an out-of-towner, since Roland, after all, was just taking his ease, whittling as he sat on a sleigh in the shade, and only when Whittlemore had given up the fight did he discover that the successful buyer was his cousin, who had made his bids by whittling on the stick. "Hey, Whittlemore," Roland was purported to have said, "you should have whittled more yourself." The satisfaction of these eight words had presumably been enormous, since the two men never spoke again.

And now, this auction was about to start, and Peale didn't want to be here. From his hiding place behind the quilt, where he pretended to be studying the count of the stitches—pushing his face right up against the musty fabric and wondering whether he could keep this up all day—Peale heard the auctioneer making throat-clearing noises and testing the microphone system. Most of the serious buyers were already here, though the main mass of interested spectators had yet to arrive, and it was the main mass that Peale especially dreaded; he needed a day off from people. Although he had always thought of himself as an extremely sociable person, since he'd become sheriff he'd been getting strangely skittish. Whenever someone approached him these days, he feared it was to ask him for a decision, and he felt completely decisioned out; he wanted deliverance from sheriffry. For the last few days, he'd been feeling especially put-upon, what with this business about the Russians. The count, he discovered, was forty stitches to the inch. He didn't know whether that was good or bad.

Over the loudspeaker, real words emerged now; the auction proper was beginning. "One dollar, one dollar, who'll give me two, one dollar, who'll make it two," came the words, still comprehensible, though as the auction heated up, likely to become a lot less so. Looking around the edge of the quilt, which was stirring slightly in a light breeze, Peale saw that the crowd's attention was riveted on what looked like a sock in need of darning. The fascination of this object was so great that all backs were turned to Peale, so he slipped from behind the quilt and ambled toward the nearby barn. Behind the barn, he found an Adirondack chair and he settled into it with satisfaction; then, staring west across the newly plowed fields that came right up to the edge of Felicity, he let the sounds of the auctioneer in the background lull him into a real contentment. The sun was pleasant on his face, and the gentle breeze was blowing; it was a lovely spring day, with the trees already leafing. From time to time, Peale would turn his attention from the fields to the road where he had parked his Corvette—it was in the shadow of a budding oak tree, where it would stay cool for hours. Traffic moved slowly along this road, but there was more traffic than usual, and now he saw a station wagon pull out from right in front of his sports car. Immediately afterward, a small red car of foreign make came down the road more rapidly than most, and then came to a stop just beyond the Corvette, obviously aiming for the newly vacated space. While Peale watched, at first incurious and then incredulous, the driver, in a series of rapid maneveurs, backed toward the curb, then continued backward some more, finally smashing with a thump and a tinkle of broken glass into his Corvette's left headlight.

Without thinking at all, Peale got to his feet and started striding off toward the road. His Corvette was the one thing in the world upon which Peale lavished the kind of attention that Ryland gave to everything he owned, and he felt a moment of happiness at his position of sheriff as he watched his dear car get damaged. Car accidents in general made him sick—whenever you got an accident report and went rushing off to the scene to investigate, you never knew whether you would find some horribly injured person lying moaning in the road, or just an exasperated driver—but this one gave him a strange satisfaction by allowing him to take some action. His day had suddenly acquired a purpose.

But when he arrived at the road, his feeling of purpose weakened as the driver turned to look at him, and it vanished entirely when she shut off her engine and scrambled into the road. The driver was a woman—well, really, not much more than a girl—and she was dressed like no one he'd ever seen, in a style that was weirdly attractive. A white jumpsuit covered with purple flowers cinched her waist in tight; around her neck hung a red satin bag, tied with blue knotted ribbon. Her socks were red, her sneakers were violet—the latter matching her eyes—and it was her eyes that really shocked him more than her clothing, since they seemed somehow more outrageous. They had a depth to them, a three-dimensionality, that was surely not normal—so intense.

"I'm so sorry," she said. "I need to have a brake job. They've just been getting worse and worse."

"Oh," said Peale.

"This *is* your car?"

"Yes," said Peale. "It is."

"I was going to the auction. Do you know if they've sold the cauldron?"

"I hate auctions," Peale said. He cleared his throat authoritatively. "I'm the sheriff."

Why he had said this he could hardly imagine, but he was unfortunately certain that he had. To say that he immediately coveted this woman would be understating the case, since—as he managed to look away from her eyes and take in the rest of her face, discovering that though there was nothing distinctively beautiful about the short cap of thick brown hair that framed it, or the broad cheekbones that spanned it, the same depth that the eyes revealed was mirrored, too, in the face—he felt something come alive inside his head that had rarely been alive there before. He had ratified his life, had validated his existence, without knowing, he saw suddenly, all the facts.

"You're the sheriff?" she said. "But you're not wearing a uniform."

"It's Saturday."

"Oh, so it is."

"But I'm always on the job. I hope you have insurance. There may be more damage here than meets the eye." That was even worse than his pompous self-introduction.

By now, Peale felt quite seriously disturbed at the tangle his life could well become. After at least two hundred women who had modeled their behavior toward him on that of the first yellow-haired girl who'd said to him, in her high voice, "Peale, I love you," a woman had come along who would probably never do that, and who he wished already he could persuade to. As she reached into her car to get a pad of paper and a pen with which to write down her name and insurance company for him, and as he watched her blunt, expressive fingers move across their papers, a little smudged as if with grease, he wanted nothing more than to get away quickly, to return to the auction and its crowd. Instead of filling out an accident report on the spot and giving her the relevant papers, he simply took the scrap of paper that she gave him, almost ripping it out of one lovely hand.

"Bailey Bourne," he said, reading the name. "Well, I have to go now, Ms. Bourne."

"I'm really very sorry."

"Never mind, it doesn't matter." Did he still have a chance to get away? Yes, he did. He hurried across the road and rejoined the crowd on the lawn.

That crowd was staring, he discovered when he got there, at a large dirty glass jar. The auctioneer exhorted them to store their pennies in it; several people seemed eager to comply. If he could just nip this whole thing in the bud—ah, there was Amanda now, his wife! She was holding three baskets, which Peale hugged as he hugged her. Then he held them while she waited for some more. Peale did not tell her that by now the auctioneer, a notorious crook with a notoriously crooked son, had undoubtedly noticed her fondness for baskets and would certainly have commanded his issue to bid on the next one in order to drive the price higher; he didn't tell her because she enjoyed auctions, and he didn't want her to be disillusioned. He wanted to protect her from all disappointments, in a sudden rush of tender feeling. When the next basket came up he urged her to keep bidding, and she ended up paying twice its worth.

Shortly afterward, Peale left the auction, promising to return for Amanda later. Driving his mutilated car toward the Sunoco station, he thought about Amanda and her baskets, the way she would spend the afternoon arranging and rearranging them on the sun porch until they exhibited the perfect harmony that she had grown fond of as a librarian. Other than interior decoration, her only hobby was bookbinding, and when she had once explained to him that there were eleven bookbinding styles, she had added that she thought there were eleven kinds of everything: eleven kinds of marriage, of cooking styles, of sex. At the time, he had thought it rather charming, but as he headed for the gas station to get a headlight, he wondered whether Amanda was all there. She did not float, and she certainly wasn't translucent, but she did have a kind of luminous inconsequence, as if she were always standing in moonlight. Why, compared with the Bourne woman, Amanda was a photograph; the other was a type of 3-D. Oh, nonsense, why was he thinking about her? Amanda was perfect, and his wife.

At the gas station, where one listless attendant sat in the shade of the front wall, his legs propped up on an empty plastic crate, his thumb in the spine of a paperback book, Peale parked and got out, while the attendant, whom Peale knew only slightly from high school, climbed to his feet with an obsequious expression.

"So what can I do for you today, Sheriff?"

"Some woman smashed into my headlight," said Peale. This phraseology, calculated to degrade that woman to the level of a sub-moron, someone who could scarcely be trusted to walk down the street without aid, and who certainly shouldn't be driving, had instead the unfortunate effect of bringing her vividly to mind, and while Eddie went strolling off to get a suitable headlight, Peale smelled her soap-horsy smell as eloquently as if it were rising right then before him, and saw that remarkable face, those eyes, as if he were taking vitamins for the purpose.

"So," Eddie called over his shoulder, "I hear a couple of Commies are coming to town."

The mention of the Russians did something to return Peale to his real situation, but not enough, since that specific concern now seemed merely part of a whole set of questions he didn't want to consider, and, feeling desperate, he decided that he would go shoot, which should at least put his mind into focus. Although shooting might have caused this whole mess to begin with; it was his shooting that had made him run for sheriff.

Still, shortly after, his headlight replaced, he made his way to his gun club. This building, a dark green metal pole barn with a firing range and an adjoining room, was situated close behind the Kiwanis Club building, but was not affiliated with it; it belonged to the gun club members themselves. So intensely had these people—seventy-five men and three women—wanted to have an inside firing range that they had each, about six years before, contributed

$300 to the purchase and maintenance of the building, and it was now rented regularly to other clubs and to the sheriff's department, as well. But Peale had been a member of the club before he became the sheriff and was, in fact, one of the founders, with a long history of good times with guns. There was something about the shooting stalls, where each man stood isolated from the men on either side of him, in perfect silence and concentration, that provided for him a needed privacy, a fine concentration of the heart and the hand. He was a member of both the rifle division and the pistol division, and his scores were regularly sent in to the NRA as some of the week's best shoots; on the firing range it was as if he could do no wrong. He had a steady, brilliant eye. After he became sheriff he had taken the qualifying test for small arms, and on a silhouette target he had qualified as a Distinguished Expert with a score of 297 out of a possible 300. But, his accuracy aside, it was at the moment when the announcement came "All quiet on the firing line" and a little later "Prepare to shoot" and then "Shoot at will"— it was at those moments when the universe seemed to contract to a pinpoint, and there was a great, almost holy silence, in which he gathered himself into a perfect purity, in which all the sophistry, the hedging, of everyday life was stilled, and he became rapt, an extension, almost, of the pistol in his hand. At these moments, he was a wholly centered being, and language did not begin to describe the reality of that moment when, his right hand outstretched and steadied by his left, his ear protectors muffling all sound, he looked at the target and tried to draw it to him, and threw his whole being into space. Although, from the time he was an infant, he had been blessed with sheer luck in matters great and small, this skill was more than luck, and more than blessing, too. It was his; it was Peale.

He unlocked the door to the firing range and flicked on the overhead lights. Then he took a deep breath of the air, which smelled always, and pleasantly, of gunpowder, and seeing that whoever had shot here last had failed to clean up the .22 shells that littered the floor, he took a broom and swept them up.

He then went down to the end of the range, where a slanting

steel wall caught the lead bullets, flattened them, and dumped them into a trough below, and he pinned a target to the center clothespin, after which he returned to the stalls. He had with him only his regulation issue .357 Magnum—loaded, at the moment, with hollow-point copper-jacketed bullets—but he, like many of the club members, kept some ammunition in a locked storage crate here, so he took out a box of unjacketed .38's. And as he pushed them neatly, one after another, into the cylinder, which he knocked out into his hand, he felt much calmer, happy and sane, well beyond the reach of decisions. Somewhere there was an auction, where both Bailey Bourne and his wife were now bidding on baskets and cauldrons, but this world, this place, was the only one that was real. Placing his ear protectors on his head, he stepped up to the firing range and slowly raised his right hand in front of him, then raised his left to support it. He drew back the hammer with his thumb, let his weight settle into the floor, and—leaving his left eye open—allowed only his right eye to see. Finally, he started to squeeze the trigger inward, the slow steady pressure as soft and gentle as a kiss, and it was only after there was no going back, only after the trigger was in the final moment of its journey and the shot about to be released, that he saw, to his horror, Amanda's face appear on the target, and appallingly, had to shoot her right between the eyes.

# 11

ADA was feeling very pleased with herself; her cleverness really was extraordinary. Three days ago, her new patient, Ryland Guthrie, had come by for a treatment and had told her, in the course of it, about the Widau auction this morning. He would be going, he had said, because he wanted to buy something for his son, and immediately Ada had seen what a perfect opportunity it would make for introducing him to Maggie.

Maggie, of course, had not wanted to go to the auction, protesting that this was supposed to be her day off, and that tonight she was already planning on going to a meeting—something, Ada thought, ·to do with Doomsday. But Ada, who certainly had no interest in buying anything they were selling—indeed, a sorrier-looking lot of useless junk she had never in her life seen—though she had come to the auction as late as she thought reasonable, was certainly not going to miss it altogether. The more she observed of that young man, the more she liked him, and the more convinced she became that he was perfect; his sperm, she thought, should be perking up by now, in its newly healthy seminal fluid. And while there was, unfortunately, no ideal way to introduce him to Maggie—her grand-daughter, deplorably, was much too acute not to suspect when something was up—there were certainly some ways that would work better than others, and this one was as good a chance as any.

As soon as Ryland arrived, Ada planned to introduce them, and then, making some excuse, to disappear. Since Maggie had driven her here, she could hardly leave without her and would be forced to spend some time with her future mate. If all went well, she would invite him to this Doomsday thing; for that, Ada had already laid the groundwork.

"You are going *alone* to a meeting with *strangers?* You had best take a friend along, pumpkin."

"I don't have a friend."

"Well, high time you made one! Maybe you will meet someone today." Maggie, at this, had looked at her suspiciously; now, Maggie simply looked cross.

"Maggie, my little one. You must make an effort. You must try to mingle, to *mix*."

"You don't come to an auction, Ada, to mingle. You come to buy something you don't need. If you don't want to buy something, why did you drag me here?"

"But I do want; of course I want to buy!"

"What?"

"I don't know. I will know it when I see it. Go sit in a chair if you are tired."

"I'm not tired, I'm just bored."

"So sit, sit, go on! There are enough ugly chairs for you to choose from."

To Ada's relief, Maggie shrugged, grumpily, then went off to sit down under a tree. This waiting around, yes, it was undeniably exhausting, but still, what a crosspatch Maggie could be. Moping and sulking on a lovely day like this!

Noticing that Maggie had not only settled herself in one of the ugly chairs under the tree, but that she had, furthermore, closed her eyes, Ada decided to take a walk around the square while she waited for Ryland to arrive. He would, she was sure of that—he was such a nice, reliable young man—and meanwhile Ada wouldn't mind a little change and a stroll around the center of Felicity. Even now, so many years after she'd moved here, she still found it a droll presentation.

First she went by Saguanay's, which had a new display in its windows, a display, it seemed, of a man's den. A big leather chair, a black-shaded lamp, a pipe in a rack—and a rifle. It was a funny-looking rifle, very old, and underneath it there was a small printed sign that read: "NOT FOR SALE. This early example of a breech-loading rifle, invented in 1856 by General Ambrose Burnside, a son of Indiana, belonged to Mr. Thomas Saguanay."

Ada had put her best hat on this morning before coming out, and now, as she shook her head at the phrase "breech-loading rifle," all the little flowers on its rim shook. What a priceless language English was; what other country in the world would invent a rifle that claimed to do nothing but fill an enemy's pants? Oh, she knew it wasn't polite to think such things, it wasn't what her beloved mother had tried to teach her—but she was old, she had earned the right to laugh in the quiet of her own mind. She walked a little farther down the square, checking out of the corner of her eye to see that Maggie was still collapsed in that chair like a sack of grain, and came to a stop in front of a Navy recruitment poster, this one trumpeting in large letters the fact that Navy Men were the Guardians of Freedom. From television, she saw that these days the Navy was advertising that it Wasn't a Job, It Was an Adventure, but here in Felicity the new posters hadn't yet arrived, and probably wouldn't for years.

The picture of the "men"—one that adorned both sides of the rather shaky display, which regularly fell onto the sidewalk and had to be propped up again with bricks holding its legs in place—showed one of the youngest boys (in Ada's opinion) who had ever been popped into a uniform. Of course, in her great-grandmother's day, in Hungary, they had collected them even younger; when the gallant bands of Hussars had come through town, their buttons gleaming, their gold braid flying, the pipers and drummers marching at their side, her great-grandmother had kept Ada's grandfather locked in a flour chest to prevent him from joining the parade. Because if he had, a smiling Hussar would have reached out to wring his young hand, and would have left in that hand a round gold piece, his first payment as a soldier in the Napoleonic Wars. And now this boy, his face like a peach, his hair cut so short that it looked as if he were worried about the top of his head coming off; *this* was to be the Guardian of Freedom, this little one with his loaded breeches? Oh, well, she was old, she had seen much, she knew more about wars and history than most so-called historians; she knew that they were always fought by children, and that both sides were always in the right. Ah, and here was the War Memorial, Dedicated to the Memory of Those Who Served Their Country; that was simple, that was dignified, there was nothing wrong with that. As long as men were going to be so crazy as to engage in wars—and Ada had to admit that though Maggie, poor dear, was a little demented on the subject of Doomsday, she was certainly right that it was wrong— well, it was good to have dignified memorials for all those handsome, peachy dead.

From across the street she could hear the sounds of the auction; the auctioneer keening about his wares. She had seen much the same sort of thing when she lived in Egypt, the vendors crooning at the bazaars, but there, of course, there had been things worth buying, instead of the refuse of the world. Oh, well, let them be happy, she was not going to grudge them that. *She* was happy, after all; she continued on around the square. Here was the sign outside City Hall, a sign with white letters set into black, the whole thing stuck behind glass. Ever since Ada had lived here, half the letters in the sign had been lying down at the bottom of the case, all in a tumble like parts of a game, and as a result, of all the rooms in the building, the only one clearly indicated was the Men's Room. Well, those men with their breeches had to go somewhere, and it was surely better that they run for the right room when the time came, but Ada never ceased to find this amusing. The priorities of a world run by men!

Inside City Hall was the Felicity Museum, and it was Ada's favorite stop on the tour. The Felicity Museum, the existence of which was announced by a huge white and red sign, consisted of precisely one glass case, set carefully against a tile wall. In this display case were twenty-nine objects, objects Ada now knew well. There was the STAMPED COLLAR, lent by Getrude Pyne, the HO MESPUN MONEYBAG, lent by the very same woman. A WEDDING SHAWL had been lent by Serena Gould, and MY MOTHER'S WEDDING

SHAWL was also from Serena. POCKETBOOK THAT BELONGED TO MY GRANDMOTHER WHO DIED IN 1850 had been lent by Barbara Peterson, and another STAMPED COLLAR was from Barbara Peterson as well. Then there were plates, purses, wooden spools, socks, huge mittens, framed photos, and wristlets—these last, something that Ada recognized from her own childhood, when her mother had tucked them up between her sleeves and her mittens to keep her wrists from chafing. Good God! If this was a museum, then Ada— who had been to the Tate in London, the Uffizi in Florence, the Prado in Madrid, the Rijksmuseum in Amsterdam—if this was a museum, then Ada was a speckled brown hen! She had nothing but derision for these old people who thought that any relic they dug out of their basement was worthy of the adulation of others. Some old things should just fall apart and blow away—and that homespun moneybag was one of them!

She came out again to the steps of City Hall and scanned the crowd across the square. She supposed she had best go check to see if Ryland had arrived yet, so she climbed back down the steps, on the way peeking into the glass wall cabinet that held the Rock County Roll of Honor and that had been awarded, of all things, by the Indiana Sanitary Commission, as if honor were in taking those breeches to the cleaner's. Then she straightened her hat, pulled her cotton gloves a bit tighter, and marched back across the street. Just as she arrived at the edge of the curb, a pickup clattered up and parked there.

At first, she ignored the truck and its contents, and set off to march right around it. But then, to Ada's surprise, she saw that it contained Howell Bourne, the dog man with whose bitch Boonskie was to mate, and she paused until he had clambered out of his truck so that she could greet him politely and so on. She had grown up in a fine family in Hungary, after all, and she knew how to act with peasants; she treated them with politeness and firmness, which was all that was really required. While the man leaned into the window of his truck to speak to his wife and children for a moment, Ada had a chance to study those children, and they weren't a pretty sight. They had white, pasty faces and dull, slack mouths, and their eyes lacked any sparkle, any fire. They embodied, in fact, everything that Ada wanted to avoid in her own descendants, and she was heartened by this reminder of what the world was full of, and strengthened in her resolve to take a stand against it. Then Howell Bourne joined her on the sidewalk and stood in silence as he summoned speech.

Ada wondered what the man could want, but she knew he would tell her fairly quickly. There would be no pleasant banter or badinage first; she had discovered long ago that these Indiana farmers had the capacity of an eggplant for raillery, and that there was no point at all in trying to liven up conversations by teasing or being humorous. Frankly, she found the tediousness of their minds an amazement, but she hoped that she had never let this show, and as Howell started to bake the sentence "Good morning, Mrs. Esterhaczy," somewhere deep in the oven of his brain, she waited patiently for it to be cooked and delivered into the air.

"Good morning, Mrs. Esterhaczy," said Howell. "What a coincidence, seeing you here. I have a proposal I'd like to make. Would you care to go sit on the bench?"

On the one hand, Ada was feeling guilty by now about leaving Maggie alone in that chair; on the other hand, she couldn't help being curious as to what this was all about. As far as she could tell, Ryland had not yet arrived—he had a dark blue Mercedes, and you just couldn't miss it if it went whizzing by—so the main purpose of having come to town could not yet be fulfilled in any case. She led the way to the bench Howell indicated and arranged herself graciously upon it, and when Howell came to sit there beside her, she regarded him with something like fondness.

"I hope you will hear me out," he said, "because this is extremely important. You know, I imagine, about the farm liquidations and the terrible plight of our land." Here he paused, and Ada, who had been fully prepared to hear him out, was left to wonder whether this was all he intended to say.

But no, he geared up again, and this time dropped a bombshell. As Ada listened, at first amused and a little condescending, and then both fascinated and appalled, Howell unraveled his theories of a conspiracy and all that they entailed. And pointing out—with more craft than Ada would have thought he had in him—that she was a woman of great experience, a woman who had traveled widely and had seen what the world could do, he suggested she help him in his endeavor to save their small corner of the earth. By this, he seemed to mean that she harbor him and some Russian professors whom he intended to kidnap and hold for ransom—because her house was so remote and inaccessible, and because they'd never suspect an "old lady." And although at first Ada's temptation was to stand up in front of the bench, even as he spoke, and to holler out this plot to the sheriff, the more she heard, the more intrigued she became, for reasons that weren't quite clear even to her. That Howell Bourne—a man she had credited with the imagination of a sugar snap pea, a man she had thought existed in the first place simply because he had a hound dog Boonskie could impregnate— that this man should be capable of such a complex scheme struck her as well-nigh incredible.

Of course, these farmers, and other simple Americans like them, had relied for centuries on their own slow wits to fabricate whatever they needed, and while in the early days of the continent's settlement those needs had been largely met once they had manufactured square-headed nails and a couple of machines that could pit cherries, now those needs were probably more complicated, in a world that swirled around them like a wind. So here she sat, privileged to be in on the genesis of an idea, a homespun idea created right in the barns of Felicity—made up out of whole cloth, perhaps, but with the same care and attention to detail for which Americans were famous. And with no embarrassment or shame—just as if this idea were as worthy of respect as the cherry pitter devised by one of his ancestors—this man had laid this newborn concept right out where she could see it.

That in itself intrigued her and made her feel a little bit flattered. But there was something else, something even more compelling: she had always *hated* the Russians. When they had come into Hungary after the Great War, they had stolen the light bulbs out of the sockets and taken them back to their tents—and then, when the light bulbs had not given light, they had rampaged and shot and raped. They had been animals; worse than that. Why slander animals? Whatever they'd been, they hadn't been men, and though Ada knew that many years had passed, some part of her still was angry. When America entered the Second World War, her darling Tibor had been stationed in Cleveland, and he and Ada had become enemy aliens; they'd been interned in upstate New York. That was fine, that was good, they had hated Hitler, too, and in this camp they were treated with respect and given a lovely big room. They were allowed to walk in the extensive gardens and were served delicious meals in an elegant dining room, but they were held for almost nine months while their case was being reviewed. At last, they were taken before a nine-man panel of examiners, and as Ada remembered proudly, she had resisted every attempt that was made to persuade her to take an oath of loyalty, not just to the United States but to *all its allies in the war*. By this time, the Russians were dying by the millions on the eastern front, but "America," Ada had said, "I will take an oath of loyalty to America any day— ten times a day—but to say I am loyal to *Russia:* this I will not do."

Impressed by her convictions, exhausted perhaps from arguing with her, seeing that they were fighting a losing battle, those nine darling men had removed "and all its allies" from her loyalty oath and made her an American citizen. During the Cold War, and again in recent years, Ada had gotten an enormous chuckle out of this.

"I told them," she would say to whoever was listening, "I told them about the Russians."

So instead of getting to her feet and shouting, she sat in silence for a while. She knew that she was too old and presumably too wise to get involved in any lunacy of this kind, yet something in her was tempted to do it, just to see what occurred. Oh, certainly the idea that anyone would give all the mortgages in Rock County to the fire just for the safe return of two Russian professors was absolutely ludicrous—money was always put before life, in every country on earth—and furthermore, this wearisome belief in a conspiracy was bound to lead to trouble. Indeed, if the Russians ever arrived at her house at all, it would be no less than a miracle.

Nonetheless, nonetheless . . . she was really tempted to do it. She had lived such a tame life in recent years, and though of course the excitement of planning for a great-grandchild had made inroads on that tameness, a baby was not the same as an intrigue; anyone could always use both. Then, too, she liked Bailey, this lunatic's sister; what if she *didn't* agree? He would go to someone else, who would surely make a botch of it, and he might even end up being killed. That would make Bailey unhappy, of course, and it would make Boonskie unhappy as well—because Boonskie was already looking forward to mating with Sam, the hound with the so-auspicious name. Why, she and this Bourne man were already almost in-laws. She hardly knew how she could refuse.

Howell was meanwhile staring at her face, waiting to hear her answer. And though in other circumstances she might have postponed giving him one until she had had time to consider the whole situation more slowly, the sight of Ryland's Mercedes whizzing by made up her mind for her now.

"Yes," she said, getting to her feet. "I think I may be able to help you. You will call me, and we will talk. And Boonskie, my darling boy—he is ready, you know, any time."

She caught up with Ryland just after he parked and before he lost himself in the crowd. At his side there stood a small boy, perhaps five years old, with enchanting large eyes and strawberry blond hair. This boy seemed to have much the same attitude toward existence as did her Boonskie; when Ada came up to the two of them she was just in time to hear the child say, "Oh, look at all the people!" in a tone of great excitement, at the same time pressing himself against his father's side, from which vantage point he seemed to feel he'd be better able to enjoy his own delight. To Ada, Ryland's having his son with him was the icing on the cake of her satisfaction, because in the week and a half since she had started treating Ryland, he had improved so much to look at that she wished she could use him as an advertisement, and now she saw what stuff he was really made of. Why, this gorgeous little boy would be her own great-grandson's half-brother, and the sooner she got Ryland over to Maggie, the sooner that would happen.

"Good morning, young men," she said mainly to the boy. "You are both looking fine this morning."

"Who's that, Daddy?" asked the child, alertly.

"Clayton, this is Ada, my new doctor."

"Your doctor?" Clayton said, and as Ada smiled agreement, she patted him twice on the head. He had good hair, soft but with toughness inside it, and a nice resilience to the scalp.

"Your father is very kind. So what are you learning? You are in school, now, I bet, are you not?"

"Oh, words and science and winged horses." Then, forgetting that Ada and Ryland were listening, he took off on this last thought, and in a soft singsong voice, with his head bobbing from side to side, as if he were carrying on two parts of a conversation, and his fingers coming together and then breaking apart again, he said: "Winged horses fly through the air so that you can ride them and go up the place where they eat their dinner. But why do we never see winged horses? Because they have the power to make themselves *invisible*. Would you like to be invisible? I would. I would like to be an invisible winged horse. When I was born I was a little baby, but I also had two tiny wings on my back, lying flat and feathery. They were perfect little wings, and they would have grown, too, but they cut them off in the hospital, because only horses and birds have wings. You're sorry about that, aren't you? Oh, sorry, sorry, sorry."

He fell silent, humming a little, looking not at all sorry from what Ada could see, as—in a perfect ecstasy of self-congratulation—she told herself that she had always had an eye for character and genes, and that if only the sperm that awakened Maggie's egg were half as marvelous as the one that had helped to form this child, she would die happy, her line in good hands, her life's last mission complete. At this moment Maggie came over to where Ada stood and said grumpily, "Where have you been?"

To Ada's dismay, she saw that Maggie, normally a beautiful girl, trim and neat, with a wild head of shining red hair and with the complexion of a saint, looked not at her best right at this moment; she was flushed with the heat and the moisture. Furthermore, she took no notice whatever of Ryland or Clayton as she said, "For God's sake, Ada, let's go home."

"Maggie," replied Ada reprovingly, "please remember your manners. This is Ryland Guthrie, a patient of mine—he runs that fine furniture store, Saguanay's—and this is Clayton, his little progeny. She is a brat," she explained to the males. "A darling brat, my granddaughter, Maggie. She believes the world is about to end. Today, that is, on April thirtieth. Can you explain to her otherwise?"

And then, as Ryland muttered something about thinking maybe he had seen Maggie before once somewhere, and as Maggie muttered something about yes, that must have been in Saguanay's, meanwhile looking daggers at Ada, Ada slapped her forehead with her palm, as if she had just remembered something. Then she pretended to feel very sad, and looked down with this sadness at her shoes.

She had decided that the best thing to do was to get away from the happy couple, and let them get to know each other, and for this purpose only something drastic would do, so she fell back on her dead husband. She explained that this was—though she had completely forgotten it until now—the day dear Tibor had passed on from the world, that sad day, April 30. Every year on this day— actually, it was February 17, but she was fairly certain that Maggie would not remember this—she went to the little Church of St. John and prayed for the peace of his soul. She must go right away to do this, of course, but perhaps Maggie and Ryland would like to stay and talk until she returned. For *her* sake—it would do her good, to know that they were together.

So Ada set off once more across the street, this time in the direction of St. John's. She moved fast so as to get past one of the deacons, a man who seemed to live in the garden to the north of his beloved church. He was a fossil of a man, his old face as translucent as the windows in the nearby rectory, his hands swollen beyond belief, each finger thick as a sausage, and he could talk about nothing but his youth, when everyone had married someone else. The few times Ada had been so incautious as to find herself in conversation with him, his comments had been limited to such things as "And he was a Whiting . . . . Course he married a Bourne. Everyone did, those days. Why, the Bourne sisters, they grew thick as weeds. Or did he marry a Johnson?" Now, as Ada hustled past him, he started to get to his feet. But she dashed inside and shut the door, and he didn't follow her in.

Ada hardly ever entered a church—maybe once or twice a year now. As a child, she had loved going to church, but then, of course, it had been to the great cathedral of St. Stephen's, at the top of Castle Hill, where the music had made your whole body soar, and the incense had made you weak. Kneeling on the beautiful velvet knee rests, her black boots buttoned painstakingly that morning by the servant girl, Poppi, she had felt like a splendid burnished object, with an outfit as fine as God's own.

Then, as the years had passed and the ritual had been changed from the fine old Latin to this ridiculous if lovable English, and as the churches she lived near had grown smaller and duller, she had gone to church less and less often. In Indiana, she had noticed that many of the people who went to church were either criminal lunatics or morons, and her attendance had fallen away to nothing. She had, anyway, a private arrangement with God; they understood one another well. She believed in Him without giving Him much thought, and He generally left her alone. They had worked this out between them years ago, and they had never seen reason to change it. Now, though, as she was determined to give the budding romance of Maggie and Ryland time to take root, she settled in for a good long chat, and while she did not kneel down—her nice knees could surely be spared that degree of verisimilitude—she stretched out, and in a position as supremely comfortable as she could make it, she started to converse with God. About a minute into this, she thought it might be a good idea to time herself—half an hour would probably be adequate—so she looked at her watch to get started correctly. It was one-thirty now—on Ada Time.

# 12

RYLAND didn't know quite what to do as Clayton babbled happily at his side. Even if Maggie had not been one of the most beautiful women Ryland had ever met—a woman who, he was glad to see, was not, today, with Dr. Minot—common politeness would have dictated that he stay here and converse with her until Ada returned. And certainly Ryland could be nothing but polite where Ada Esterhaczy was concerned, since, in the scant ten days since he had first seen her, the pain in his testicle had completely vanished. Try as he would—lifting his leg slightly off the ground and backward in order to encourage any latent painful tendencies to manifest themselves—there was simply no prick, no twinge. The pain was gone. He felt better than he'd felt in months. This morning, when he woke up overly early to the sound of his son in the next room singing, "I'm a bird, I'm a big red bird, I'm a bird, I'm a big red bird," Ryland, who normally needed his sleep, had bounced up, ready for anything. Incredible as it seemed, this *must* be the result of that vile herb mixture he'd been drinking three times a day, and those four relaxing "treatments," and Ryland had a bad case of hero worship for the woman who had helped him so effectively. But he'd promised Clayton that they'd buy something at the auction, and it was already past noon.

Well, he would find something later, that was all. For now, he would talk with Ada's granddaughter. She stood in front of him, looking hot and flushed and miserable, dressed in baggy blue jeans and a jade-colored T-shirt, clearly very annoyed. Her shoulders slumped slightly, she had large circles of sweat under her armpits, there were smudges under her eyes, and her red hair, naturally curly, looked in need of a washing. She had, as he had noticed before, green eyes, which stared at him resentfully, though the more Ryland looked at her, the less angry she seemed.

"So what do you do?" he asked.

"I'm a kind of psychologist," Maggie said, thrusting her hands in her pockets. "Don't worry, I'm not mad at you. It's Ada. She's quite an operator."

"She is?"

"She is. She set us up. Umpa died in the winter. But never mind, it doesn't matter now."

Ryland felt that it would be impolite to Ada as well as to Maggie to pursue this subject further, so he went back to the first one, and murmured, "A psychologist?" while trying to look suitably impressed. He really *was* impressed, but he also felt rather awkward.

"It isn't hard, believe me," said Maggie.

"It isn't?"

"Not at all. All you have to notice is that, first, everyone feels that their parents treated them like dirt; second, that everyone feels they're about to die at any minute; and third, that everyone is scared to love anybody; and you've basically got it in the bag."

"Is everyone scared to love anybody?" Ryland asked.

"Not kids, of course. Or dogs. Just anybody their own size."

"And everyone feels their parents treated them like dirt?" he asked, stupefied.

"Oh, everyone, believe me, everyone. You could be the son of Saint Francis of Assisi, and you'd still have to be in analysis."

"And everyone feels they're just about to die?"

"Well, no, there I was oversimplifying a little. It's more that you either feel you're about to die any minute or you've hidden that fear so deeply you think you could never die. In me, you get the first; in Ada, the second. The second is a lot more fun."

"Does everyone feel they've been *gypped*, too?" asked Ryland, glancing down at Clayton just long enough to see that his son had fallen to the grass on his knees and was poking the dirt with his forefinger.

"Not exactly," said Maggie. "That's a rather sophisticated combination of one, two, and three. Why? Is that how you feel?"

"Me?" asked Ryland, taken aback. "Well, not exac— well, not always . . ."

"Ah," said Maggie. "That's probably why you run that fancy store."

"Oh," said Ryland. "Ah."

It seemed to Ryland things were getting out of hand, but he wasn't sure that he wanted to secure them. It was amazing how rarely in everyday life the conversation ever reached any point, how few people you ever met talked about reality. Pain, suffering, hatred, death; in Felicity, and presumably in most other places as well, there seemed to be some kind of unspoken agreement never to admit they existed. And while the possibility of physical health had always seemed to him elusive, the possibility of psychological health had frankly never occurred to him. So—albeit cautiously— he decided not to change the subject.

"What about you?" he asked. "Are you afraid you're going to die?"

"Of course."

"In an accident or what?"

"Nuclear war," said Maggie tersely.

Nuclear *war?* thought Ryland with a flush of sympathy. Why, that was even worse than cancer! Cancer at least you had a chance of surviving, but nuclear war was always fatal.

"I'm so sorry."

"Oh, well, there it is. That's why we study psychology."

"But can't you get rid of it?"

"You *can*. It's just hard. I think maybe I may finally have started."

"Getting over it?"

"However you like to look at it. Guthrie. Guthrie? Are you related to the sheriff?"

At this, Ryland's interest in the conversation waned, and threatened to disappear entirely. One of the reasons he had come late to

the auction, despite his promise to Clayton that they would buy
something—something *good*, he had assured his son—was that he'd
been afraid that he'd see Peale here, since Amanda was fond of
auctions. And while it seemed, luckily, that this ploy had worked,
and Peale had already departed, just the mention of "the sheriff"
made Ryland feel nervous and troubled, but while he wanted to
feel a sudden surge of distaste for Maggie, who was, he remembered
now from his brother's account, at least partially responsible for the
business of the visiting Russians, he found that he was tempted
instead to reassess it. After all, if Maggie was helping organize the
security for the foreigners, then maybe the idea had some merit.

"He's my brother. I remember him mentioning you. So why do
you think these professors will need security?"

"I don't know. When it comes to Russians, most people around
here are . . . well, they're mostly all crazy."

Ryland wasn't sure whether this was offered as a professional
opinion or was simply a concerned citizen's exhortation, but he felt
strangely agreeable to letting it be both; he was really getting to
like this woman. She seemed to anticipate bad things even more
effectively than he did; where he was afraid that his testicle might
have to be removed, she was afraid of the bomb; where he was
afraid that his brother would make a fool of him, she was afraid of
high crime. She had an industrious approach to impending doom
that was both simple and complete. Not only that, but she had an
acuteness of intellect that had, in one sentence, summarized neatly
for him the major concerns of his entire existence, and while it was
hard to believe that he had not been able to do this for himself long
before, the triple whammy of parents, death, and love was new.
Didn't her theory sort of explain the disaster of his relationship
with April, who had been closer to his own size than anybody he
had known up to then, and who had therefore needed to be constantly measured, against charts and salaries and time slots?

Meanwhile, just behind them, the auction was winding up again—
the house itself and the land it stood on were to be auctioned off
at one o'clock. Since a lull had occurred in the conversation as a
result of Ryland's recent musings, they could hear the auctioneer

quite clearly as he exhorted them to gather round. Maggie and Ryland glanced at each other and agreed that they might as well do so, so Ryland urged Clayton onto his feet and took his son's left hand. Without being encouraged, and without any sign of interest on Maggie's part, Clayton held up his other hand for her, and she took it with a little squeeze. So Ryland found himself walking once more, as he had often done with April, as one half of a pair of human bookends, with his son the sweet little book.

They stood and listened to the auctioneer, and Ryland glanced through the crowd. He loved auctions, he always had, ever since his mother had first taken him to one and it had appeared to him that they were giving out presents to anyone who stuck up his hand. He himself, though he had waved his hands wildly, had never, of course, received one; but for quite a while he was merely convinced that he was waving his hand a little wrong. Now, as he lifted Clayton high on his shoulders so that he could see everything that went on, it struck him that his son, dreamy as he was, might not like auctions as much as Ryland himself had. But Clayton squeaked in excitement, happily and reassuringly, and Ryland wrapped his fingers around his son's ankles.

Several items were held up and sold—a vase, a radio, a table. With each of them, Ryland asked Clayton if he was interested, and with each, received a definite no. Now, however, as the auctioneer held up a sword—"pre–Civil War era: a genu-ine piece of Amer-icana"—Clayton suddenly started to nod his head furiously, making Ryland's shoulders shake. Well, at least his son had taste, though God knew the bidding on this could go into the hundreds of dollars; some people in the crowd might *believe* it was pre–Civil War, though it'd be lucky if it was pre–World War One. Tentatively, Ryland started the bidding at ten dollars, and found himself quickly engaged in a hot competition; one of his competitors, he noticed, was that crazy Bailey Bourne, the one who had lived in the wrong house. But she dropped out quickly, leaving Ryland one-on-one with a dealer, someone Ryland didn't know. At this point, Ryland asked Clayton *sotto voce* whether he was sure this was really what he wanted; his son nodded so hard he almost fell off, so Ryland kept up with the bidding. When he finally got the sword, at a figure just short of a hundred and fifty dollars, he lowered Clayton to the ground and went to pick it up. He returned, knelt down, and handed the thing to his son, who, grinning from ear to ear, cradled it in his arms as if it were a cat.

"Clayton," said Ryland, "why did you want this?"

" 'Cause it's the Sword of Communism!"

A little later, after Ryland—both appalled at this evidence that April not only was leaving her pernicious tracts lying about the house, but was reading them aloud to Clayton, and simultaneously delighted that she was doing something so obviously irresponsible, which would give him a better chance of winning the custody suit that he was more and more inclined to bring against her—had managed to explain to his son that there *was* no sword of communism, he and Maggie saw Ada returning and went walking off to meet her.

As they walked, Ryland thought quickly; he wanted to see Maggie again, and soon. When he had first met Ada, he had been uneasy because he was almost attracted to her, but now, he felt, all that was quite explained. He had *actually* been attracted—in advance and without knowing it—to Maggie, of the same blood and many of the same genes. He thought Maggie bright and funny, as well as gorgeous and sexy, but it was hard to know just where to start; and Maggie didn't make it easier by broaching, just then, the subject of some political meeting she was going to that night.

"It's at the house of some minister or other, and is probably going to be excruciatingly dull. But it sounds nice, doesn't it? Beyond War? What a pipe dream. I'm losing my mind."

"What minister?"

"I don't know. Wittenham? Wickenham? Something like that."

"Wickenden. She likes rugs."

"Well, anyway . . ."

"Listen, could I come with you? Uh, I'm interested. In getting beyond war."

"Yeah, sure, I guess so. But what about Clayton?"

"Oh, that's true. We were going to stay home."

Ada, however, who had come up to them just in time to hear this last exchange, although it was quite impossible that she could have heard anything that led up to it, greeted them by saying in a pleasantly firm tone, "I will take care of your little boy."

And while it took a little explanation back and forth before it became quite clear to all concerned just what was going to happen when, eventually they had it straightened out: they'd break into pairs for the evening. And since Clayton seemed excited by this prospect—Boonskie and Raga had been dangled alluringly before him—Ryland didn't even feel guilty at his uncharacteristic artifice in arranging this fail-safe date. He had always been completely apolitical, and hated meetings of any kind, but Maggie couldn't know that, not yet, so there was satisfaction all around. While Ryland was making his way back to his car, the Sword of Communism clutched in one hand and Clayton in the other, he saw Bailey Bourne, lugging what appeared to be a cauldron.

By the time he and Clayton had finished lunch, Ryland felt completely happy all over. After Clayton's nap, they polished up the sword with a little steel wool and a lot of drops of bicycle oil, and then they took Molly for a walk.

Molly was now close to fourteen years old, but she still loved to go for walks. Ryland had never been able to comprehend the motives that led his house's previous owners to abandon their dog when they moved—not only to abandon her, but to lock her in the kitchen, with some water and a couple of bowls of food. When, a week later, Ryland had let himself in the back door and discovered Molly inside, she had wagged her tail at him and tried to lick his hand, though she was by then very weak. But although she could hardly walk, she tried to apologize for the urine and the feces; she wiggled and grinned and looked embarrassed and then collapsed in a heap on the floor.

In the years since, though she had been as devoted to him as she found it possible to be, she had never really recovered from the experience of abandonment, and whenever Ryland found it necessary to leave her alone in the kitchen, he could expect to find large gouges in the kitchen door when he returned, gouges that Molly had made as she tried to claw her way through solid oak. Not only that, but if she couldn't finish a whole bowl of food at one sitting, she would try to bury the remainder for later, which meant that she would thrust her nose into the bowl of dried nibbles and then shove them out all over the floor, attempting, if possible, to push them *under* something—her blanket, the radiator, or, if all else failed, her water bowl, so that spilled water and soggy food were excessively common in Ryland's kitchen. Not only that, but on the few occasions when Ryland had a visiting animal in the house, Molly would bare her teeth and growl if that animal came within ten feet of her food or water, her eyes wild with paranoia, her hackles straight up on her back. Finally, there was the little matter of linoleum; whether because of advancing age and arthritis, or because she had come to associate linoleum with the inability to escape, the kitchen floor made her very nervous; she was convinced that she couldn't walk on it. When she was forced to, she would tense her feet up so much that the nails stuck straight out and the pads retracted, making her skid around like crazy.

*Outside,* however, she was always happy, and neither cataracts nor arthritis could disturb her. Her joy in a romp was made even greater when Ryland kicked leaves into the air; she would do an arthritic half back-flip as she tried to bite them. She would do this, if possible, all day.

When they got home, they had dinner and then Ryland and Clayton took a bath together, soaping each other's backs and chests and carefully taking care of their other parts themselves. Then Ryland wrapped them both up in towels, and took Clayton into his room. This room was decorated with a wallpaper he and April had chosen when Clayton was an infant, wallpaper with bunny rabbits and ducks marching happily around in circles. On the walls were framed prints removed from an old copy of Robert Louis Stevenson's *A Child's Garden of Verses*, and matted in cheery pastel colors. The bed, which had a white wicker headboard and was covered with a fluffy white spread, had several of Clayton's favorite stuffed

animals permanently residing upon it. Now, after Ryland had helped
him into his blue jeans and T-shirt, Clayton joined the animals on
the bedspread, and since they still had twenty minutes before they
had to leave for Ada's, Ryland offered to read to him.

"What do you want me to read?" he asked.

"The sieve, the sieve, the sieve!"

So Ryland got out Edward Lear's book from the shelf underneath
the window and, turning to the well-worn page, began to read "The
Jumblies:"

> They went to sea in a Sieve, they did,
>     In a Sieve they went to sea:
> In spite of all their friends could say,
> On a winter's morn, on a stormy day,
>     In a Sieve they went to sea.
> And when the Sieve turned round and round,
> And every one cried, "You'll all be drowned!"
> They called aloud, "Our Sieve ain't big,
> But we don't care a button, we don't care a fig:
>     In a Sieve we'll go to sea!"

Ryland didn't know why Clayton loved this poem so much, but
as he read he noticed that his son's lips were moving along in time
with his, and though sometimes Ryland paused in front of a word,
Clayton never did. He was sitting in his little blue jeans, his legs
crossed, his head propped up on his hands, staring at Ryland wide-
eyed, waiting for his favorite stanza. Ryland read the refrain, and
then the next verse and the refrain again, and when he got to the
third verse Clayton, who had been silent in his accompaniment up
to now, burst out loudly in a series of toneless yelps that almost
drowned out Ryland's modulated voice.

> The water it soon came in, it did;
>     The water it soon came in:
> So, to keep them dry, they wrapped their feet
> In a pinky paper all folded neat;
>     And they fastened it down with a pin.

And they passed the night in a crockery-jar;
And each of them said, "How wise we are!
Though the sky be dark, and the voyage be long,
Yet we never can think we were rash or wrong,
    While round in our Sieve we spin!"

Here Clayton, whose voice had risen to a perfect shriek of joy, collapsed backward against the pillows to listen silently to the rest, and while Ryland read it, he marveled once more at the wholeheartedness of this son of his, who had known from the age of two what Ryland had not yet really learned—which was just to enter into things, not measuring their possible ends.

# 13

MAGGIE was heavily pissed at her grandmother as she got ready for Ryland's arrival. "Getting ready" involved little that she would not ordinarily be doing at this time of day—taking a bath, brushing her hair, changing from a T-shirt to a button-down—but somehow she felt that it was Ada's fault this was all happening. To be fair, Ada had never suggested that Maggie go to this Beyond War meeting—that had been Maggie's own stupid idea—but there was no doubt in the world that she had arranged for the encounter with Ryland, and had expected he would invite himself. Even so, she couldn't imagine what had possessed her to say yes to him, except that she had felt sorry for him after that Sword of Communism mistake and had wanted to reassure him that she liked him and wouldn't mind seeing him again sometime. Fine, well, and good—but had it really been necessary for her to agree to take him with her to some strange place for what would undoubtedly be a strange experience? No, it hadn't; Ada had forced her into it, even though Ada hadn't been there at the time.

When Ryland arrived, there wasn't a lot of talk; they were all too involved with supervising Clayton. And on the ride into town, while there was some polite chitchat, Ryland and Maggie sat mostly in silence. In fact, so awkward did Maggie feel at being seated in the front of this man's Mercedes that by the time they arrived at the house where the Wickendens lived, she was quite relieved to be there, freed from the awareness of her own presence.

But her relief lasted only a moment, just until she had time to take in that the Wickendens apparently had a conviction that plants should be disguised as animals, since a number of large bush-based starfish were fastened to their white clapboard walls. As Maggie climbed from the passenger seat of Ryland's car, she wondered what on earth she could say about this grievous state of affairs, for which she felt personally responsible, but Ryland, who had come round to help her out and was now extending his hand toward her to help her to the curb, said, as if he were reading her mind, "Well, they like to sculpt their shrubs. That isn't so deplorable."

Maggie, as she gripped his hand—a nice, dry, firm hand, quite warm—smiled up at its owner, pleased and surprised, then, leading the way up the walk, she had again the sinking conviction that this evening was going to end very badly. And when the door was opened by an extremely elderly man with a hearing aid, who looked at her and at Ryland with such obvious disbelief and mistrust that Maggie was certain he could somehow see at first glance that she was an atheist and a skeptic, she couldn't even find it in her to remind the minister that he had invited her to come tonight, and to bring a friend. They stared at each other dumbly until an elderly woman behind him said, clasping her hands together kindly, "David, let the young people by."

Then he moved out of Maggie's way, permitting her to set foot on an entryway floor so polished that she could actually see her face in it; Maggie was detained for a minute by that face, which was paler and thinner than her real one, but which she wished nonetheless she could join there, under the floor. As Ryland followed her into the house, the woman said, "Why, Mr. Guthrie! What an unexpected pleasure! I didn't know you were interested in the Movement!"

For a minute, Maggie was so distracted by the term "the Movement"—good heavens, what had she gotten herself into, she who hated causes of any kind and the groups that such causes created—that she could not pay proper attention to Ryland, who was gravely and courteously explaining that he had come mostly as a guest of Ms. Esterhaczy's, but that it would be such a pleasure to see Mrs.

Wickenden's Turkish rug collection at last. At this, Mrs. Wickenden
seemed effortlessly to change gears—from the Movement to Rugs—
and started conversing with Ryland about thread count and nap
cut, while the Reverend Wickenden stood staring dumbly at Maggie. She was now convinced that he had focused on some aspect of
her character or personality or looks so heinous and reprehensible
that even the word "skeptic" didn't cover it, but Ryland, who was
acting with extraordinary poise, held back for a minute, as Mrs.
Wickenden led the way into the living room, and whispered to her,
"Don't worry, Maggie. It's just that we seem rather *young* to him."

Maggie, rounding the corner from the hall into the living room,
was persuaded of the essential rightness of this judgment as she
looked into a perfect sea of white hair. The owners of the hair
subsided into silence at the entrance of Ryland and Maggie; they
presumed, she could see, that they were here by mistake. Or perhaps they needed to use the phone?

Later, Maggie realized that the people came in matched sets,
but in the first blur of embarrassment they all seemed the same
sex, a sort of plain functional sex that was neither one thing nor the
other, but that would do, at a pinch, as either. The only thought
that Maggie had just at first, though, was rather an uncharitable
one: she was glad, she thought to herself ironically, that the world's
safety was in such good hands.

Now one of those matched sets detached itself from the herd and
came toward Ryland and Maggie. The male half of the unit introduced them as the Jeffersons, another retired Presbyterian minister
and his wife, and as Maggie and Ryland reciprocated with information about themselves, the whole room broke up like a river
thawing, and the chunks of ice bobbed around them. Clearly, Maggie and Ryland were the most exciting thing that had wandered
into these people's lives for a long time, and even if they *were* here
just to use the phone, they were certainly going to be welcomed.
When it was divulged that they were actually here to attend the
meeting, the dizzy heights of silent rapture were climbed by all
who heard this. Others—those with hearing impairments—seemed
also to be pleased.

When Ryland went off with Mrs. Wickenden to examine her Turkish rugs, Maggie was surprised by how deserted she felt, how inhibited she felt without him. All around her, people were drinking tea, and she took a cup herself, then sat on the edge of a wooden chair and listened to people talk. To her left, she heard two of the stronger male specimens in the room having a discussion about philosophers. One of them, testing the other's knowledge, said, "Name all the philosophers whose names begin with P," and, when his correspondent couldn't come up with any names but Plato, said in a tone of smug satisfaction, "Parmenides, Philo, Peirce, Plato, Plotinus, Protagoras, Pyrrho, and Pythagoras." Elsewhere in the room, voices rose and fell, discussing everything from the monthly DAR meeting to the pothole on High Street, but not touching on, from what Maggie could hear, either nuclear weapons or war. Since that was the topic of the meeting, it seemed to her peculiar that no one was talking of it, but perhaps in this group it would be impolite to anticipate the main speaker.

At last Ryland reappeared, followed by an ecstatic Mrs. Wickenden.

"Silk?" she was saying. "Do you really think so? Silk! I never imagined!" Just then, the Reverend Wickenden started rapping on the top of the piano with his knuckles, and silence fell on the room again as the assembled company sat down in the hard-backed chairs, which had clearly been borrowed from some church and arranged in a circle around the living room. Maggie made certain that she ended up next to Ryland—whose renewed presence was remarkably comforting, considering that she had known the man for only half a day—and then she tried to focus on the room.

On the piano that the Reverend Wickenden had rapped were set pamphlets and informational literature; an easel was covered with a thick wad of charts; on the wall hung a picture of the earth from space. As the Reverend Wickenden began the meeting by asking everyone present to introduce himself or herself and to explain his or her prior involvement with the issue at hand, Maggie found herself staring at this picture; she stared at it continuously while she listened to twenty or more self-introductions, which all began with variations of "Well, of course, Dave is an old friend"—old, and how, thought Maggie each time she heard this, perversely adding an extra year onto the age with every introduction—and ended with variations of "I can't imagine that the Lord God doesn't want peace on earth." When the time came for Maggie to introduce herself, she felt at a distinct disadvantage, as she could use neither the beginning nor the ending of this formula, and the middle, which might have served as a model, had somehow escaped her attention. So she swallowed, and fixing her eyes on the part of the earth where the blue and green swirls of sea and forests seemed the calmest and most well-ordered, she introduced herself, for reasons she couldn't have explained, by talking about the air raid drills in second grade.

"And then for *years*," she found herself saying, "I was so scared of hot water radiators that I wouldn't go near them, not even in the summer when they were turned off. It took a long time to feel the full effects of that, but this winter I saw that movie *Threads*, and all anyone could do was grunt, and I thought, OK, that's enough. At least *I* could feel *scared*, you know what I mean?" It was clear, when she tore her eyes away from the picture of the earth—she thought it must have been the tip of South America she had been focused so intently on—and saw that all the white heads in the room were fixed in her direction as intently as she had been fixed on the Cape of Magellan, that they didn't know what she meant. Ryland, when he took over, said simply, "I came because I'm a friend of Maggie's," and at this there was universal approval. Now the meeting could begin. But as it began, Maggie found herself so entranced by the words that Ryland had just spoken—a friend; he had called himself her friend—that she had some trouble concentrating.

The Reverend Wickenden stood up, adjusted his hearing aid, and looked around the room. His wife handed him a pointer, the old-fashioned wooden kind with a black rubber tip, and he held it as he flipped through the charts, choosing one to land his pointer on. This displayed a statement, signed EINSTEIN 1946, that read THE UNLEASHED POWER OF THE ATOM HAS CHANGED EVERYTHING SAVE OUR MODES OF THINKING, AND THUS WE DRIFT TOWARD

UNPARALLELED CATASTROPHE. The Reverend Wickenden read the quote aloud to the company, helping them to follow it with his pointer. Then he added, looking modestly down at the floor, "Einstein realized, you see, that the splitting of the atom changed our world completely. Because our thinking hasn't caught up with this, we have drifted to the brink of extinction. 'Drifted' is important, here—something that happens so slowly and subtly you don't even notice it's happening, and by the time you do, it's often too late. Or at least it's a real emergency."

Here he stopped and scanned a series of little tabs on the pages of the charts, searching for the next one in his presentation. He tried one, but it was not the one he wanted—Maggie had just time to see a circle with "New Mode of Thinking" written in its top half and "Old Mode of Thinking" in its bottom half, and then the Reverend Wickenden flipped it away apologetically, locating the correct one on the next try, while everyone waited in sympathetic silence.

"Now," he said, adjusting the chart on the easel and rallying his pointer to the task once again, "why do we drift? We drift because we have the following illusions. One, the human species can continue to war and survive. Two, 'They' won't let it happen. Three, one person cannot make a difference. Let's start with the first illusion. For that, we have two visual aids, the Dot Chart and the BB Experience."

Maggie, at this, glanced over at Ryland, who smiled at her slightly. It was a deprecating smile, a hapless smile, a smile that said, somehow—at least in Maggie's reading of it—"Ah, well, as luck would have it . . ." And she could only hope that he was referring to the three illusions, and not to having come with her this evening.

But now, the Reverend Wickenden was displaying the Dot Chart, a huge sheet of paper entirely covered with dots, just *one* of which represented *all* the firepower that had been released in *all* the wars that men had fought since the dawn of mankind. The other two thousand or so represented the arsenal man presently had in reserve. Maggie's stomach was still doing a roller coaster dive on that one—for the moment, she was wrenched away from her concern that Ryland was having a miserable time to her more familiar concern that she was going to die at any moment—when the Reverend Wickenden moved on with relative speed to the BB Experience.

He picked up a container full of BB's and an empty galvanized steel pail and, picking out one BB, dropped it alone into the pail. It rang, as it struck, in an irritating manner. Wickenden said, "That's the dot you just saw. These are the other dots," and started to pour the other BB's after it. The noise, which grew steadily in volume and obtrusiveness, was one of the most unpleasant sounds Maggie had ever heard, and it went on and on until she thought she would scream. Even those in the room with reduced hearing seemed to be able to hear *this* sound quite well, and when the Reverend Wickenden had finally transferred the last BB and the sound had ceased, it was obvious that his audience was putty in his hands; *anything* to get rid of those BB's. Maggie's ears were ringing so hard that she missed part of what the clergyman said next, and when she was able to tune in again, he had moved on to the third illusion.

"The most significant changes in history began with individuals who had a vision and acted on it. For example, individuals were responsible for the abolition of slavery, women's suffrage, the civil rights movement, the environmental movement, et cetera. Without the sustained efforts of lots of different individuals, these movements would never have succeeded."

The meeting was now turned over to one of Wickenden's cronies, a tall man with huge cauliflower ears that stuck out from his head like dish satellites. This man—who introduced himself as the sexton at St. John's, Ada's church, as Maggie recalled—was invited to give a personal response to the idea of nuclear war, and he had come prepared to do so by bringing his file full of clippings. His personal response consisted of lifting these clippings out, one by one, and reading them aloud to the listening heads, prefacing his presentation with the remarks: "I find one of the most exciting things to do is to keep clipping things, and then storing them. Storing them is just as important as clipping—and then you can read them whenever you want. Last week, for example, I came across an article that showed how *shellfish* are involved with rain. Way down at the bottom of the ocean, they somehow know all about rain, and they respond.

I don't know, it's osmosis or something, but they kind of expand and shrink when they want to. So I clipped it. And here it is."

He passed it to his left and then, while Maggie wondered what on earth shellfish had to do with nuclear war—except, presumably, that they wouldn't like it much—the man went on with his clippings, pulling first one and then another out of his very thick file: one about Margaret Mead, one about the Palace of Knossos, one about "Peace Links," one about a new encyclopedia. Everyone present nodded their heads, as if they completely understood. Maggie, however, did not understand, not until—the last clipping lying on his lap—the man took hold of his cauliflower ears, one in each hand, and, staring intently in front of him, said: "And this one here explains it all. It's called the Gaia hypothesis. There's a British scientist who is proving that the earth is self-controlling, a unified, single system. Like a big, well, a *creature*, with nothing partitioned. *Everything is all one thing*. It's all trussed together, all cinched up. You've got to see it all as *linked*."

And since Maggie had also read about this theory and the man who thought life was self-regulating, she did not, as she might have, diagnose schizophrenia, but instead felt profoundly touched.

When the meeting was over, and Maggie and Ryland had had some more tea, they managed a gracious departure. At the door, the Reverend Wickenden thanked them at least four times for coming, and suggested that they come again sometime soon; Mrs. Wickenden had on her Rug Face as she pressed Ryland's hand goodbye.

Maggie went down the walk first, in perfect silence, and Ryland helped her into the car in the same state, and then he started up the engine, and still neither of them said a word. Maggie felt such a deliriously conflicting set of emotions that she hardly dared breathe, much less open her mouth and say something. The whole thing had been so unbelievably affecting—these white-haired old people, all of them born long before the atom had become a threat, all of them schooled in a politeness so profound that it would clearly be crippling in any emergency at all, giving to this problem, nuclear war, the same sort of attention that they had no doubt given to their elementary school teachers sixty years before, when they were memorizing the Preamble to the Constitution—and at the same time so utterly ludicrous—that in this diminutive town of Felicity, Indiana, in a house surrounded by sculpted starfish, a group of people who were, by virtue of their age and through no fault of their own, entirely outside the functioning of the society they lived in should think they could save the world. Between pathos and comedy it just about broke her heart, and when Ryland finally broke the silence, to say "Peace Links. A new breakfast sausage?" Maggie exploded into laughter, spraying the dashboard of Ryland's car with a wild burst of spit, and Ryland exploded, too, and the two of them sat in his car, the engine running, the windows closed, clutching their stomachs and shrieking with relief, and when at last the tempest subsided, Maggie found that she had, at some point, in the midst of violent convulsions, thrown herself into Ryland's arms and now had to disengage herself while occasional gusts of laughter continued to galvanize her body, and Ryland gunned the car and drove away from the Wickendens' white clapboard house. Finally, Maggie could speak.

"It was so f-f-f-funny when that man with the ears was going on about the Palace of K-K-K-Knossos," she said, surprised to find that the water did not stop streaming from her eyes but kept coming as if it was tears.

Maybe it *was* tears. Thinking about that man, clutching his ears and staring in front of him, and the Reverend Wickenden, with his rubber-tipped pointer and his charts, she suddenly started to sob aloud, her breath coming in gulps. When Ryland, who had stopped laughing just before she did, glanced over at her, concerned, it was as if he had seeded the clouds of grief, and she began to sob all the harder. Dimly, she heard Ryland saying that he thought he'd better take her back to his house rather than going immediately out to Ada's, and she gulped and nodded her agreement to this while she continued to sob uncontrollably.

At the top of one prolonged wail of sorrow, while her voice was hanging in the upper registers of despair, she suddenly thought once more of those sensitive shellfish, so deeply *involved* with rain.

And at that, she started to laugh again. While there was absolutely no question, at this fourth reversal, that she had a genuine case of hysterics, there seemed to be nothing she could do about it except to let it take its course, but by the time they pulled up in front of Ryland's house—a lovely white house with a wraparound porch, and tall clean windows shining with light—she had almost worn herself out with emotion.

Ryland led her through the hallway into the kitchen, which featured an antique lion-footed table and a cheerful potbellied stove. He got down a wineglass from the cupboard and poured her out some red wine. Then he led her to one of the two oak armchairs on either side of the stove and, putting his hands on her shoulders gently, urged her to sit and drink. "Hi, Molly," he said to a black and white dog who wagged apologetically up to them. Maggie smoothed the dog's head with one hand while she raised her glass with the other.

The first taste of the wine was very calming, and with the second, she could almost breathe. Strangely enough, she didn't feel embarrassed, just grateful for the wine and the chair. And when Ryland had poured himself a glass of wine and joined her on the other side of the stove, she looked at him steadily, still wiping her face; he looked just as steadily back. Then he leaned over and stroked his finger lightly across her forehead, bringing it down around the side of her cheek. She smiled at him openly, her sorrow gone, her lugubriousness dissolved. For it struck her that here she was, sitting in one of the loveliest houses she had ever seen, with a man who was clearly both gentle and good, in a place that was, tonight, Nuclear Safe. And while she hadn't brought her diaphragm along—indeed, why would she have, to a meeting of Beyond War?—she felt fairly confident that she would sleep with Ryland anyway, fairly confident and rejoicing in the thought. It crossed her mind that Ada was still baby-sitting for Clayton and would have to be relieved at some point before the night was through—Ada, what a sweetheart, wouldn't *she* be happy, Ada with all her little plans—but it was only nine-thirty; surely that could wait. She reached up and took Ryland's hand.

## 14

THINGS were heating up in Howell's mind. As he got ready to go to church early on the morning after the auction—outside in the barnyard Charlene and the twins were already sitting in the front of the truck, waiting for him as patiently as cornstalks—he thought about how far he had come, how little he had left still to work out. Now that Mrs. Esterhaczy had agreed to let him bring the Russians back to her house after he had captured them—whenever he thought of these Russians he saw in his mind's eye a set of Siamese twins, wearing overcoats, attached near the shoulders and hips—all he had to work out were the details of the kidnapping, and that shouldn't really be so hard. Not only had the precise dates of their visit been printed already in the *Felicity Companion,* on the Coming Events page, along with Women's Aglow meetings and various pig roasts, but his moving truck was in tiptop shape, and he had right on his side as well.

It was funny, though, that while the whole idea had been God's to begin with, He hadn't said much about it since, and now, as Howell ran a brush through his short bristly hair, looking at himself in the mirror with the pleasant certainty that soon his face would be on the front page of all the newspapers in the Free World, he suggested to God that He give Howell an update on just how to pull the whole thing off. But although, after a rather prolonged and doubtful pause, God appeared in the mirror over his left shoulder, floating in the air like the head of a sunflower, when He showed up He had his eyebrows raised, as if to say "Hey, *I* don't know."

From the yard the sound of the truck horn interrupted the consultation, and Howell straightened his tie, drank down his coffee, and went out to join his family. When he climbed into the front of the truck, there was an almost imperceptible universal scooch to the right, but Charlene and the children didn't turn to look at him; they stared calmly, directly, ahead.

Howell turned on the engine, then backed the truck slowly around. Maybe it was just his imagination, but it seemed to him that ever since Friday night Charlene had been even more silent, more secretive than usual, and he wondered what it could be about. He couldn't believe she disapproved so terribly of his plan to kidnap the Russians, particularly because when she had married him she had said that one of the things she liked about him was the way he had so many plans. She'd said—in one of the longest speeches Howell had ever heard her make, before or since—that he seemed to want to *do* something with his life, to accomplish something, and she liked that, because it was so different. Most men, they let things happen; but he had targets, things that he aimed for.

Well, she'd been right about that, certainly; as far back as he could remember he had been unable to rest. When he was eight years old he'd already been getting up at seven in the morning in order to watch "Modern Farmer," and in the 4-H Club he'd given his yearly pig production the same care a doctor might give to a dying patient—which was, of course, what a pig really was. While other kids were wasting their time reading storybooks, he was reading *Farming Fun* or *Popular Mechanics,* learning about grain yields and projects for the home, and though, when he was a grown-up, things hadn't always worked out for him, he had kept on having goals. So he couldn't imagine that Charlene was quiet because she was disapproving, especially since one of her own two brothers was about to lose his farm. And one thing she had pointed out Friday night was really bothering him: in order for him to be able to park his truck in the middle of the road around Felicity Pond, and then get the car with the Russians to drive into its back, that car had to be *on* that road, and no one had told him that it would be. No one, in fact, had told him anything, so what was he going to do?

At the moment, he was simply going to church, and he put the truck into first. The hounds howled and strained at their chains as he pulled down the driveway and turned north at the road, heading away from town. Howell's new church was quite a distance from Felicity, but it was his favorite one yet; Mitch and Billy Bob were also members, which made it especially nice. One of the churches he had gone to for a while had been a Pentecostal, with only fifteen members, and had consisted of just the Bournes and one other family, who all could speak in tongues. For a while, it had been rather impressive to hear eleven people, all of them with the same jaw line and the same slightly protuberant eyes, speak very rapidly, one after another, in eleven different tongues, but eventually he'd felt as if he was at a school for linguists, and had decided to find someplace else.

Howell had finally fastened on the Church of God, which not only had a preacher who was almost as interested as Howell was in politics and the world situation, but also had a kitchen and a fellowship hall, and in the year or so since he had started attending (going also to the Christian weenie-roasts, where they all ate hot dogs while one of the members sang anthems, occasionally stopping because of smoke inhalation), he had really become very much a part of it, one of the important voices in the congregation. Now, as he pulled up into the parking lot, letting the truck, which needed tuning, cough itself into silence, people waved at him and called out, and he waved back as he clambered down. He loved going to church, he always had. It made him feel good about himself.

It would still be a while before the service got going, so Howell went to talk to Billy Bob. Mitch came over, too, and the three of them stood beneath a tree for a minute in friendly silence. Usually, it took them five or ten minutes to really warm up to a topic for conversation, and since they probably didn't have quite that long before the bell rang for church, Howell didn't try too hard to think of one.

"Nice day," he said instead. "Looks like the frost is really out," and while this meant that planting could begin, and that they therefore could get into an animated or semi-animated discussion of the best kinds of pre-emergent fertilizers, Billy Bob changed the subject abruptly by saying, "Didja know your sister's a witch?"

"What did she do this time?" asked Howell, resigned.

"No," said Billy Bob, curling his lip indignantly, "I mean a real *witch*. Phyllis went to her house on Friday night for some kind of meeting—she didn't know what it would be beforehand, course— and Bailey had spells and kettles and dancing. Witch stuff. Really. No shit."

"Dancing?" said Mitch. "Janet went too and she didn't say anything about *dancing*."

"Well, maybe not dancing, but certainly spells. Like for what they used to hang 'em."

"Janet said it was funny; not really like what they'd hang 'em for."

"Point is, your sister's a witch."

These last words Howell finally absorbed; Bailey, his sister, was a witch. He was surprised only at how little this surprised him, and how much it delighted him. First, it explained the cauldron episode, and the fact that she had actually spent fifteen dollars of her own money at the auction to buy one; and next, it was incredibly typical of her; it confirmed what he had always suspected. He had spent much of his adolescence and early adulthood troubled by her continuous attempts to pretend that things were something they were not—that pigs were playmates, that the woodshed was a jail—and while he had eventually accepted that this did not mean she was really insane, he thought she came pretty close to it. Now, insane or not, look where it had led to; she was trying to practice magic, which was forbidden by God and everything.

Why, in a way, God Himself was a great magician—He could make a plant look first like a little dot of nothing, then like a small green stick, and finally like a cornstalk or a tomato—but if you let anyone else have this power, if you let what had been exclusively the domain of God pass into the hands of just anyone, then the whole world could be ruined. Things *had* to be centrally controlled by God; otherwise everything would be unbalanced. What a mess someone could make in no time at all if they didn't know what they were doing. Why, the cows might end up able to fly, or the pigs could become deep thinkers, or what if they just made plants a lot bigger so that corn grew twenty feet high? And this was what Bailey, his sister, was doing! Though probably still as a recruit.

"A witch," he said. "Well, that doesn't surprise me. I wonder if it's against the law?"

"Bound to be," said Billy Bob.

Now the bell rang for them to go to church, and they proceeded to round up their families. Howell liked to sit near the front, so he hustled Charlene right along. On the way in, he picked up a pamphlet from the table, a pamphlet in comic book form. Recently, the church had started to send these out to everyone in Felicity with a mailbox; they were extremely readable, with bubbles in people's mouths, and just one statement per page. This one, on the cover, read SOMEBODY GOOFED, and by leafing through it as he walked down the aisle, Howell saw that it was about Satan and Hell. But he didn't have time to read it now, so he thrust it into his pocket, and then settled his family down in the pew to have a prayer before the service.

Howell, however, had difficulty praying. Things were hotter than ever in his mind. His sister Bailey was a witch, and she didn't know that he knew it, which really gave him something on her, he felt, something that he might use. She couldn't possibly take half the farm if she were sent to jail. Was there some way that he could get her sent there? Or at least make her leave the state? Why, maybe he could blame her for the Russians' disappearance, thus killing two birds with one stone!

In a way, this *was* praying, thought Howell as he knelt, and welcomed this insight with wonder. In the original story where the car was kidnapped by being driven into a truck, everyone in the town had thought it was magic; since the whole town had thought it a disappearance, they hadn't searched as well as they should have. And that would certainly help Howell, too, if it kept them from finding him too soon. When he had the Russians under lock and key at Mrs. Esterhaczy's—Lock and Key, he saw it in his mind—he would make an anonymous phone call to the sheriff, and report Bailey as a witch. He would imply that she had turned the Russians into rocks or small trees or something, and while the sheriff would no doubt be too sensible to believe such a thing—though you never knew, you never knew—he would still be forced, under the circumstances, to investigate, which would make things sticky for Bailey. She even *might* be arrested, though being taken in for questioning was the best Howell could really hope for. Still, by the end the whole town would know her for the lunatic that she was.

He wrenched his attention back to the service. The preacher had chosen as his subject today the boring topic of the low voter turnout in the last election, but as he warmed up, getting past the bare statistics and the initial admonitions, Howell found, to his amazement, that God was *again* trying to encourage him to proceed with his kidnapping plan, since Brother Murphy was talking now about Russia.

"Think of it," he roared in his usual thundering style. "Just think of it, brothers, I ask you. In the Bible we are told that anyone in whom the Lord Jesus Christ does not dwell will be left on this Earth after the Rapture and will go through the Great Tribulation spoken of by Jesus Christ. The Rapture is the next great international crisis—it will occur in the next few years. It will disrupt communications and transportation like no major war has ever done, since during the Rapture over four million people will depart from this earth in less than a fifth of a second! The Rapture will herald the coming of the Antichrist to take over the United States through the United Nations. And here we are, as a country, pouring millions of dollars into that United Nations, which is nothing but a spy headquarters for the Soviet Union. We allow the Soviets to infiltrate our society; we don't restrict their movements! It might surprise you to learn that the UN Charter supersedes our own U.S. Constitution; this should scare you to death! There are some in power who want and are working for a 'world government.' I am an American and I want to stay that way. America is the country of God.

So VOTE next time Election Day comes, and know that you are voting for Him! Don't make it easy for the Antichrist of Russia! Dear friends, Hell is real!"

When the sermon ended, they all sang a hymn, "The Lonely Trail of Faith." And as Howell helped Daisy and Darell—who were still mighty short—up onto the knee rests, where they could see better, he thought about the sermon and the idea that God was, well, a citizen of America. Howell had never thought of it in precisely those terms before, but of course it made sense; where *else* would He live if He had a choice? Where else would *anyone* live? And then also, all that business about restricted movements and the infiltration of society; it was almost as if Howell would be just an immigration officer, making sure there were no enemies running loose.

After the hymn, they all sat down again; Brother Murphy was doing some praying. Howell's thoughts now returned to Bailey and her witchcraft, and how he could use this against her. It had been nice of Mitch and Billy Bob to tell him; maybe he should do something for them in return. Maybe he should pay them back by letting them in on the kidnapping—that way they could be heroes, too.

By the time the service was over, he'd made up his mind that he would give them the chance to join him. When the preacher had had his final say—"They that have done good and have followed after Christ shall have everlasting life, but they that have done evil and rejected the grace which is in Christ shall be condemned to eternal agony!"—and everyone had popped up from their seats, congratulating themselves on the way that they were going to escape eternal agony, Howell started scooting toward Billy Bob and his family, and ran into them near the back door.

"Talk to you a minute afterward, Billy?" he said, and when Billy nodded, he moved to intercept Mitch as he hurried also toward the rear. Charlene and the twins ignored this, as they ignored much of what he did, and they went to stand on the grass below the church, where they were joined by some of their neighbors.

When the three men were once again grouped beneath the oak tree, Howell hardly knew how to proceed. He remembered that

Billy Bob had said at Rosie's not too long ago that he thought the Russians should just be blown off the face of the earth, and that seemed like a good enough starting point, but then Mitch was just about to lose his farm and would be more interested in the burning of the mortgages. So he started with the mortgages, and after explaining just enough of the Bankers' Conspiracy to get on with, he moved ahead with the Russians. And while Mitch and Billy Bob's families—seeing that their men were in earnest consultation and shouldn't be disturbed—gravitated toward Charlene and the twins, where they all stood talking softly and waiting, Mitch and Billy Bob got really enthusiastic and punched their hands in their palms.

"*That*," said Billy Bob, "sounds like a hell of a lot of fun!"

But Mitch said, "Jesus. I could get my farm back!"

When Howell and his family were back in the cab of the pickup, Daisy asked if they could go get ice cream. Sometimes on Sundays, after they had had their Sunday dinner and before Howell went out to check on the stock, they would take a little drive into town and visit the Dairy Shack, where they would each have a vanilla softie. But of course they never went *before* dinner, and Howell was just about to say that, when, so great did he feel, so mirthful about the future, he said instead, "Why don't we get burgers? We'll have lunch out today. You like that, kids?"

"Oh, yeeessss!"

And when they both said "Yeeessss!" he felt even better, magnanimous as well as very clever. But as a little time passed, and Howell had a chance to think everything over in his mind, he started to feel less happy; at the Dairy Shack, munching on a double cheeseburger with mayonnaise, he even wondered if he'd done the right thing. He had had this great idea, or God had had it for him, and that was all well and good, but then he'd gone and told four other people about it, and that wasn't really much like him. He stabbed at his root beer float with his spoon. He had never been good at leading others. As a Boy Scout, for example, when he had had a brief tenure as the head of his patrol, he had been thrilled at the responsibility and had spent days before a camping trip making lists for his patrol, assigning chores and suggesting merit badge work. When they got to the woods, though, he'd found no one who would listen as he tried to communicate his vision. As he was sitting trying patiently to explain it, they had decided instead to have a circle jerk.

"Hey, guys," Tommy Widau had said, "let's all go into the cook tent and jerk off; we'll leave this bozo here with his lists." Whooping approval, they had all taken off for the tent, and laced it carefully behind them. Howell had stayed where he was, but he hadn't been able to help overhearing the *whack, whack, whack* they made as they went about their fun, and he'd been left with all his plans and no one to carry them out. It hadn't taken him long to learn that it was better to do things on his own; that was when he dropped out of Boy Scouts and joined Future Farmers instead. Of course, this kidnapping wouldn't be like a camping trip, but it seemed to him, as he sat sipping his root beer float through a straw, that there was probably some potential for having the others ignore him; Billy Bob in particular might be a handful.

And as Howell sat there brooding, another discouraging thought struck him. If he *did* turn Bailey in for witchcraft, and she was arrested as a result, she would probably be pretty mad at him afterward—less eager than ever to give him the whole farm, no matter what she might say about it now. If he could, he should get it settled before the whole matter arose; he should get her, quite simply, to sign something. So exciting was this thought, the thought that the farm ownership would be settled for once and for all if only he could get Bailey committed on paper, that he jumped to his feet and marched out to the truck, where he found a dusty pad of paper and a pencil. He thought for a while and then started to write: "I, Bailey Bourne, promise never to bother my brother about the farm, which should have been left to him. It is his now, that is all there is to it, since he is the one who works it, and everything on it too." He studied this for some time, then went to get his family. At least *this* he could settle up right now.

"You want to go see your aunt? Pay her a little visit?"

"Oh, yeeessss!" said the twins again.

# 15

BAILEY was out at Grey Rock grooming horses and, at the moment, trying to deal with Joel. Since it was Sunday, show day, many of the stable's riders were in Terre Haute for a large regional jumping competition, and she had been looking forward to being the only one in the barn, as she had been going a hundred miles a minute since the debacle two nights before, picking up the cauldron at the auction, teaching two classes on Saturday, all of which had prevented her from thinking about what it was that had gone wrong. Not that she didn't already know—what had gone wrong was that she had tried to form a coven in Felicity to begin with, the most unimaginative town, she had to suspect, that had ever been put on a map—but still, she just wanted to be alone right now, and Joel wouldn't let her. He was the handyman here at Grey Rock, and was supposed to be fixing the fences up in the higher pastures this morning, but he had decided instead to come down and pester her; he was in an unusually animated mood. His soon-to-be-ex-wife had dropped her demand for a new car, saying that she would settle for a used one, and Joel, in delirious contemplation of all the ways in which he, an experienced mechanic, could rig this "used" car so that it would, immediately after the divorce was final, completely self-destruct—the piéce de resistance was to be the way the engine would fall through the bottom of the vehicle, entirely detaching itself from its moorings—had managed to transform his usual lethargy into something that resembled high spirits.

"So I thought maybe we'd go out and celebrate one of these nights, what do you say, Bailey? I'm going to be a free man, I'll have more time for partying."

"Well, I don't know, Joel," said Bailey. Chance sat on her small haunches on a nearby bale of hay, her two front paws turned slightly outward, her ears a tiny bit cocked. In the short time that Bailey and Chance had been together, Bailey had come to depend on Chance's judgment, and now as she stared intently at Bailey, her eyes preternaturally alert, she seemed to be asking, "Why don't you unload him? Why don't you get rid of him for good?"

"What do you mean, you don't know?" said Joel, who by now had his hands crossed on his chest in a defensive posture and was staring at her with a look of wounded outrage that was almost comical.

"It all depends on when. I'm busy. And you know I don't drink at all."

"Is this a brushoff?"

"Oh, come on, Joel."

"No, no, I mean it. You don't like me?"

"It's not that I don't *like* you."

"Oh, then what is it?"

"Listen, give me a break. I'm working."

"I'll give you a break. I'll give you a *big* break. Just don't come sniveling to me afterward." With that, his high spirits now gone, he stormed his way out of the barn, calling out, on the way, to his own two dogs, who would also be going to his ex-wife. One was a miniature dachshund and one was a brindled hound, and they were much more sweet-natured than he was. They ran after him cheerfully; Chance watched them go, then rested her chin on her paws.

Well, that was that, and good riddance to it all, but it was really very strange. You'd think that by now, after who knew how many partings of the ways, she would have figured out a way to tell these men that she really didn't want to see them anymore, that she would far prefer the company of a newt, but she hadn't; she made a mess of it, every single time. Though she had, in plays and films, run into innumerable admirable characters—men and women of strength and courage, of vision and compassion and grace—in real life such people hadn't often come her way; it was just the opposite, in fact. Animals were *invariably* nicer than humans—she included herself in this assessment—and it seemed more and more obvious to her that not only did people delude themselves into thinking that there was a power that was beyond and separate from them, they did it largely to justify their own incredible self-obsession as a species, their totally unfounded claim that they were of more value than other creatures. That humans were clearly of *less* value— the most savage and rapacious, the most petty and quarrelsome— well, this explained nicely the invention of "God," who would single them out for special attention anyway.

"Hey, Chanceo!" she said. "How're you doing, kid?"

Chance wagged her stump of a tail.

Now Bailey urged Scout, a large bay gelding, up onto the concrete grooming platform. She clipped his halter between two steel chains that would hold him in place while she worked. Scout was a little bit shy about his hooves, and sometimes resisted picking up his feet, but today he seemed eager for attention, and he looked at her expectantly. Horses didn't have a lot of facial muscles with which to work, and whatever they managed to communicate generally got communicated with their lips or their eyes or their ears, but Scout operated splendidly, despite this difficulty, by exaggerating everything he did. He was an absolute master of lip movements, able to stretch out the top and bottom lips farther than one would have thought possible, and to make them quiver independently of each other; he knew the effect was funny, however, and saved it for moments of humor. His sorrow he communicated with his eyes, arching his neck around to the left or to the right when someone was standing beside him, then staring at that person with a widened eye, unwinking, fathomless, and grave. Gritting her teeth, Bailey started on his toenails, sinking the pincers deep into the nail.

Bailey had gotten her first horse as a present when she was nine years old, and when they had, at their meeting, breathed into each other's nostrils, Bailey had fallen permanently in love. Together, she and Roby had learned how to ride, how to veer together through the world; soon Roby had become more real to her than her family—which Howell, in particular, had hated. "She believes that horse is human," he had often said to their parents when he thought that Bailey was not around. "That it has the same rights that we do. And it says in the Bible, clear as clear, 'Let us make man in our image, after our likeness, and let them have dominion over the fish of the sea, and over the fowl of the air, and over the cattle, and over all the earth, and over every creeping thing that creepeth upon the earth,' and Roby is just a creeping thing." It was then that Bailey had stopped believing in God, since it seemed clear to her that anybody so insensitive to the rights of animals could be only a human being in disguise; Roby a creeping thing, indeed! Roby was dead now, and Bailey didn't have a horse of her own anymore, but she felt, in a way, that all the horses at Grey Rock were hers, and now, as she finished off Scout's toenails, she decided to take him for a ride; he was staring at her expectantly and winking a bit.

Leaving him for a moment on the platform, she went to the tack room for a bridle, and when she returned he whinnied happily, in anticipation of a run. But before Bailey had the chance to slip the bridle on him, and to her great—nay, enormous—astonishment, she heard a truck clambering up the dirt road, and she knew that its engine was familiar. The truck made an enormous crash hitting a bump, and then snarled and growled its way onward, and Bailey stood transfixed as she confirmed that it was Howell's and that his whole family was packed inside. Grinding to a stop, the truck slowly and painfully died, and Howell climbed out of the driver's seat; the bright sunshine outside kept him from seeing into the barn, where both Scout and Bailey still stood, silent. At last Bailey called out, "I'm in here, Howell. In the barn." Then she took Scout to the door. Chance followed.

"Hello, Bailey," said Howell when she appeared. "We stopped by your residence first."

"I always work Sundays. You know that," she said. "We had a big fight about it, remember?"

"I try not to remember arguments," he said as the rest of the family climbed out.

"Hi, Aunt Bailey! We just had Dairy Shack!"

"Hi, Daisy, Darell. That sounds nice."

"Don't let us interfere with your duties," said Howell.

"No," said Bailey. "Hi, Charlene."

Already she was beginning to feel angry, though for a moment the surprise had been pleasant. Daisy and Darell were looking wide-eyed up at Scout's nose, and that was nice, as far as it went, but Charlene seemed distinctly uncomfortable, and Howell had begun to readjust his body into the pose that indicated he was settling in for a long conversation—for this pose, his feet were moved more widely apart than would be practical for walking, and his arms were slung across his chest, loosely intertwined. Charlene, who obviously knew this stance also, went back to sit in the front of the truck, and the twins, after starting to reach their hands up to touch Scout's nose, and being scared off by a sudden movement of his eager, flexible lips, drifted away toward the upper dressage ring, where Billy, the goat, was grazing. Bailey decided to hang on to Scout; it would keep the discussion short.

"What's this about? I have work to do."

"I came to discuss that cauldron."

"What about it?" asked Bailey.

"Well, I changed my mind. You can have it if you want to. That's all."

"I already have one. I got it at the auction."

"Ah," said Howell. "That's too bad."

Here they stopped and stared at one another in silence while Bailey tried to decide what to think. She found it pretty fishy, to put it mildly, that Howell had suddenly decided to be generous, particularly when she knew he had been at the Widau auction and had probably seen her bidding. But if by some unlikely chance the offer was made in good faith, it would be mean of her to be totally ungrateful.

"But thanks for the offer," she added shortly. "If I ever need another one I'll remember it."

This seemed to satisfy Howell, as he disposed of the subject at once, broaching another one instead.

"I hear there's going to be some visitors to town next month. Some Russians coming to the college. That'll be real unusual, won't it?"

"Unique. By why are you interested in *that?*"

"I'm interested, Bailey, in a wide range of topics."

"But Russians?"

"As a Christian, I'm supposed to love my enemies."

"You're not a Christian, you're a fundamentalist."

Howell frowned at her in disapproval, and Bailey looked back with some alarm. This was the first that she had heard that there were Russians coming to Powell College, and that Howell knew about it was in itself fairly surprising; but that he would bring it up without simultaneously damning it—that was genuinely suspicious, even weird.

"Why aren't you having a fit?"

"Why should I? They're only professors."

"*Only* professors? You *hate* professors."

"One of them gave me a couch."

In the dressage ring, Daisy and Darell were running, pretending to be horses themselves, and Scout at her side was getting impatient; he shoved his head under her arm. But Bailey didn't move, since the more she considered it, the stranger it seemed that Howell, who had always manifested every sign of paranoid hatred of the Soviet Union, should be anything but hysterical with rage at this visitation, practically frothing at the mouth. Howell managed to blame the USSR for just about every bad event that took place anywhere in the world at any time; when four Russian diplomats were kidnapped in Lebanon, he'd asserted that the KGB had arranged the kidnapping themselves to make it seem that the Soviet Union *wasn't* behind the whole Middle East mess (as Howell knew for certain that it was). Going purely on her knowledge of Howell's psychology, which required a limited identification with his immediate family (sans Bailey herself, of course), his church (whatever that happened to be at the moment), and sometimes the local Republican party (though he had his disagreements with it, too), she found it almost inconceivable that Howell's most hated enemy should suddenly be the topic of a little friendly chitchat, particularly with *her*.

"Howell," she said, "just what is going on?"

"You're right. That's not what I came to talk about. I came to talk about the farm."

"So talk."

"Well, as we both know, our parents died intestate. And since we live in a world of written documents, just sign this one, if you would." He removed from his pocket a careworn sheet of paper with a few lines on it in pencil. When Bailey had had the chance to read them, she ripped the paper into pieces. They scattered into the light breeze that was blowing, which whipped them toward the barn. Chance pounced on one of them, worrying it in her teeth. Bailey felt like doing the same to Howell. She had never disliked him more intensely than she did at this moment, while he looked at her with shock.

"OK, Howell, you've gone too far. I'm going to see a lawyer. I'll give you a paper of my own before long. Now leave me alone. Get lost!"

"You'll be sorry for this, Bailey."

"Out! Out! Just go away!" Scout backed up a pace and then stopped.

Daisy and Darell came charging back at this moment, both of them very excited. Daisy was shoving Darell in the right arm, and he was shoving her back in the left, and they were saying "Yes, you did" "No, I didn't," "Yes, you did," "No, I didn't," as if they'd invented the phrases. Howell, who obviously could not have been more pleased at the timing of his children's return, which relieved him of the need to seem to be doing what Bailey had told him, now rounded them up toward the truck.

"Say goodbye to your aunt, children."

"Shit," said Bailey. "Shit."

*Smash* BANG the truck choked to life, then chugged assertively back down the gravel road.

———

Bailey worked with the horses for two and a half more hours, and a hard two and a half hours she made it. She had been upset by Howell's visit in so many ways at once that there seemed no way to tackle her feelings; the one thing that was clear was that she should take some kind of action, but right now she would think of nothing but the horses. Joel came by once, on the way to his car, slouching in a way that indicated he would like another chance; Bailey waved to him in a way that said "Forget it," and he fumed and opened the door for his dogs. They loved riding in cars and never needed a second invitation; they hopped in, and he slam-banged away.

Scout had a nice workout, and then Bailey put Dino on the longe line, and kept him there for at least half an hour; Starburst she groomed first, then put through a complex series of show moves until he was happily exhausted. And while she worked and the day grew warmer—the beginning of May had never been Bailey's favorite time of the year, as she invariably got too hot and felt bedazzled by the sun—she managed to succeed in thinking only of horses, in letting her focus stay complete. But eventually she was finished, and she called Chance to her side; the dog had, foxlike, been hunting mice beneath a tree, lifting up on her haunches so that her front paws dangled, and then thrusting her forebody downward. Her nose was iced with a rime of dirt, and she panted with pride and satisfaction.

Back in her apartment, Bailey stripped off her work clothes, leaving them in a pile on the bedroom floor. As usual, she smelled strongly of horse, and when she climbed into the shower—leaving the bathroom door open so that Chance, who was a little uneasy around water, could nonetheless be with her—she grabbed a scrub-brush and a loofah sponge, vigorously scrubbing herself all over. She kept trying not to think, as she had at the stables, but this time with little success; the truth of it was that her life was going nowhere, and that she was probably too smart for her own good. She loved animals first, and riding second, but she was stuck where she was, without money; and witchcraft—well, witchcraft was all very well, but it was hardly a practical practice. She should certainly leave Felicity, but for where? And to do what? California was too expensive, she had heard, and New York was too polluted. England? There she might visit Stonehenge. Neo-paganism was flourishing in England. And there was a lot of riding there, too. Yes, maybe she should move to England. But the whole point was, wherever she went, she couldn't get settled without money.

Now she washed her hair, holding her head back under the nozzle, letting the spray flatten her hair against her scalp. Whether she liked it or not, she was going to have to ask Howell to take out a loan on the farm. If he didn't want to sell it, he was simply going to have to mortgage it so that he could pay her her share of its worth. Why she had avoided seeing this for as long as she had, she really couldn't imagine. Oh, yes, she could—it was because he'd *expected* just this; it would confirm everything he'd always thought. That she was selfish, not a farmer, with no sense of family. That he had been punished from the moment of her birth. And she really hadn't wanted to give him the satisfaction of being able to hold the whole thing against her. How they could be *siblings?* It had always amazed her. True enough that you couldn't pick your relatives. And that stupid, stupid paper had been the crowning blow. He *deserved* whatever he now got.

By the time she got out of the shower, Bailey was feeling a little bit calmer, having tackled what she'd avoided long enough. But she wasn't feeling good, and she decided to cast a spell to focus her mind and lift her spirits. Chance loved the witchcraft and insisted on sitting in her lap, where she could get a good view of the proceedings; now, as Bailey got dressed, then pulled the shades and locked the front door, the dog seemed to sense what was going to happen. After lighting some candles and incense, Bailey settled herself cross-legged in front of the altar; Chance jumped ever so lightly into the triangle between her legs and rested her head on Bailey's left knee.

This was the first time she'd used her new cauldron, and she thought she'd do a cauldron meditation, which was one in the book that had always appealed to her. The cauldron was the Cauldron of Ceridwen, the womb of the Goddess and the gestation ground of all birth, and the meditation was supposed to be about creation— your power to create, to give life to new things, to die, and be reborn in new directions. She tried to hold the cauldron, but Chance was in the way, so she decided to start with a circle visualization. Atop the altar all her tools were neatly laid out on a piece of red satin, with images of the Goddess—shells, sand, a small mirror, a carved ironwood turtle—clustered in the middle, and the athame, the chalice, the wand, and the pentacle resting in the directions to which they corresponded. Now, grounded and centered, she lifted the athame from its place, held it away from her body, and then, shifting east, drew a pentacle in the air. She imagined that the pentacle was burning with blue fire, and in her mind she saw herself climbing through the pentacle, lifting first her right knee and then her left one to scramble through and find herself in a glorious field, a pasture full of flowers and swept by a strong east wind. She breathed hugely and felt the wind caressing her all over as the sun, which was rising just behind the wind, tossed its gold and silver rays all around her. She hated to have to leave, but after a while she walked back through the pentacle, turned south, and drew another one; this time, when she climbed through, she found that the sun was lazing on the earth, hot hot on her skin and baking her with fire. And by the time she returned from the south and visited the oceans, crashing and pounding in the west as the sun went down, and then the midnight landscape of the north, with its small bright stars bejeweled overhead, she felt ready for whatever she had to do, calm and at peace with her own future. Her circle was a cone of light that began at the far reaches of the earth, and though closer at home, here in Felicity, it included many puzzling things— her horses and her brother, Ada and her parents, poverty and imagination and death—it began out there where the stars formed a wheel, and where everything in the universe was clear. It was just like horses, really, training horses. Belief in the connection between things.

# THE
# CONE OF POWER

# 16

PEALE sat on the porch of the Powell College Guest House, fanning himself with his clipboard. Today was already the thirty-first of May, and the weather was unpleasantly hot. At this time of year, Felicity was sometimes blessed with warm but lucid days and mild nights—the kind of weather that made plants substantial and all one's troubles unreal—but for the last two weeks the weather had been awful, more like August than May. During the Memorial Day parade the previous afternoon, marching at the head of his men, Peale had once felt almost overcome by the heat, and today things had simply gotten worse. You could see the moisture in the air— it hung over the fields like a fog, thick at its base and a little thinner as it reached the upper atmosphere—and you could feel it in your clothes, which seemed tight and constricting, so that you wanted to tear them right off. They had had two small thunderstorms, one the night before, but the air was still thundery, heavy with its own discomfort, and the wind was abrasive, not soothing.

And Peale's troubles seemed anything but easy to solve, though at least the Russians had arrived. They had flown into Indianapolis the night before, where Dr. Minot had picked them up, and they were staying now above the porch where Peale was sitting, waiting to meet them. As a student at Powell, Peale had spent a number of evenings sneaking around this porch, a fanciful gingerbread affair with brackets and corbels, balustrades with large turned posts and a screen door with white stencil work; one of the games students had played in his time had been baiting the house's caretaker. Mrs. Wick, as spare as her name, was the last living member of her family, and she had sold this house to the college only on condition that she be retained as its caretaker. This was a peculiar arrangement, since Mrs. Wick hated guests, and she always made their stays as unpleasant as she could, in the hope that they would leave early. When Peale and his deputy Johnson had arrived this morning, she had opened the screen door only wide enough to inform him that the Russians had been delivered to her at one o'clock in the morning, awakening her from a sound sleep, and that since she was seventy-nine and this was her home, she deserved a lot more consideration. Though it had been made clear to her at least three times that the Russians wouldn't be arriving until after midnight, Peale had apologized profusely nonetheless, remembering his days as a troublemaker. On several occasions, successfully baited, Mrs. Wick had emerged onto this porch to hurl heavy objects toward the chortles in the night, and one of them, which hit Peale in the chest, had turned out upon examination to be a lead-crystal paperweight. For over a week, he had carried a bruise. Ever since, Mrs. Wick had scared him. So he'd promised her that tonight, whatever happened, he would get the Russians back early.

"See that you do!" she had said. Then she'd sniffed and banged the door behind her, and Peale had settled cautiously into a chair. Johnson sat on the steps, very earnestly, waiting until he could start to Secure.

The weather seemed somehow like bad luck to Peale—he fanned himself again with his clipboard—but it was hardly out of keeping with his luck these days in general, which was going from bad to worse. On the bad side, there was his marriage to Amanda, whom he continued, at the pistol range, to shoot twice a week. No matter how much he resisted, just as he squeezed the trigger her face would inevitably appear. He had not seen that curly-haired woman, that Bailey Bourne, since the afternoon of the auction, and moreover—he felt glumly proud of it—he hadn't even tried to do so. But he had thought about her a lot; it was as if he had spent his whole life to date without a sense of smell and then had gotten a whiff of fresh grass; Amanda seemed more and more odorless to him, more and more ethereal and unreal. On the worse side, there was his feeling about his job, which he was coming, quite frankly, to hate.

It was not that Peale did not *get* the concept of Law and Order; it was just that it contradicted his experience. He himself had learned how to be kind and considerate of others, after all, not because there were laws that suggested such things, not because there was an authority that commanded them, but because he had *felt* like it; it was really that simple; he had experienced the desire to be good. And it was absurd to suppose that if people did not experience that desire, laws were going to convince them otherwise. Why, last week there had been a case of statutory rape brought against Willard Smith, and when Peale had gone to arrest Willard, a construction worker who lived in a trailer three doors down from the trailer of the girl, that very girl—Chris Muncie, who was slightly retarded—had wept and begged him to arrest her *too*. The parents had looked on with great satisfaction. What kind of a law was that?

Well, that was an extreme case of a pretty bad law, but in fact *no* laws were good. It seemed that the worse people were, the more antisocial or violent, the more laws were made to try to correct this, and the more people depended on those laws. Instead of changing the way that the Powell students put their stereo speakers into the windows of their dorm rooms and played extremely loud music late at night, keeping everyone in the neighborhood awake, instead of going over and *talking* to the students, everyone said, "There ought to be a law!" And even now there was, before the town council, a proposal to enact a noise ordinance. No doubt another law would be the result, and another one to follow that. Because once you started to depend on laws, those rigid and unresponsive principles, there was really no end to it; life always squeezed through them. It was like trying to hold water back with your hands.

And yet everyone believed in them, no one even thought about them, there were already enough to last a millennium. Everyone thought that the laws could put things to rights—but maybe the laws themselves were wrong. They were, after all, just general commands backed up by the threat of force. Maybe they actually *caused* people to be bad. If you thought about it in a certain way, you could see that it was at least possible that people all over the world had been perverted by their own societies, which had tried hard to develop in their citizens an attitude of submission to authority. Why, it was even possible that the main causes of crime were laws and authority and the threat of punishment; since it seemed clear these things hardly acted as deterrents, why should they not act as stimulants? Peale himself and other authority figures like him—they were all implicated in this mess.

Then, too, the whole idea of punishment and prisons was coming to make Peale truly sick. His little jail, where men were rarely kept for more than a few weeks, and which, therefore, you might think was not so bad, was, in microcosm, everything that a prison was: a destructive, hypocritical place. Prisons did not stop violent or antisocial acts from taking place—on the contrary, they seemed to increase their number. Prisons did not make people better—on the contrary, they generally made people worse. Well, no wonder, when every one of the prisoners Peale had had pass through his hands—*every single one of them,* from the men who had gotten into shoving matches with friends to Jeff Metz, who had stabbed his own brother—had failed to recognize the justice of what was being inflicted on him. Every one had felt himself misused. They all believed that jails had been created for the unlucky or the unskillful, not the particularly evil; they all suspected that the really bad ones were living it up in the State House. Who could argue with them? They were no doubt right. It was just a disaster all around.

And the worst of it, the really sickest thing, was that jail destroyed a man's will. It was just so *illogical,* since most of the people who went to prison in the first place were there because they lacked will power—they had been tempted to do something, had been overcome with passion, they had succumbed to a weakness in their own souls. And then, in prison, everything was done to further weaken a person's will. Life was entirely regulated; choice was rarely possible; an already weak will was made weaker. Naturally, it was absurd to think that when the person was out in the world again, and beset with the same dilemmas or troubles or temptations that had put him in prison to begin with, he was better prepared to deal with them; he would almost inevitably be worse. What should Peale do? He was the sheriff. Everything about it was wrong.

Peale's thoughts were interrupted by a thumping behind him on the stairs, and the screen door was pushed open once again. When two men emerged from it, Peale jumped to his feet and Deputy Johnson followed suit. The first man, a short one, with a shining bald head and a round face set with large round eyes, grabbed Peale's hand and shook it enthusiastically, then held on to it with both hands while he spoke.

"Hello," he said. "I am Josef Drubetskoy, and this is my colleague, Nicolai Rostov. I understand you are the sheriff of this town. We are both extremely pleased to meet you." Here he paused to beam, and Peale, who had been trying to identify the precise emotion that was gripping him, noticed that Mr. Drubetskoy seemed to be winking. The wink, however, was of grotesque proportions— it looked like an exaggerated movie wink, with the whole mouth on one side of the face opened wide to allow for the eye's contraction. He had scarcely had time to get over the first wink, and to assume that it was some regional Russian expression of friendliness, when a second wink came close upon its heels, and a third wink swiftly followed: WINK, pause, WINK, pause, WINK, pause, WINK, pause. It looked as if the face were being kneaded.

"We have never been to your Midwest before. We are pleasantly surprised—so warm." WINK. "What a gracious little house this is." WINK. "You have met our charming hostess?"

Somehow, prior to this moment "the Russians" had simply been objects to Peale, items that he had to Secure. He had never bothered to try to formulate an appraisal of who or what these men were going to be—why two Russians would *want* to come to Powell, or what they would hope for once here. Now Peale felt deeply abashed, as if he'd been rude to the handicapped. He mumbled something awkward and looked down at his shoes while Johnson came up and introduced himself.

"I am Michael Johnson," he said, in a speech that had clearly been rehearsed, "and it will be my pleasure to guard you from whatever untoward occurrences may occur while you are staying with us in our fine town."

To this, Nicolai Rostov, a tall man with shocks of blue-black hair and a lean, almost craggy face, said, "Untoward occurrences. Also smashups."

"Nicolai," said Josef sternly. "You must say hello. He's a linguist, you see. Very brooding."

"Hello, of course," said the other, staring at the corbels. "I stand like a stuck pig—a colloquial expression. For keeping still, being quiet."

"He's studying idiom in English, you see. This year, the Midwestern American."

"Ah", said Peale, although all the stuck pigs *he* had ever seen had been shrieking and thrashing around like crazy, "that sounds very interesting, a fascinating study. And so, are you ready for your day?"

"Oh, yes," said Josef. "We have been ready for months."

"We are ready. We are loaded for bear."

Wherever Nicolai had learned these idiomatic expressions, thought Peale, there had been a heavy emphasis on animal slaughter, but he just said "Good," and checked the agenda he'd been given by Maggie Esterhaczy. To his frank incredulity, Peale had discovered several weeks earlier that his brother Ryland was having an affair with Maggie, Ryland's first since his divorce, and that she had been able to persuade Ryland, who hadn't given a dinner party for years, to host a huge reception—catered by the college food service—in his own home, this evening. Not only had Ryland agreed to do this, but he seemed to be looking forward to it. Distracted and worried as Peale had been, he had not failed to notice that his brother was looking better these days than he had looked in years—far from an unmixed blessing as far as Peale was concerned, since, with his newfound health and well-being, Ryland had proved a good deal less helpful recently; his natural pessimism and gloominess had lessened, leaving Peale without a mental Taster.

But the party was the last thing on the day's agenda, an agenda that outlined every minute of the Russians' four-day stay in Felicity and that began, in about ten minutes, with breakfast with some Powell College students. The students were involved with political science, and little as he knew about the field, which he himself had avoided when at Powell, Peale had a feeling that the students were in for a shock. He was very glad that he had decided to delegate the responsibility of shepherding these two to Johnson, and then to Davis, and then back to Johnson, and so on; his own contact with them, today at least, would be limited to the dinner in their honor.

Just then, Peale looked up to catch another wink. This one surprised him, and he winced. Josef, unfortunately, noticed the wince, and said in a comforting tone, "I see that my eye has troubled you. I am sorry, but it is not to be helped. I had, some years ago, a frightening experience. I have never fully recovered."

At this, Peale's thoughts took an alarming turn, in keeping with his new distaste for authority. Stories about the KGB and the psychological torture it inflicted on political prisoners began to crowd into his thoughts until Josef interrupted them, taking out a pack of Marlboros and knocking one into his hand.

"Not the sort of experience you may be thinking about. I was lost in a cave for ten days. I am, as you know perhaps, a geologist— that is why I have come here, because of your Felicity Pond—and I was spelunking once in the Pamir Mountains when I got separated from my group. Ten days later, after drinking nothing the whole time but the condensation off the rocks, I stumbled back out into the sunlight. And my eye did this. It's been doing it ever since. It reminds me how surprising life can be." He struck a match and lit his cigarette, drawing the smoke deep into his lungs. "Marlboros," he explained. "This is Marlboro country. How splendid to visit America."

"Rock music, disc jockey, sex appeal, ice cream. These are all Russian words now," said Nicolai.

"Is that so?" said Peale. "Well, we might as well go," and he led the way off the porch. He looked back to see that Nicolai, with enormous forethought, was lifting each leg separately to climb down off the porch. Josef followed, and then came Johnson, the weight of his cares upon him. As he led the way up the hill to the dining hall, he was obviously searching his head for something to say, but couldn't find anything that looked at all likely, hard as he was obviously trying. That in itself, Peale felt, proved what a good choice Johnson was for the job to which Peale had appointed him: he was not very imaginative, and in this case that was fine. He would not turn this job into a lark.

When they reached the dining hall, Peale clapped him on the back and handed him his clipboard with the agenda.

"They're all yours, Mike. I'll see you at the party." Johnson nodded earnestly, and Josef and Nicolai, who had been speaking to one another in Russian, Josef animatedly and at great length, and Nicolai in short clipped sentences, stopped their conversation long enough to thank Peale. For this, Nicolai had no idiom.

"I think I can assure you, though, young man, that after my ten days of licking condensation off the rocks, Felicity will present me with nothing difficult, nor half so surprising as the sunlight." Peale certainly hoped so, and while he made his way back down the hill toward his Corvette, sweat trickling down the back of his neck, moisture forming on his forehead, he hoped, too, that the weather would break soon; in this weather, people went crazy.

Back in the office, Peale was met with a barrage of questions, and he fielded them as best he could. He had a lot of paperwork to catch up on—gun permits, tax warrants, subpoenas, and so on—so he made his way to his inner office and closed the door behind him. He had just started working on an accident report when his secretary buzzed him on the intercom: "A young woman to see you, sir. Bailey Bourne. She says she has information for you."

"Bailey Bourne?" he said stupidly. "I don't know a Bailey Bourne." But a thin feeling swept through his chest.

It was funny, but when he saw her, marching into his office, it was almost as if a month had not passed. Although, in fact, these last four weeks since the morning of the auction had been the longest four weeks he'd ever lived through, now, with her eyes staring intently in his direction, now they had simply not been. He tried, even as he was getting to his feet to say hello—the chair making sounds as it was pushed back that were a bit like two train cars unlinking—he tried to recapture them, like a familiar illness, but it was no use; he was suddenly too happy. It was her, oh, yes, it was really her. Today, she had on an outfit even more outré and irresponsible than the one she had had on the last time, a shocking pink smock belted with a thing that looked like a melted American flag. Her clothes, her clothes were really outrageous. He wished he could take them all off.

"I don't know if you remember me . . ." she began, and he interrupted her to say, gruffly, "Of course I remember you. You cost me twenty dollars."

He couldn't believe he had said that.

"Gosh, I'm sorry. I'll pay you back. I just forgot."

"Never mind. How can I help you?"

"It's not *me*. It's the Russians, the ones up at the college. I have a feeling they may be in danger."

While one part of Peale's mind was, at the moment, still groaning under the weight of his own stupid remark about the headlight, and another part of his mind was, to his own amazement, happily occupied with the mental removal of Bailey Bourne's clothing, beginning with the flaglike belt, at this remark both parts gave up their pastimes and focused, as one, on "in danger." Bailey sat down across from him, looking almost purposely worried, and the thin feeling dissolved and was replaced by a thick one, a kind of huge lump of dread.

"What kind of danger?" he said dismally.

"That's just what I really don't *know*."

"They'll be guarded round the clock. I have a deputy with them now."

"That's good. But it's the farmers I'm afraid of."

"Yeah? Why?"

"I don't know. I just have a feeling, that's all it amounts to. I just thought I should come and let you know."

At this point, a real honest-to-God sheriff would have pressed this woman until she talked; she obviously knew something, though she was trying to pretend she didn't. No one on earth would come in here just on a feeling. And if all had gone according to plan, at this moment Nicolai and Josef, having finished breakfast with the political science students, were about to attend their first class, a seminar on the political implications of Marxism, and they would be sitting, within minutes, in a room with *glass windows!* But, not being a real sheriff, and having, as he had already discovered, no right at all to wear the badge or carry the gun, he didn't know *how* to press her, he just said to her—politely—"I'd appreciate it if you'd tell me more."

"I don't really know anything. I've just heard some nasty talk."

"From whom?"

"Oh, people, you know, in general. At the market, at Rosie's, all over."

"I see." But he didn't, even though he was trying. He saw nothing clearly but her.

When, a little later, she stood up to leave, he followed her to the door. There, successfully contesting his own sudden desire to thrust her up against the wall and kiss her, he nonetheless found himself unable to resist reaching out his hand to shake hers, and holding that hand for quite a while as the thin feeling came back into his chest. At last he let her hand go, and watched her walk across the main office, then turn and nod to him from the front door. He nodded back, then sank down at his desk. Oh, Lord, what was he going to do?

If he had been the FBI, or even the state police, he would have had lists to consult at this point, lists of suspicious characters. As it was, he didn't have anything but his own knowledge of the town, and though that knowledge told him that if there was going to be trouble, it would probably start down at Rosie's, what was he supposed to do with that: arrest all the farmers for hating Russia? Maybe he should call Ryland and ask him what to do. If only it weren't so goddamned hot. And thundery, almost like tornado weather. No, that would be simply too much.

# 17

THE WEATHER was affecting Maggie, too, though a good deal more pleasantly somehow. She was lying in Ryland's bed, next to an open window through which blew the humid, thundery air of a morning that was starting off much too warm, and this gave her a delightful excuse for staying just where she was, with one leg draped comfortably over Ryland's thigh and her hair sprawled across his chest. That hair was rather dirty, as Maggie had a theory that washing one's hair more than once a week expanded the pores of the scalp grotesquely, which was what made the hair get dirty in the first place; she saw it as a conspiracy on the part of the shampoo companies to *addict* the hair to washing. This turned out to be a lot like one of Ryland's theories; when she had explained her situation to him, and why her hair was likely to be dirty at least half the time, he had told her that *he* had always thought that the soap companies put a small amount of grease into their bars of hand soap so that after washing your hands you never felt quite as clean as you had before you started.

That was so like him—she really loved him so. She ran a hand over his chest. He smiled down sleepily at her from where he was propped contently on two enormous pillows, his hair damp and clinging to his forehead. That was partly from the heat, and partly from the lovemaking they had just engaged in. Maggie had never had a lover with whom she felt so friendly, and with whom sex seemed so kind and almost jolly, and she was almost reluctantly forced to admit that she had never felt so happy in her life. Just a month had passed since she and Ryland had attended that Beyond War meeting together, and in that short month she had moved perilously close to feeling "settled down." Not that there was anything wrong with settling down, either as an actual or a psychic move, but such a thing had always been inconceivable to a person who was preeminently of the nuclear age. Not since she was five years old, and had, in the pre–Cuban missile crisis days, seen being alive as a real opportunity of sorts, had she enjoyed so much just waking up in the morning and encouraging the sun to keep moving.

And part of the reason for this, strange to say, was that Ryland was apprehensive enough for both of them. Oh, she hoped, and was half convinced, that since he had met her his own fears had been reduced, subsumed by a degree of new contentment, but he was still rather scared of both intimacy and dying, as if they were somehow the same thing. In comparison with the degree of trepidation that Ryland was able to maintain about life at all times, her own abilities seemed minor, more amateur renderings of fear. To anticipate the end of the world, as she had always done, simply required a generalized gloominess, a sense of things spiraling toward dissolution; but to fear constantly your *individual* end, that was really quite special. Ryland had not only perfected his crystals of consternation until they worked as remarkably well as a child's handmade crystal radio, but he didn't even know he had done it; he was a pure, old-fashioned neurotic. She squeezed his middle.

"I love you so. You're so different from all the men I've known. They were, well, so *thinky.*"

"I'm not thinky?" he asked, looking hurt, and scooting himself more vertical.

"Well, sure you are, in a way. But you don't care if you're crazy or not. You're normal; that's all that I mean."

"I'm normal?" Here he looked faintly outraged, and sat up entirely against the headboard.

"It's a *compliment.* You're not *normal.* You're just not in analysis. They usually get so much *help.*"

"You think I need help?" Now Ryland looked interested. "You think I should be in analysis?"

"God, no. But you could be. They wouldn't believe their good fortune. You'd send their children to Harvard."

"But what would we talk about?"

"You could start with your mother and the baby scale. The way she measured and weighed all your food. But don't; that's all right. I like you the way you are. It's like finding a mental virgin."

Here Ryland began to look *really* interested, and Maggie was sorry she'd started this. Most of the men she'd been with had spent, as she remembered it, at least ninety percent of their time going off to their therapists and coming home red and weepy, and the last man she'd been with, a commodities broker named Peter Green, had been in analysis and had rushed off what seemed to be every two minutes for another psychic detonation. He had been fanatical, almost savage—a horrible Freudian Moonie.

"Your neuroses *work* for you. Why should you meddle? You're nice just the way you are. In fact, I don't ever want to leave your side. I want to be glued at the hip."

Ryland smiled, looking a little faraway, and just then the phone in the hall rang. Disentangling himself from Maggie and the sheets, he padded naked out the door.

"Hello? Oh, Peale, hello. What is it?"

It was his brother, probably calling about the Russians. This he had done almost daily for a week, and though there was certainly something affecting about his need for his brother, a need that Maggie was quickly coming to share, it was annoying to be constantly reminded of these Russians. As always when she was in the first throes of a love affair, she wanted nothing to do with the world beyond it, she wanted no duties, or even thoughts, and for the next four days she was going to be tied to these Russians; there was no getting out of it now.

Of course, if she had had any idea when she volunteered to help organize their visit that she would be in *love* when they arrived, she would never have volunteered; she would have taken Ada's advice and simply left well enough alone. Ever since Maggie had started seeing Ryland, Ada had been in a state of self-congratulation that had to be seen to be believed; she took all the credit for finding Ryland to begin with and for "softening him up . . . his shoulders." She gave no credit at all to the Beyond War meeting—Maggie's idea—which had done, in her opinion, most of the real softening up. It had drawn them together, like any catastrophe; had thrown them into each other's arms.

Thinking of the meeting made Maggie feel a bit guilty. Her political convictions had been brief. The embarrassing truth was that since Maggie had started seeing Ryland, she had sunk back into her former political stupor, and though she *had* managed to convince Ryland that he should hold a reception for the visitors tonight in his house, and furthermore that the Beyond War contingent should be invited, her motives in this had been anything but pure; she had wanted to go to a big party. She thought that it was about time she and Ryland appeared together in public, and what could be more public than this party? It would be the perfect occasion to celebrate their good luck. Who cared about the damned Russians? At the moment, she wanted nothing more than to spend the day with Ryland—let the Russians vanish off the face of the earth. But she was supposed to get up and go spend the *whole day* with them. Probably that was why Peale was on the phone.

"Bailey Bourne?" said Ryland after a long listening silence. "Well, Peale, I really wouldn't worry about it. She's a well-known nut. I was going to do her apartment in a lovely country estate look, but then it turned out she was broke. Whatever she thinks is going to happen, it isn't going to happen after all." A pause. "Yes, I'm sure. Right, all right. Well, fine, then. Yes, Maggie's on her way there right now."

He hung up.

"What was that about?" Maggie asked.

"Oh, nothing. Some crazy woman. She reported an incident involving farmers."

When Ryland came back, he didn't climb into bed, but instead started to get dressed. Maggie loved to watch the careful way he laid everything he was to wear out on top of the covers first, counting all the items once they were assembled and before he started to don them. First he put on his socks, and then he put on his shirt; his penis hung naked below it.

Fondly, she asked, "You mean an incident with the Russians?"

"Yes. And of course he's in a panic."

"But I thought there was going to be a deputy always with them?"

"Yes, yes, the whole thing's only a fantasy. At least . . . you don't think there could be something in it?"

"Good grief, no. I'm sure it's just a fuss about nothing. What on earth could happen to them here?"

"But weren't you the one who was originally worried?"

"I guess so. But that was *before*." Here she got out of bed and flung her arms around him. "It all just seems paranoid now. But what a pain in the *ass* that I have to go meet them. Couldn't I just stay with you instead?"

"I'll see you tonight. That'll just be seven hours."

"Seven *hours*. That's . . . what . . . four hundred and twenty minutes!" But she let him go and started hunting for her clothes; she supposed she'd really better get dressed. And as Ryland, looking relieved, went downstairs to start getting the house ready for the sixty people whom he expected that evening, Maggie ran his brush through her hair, studying herself in the mirror and wondering if she should give in to the shampoo companies. She was surprised at how healthy she was looking, since she hadn't been getting much exercise—unless you called lovemaking exercise, which she didn't. She looked rosy and taut and fit, which, to her mind, was unusual, since, although men had always found her beautiful, she usually thought she looked, well, a little dried up. Now she looked anything but. She knew that this probably *was* the result of regular sex, after over a year of celibacy, but still it was nice. Well, she *would* wash her hair. In fact, she would do it right now.

A half hour later she pulled up to Powell. It was almost lunchtime, so she made her way to the faculty lounge, where there was an informal buffet for all the students of the "language arts," and as she entered the room—a rather stuffy room at the best of times, with heavy velvet curtains and a high ceiling painted an unpleasantly dark color, today it was almost unbearably hot, after Ryland's breezy white house—she was struck by the horde of students crowded near the lunch table. They seemed to be admiring two men, one tall and dark-haired, the other short and bald, and they were uncharacteristically silent and attentive as the short bald man said in a loud ebullient voice, winking hugely as he spoke, "So in the Soviet Union, there is much research into ESP. You can see how useful this would be."

"You mean mind reading?" asked one of the young male students—the sort who could be immediately identified in any group as a devotee of science fiction just by the peculiarity of his shoes.

"Mind reading, yes. Psi research, more accurately. Remote viewing, for example, is part of it."

"I've heard of that," said another, more conventionally shod student. "They get mostly visual images."

"Yes, we prefer this, on the whole, to mind reading. We should skate on thin ice otherwise," said the tall man.

To this, one of the students, a young woman with pewter hair and round glasses, said, "That's correct. Though it might be a little too weak in this case. You could also say 'Sit on a barrel of gunpowder.' "

"Sit on gunpowder," said the tall man thoughtfully. Drawing a small black notebook out of his jacket pocket, he opened it to a fresh page and inscribed something in a minute hand, adding, "We have a similar expression in Russian."

Psi reseach? thought Maggie. Skate on thin ice? This was not, somehow, what she'd expected; she went up to Minot, who stood at the edge of the group, and asked him, with her eyes, to introduce her.

"A little late, aren't you, Maggie?" He was annoyed by her affair with Ryland.

"A little. What's going on? This seems like a success."

"I'd say so, though they're hardly fine *minds*. That's a tic, by the way, that winking. Ignore it. Josef Drubetskoy, this is Maggie Esterhaczy."

"Hello," she said, trying to summon up some warmth. "We've been looking forward to your visit." He kissed her hand, to her surprise and not to her pleasure.

"Esterhaczy. This is Hungarian?"

"Yes, it is. How did you know?"

"Well, Nicolai is the linguist, but I have been to Hungary. Hah. I can see that this surprises you."

It didn't surprise her much, but she managed to look a bit startled. This seemed to gratify Josef, as he beamed and then winked at her several times. Now Minot introduced the other man, who also kissed her hand.

"I am delighted to meet you, Miss Esterhaczy," he said. "I am in the Bower of Bliss." And whereas the first man, Josef, had left Maggie with only a vaguely unpleasant feeling after his warm introduction, this man, Nicolai, somehow really repelled her; she wanted to wipe off the kiss. Four days with these clowns? She'd go out of her mind. And while she was trying to think of a suitable response to this ridiculous statement, the young woman who had told Nicolai about the gunpowder put in, to Maggie's relief, "No, no, that's far too strong."

"How do you know it's too strong?" asked Josef. "Psi powers?"

"It just *is*. He could be tickled pink."

"We are all tickled," said Josef.

"Yes, yes, tickled pink." And everyone stood around, looking tickled.

Maggie, though, needed some time to recover, so she turned away to get a drink. Well, this would teach her about political convictions—she really *hated* these Russians.

"Like them?" said Richard Minot, joining her.

"Just don't start in on me, all right?"

After lunch, they took a tour of the campus, and then a tour of the town. Michael Johnson, a rather solemn and petite man who seemed to be the end result of Maggie's request for Security—a request that she felt grumpily she would never have made had she been able to read the future—was driving a small van borrowed from Saguanay's, and Josef and Nicolai loved it. As they climbed in, they exclaimed about the molded front seats, the bright, white upholstery, the sheer size and solidity of the thing, and though Maggie knew that she should be able to sympathize with their childlike excitement, she could only wish them somewhere else. If Ryland were driving the van . . . and they had a cooler of wine . . . they could go off for a day alone in the country. But instead, Nicolai and Josef settled into the seats behind the driver, from which they could "see everything," and Maggie and Richard Minot had to climb into the back, where they had a perfect view of the Russians.

The afternoon dragged on—Maggie kept glancing at her watch—as they toured from pillar to post and back again. They had an excruciatingly detailed journey around Felicity itself—they stopped at City Hall to view the memorials and the so-called museum, and to "see a typical American government in action," by which was meant a boring visit to the county tax assessor's office in the courthouse; they took a walk around the downtown district and stopped in several stores, including Saguanay's, from which Ryland was sadly absent; they went to the high school, for some bizarre reason, where they got to see a rehearsal of the senior play; and then they went to Rock County Park, where there was one disheveled Indian mound. The heat in the van was fairly intense, because the air conditioner was broken, but though this, coupled with the mind-dulling quality of the exhibits, would have reduced most people—even people who weren't Maggie—to a state of somnolence or despair, the Russians seemed indifferent to the heat and absolutely pleased with everything. Josef was an especially strong sweater, and as the water poured off his head in perfect rivers, he admired the museum, he admired the play, he even admired the mound. So emphatic was his admiration of the most unadmirable of things that it crossed Maggie's mind at one point to wonder if he could be a spy; who but a spy could put on such a show? But Nicolai was worse.

Not that Nicolai was so emphatic, but he spoke in nothing but clichés. And they were often so skewed, so somehow tilted, that their meaning was lost; it sounded after a while as if he were talking gibberish. Maggie would have loved to wring his neck. When they finally left Felicity behind and headed out into the country toward Felicity Pond, whose Josef was to get his first view of this natural wonder, Josef said rhapsodically, "What a wonderful landscape!" and Nicolai added, "Hot dog!"

Only one more hour, Maggie told herself, one more hour to go. And it couldn't be so bad, out in the country, where at least there were the trees to look it. To get to Felicity Pond, you went down a long hill, that curved around a small river, then climbed a hill on the other side, and entered a stand of thick woods. On the other side, the woods suddenly cleared right away, and from the meadow they left, you could look down the valley, at the bottom of which was the Pond. On its far side, a cliff rose violently, practically right from the water, though a road had been blasted along the cliff, a thin spidery line of white. Maggie knew this route well, of course, because it was the road she took to get home, and she always liked the view, even now; *less* than one hour to go! The Pond itself, still and dark, was a perfect mirror for the sky, and even from the hill you could see the clouds reflected. There were some dark clouds coming up now. Johnson, who had said hardly a word since they left Powell, paused in the clearing to let the view speak, then dived down into the trees, and so took them to the south end of the Pond, where they parked for a while and got out.

Josef took his geologist's hammer and started chipping about in the rocks; Maggie took off her shoes, got well away, and stuck her feet in the water. This afternoon had had the unforeseen and unfortunate effect of bringing Maggie and Richard Minot together, since they shared a common feeling, and also since they had had to take turns finding something to say to Nicolai. Right now, Minot was engaged in a conversation with Nicolai about, naturally, his theories of punishment, and he was finding it pretty heavy going, as Nicolai's only apparent interest in the subject was in the idioms that surrounded it.

"I don't know," Minot said in a frankly annoyed tone. "Come-uppance, I suppose, though that's not very strong."

"Comeuppance?" asked Nicolai.

"Why don't you get a thesaurus? You'd save yourself a lot of work."

Josef, meanwhile, was grunting as he chipped a bit of rock here and there. He was also, from time to time, muttering things to himself, like "Very mysterious, very mysterious," and "Hah-ha! And here's another one!" It probably *wasn't* all that mysterious; Maggie had heard a number of times that the best explanation for the existence of Felicity Pond was the fall of an ancient meteoroid—*that* would have been a surprise to whatever may have lived here, a small planet suddenly falling out of the sky. Anyway, she was glad that she had her feet in her water, because the humidity was rising by the minute—let Josef get rocks for as long as he liked, as long as they got home on schedule. If they didn't have a storm before long, she was going to be very surprised. Ada would like that; Ada loved storms. She said they were the only redeeming thing about Indiana.

About twenty minutes passed while Josef played with rocks and Richard talked with Nicolai. Michael Johnson, who had not grown more loquacious as the day went on, but who seemed at least to have relaxed, was now skipping rocks, standing on top of an outcrop where he had piled three little pyramids of flattish stones that he took up one by one and whizzed, straight-armed, away. When at last Josef called out, "All done for now," and everyone climbed, rather sluggishly, back into the van, Johnson put a few of the best stones in his pocket, presumably for future use.

Well, finally they were heading home, though they were taking the long way around. Soon she would be in Ryland's arms, and all this would be over for good. She leaned her head back against the seat and tried, not seriously, to doze while Johnson took the cliff road slowly, curving and twisting about. Suddenly the van slowed still more, and Maggie opened her eyes. With a jerk the van stopped. "What's this?" said Johnson, in a high, uncertain voice.

A truck was parked in the road, blocking any further progress.

A couple of men were tinkering around, desultorily, at the front wheel, and one of them lifted his hand to signal them, though the nature of the signal was unclear.

"Somebody in trouble," said Josef with interest, looking back at Maggie to wink.

"Great," said Maggie.

"I have no instructions to cover this," said Johnson.

Richard Minot, leaning forward, said, "Oh, it's Howell Bourne. He's a moving man. I gave him my old couch."

Johnson still seemed to be in a quandary, but Josef and Nicolai were not. Reaching over to the van door, Josef expertly twisted the handle up and sideways, letting the door slide back on its rails, and then he and Nicolai clambered down to see, presumably, if they could help. At that, Johnson scrambled out, too, hurrying after the two Russians, and Maggie decided to get out as well, since this was clearly going to take some time. So they were quite a herd as they approached the truck and the men bent over its wheel, and Maggie was in a position to get only a partial view of what happened next, which probably contributed to her sense that it wasn't really happening, that she must be making it up. One of the men opened the door of the cab above him, as if to get a needed tool, and emerged instead with a double-barreled shotgun, which he swung directly toward Johnson. The other crouching man, at that point, mimicked his behavior exactly, and now a third man emerged from around the front, holding not a shotgun but a rifle. The whole group stopped walking, and Johnson, who might have been expected to do or say something in these circumstances, instead took one look at all those guns and fainted dead away. Luckily, he was standing at the time near the soft shoulder of the road, so he fell on dirt, not on asphalt, but it was amazing what a thump he made, hitting the ground. The bandits, or whatever they were, looked shocked.

And Maggie, who had just spent the last five or so hours wishing bad things upon the Russians simply because they bored her and because she was in love and wanted to be close to her lover, and yet who had lived through a brief period in which she felt it was her duty to protect these now-arrived visitors from the xenophobes and paranoids who she knew were crawling around the woodwork of Felicity, now could only wonder if this—this event—was some kind of strange punishment for the one set of feelings, as it was certainly a justification of the other. But that was absurd. What was less absurd was the possibility that she had all along misinterpreted the nature of her own eventual doom, with a grandiosity that bordered on the delusional, and had thought that she was going to get sucked into the grim cosmic joke that was the history and early demise of the earth itself, when all that was going to happen to her was that she would be shot by some lunatic farmers. And, irony of ironies, this was going to happen in the company of Richard Minot, whose theories of punishment suddenly took on a whole new substance, as she imagined her own simple funeral, up in the cemetery on the hill, with the late May lilies trumpeting through the grass, and Ada and Ryland weeping. The sun would shine, the sky would be cloudless, the breezes would play through the leaves—but she would not see them; she would be gone.

"What the fuck is this?" she said.

# 18

HOWELL was feeling sick to his stomach as he stood there clutching his shotgun. Although she had apparently not recognized him, that red-haired woman who had just questioned them so angrily and who was now staring incredulously toward him was, almost certainly, Mrs. Esterhaczy's granddaughter, and that was very bad news. He didn't like to think what Mrs. Esterhaczy was going to say when he showed up with her own granddaughter as a hostage; even his bringing Sam along would probably not make up for it. Sam had come into heat six days before, but only today had the blood turned thin and pink to indicate that she was ready to mate, and Howell, delighted that he could accomplish two things at once, had thrust her into the back of the truck, where she was now whining and making little scritching noises with her claws. Then, as if the granddaughter weren't enough, here was Richard Minot, too, and though he had never considered the man to be a friend or anything, he *was* indebted for the couch. And finally, Howell was profoundly embarrassed by the fainting of the deputy. He had never in his life seen someone faint; when they went, they really went *down*. For a moment, while everyone stood stapled in place, the only movements the slap of hot wind on rock and the slight sucking of the branches, Howell thought of calling it off, pretending this was all just a mistake. He and his two pals had been hunting rabbits, the story went, and they had had a flat . . . but Billy Bob made this impossible by saying, "Hi, folks. We've been waiting for you."

One of the men now spoke in an excited voice. "Are we being robbed?" he asked those around him. "Are those American robbers?"

"You're being kidnapped," said Mitch somberly. "There's something we'd like you to do."

"And don't get excited, lady," said Billy Bob to the granddaughter. "This has nothing to do with you."

"Oh, fine," she said sarcastically. "Then would you mind very much if I left?"

"Now, now," said Howell. "Now, now. There's no need for alarm. I've worked it out very carefully." For a moment, though, he couldn't remember just how. Then, luckily, it came to him, and settling carefully into his conversational stance, he explained that the van was to be driven into the back of the truck so that no one would be able to trace its movements from here on out. The cleverness of this conception, the mind-dazzling mysteriousness of it, reminded him of the circumstances in which he had discovered it, and the way that God had guided him. Indeed, as he spoke, God appeared in a corner of his mind, small and discreetly defined like one of those people in a corner of the TV, signing for the hearing impaired. Only instead of speaking in American sign language, madly twiddling His fingers, God merely circled one thumb and one forefinger, as if to say "You got it, Howell." He vanished abruptly from Howell's mind, however—went off the air as suddenly as if the electricity had been cut at the source—when the same bald man who had spoken before said happily, "Oh! That old Prohibition trick!"

Now everyone was talking at once, and Mitch and Billy Bob were moving forward. Billy Bob, with a swaggering look, relieved the deputy—who was, to Howell's extreme discomfort, still lying on the ground in a heap, a heap over which the second Russian was bending inquisitively—relieved the deputy of his gun, and commanded him to climb back into the van. Meanwhile, Mitch lowered the truck ramp. The minute it clanged down, however, Sam— whom Howell had somehow forgotten to tie up—leaped out of the interior darkness into the growing darkness of the day, yelping hysterically and flapping her long ears. Howell had barely the presence of mind to drop his shotgun onto the ground and spring toward her to grasp her collar. She calmed down a bit at his touch and stared up at his face, her dark brown eyes questioning and hopeful. The van was driven up the ramp, the hostages climbed after it; Howell just looked at Sam's brown eyes and patted the top of her head.

While Mitch and Billy Bob were eagerly congratulating one another on the smooth completion of Stage One of their plan, Howell was afraid that it was time for Stage Two, which meant *his* climbing into the truck bed. He had decided just that afternoon that he would ride there, with the hostages, since someone had to keep an eye on them, but now that the time had come, he didn't feel eager. What if he had to converse? But, saying to Mitch, "OK, I guess that's it. You might as well close her up," he mounted the ramp, dog in hand, and let Billy Bob hand him his shotgun. The five hostages were now all sitting in the van again, like children waiting for an amusement park ride, and that made Howell feel a good bit safer, until Billy Bob said, "Be careful! They're Communists, remember."

"I'm fine," said Howell. "I'll knock if I want something. Four raps, like we agreed."

"What's wrong with that guy, anyway?" asked Mitch. "Is he an epileptic or something?"

"Who?" said Howell.

"That bald guy. His face. You know, the way he keeps winking."

"Oh, that," said Howell, who hadn't even noticed it. "Got something in his eye, most likely."

He stepped back in order to allow the ramp to come up, and the rear door crashed down after it. In the semidarkness that followed, a semidarkness still echoing with the reverberations of the crash, and stuffier than Howell had expected, Howell let go his grip on Sam's collar, and she immediately bounded up onto his chest. Whimpering and snuffling, she placed her paws on his shoulders, almost knocking the shotgun out of his hand, and though he said, quite firmly, "Down, girl, down," she paid not the least attention. Since she had spent most of her life straining desperately against her solid linked-steel chain, now that that chain had miraculously released her, she would certainly make the most of it. But when the truck lurched to a start, both Sam and Howell were knocked off balance, and though Howell managed to grasp a canvas strap, the dog was slammed to the floor. So emphatic was this slamming that the bitch did not bother to argue with it. She stayed flattened on the truck bed, trying to dig in with her nails, but sliding with the skittishness of the truck. Howell slid down to sit on his haunches, trying to clutch at the wall.

So here he was, with his plan coming off, and he tried to feel suitably pleased about it. After all, going down in history as the man who had blown the lid off an international conspiracy was no small accomplishment. But the strange thing was that when that van had finally rounded the corner of the road, and those people had poured from it so helpfully, if he hadn't known Minot, and the deputy by his uniform, he wouldn't have been able to identify the Russians. Even when, by the process of elimination alone, he had figured out that they *must* be the two people who weren't the deputy or the granddaughter or Dr. Minot, they still didn't look at all as he'd expected; they couldn't have looked more different. And now, instead of being silent and secretive as he had anticipated, they were, as was obvious even through closed windows, chattering away like crazy. In fact, everyone in the van was talking at once, and as the truck was presently traversing a relatively straight stretch of Pond Road, and Howell, thus, was able to move, he went over to the van, feeling left out. He knocked on one of the windows.

At his knock, everyone in the van immediately shut up and re-garded him with real surprise, and the short bald man—ah, there was the wink—rolled down the window beside him. "Yes?" he said. "What would you like?"

"Oh, nothing," Howell said.

At this, the man stuck his hand out the window in so natural and subtly insistent a gesture that Howell found himself taking it.

"I am Josef Drubetskoy, but you may call me Josef. I am happy to meet an American desperado." His grip was firm and warm.

"I'm Howell Bourne. But I'm not a desperado."

"You are too modest! Why not?"

"Well, I've never done this sort of thing before."

"What sort of thing is that, exactly?"

"Kidnapping. You know. Holding someone for ransom."

"For ransom!" said Josef. "How much?"

"Are you not going to introduce us?" said the man to Josef's right, and Howell, who was feeling more peculiar with every passing minute, looked past the bald man and his tremendous wink.

"Nicolai Rostov," said the other man grimly. "And what does it matter what ransom? They will not pay it. They never do. And then we will be 'rubbed out.' "

"Of course it matters what ransom," said Josef. "They would pay a hundred dollars!"

"A hundred dollars? I am splitting my sides. He probably wants asylum in our country."

"I certainly do not. I'm a patriotic American."

"Of course he is," said Josef. "He wants money!"

While this odd conversation meandered along, the truck was not doing the same. Billy Bob, who had always been a reckless driver, famous for frightening students by bearing down on them in the huge mowing machines at Powell, seemed to be injected with an extra shot of wildness by the excitement of the recent events. He was barreling around the curves of Pond Cliff like a racing car driver while Howell desperately gripped the top of the van door with his shotgun-free hand, trying to think of a suitable response to Josef's last comment about money. But there was no way that he could easily communicate with Billy Bob at this moment, tell him for God's sake to slow down, so he just tried to keep his balance, and his mental equilibrium, as well.

Because it struck him as incredible that these two men were the Russians. Whenever he had imagined this moment, he had, he clearly remembered, pictured the two as a set of Siamese twins, attached somewhere near the shoulders and hips, and wearing specially made overcoats to permit this. He had visualized these two synchronized swimmers as practically speaking with the same mouth: "Comrade, comrade" would be most of what they'd say. "Comrade, we come. Now we go."

Instead, not only did they look just about as different from each other as it was possible for two people to look and still be part of the same species, but they couldn't seem to agree on anything, not even whether they would be ransomed. Why, even *Americans* would probably have agreed on *that* point—as a way to keep their spirits high, their belief in the future intact—but these two had set their minds on opposing positions, one of hope and one of hopelessness. If these were typical Russians, then Howell's whole idea of Russia might need to be revised, at least to include two different halves, like the Democrats and the Republicans.

But now the Russians started talking *in* Russian, which was something of a relief. It was soothing to hear all those nice guttural sounds and not to have to make the effort to process them in his brain; it was also reassuring to catch them plotting, which was what a conspiracy required. Howell didn't even tell them to be quiet; he turned his attention to the Esterhaczy woman, who was staring at him incredulously once again. The problem of bringing her to her own grandmother's home, as part of a kind of case-lot of hostages, was one that was simply not going to vanish, and he wanted to solve it soon. It crossed his mind that maybe he could get her on *his* side, somehow, since, after all, Mrs. Esterhaczy had been eager to help him against these Russians—and this woman, she shared the same blood, why would she not have the same feelings?

But then it crossed his mind, heading the other way and with equal or greater velocity than the first thought, that the fact that the woman was here at all indicated that she must be a peacenik— oh, people in the same family could be very different. He should know that, with Bailey and all. Thinking of Bailey made him feel even more disoriented than he already did; all during the last month, while he had been getting the corn crop in the ground, he had been haunted by the possibility that he would not get to harvest the crop himself, that some stranger would come in and steal those plants from under his nose, just wrest them out of the ground. When he had gone to see Bailey at Grey Rock, she had told him she was planning to visit a lawyer, and his worst fears had thus been completely confirmed—though, of course, that was why he was here. If the existing mortgages could be burned as part of the exchange for these Russians, then he himself might be able to *afford* whatever it was Bailey tried to do now. There was nothing for it, he realized, but to try to talk with this woman, but just as he formulated his opening sentence, there was a WHOMP, and the truck started fishtailing wildly. Howell had barely time to identify a blowout when he was slammed back against the wall. For the second time that day, he dropped the shotgun. This time, it went off.

When it did so, it blew a hole in the truck's side. Luckily, it missed Sam. For that matter, it was lucky that it missed Howell's foot, which was perilously close to the barrel. Meanwhile, the truck was shaking terribly, as if it were being vibrated apart, and when the whole mess careened to a stop, Howell's ears were still ringing with the shotgun blast. In that enclosed space, it had been so loud that it hadn't been like a sound at all; it had been more like a new condition of existence, one that left Howell irradiated with noise, transfused with sheer loudness and din. In the aftermath, Sam, acting on an instinct that Howell shared, tried to bolt out the newly made hole in the wall, but couldn't fit through its ragged metal edges.

By the time Mitch and Billy Bob opened the back, Howell had partially recovered. Sam charged outside, despite Howell's attempt to stop her; the people inside the van had climbed cautiously out when the truck was finally still, and were now standing staring at one another doubtfully, for which Howell could hardly blame them. By his own count, so far five separate things had gone wrong, if you counted the Esterhaczy woman and Dr. Minot as two separate ones: *they* had come along, the tire had exploded, there was a hole in his truck, and Sam had run off. But when Billy Bob, obviously shaken, called up assertively, "Jesus, that was quite a blowout,"

Howell tried to do his part by saying, "It's lucky we weren't on Pond Road."

"But what happens now?" asked Mitch, looking worried.

"We change the tire and go on. Or you change the tire. I've got to find Sam—she cut loose when the shotgun went off." And while the hostages, on command from Mitch, climbed back into their van, and Billy Bob, without any particular encouragement, got down on his back to unscrew the spare tire, Howell climbed down and started looking for Sam, who had vanished completely from sight.

Here, about a mile west of Pond Road, just past the Sizemore place and just before the Dickensens' pig farm, what had once been pastureland had now returned to woods, woods that concealed Sam nicely. Although he had no idea which direction she had set off in, once her precipitate departure had landed her on the ground, Howell set off toward the Dickensens' pig farm just to get away from the truck. He found it pleasant to be walking, particularly since the heat, which had been pressing on him all day like a warning, was starting just a little to break; the wind was picking up out of the west, and a storm was certainly coming.

Howell almost wished he could just keep walking, walking away into the woods. "Sam," he called, "Sam, Sammmm!" But Sam did not appear. Instead, Howell came upon some pigs, a few hundred yards down the road, and he stopped to look at them—fellow creatures, and ready to strike up an acquaintance. Here, in this netherworld of woods and ancient pasture, each sow had been provided with a half length of drainage culvert, round side up, to shelter in, and as Howell eased along the fence he found one that contained a sow and a whole litter of newborn piglets.

The sow was tremendous, her breasts a furious red, her nipples spread to either side as if by a hand; beside her in the straw her piglets were asleep, twelve little curls of clean white flesh. Howell, momentarily forgetting Sam and, had he realized it, all his troubles, said gently to the mother, "Good sowie, good sowie." The sowie shifted her huge head. She was encrusted with dirt and had that look of malevolent mistrust that is so common in mother pigs, who have plenty of time to think; the lumbering alarm with which she moved her head woke all the little piglets from their sleep.

But to Howell, relieved as he was to be once again dealing with something he understood, it was almost sweet, the way the sow raised her front body on the points of her trotters and glared at him with mean red eyes; and as the piglets all sprang to their feet, one after the other, like foam that has been compressed and then released, he watched them mill about in front of the drainage culvert, each one pink and white and glowing. Though Howell could hear the voices of Billy Bob and Mitch behind him on the road, raised in acrimonious debate, he managed to ignore the import of their words as he focused on these nice little animals. Their ears were folded and clipped to the sides of their heads, straight up, and their mouths smiled placatingly right around their snouts, as if they were ready for bad news. They were compact packages of plump alertness, their tiny trotters in place, their tails like small shavings of fresh-cut wood, their eyes two happy almonds.

Howell stood very still to watch them as they all decided what to do. Should they go back to sleep beside their mother, or should they run and hide in the woods? Run and hide in the woods was the vote at last, and they all started off through the grass with their springing, prancing gait, the first one selecting, quite at random, a route that led between the drainage culvert and a tree, and all the others close on that one's heels—each one appearing independently to consider an alternate route and each one seeming to decide that really, that way *was* rather nice—so that as they poured back into a slightly safer part of the world, they looked as if they were a miniature herd, stampeding on a miniature earth. That was the thing about pigs, it occurred to Howell suddenly, that set them apart from msot other species. They looked most like *pigs* when they were small; firm and completely formed, they were modest but assertive manifestations of the perfect idea of the Pig, an idea that would get distorted as they grew older, an idea that would almost be lost. For just a moment, he imagined himself as one of the piglets. How happy to prance thus on tiny trotters, to swing an insouciant ham.

Then Billy Bob called his name, and unhappily he turned away. The pigets, now in the grass at the edge of the woods, looked at him in surprise, as if to say that if they'd known he'd be leaving *this* soon, they'd have simply gone back to sleep.

"Bye, piggies," he said apologetically, and then turned back toward the truck, remembering Sam's disappearance as he did so, and wondering what he should do. "Sam, Sammm," he called once more, but Sam did not appear, so he tramped back down the road to the truck, where Billy Bob and Mitch awaited him.

"The damned thing's flat," they said almost together. "You let your spare go flat." And Howell, foreseeing in this one incredible circumstance the ruination of all his plans, felt betrayed by God, Who should certainly have made sure that the tires at least would function. But, with a kind of grim determination very much like the determination with which he always tackled the recalcitrant, he suggested that they all climb into the van, have the deputy drive the van down the ramp, and then proceed to Ada Esterhaczy's, leaving the truck behind. He could see that Mitch and Billy Bob were impressed by his ingenuity—they had not thought of this solution themselves—and Howell was too discouraged to bother to point out that the truck, which could not be moved and could not be concealed, would practically act as a signpost, and whatever happened, the "mysterious disappearance" had been scotched before it had occurred. He had a moment of renewed hope when Sam came charging down the road from the Sizemores', tail between her legs, ears flapping like laundry before a storm, for all the world as if *he* had deserted *her*.

When they got on their way again, crowded—stuffed—into the van, Sam was riding in Howell's lap as he crouched against the rear door. Although he had known the dog for six years, and had had full care of her for one, they had never before been so intimately together, and he felt a little embarrassed. Sam kept panting, for 'one thing, and then licking his face, and her heart was beating very fast, and when Howell leaned forward to get away from the hinge, she squirmed delightedly in response. In this position, he felt the same sort of discomfort with Sam that he usually felt with his children—a vague shrinking feeling, a mystification, as if almost anything might happen. He wished that the whole thing was over and done with, the mortgages burned, Sam pregnant, the Russians back home in Russia; and even the thought that in a few hours—when they were safely settled in at Mrs. Esterhaczy's and Howell had had the opportunity to call the police and turn Bailey in for witchcraft—his sister would be answering to the police for her misconduct, even this thought did not greatly warm his heart; what was the point of it, anyway? He tried to remind himself that there was a time during every project when it seemed too hard to accomplish—why, when the corn drier had broken, it had taken him *weeks* to fix it—but with Sam still panting and licking his face, the corn drier seemed far away.

At last they were turning up the Esterhaczy driveway, to the granddaughter's vocal dismay. Billy Bob, who had seemed a little more subdued than usual since his accident with the truck—and who, furthermore, kept looking sideways at Josef and Nicolai as if he, even more than Howell, were filled with a sense of disbelief at the way they looked—asked Howell if they should get out, or wait, or go somewhere else, or what? But Howell, who had somehow not managed to think beyond this moment, and who was still holding Sam, a great dog bundle, on his lap, asked the granddaughter if she knew where her grandmother was—he had told her he would be here at four.

"What!" she said, looking at him even more incredulously than usual, her red hair looking incredulous, too. "You're not trying to pretend that *Ada* is in on this? If you do, I swear to God I'll kill you."

And Howell, who at some other time might have gotten upset at this, at the profanity and the threat as well, just sighed and said, "We'd better get out. This storm is going to break soon."

So one after another, the crew piled out onto the driveway, and as they all stood around looking blank, Sam peed on everything in sight, the sky continued to get darker, and nothing else happened at all. Boonskie, who should certainly have appeared at the first whiff of Sam's blood, did not—all was silent but the wind—though for a moment Howell thought Nicolai was reassuring him when he said, "It will soon rain dogs, perhaps."

# 19

OH, YES, this was going to be quite a storm, and Ada was getting ready for it. While she knew that the dog man, Howell Bourne, would be arriving with his Russians any minute—he had told her four o'clock, and it was already four-thirty (five-thirty, actually, on Ada Time)—it was more important right now that she take care of Boonskie; the poor dear was terrified of storms. It was hard to judge whether it was the thunder or the lightning that scared him more, but although he had gotten over most of his other childhood fears, when the first rumble of thunder rolled across the sky, Boonskie would race for the nearest object and thrust his huge head, up to the shoulders, as far underneath this as he could, and every time there was a bolt of lightning, he would quiver from head to tail. Well, naturally, he preferred that the object under which he hid be Ada, and though Ada had no theoretical objection to that, practical experience had shown her that she was liable thus to end up on the ground, at which Boonskie, unable to get under, would simply climb on top of her and stretch to full length. As he weighed almost as much as she did, this hurt, so she was locking the dogs in the barn with the hay.

"It's all right, darling," she said comfortingly to Boonskie. "Raga will see that you are all snug." And little Raga—who worshipped Boonskie and was not scared of anything, though he tended to get overexcited when the opportunity arose—settled himself sympathetically next to his friend.

Ada, turning to leave, rubbed them both under the chin, then unhooked the side door of the barn to exit. As she did so, an errant gust of wind from the north blew through it, and Boonskie—who had been sitting on his haunches with a glazed expression in his eyes, panting as furiously as he could, as if panting were a specific against thunder—suddenly slurped his tongue back into his mouth and looked a lot more alert. So did Raga, who jumped to his feet and stared quizzically toward the driveway, his white duster of a tail shaking slowly, his head held over to the side. Ah. No doubt the guests had arrived. And though Ada was not precisely looking forward to their visit—she had agreed to act as hostess, after all, before Maggie started seeing Ryland and at a time when her own life had simply seemed too *boring*—she had better get out to supervise things and make sure that everyone stayed dry. She herself loved a good storm, though she knew there were many like her Boonskie. How odd, though, that the dogs had smelled people, with the smell of the woods now so strong. And now they were acting even more deeply interested, both of them up on their feet; before Ada could react, they sprang into flight and burst out the door, tails leaping.

Well, Ada liked that! What disobedient dogs! Humph, she would say a thing or two to them! But when she got to her house, that intention disappeared and was replaced with a high level of astonishment. There were three men with guns standing on her lawn—with guns, thank you very much! No one had said anything to her about guns, and if they had she would have scotched that idea firmly and decisively. And there were four other men without guns, and her granddaughter as well; what on earth was Maggie doing here? Why, right from the first she had sensed that Maggie would disapprove of any impulse on Ada's part to get involved in this incident, so of course she had failed to inform her, and yet here she was, despite the secrecy. She was supposed to be over at Ryland's. Of all the tasks that faced Ada at this moment, dealing with an irascible granddaughter was by far the most intimidating; luckily, there was a major distraction at the moment, in the form of Boonskie and Raga. That lunatic Howell Bourne had brought his bitch at last—she was long of nose and mournful of eye and seemed presently stricken with despair. Boonskie and Raga milled around her, indifferent to everything else. Friends even at this crucial juncture of their lives, they had apparently agreed not to let Sam come between them, and were both trying to mount her at once, Raga with his paws perched on her shoulders, and Boonskie grappling with her ribs; they were having trouble getting a solid purchase, as Sam was hardly holding still. Howling like a damned soul, she was turning from right to left and left to right, too unhappy even to try to bite—but Boonskie and Raga were like heat-seeking missiles, the kind that Maggie so hated.

Ada grabbed Raga. "For you, to the shed. These are going to be Boonskie's babies. Maggie, will you help me?"

"What do you mean?"

"With the dogs. With Raga."

"Ada, are you in on this?"

"Maggie. What a thought! Well, in a way. But we will discuss it later. For now, you must take Raga."

Unwillingly, Maggie dragged Raga away. At least she was, for the moment, disposed of. Now Ada could greet her guests, although several of them—loutish men that they were —seemed to be more interested in the private life of Boonskie and Sam than they were in responding civilly to her greeting; as Sam broke loose and loped away howling, one of them said, "She's just like my wife," then chuckled rather crudely.

Ada did not deign to notice this, but welcomed the other men instead. And here she met with greater success, for while Howell attempted to apologize for the way that Maggie had been inadvertently swept along in this kidnapping, and Richard Minot reminded Ada—as if she were an idiot!—that they had met before, the two Russians proved to be so delightful, so polite, such thoroughgoing *gentlemen*, that Ada, though she did not, of course, forget completely what Russia had done to Hungary, immediately forgave these two particular Russians for any part they might have played, active or passive, reminding herself that there are many extenuating circumstances in the world, and that, in any case, these men could hardly have been born. So completely did Josef and Nicolai charm her with their bows and their hand kisses and their complimentary remarks about her "lovely estate" and her "mature beauty" that in the space of the minute or so during which she stood there conversing with them, while Boonskie chased Sam around, a lovelight in his eyes, Ada managed to convince herself that the only reason she had ever agreed to participate in this incident to begin with was that in this way she would have a real opportunity to persuade the two gallant Russians to *defect*, to move to America—perhaps to Felicity—where they could be neighbors and friends. Why, she herself, a Hungarian by birth, had found a happy home in this great country, and there was no reason why others shouldn't share her opportunity; it was her duty, really, to try to persuade them, and they'd thank her for it, she was sure. It did cross her mind, of course, that this approach would be an excellent one to present to Maggie when her granddaughter returned from locking Raga in the shed, and might, if she was convincing enough, get her completely off the hook. But the real reason it appealed to her was that she was flattered—and no one had said anything about guns!

"Do come in," she said. "We will all have some sherry. Those guns can remain outside."

"But Mrs. Esterhaczy . . ." said Howell.

"Well, your friends can stay there, too. They can guard all they want to from the porch. No, not another word. This is my house. I will make the rules here. People in, guns out; that is final."

Then she led the way to the house, pointedly skirting that part of the yard where Boonskie and Sam were still trying to reach an accord; Maggie overtook her, as she opened the kitchen door, and hissed at her, "What do you think you're doing?"

"Serving some light refreshments. Some biscuits, perhaps, and sherry."

"You know that this is a criminal act?"

"Do not jump to conclusions," said Ada reprovingly. "It does not become a young woman."

"Oh, it doesn't, doesn't it? They kidnapped us on the highway. They stuck *guns* in our faces, Ada. And then it turns out my own *grand*mother set us up. And I thought all the nuts were in Washington!"

"I did not set you up. You don't understand at all. I intend to help these men defect."

"Help. . . what . . ." Maggie was inarticulate.

"So now, may I proceed and serve the sherry?"

Maggie was such a dear, but she had no real spirit of adventure; she clearly did not see the rich possibilities. And her temper— well, her temper had always been her bane. But now she was preceding Ada into the kitchen, and while Howell instructed his crude friends to stay outside and watch the driveway, she led everyone else through the kitchen into the living room, where she invited them all to find chairs. One of the men—an extremely silent policeman of some kind, who appeared to be a deaf mute—sat down on the floor, his face between his hands, but the rest settled sensibly on the furniture. When Ada had provided everyone with a nice glass of sherry and some expensive water biscuits to go with them, she took out her linen serviettes from a drawer in the sideboard; after all, this was a very special occasion! She then filled tumblers for the two men on the porch, since, while she had certainly never been an alarmist—she, who had lived through two world wars—it was as well to be sensible, and getting those men drunk struck her as a sensible idea. Unless she missed her guess, they had probably never drunk sherry before in their lives, and if they were like most American men—big lummoxes who drank *milk*, for heaven's sake, and sweet sugary drinks like babies—they would guzzle it down with an absolute lack of sense. And then they would be sorry later on.

"A little pick-me-up," she said, handing them the tumblers. "I will bring you more in a little while."

"What is it?" asked one.

"Some of this. Some of that. A tiny dash of rum to give it an edge."

He sniffed it. "Well, all right."

"Yes, yes, it is fine. You will like it. Keep an eye out," said Ada, and then left them.

Back in the house, Howell was wandering about, clutching his glass of sherry in both hands. He had, at Ada's request, left his shotgun on the porch with his two friends, and he seemed now like someone hypnotized. He made several moves toward the phone, which was bolted to the wall in the kitchen, but he couldn't bring himself to pick up the receiver; when Ada suggested that he should, he agreed with her completely but remained in place, clinging to his sherry. Though Ada still found it ludicrous that he could have believed, even for a moment, that he would succeed in getting all the Rock County mortgages burned, she found it endearing that he had thought the idea up, just like his ancestors and the cherry pitters. And since it would give her more time to talk with Nicolai and Josef, to convince them that they should defect, she didn't much mind if he kept on wandering about before he could bring himself to act.

In the living room, Richard Minot was reading, and Maggie was talking with the Russians. When Ada settled herself near the group of talkers, she found they were talking about Hungary, and Josef turned to include her in the discussion, just like the gentleman he was.

"Ah, Mrs. Esterhaczy," he said "I admired Budapest so much. The Hungarians are so fun-loving, so passionate, so hospitable. They made me feel right at home. They say that Hungarians love to do three things: cook, dance, and romance. Very different from us Russians . . . except, of course, for me." He winked at her, then winked at her again.

"I, for example, am a real 'worrywort,' " said Nicolai. "I am always prepared for the worst. Right now, for example, what is going on? This is surely not a common custom?"

"It certainly is," interjected Minot, looking up for a minute from his book. "It's called breaking the law."

"Oh, Richard!" said Maggie. "Can't you just read your damned Kierkegaard?"

"I understood that kidnapping wasn't done anymore," said Josef. "That it was a dying crime, what with electronic surveillance. Of course, there are always exceptions."

"It's not," said Minot. "We're a little behind the times here. Here, they still do things with shotguns."

"Just get this straight," said Maggie to the others. "Ada is *not* an accomplice. Mr. Bourne, can't you threaten her or something?"

"Maggie, darling, I appreciate the thought. But really, that will not be necessary. Nothing will come of this, you will see. And after all, at least this isn't Doomsday!"

"Nothing will *come* of it?" said Maggie.

"Nothing bad, you will see. Now, now, let us talk of something more pleasant."

But a kind of trance now fell on the group, and even Ada did not know how to break it. All this talk of laws and crimes, of Doomsday and electronic surveillance; well, no wonder they all felt a bit subdued, unable to just swing back to Budapest. Outside, the storm had not yet broken, and despite the wind, it was still hot; Ada felt hot right down to her toes, and she noticed Josef's bald head sweating. And much as she would have liked to plunge right into her Defection Persuasion, to regale her guests with laughter and song, she could see that now was not the proper time, that the attempt would be inauspicious. In this silence, this heavy, hypnotic, pre-storm silence, Ada herself felt suddenly uneasy. What if something *did* go wrong? It had happened before in the world.

"Excuse me," she said, "I will just go check things," and she got defiantly to her feet. In the kitchen, Howell Bourne was still standing staring at the phone; outside on the porch, the louts had drained their tumblers. That was all good news—she felt somewhat reassured—and then she located Boonskie. He had finally managed, the darling, to get himself into the correct position behind the future mother of his children; that mother looked right now utterly aghast, and Boonskie looked quite shocked also. Hundreds of practice sessions on Raga had not prepared him very well for the real thing, it appeared, and as he gripped Sam's midsection with his forelegs, and balanced uncomfortably on his two hind legs, he seemed to be reconsidering the whole idea, which had recently seemed so appealing. So all was well; Boonskie was mating, and the storm would break any minute. If only Ada hadn't had her guests to think of, she would go out to enjoy the coming rain.

"I love a good storm," said Josef at that moment. "I love to stand in the rain."

"Come with me, then," said Ada impulsively. "We will go and stand in it together." As he joined her, he slipped his arm through hers.

Together they proceeded past the crude men with guns and Ada kicked off her shoes. In the west, it looked as if a cape were being tugged up over the sky, but there was an odd sparkly lightness mixed in with the gloom, and the wind was picking up very fast; it blew Ada's dress from side to side, and it knocked her against Josef's shoulder. As she passed Boonskie, he looked at her appealingly, but she politely pretended not to notice—it would be harder in the storm, but it would be over soon, and then there would be all those babies. Now the sky was shifting, the darkness cracking, and the whole southern sky had gone pearl; a shaft of sunlight dropped down through the lightness, but thunderclouds collided in the north.

"What a marvelous country!" shouted Josef over the wind.

"That is true!" shouted Ada back. "You would love it if you lived . . ." But no, now was not the time. It was too hard to make herself heard.

And now, the first lightning struck down the sky, a firebolt that clove the wind to stab to the heart of the earth. A mushroom of light exploded around its tip, like spores that were spreading their seed. Shortly after, the thunder followed, a tremendous detonation that practically rocked her as she stood, and then the rain hit, a drop, ten drops, and suddenly a cascade. Crack, crack, crack, the bolts sizzled their way down, to the right, to the left, and all around them—instead of moving into the shelter of the trees, Josef and Ada were drawn farther into the open. The trees behind them started to bend toward the earth with the force of the wind, and then turned their leaves placatingly to the sky, like dogs showing their bellies. Oh, how it bent, the whole earth bent, to do homage to this wind that surrounded it.

"It hurts!" shouted Josef, stamping his feet, and turning his face toward the sky.

"Yes, yes," said Ada, squeezing his arm with hers; he removed it and put it around her shoulder.

And so they stood, while the thunder boomed and slammed, and the lightning fenced with the earth and the sky, and everything green turned very very green, and the whole world came totally alive. But the storm, which had been so long in coming, seemed also in a hurry to move on, and it wasn't long before it passed away to the east, the drumbeats of thunder announcing its arrival there.

Soaked to the skin, Ada and Josef looked at each other.

"Your head!" said Ada. "Your poor head."

"No, no, its tough." He beat on it with his hand. "You see? It's really very tough."

"Well, mine isn't. I'm cold. Let's go get some dry clothes. I think you can wear some of Tibor's."

So they turned and hurried to the kitchen, where the louts had taken shelter from the rain. Boonskie, poor sweatheart, had finished with his business; what a triumph to have managed it through the storm! The minute Ada appeared, he rushed up to her and tried to throw himself into her lap, his ears cupped hysterically against his head, his whole body trembling with upset. How *could* she have done it, he clearly was asking. How *could* she have put him through such torture?

"Now, Boonskie, darling, most men love it. Come in, you come in and dry off."

Inside, she rubbed Boonskie down with a towel, and then found Josef some dry clothes. She encouraged him to take a bath, but he would not, and so, after refilling the louts' tumblers with sherry, and making sure that everyone else had what they needed, she went into the bathroom to bathe herself; she really felt chilled to the bone. As soon as she had started the water pouring into the old claw-footed bathtub, she climbed right in, and let it fill up around her as she studied her body submerging. For a while, she had added a bubbly soap mixture to the water—she had enjoyed the way the bubbles felt when they burst against her skin—but she had discovered that the bubbles prevented her from looking at her own body. Oh, it was not that it was such a pretty body, all loose and wrinkly as it was, but it was hers, and everything was familiar about it; it was hers, and it was there, and it was moving. Those nice knees she remembered from her childhood, when she had learned to dance some violent Hungarian dances; they were there, with their splendid caps, and those cavities at the side. And the shinbones, how pleasant, very sharp and precise, leading from the knees to the feet. There, the toes curled like grapes, ripe to be plucked, and she wiggled them all a hello. The body was a marvelous thing indeed, and though sometimes lately she had speculated on what it would be like if she could trade this one she was wearing for a nice young one, twenty years old, the thought was grotesque. Such wisdom would look silly in a youth!

Twenty minutes later Ada was settled again in the living room, which was now cooler and much more pleasant. Howell, who had finally called the sheriff's office, only to discover that the sheriff himself was not there—and who had been so unprepared for this contingency that he had simply hung up in alarm—was now cogitating about what to do next, sitting staring at his knuckles. Mitch and Billy Bob had taken their again-refilled tumblers back outside, where they could spit tobacco in peace, and Ada had settled herself next to Nicolai; Josef was in earnest conversation with Maggie. While she was in her bath, Ada had decided that a good way to get into the whole defection business would be to bring up the fascinating subject of the English language, since she understood that

Nicolai was a linguist, and she thought that they could chuckle together over some of the more amusing expressions, then move to the grand opportunity for study that would be afforded by a permanent move.

But before she could get her teeth properly into this, Nicolai asked her about television. He saw she had one. Could they turn it on? Ada had to graciously agree.

Naturally, there was nothing on, except at the moment a beer commercial. The commercial was, specifically, for Miller beer—a very patriotic beer, according to the ad: "Born and Brewed in the U.S.A." A lot of men were sweating hugely and shaking one another's hands in an emphatic way, and much as Ada loved America, she felt embarrassed at this macho display. But Nicolai seemed to enjoy it—in fact, he even seemed to know the little jingle that went along with the ad, and in a grim and rather pessimistic voice he sang it, just above his breath, along with the TV voices.

It was while he was singing that Josef got up, strode forward, and switched the television off again, saying as he did so, "Television is very bad for Nicolai. He is a television junkie. He particularly likes American television, but it is an addiction that is good not to indulge. He glazes, you see. Nicolai!"

And Nicolai, who was, Ada had to admit, looking not unlike Boonskie in some of his stupider moments, stopped singing abruptly and appeared slightly sorrowful.

"American TV?" asked Maggie. "How do you get American TV?"

"Oh, we watch pirated videotapes on smuggled Japanese VCR's," explained Josef. "It's very simple."

"From friends," added Nicolai. "All good things come from friends."

"From comrades," said Josef. "You know."

At the word "comrades," Howell Bourne, who had been leaning disconsolately in the doorway watching the TV for the few moments it was on, looked up with something that seemed almost like pleasure, and nodded twice to himself. And while Ada returned to plotting her strategy for defection, wondering how she could use these new bits of information to greatest effect—American TV, well, where could you see it so easily as in *America?*—she noticed that the storm, which should have cleared the air completely, had not done so; instead of the blue sky that normally followed such cloudbursts, there was a grayish-yellow dome overhead and a strange heavy feeling of alertness. It *was* cooler, there was no doubt about that—but there was still an accumulating fierceness.

# 20

RYLAND, too, thought the storm wasn't over, and it was making him feel a bit crazed. A party was always hard enough without mud being mixed in with it; luckily, at the last minute before the rain came, he and Peale had moved the tables in from the lawn. Now, as he spread those tables with damask, and arranged the china and cutlery in neat little fans upon it, Peale and Amanda hovered nearby, not being a great deal of help. It was Maggie whom Ryland wanted with him, but Maggie, for some unfathomable reason, hadn't yet managed to show up, and this first symptom of unreliability had given Ryland a pain in his side. In the soothing and cheerful weeks since they had started seeing each other, Ryland had felt awfully healthy, awfully awake and alive. But he had not been able to prevent himself from looking for a symptom, something that would ruin everything and confirm what he'd always suspected—that happiness was not for him, that he would die if he ever got close to it. Now, as the pain—which might, admittedly, have been caused by that ice water he had drunk down so rapidly, with some ice shards inadvertently included—poked him tenderly in the side, he could not decide whether it was pancreatic cancer or Maggie's being late. Either way, it didn't look good.

Ryland had hired a maid for the occasion, and she seemed to have things well in hand. Since the food service at the college was providing the dinner, and since all the glassware and china had been borrowed from them also, the only thing Ryland had to worry about was that the house look clean and festive. As he turned all the glasses upside down on the sideboard, first examining them briefly for spots, Molly suddenly backed out from underneath it; she had hidden there during the storm. Recently, she had decided that she could no longer trust her own paws, and so—like a Cheyenne Contrary, perhaps—she backed about her business. If someone came into the room unexpectedly, she backed at top speed out of it, staring at a point about four feet from her nose as if it were chasing her. In order to approach her food bowl, or anyplace else where she truly desired to arrive head first, she would engage in a complex series of circumnavigations, first racing backward for a chair that lay in quite a different direction from the spot she wanted to attain, then scuttling, claws extended as if mummified, sideways to some other shadowed place, and finally, in one desperate burst of hope, scrabbling with her front claws until she found a purchase, and sliding forward toward her goal. To Molly these days, every flat surface had the configurations of a cliff, and every journey the risk of a quest, and Ryland was afraid that sixty people in the house might push her right into madness. But she wouldn't go into the basement—her paranoia was stimulated by stairs—so he supposed she'd just have to back about, bumping into a number of the guests. Those guests would be arriving any minute—in Felicity, it was considered extremely bad manners to be more than ten minutes late—and he still had to select the evening's music and put out some conversation pieces.

He had decided that the theme for the evening would be Russian Cultural Achievements, a nice safe theme, all things considered, and one he knew something about. From his large record collection, he extracted Rachmaninoff, Tchaikovsky, Rimski-Korsakov, Moussorgsky, and, with some reluctance, Stravinsky, and he set them in a neat stack beside his turntable, each to be used in turn. Then, in something of a rush, he went whizzing through his library, driving Molly before him backward, her claws creating furrows in the oriental rugs as she put on a burst of speed. He found Tolstoy, Dostoevsky, and Chekhov; he considered Solzhenitsyn, but chose Sholokhov instead. Then, books in one hand, marble and cork coasters in the other, he visited all the tables in the living and the dining rooms, dropping some offerings off on each. Finally, he turned on the stereo, and set Rachmaninoff on the turntable, letting the needle find its place, and adjusting the volume and tone. As the first pounding piano chords filled the room, their brooding, hostile Romanticism creating, admittedly, an unusual atmosphere for a dinner party, Amanda called out, "There's somebody here," as she passed by the front door with wine.

Briefly, Ryland debated changing the record, then left it and went to the hall. At the curb, the Wickendens were climbing out of their car, the Reverend Wickenden's hearing aid visible even at this distance, Mrs. Wickenden wearing high heels, which were seemingly giving her trouble. Maggie had requested that the Beyond War contingent be invited to this affair, and while Ryland had had no objection to this, he wished that these two had not arrived first, given Mrs. Wickenden's penchant for oriental rugs. If he had been hosting visitors from the People's Republic of China, it might perhaps have been acceptable to spend fifteen or twenty minutes going over the finer points of thread count and design with one of his guests, but since the evening was to be Russian in theme, he felt this would be out of place. Perhaps the Rachmaninoff would discourage her; it was roaring in the background like a wolf of the Siberian steppes.

But no, the first thing she said was "At *last* I'll get to see your rugs!" and Ryland had the distinct impression that she felt almost uncomfortable at the thought.

As a host, he knew his duties, and he suggested he act as her guide. Leaving Peale and Amanda to guard the door, should any other guests arrive, he took Mrs. Wickenden on a tour of the house, starting with the library and their Tibetans. Here Ryland's impression that Mrs. Wickenden was uncomfortable grew more pronounced; her face was drawn and her hands were clenched as she murmured an admiring "Lovely!" In the dining room, things got even worse; she seemed almost to be having a seizure at the sight of one Turkoman Bokhara, very old and faded, that hung on a wall and was a rarity, though not the prize of Ryland's collection; she

gasped and drew her hands to her chest, making small breathy
noises. Even the years of genteel covetousness at Saguanay's had
not prepared him for quite *this* exhibition, and politely he looked
away until Mrs. Wickenden regained her composure and followed
him up the stairs. She had a little trouble negotiating them, but
she made it to their top at last, and Ryland headed for the rear of
the house. There, in the master bedroom was the finest rug he
had—a Turkish Tree of Life, circa late nineteenth century, its colors
as vibrant as ever.

Together, they looked in silence at the rug, Mrs. Wickenden
now almost goggle-eyed—the fruits on the tree were each works
of art, and indeed might make anyone weak. But while Ryland was
staring pleasurably at the floor, listening to the opening and shutting
door, he heard at his side a deep frothy gurgling, and looked at
Mrs. Wickenden in alarm. Now, she was clutching her chest, gasp-
ing, and was also doubling over in place, and as he watched she
toppled forward and grabbed at the rug like a fruit picker. Good
heavens! This was not at all what Ryland had hoped for—perhaps
she was mentally unbalanced? Or perhaps—oh, no— was she having a heart attack? Right on his Tree of Life rug? If he'd known the
effect it would have on this woman, he would certainly never have
risked it.

"Help, help!" he shouted. "Get an ambulance up here! Mrs.
Wickenden's going to expire!"

Though the command in this speech would have been hard to
execute, and the declaration hard to yet judge, they certainly had
the desired effect, as people came pounding up the stairs. Ryland
stood ineffectually by while Peale administered first aid. Amanda
made the call to the hospital, which promised an ambulance soon.
When the ambulance pulled up, siren shrieking, tires squealing,
and Ryland saw through his bedroom window two white-coated
figures with a stretcher dash through his back garden, he wondered
deliriously whether they would wrap her in the rug; she was stretched
upon its branches like a martyr. Only when she had been successfully transferred to the stretcher, as rugless as she had arrived, did
it occur to Ryland that perhaps the rug wasn't solely responsible

for the tragedy. The woman had seemed in trouble from the moment she emerged from her car, and if she'd already, when she got here, been having a heart attack, the rugs could hardly have made it any *worse*. Best of all, she seemed better already; it looked as if she'd survive.

The ambulance left, the Reverend Wickenden aboard it, and Ryland returned from the curb to the house. At the front door, the maid was letting in fresh guests—perhaps twenty had arrived during the confusion—but Maggie was not here yet, and neither were the Russians, and that was really strange. Still, he had his party to attend to; he, as host, must be its lodestar.

He picked up a tray of hot cheese pastries and offered them to the nearest man, an elderly man whose cauliflower ears looked remarkably familiar.

"Ah, Dostoevsky!" Ryland said enthusiastically. "What a wonderful Russian writer." He nodded to *The Brothers Karamazov* nearby as the man forlornly chose a pastry and said, "She's such a good woman. I can't understand it."

Ryland murmured some reassurances. Of course! This was the Clipping Man, one of the Beyond War-ers. Things weren't going well at all.

Ten minutes later, having struck out with Dostoevsky, he had at least exhausted the cheese pastries. He was beginning to feel distinctly annoyed, not only that no one in the room seemed to want to talk about anything but Mrs. Wickenden's heart attack, not only that Maggie hadn't yet gotten there, but, most aggravating of all, that the Russians themselves were still absent. He didn't know what things were like in the Soviet Union, but here in Felicity when you were the guests of honor you were supposed to show up, and they were now almost a half hour late, which was certainly not helping the party. Nor was Molly. Even at the best of times these days an unexpected sound, a sudden movement, both the presence and the absence of food, any door—no matter which side she stood on— she saw as pitfalls for the unwary. And now, as she backed from room to room, continually surprised by sound and movement, continually confused by food, there was an air about her of "As I suspected! Yes, yes. I surely should have known!" When Ryland knelt down to try to reassure her, she looked at him with glazed eyes—she was clearly slipping into full-blown psychosis. He would carry her down the basement stairs and put her in the tornado cellar. There, she could sleep on the army cot until the terror above her subsided.

When Molly was settled, and he had drawn her some water, Ryland returned, exhausted, to the kitchen. There, he found Peale sitting alone at the table and staring miserably at the telephone.

"They've been murdered. I know it," said Peale.

"They have?"

"The Russians."

"How do you know?"

"I tried calling Johnson on the radio."

"Maybe they had a flat."

"He didn't answer the call. God, I wish I'd never run for sheriff."

Ryland, who had, of course, wished this also—many times—looked at Peale with real alarm. His brother, who had always defined for Ryland the essence of easy, winsome charm and confidence, had wrenched his eyes away from the telephone only long enough to look despairingly up at Ryland as he made this last remark, and now had returned to his contemplation, like someone under a spell. But he couldn't be right . . . *Maggie* was with them. And things already had gone wrong enough.

"Now, Peale—" he'd begun when the phone suddenly shrilled and Ryland knocked a tray onto the floor. There it bounced with an ear-rending clang while the phone continued to ring.

"You get it," said Peale. "Tell them I'm gone. Tell them I died or something."

So Ryland, his heart by now whanging in his chest, picked up the phone and said, "Guthrie residence."

At the other end, there was a silence, though the line was clearly open. Eventually a voice said, "Yes. Sheriff Guthrie. I've got you an amonomous tip."

"Who's calling, please?"

"I said I'm amonomous. You know those Russians up to the college?"

"Yes?"

"Well, they've been spirited away. And it's no use looking for them now."

"It isn't?"

"No. They've vanished from the earth. They've been turned into trees or something."

"Turned into trees?"

"By a witch, you know. She lives at One-oh-two West Walnut."

"She does?"

"You could visit her. Her name is Bailey Bourne. But it won't do you any good."

"Why not?"

" 'Cause you're not going to find them. Well, I guess that's all. Goodbye for now, Sheriff Guthrie."

"For *now?*" But the phone line had gone dead, as had part of Ryland's mind.

Oh, Ryland had given many dinner parties in his life, and he knew how complicated they could get, but he had never before given one where a guest had a heart attack, and three others were abducted by a witch. The theme of the evening—Russian Cultural Achievements—was certainly going to have to be changed, and probably the whole party would simply dissolve when this latest news was spread. But that wasn't the point, really, was it? The point was that this was *bad*. Bailey Bourne was that crazy woman, with the candles and the incense and the dog. And while kidnapping surely was better than murder, it could end in much the same way. And Maggie was with them . . . Maggie was with them! Why hadn't he asked about her?

Peale had been gazing at him with a look of desperate hope ever since he'd picked up the phone. As the sounds of the party began to filter back into Ryland's consciousness, and the maid came banging through the swinging door with a tray of empty glasses, Ryland wondered just how to break the news to him; he seemed already on the verge of a collapse.

"Well?" said Peale.

"They're OK, I think. They've just been kidnapped. By a witch." And while the maid—who had been trained, no doubt, to ignore the strange remarks and bizarre behavior of her multiple employers—proceded calmly to wash the glasses, rinsing them with an efficient *swoosh*, Ryland retraced his steps and repeated the conversation as accurately as he could. When he got to the witch's name, he was surprised to note that Peale perked up just a bit.

"Bailey Bourne? He said that her name was Bailey Bourne? But that's Beware of Farmers!"

"Excuse me?"

"The woman who came to see me this morning. I called you about it, remember?"

"Of course, but I don't see why *that's* good news."

"Because . . . well . . . because she's just *nice*."

"Nice? She's insane! And *Maggie* is with them. Peale, you've got to *do* something."

"Yes, yes, of course. I'll get on this right away. I should probably put out a general."

The maid now asked whether she should start to serve dinner, and, distractedly, Ryland nodded. While Peale disappeared out the front door to his car, muttering, "What was their *route?*" he even helped her to carry out the bowls and set them on the tables in the dining room. Then he walked around the house, letting his guests know that, although unfortunately the Russians had been delayed, dinner would proceed in their absence. He concentrated on staying calm and hostlike while Peale set his plans in motion. Moussorgsky, he thought, would be the perfect dinner music—he made the adjustments on his turntable—and then he returned to help with the serving, stationing himself by the buffet.

"Chicken salad?" he asked. "May I give you some fruit? No, no, it's nothing serious. Potatoes, then? No, merely a delay." Five or ten of his guests looked relieved.

But meanwhile, a police car pulled up in front of his house, and rumors were beginning to fly. Within five minutes, the consensus of those in the room was that the Russians had drowned in the Pond, and the Beyond War-ers in particular seemed undone by this news, so Ryland told everyone the truth, first clearing his throat for their attention.

"Ah, I'm afraid," he said, "ah, the Russians have been kidnapped. That's all we know at this time. That is, they've disappeared. We *think* they've been kidnapped. That is . . ." Here, chaos erupted.

And it was the nature of the chaos—hysterical chatter—that jerked Ryland out of his stupefaction. This wasn't a joke, it wasn't a glitch—they'd been *kidnapped,* for God's sake, and Maggie with them. Some insane humans, who thought they were witches, were at this very moment holding Maggie; perhaps they were terrorizing her; and he, Ryland, could do nothing. Though Ryland had spent most of his life steeped in universal gloom, there had never really been a reason for it before, not a reason like this one. And though he had always been wonderful at predicting catastrophe, at seeing it lurking everywhere, *this* catastrophe had arrived unannounced. He was paralyzed. His whole body felt sick, even his ankles, on which he was swaying a little—his breathing was shallow, and his eyeballs ached, as if they were being rammed from behind. The fact was, he loved Maggie; why hadn't he noticed that? Why hadn't he ever told her? He loved her, he loved her. Oh, this was the worst. And the noise of the party was growing.

On a sudden impulse to get away from people, Ryland turned and headed for the basement. His house had been built in 1880, and the basement was extensive and well built; dry and silent, with masterly stonework and a pleasant echo to the floor. The air was cool, almost breezy, after the strange lingering heat up above, and although the party was hardly abating, its noise here was merely a rumor. In the silence, lingering from another age, in the peace and tranquillity of a century, Ryland was able to think what he needed to think: *Give her back to me, and I will do anything.* Had he believed in God, he would have promised Him this now; as it was, he promised it anyway. And he found, as he did so, that he'd spoken the words aloud—Molly woke up from her sleep in the tornado cellar. Tail wagging, she came out, pleased to join him; she smiled and panted at him in greeting. She was calmer, much calmer—she even pranced a bit.

"Molly, oh, Molly," he said, wrapping his arms around her. He found that he was beginning to cry. She—or an ancestor—had thrown in her lot in with man, had offered up her wildness for his friendship, and man had betrayed her, had abandoned her and starved her, had confined her until she was almost dead. And she? She had thought it was *her* fault, this terrible betrayal; that she had somehow failed man, as his dog—and the wildness she'd abandoned had begun to call her back, until there was a rift like a river in her soul. It had driven her half mad, that tantalizing vision of the woods and the wild, where things were clear—but she hadn't deserted him; she had stuck with him to the end, though she dwelt in unspeakable darkness.

# 21

PEALE, meanwhile, was feeling slightly relieved, though also more than slightly disquieted. On the relieved side, his deputies had arrived, and the hierarchy of the sheriff's department, which had always before seemed to him a little overwhelming—with its over-abundance of chiefs and its low proportion of Indians—now seemed to him rather marvelous, comforting, if still a little bit absurd. His chief deputy, Tom Webster, was here, as was his captain, Crane Sizemore, and he had two lieutenants, both of them squad leaders in charge of three other men. Only his major, the jail commander, was missing—he was over at the jail. Otherwise, everyone and his great-uncle had answered this call, and they were now milling around, looking hopeful. Not only did none, presumably, have anything else to do right now, but this was, from the looks of it, probably the only crime that had ever been committed in Rock County that was not alcohol-induced. His men, in fact, were so excited by the prospect of a real crime in their jurisdiction that, though they agreed that the Feds should be notified as soon as it seemed certain that the Saguanay's van had left the county, they were, to a man, reluctant to call in the state police yet, no matter *what* police etiquette required. Enormous adolescents that most of them were, they considered this the best thing that had happened in Rock County in a dog's age, and if their spirit was not exactly infectious, their presence was certainly reassuring.

Then, too, although the emergency that Peale had feared since he'd taken office had finally happened, it was really almost a boon. Dreading the future was far and away the most difficult thing that Peale had ever done, and though he had, in his short tenure in office, moved from a position of total mystification at the motives that impelled people to commit criminal acts to a sense that he, and authority figures like him, were at least partially to blame, he had not yet figured out how to cope with the result, which was a fear that he would make things even worse. Surely action of any kind would be preferable to these fears, and now he could at least take action—precisely *what* action he had not yet figured out. As he briefed his deputies on the circumstances known to date, he was glad that things were not worse: murder, a terrorist bomb, these were what could have been; simple disappearance was a lot more hopeful, as he tried to communicate to his men. But his men could not have cared less—murder, disappearance, what difference? As long as they got to give a Signal 10—both the red light *and* the siren.

On the disquieting side, there was the stuff about witchcraft and the mention of Bailey Bourne. He had sensed, when he let her leave his office that morning, that he was making a terrible mistake, and that she knew much more than she had told him, but he couldn't quite believe that *she* was responsible; and nobody, anymore, was a witch. Still, it didn't seem fair, somehow, that the two major tribulations of his life right now should be acting in concert—but that was what was happening, and the best he could do to get through it was to take things slow. Peale suspected that if he paid a visit to this woman immediately, she would somehow hornswoggle him into believing that she really knew nothing more than she had already told him—ridiculous as that was. It was also likely, more than likely, that if he went there he'd get distracted. Distracted from his clear and pressing duty, which was to locate the Saguanay's van and not get all engrossed by this Bailey and her clothes, and the effect her face and body had on him.

As a matter of fact, if he hadn't known better, he might have believed she really *was* a witch, because only a witch or something like it could have waltzed into a perfectly happy life, one that had always been almost indecently well organized, and thrown it into such confusion of soul. And while he had spent most of his brief married life mildly surprised every time he saw Amanda, twice now in one day Bailey Bourne had shown up, and neither time had she surprised him at all. The first time, her melted flag of a belt had certainly been seditious, and the second time, she had been accused, in absentia, of a felony. So why was he, the *sheriff,* even thinking about her now? He should just arrest her and be done with it.

"All right men, we've got a lot to do," he said, feeling guilty at not mentioning the witchcraft. "First, we have to trace the van. We've got an advantage there, since it was driving on back roads, and since it's white and clearly marked. You, Tanner and Sizemore, take your crews onto the roads. I'll go back to the office with Webster and make some phone calls, then radio."

Several of Ryland's guests were standing on the porch, staring as Peale gave his men their orders. The recent violent storm— which, Peale thought glumly, was certainly not going to make things any easier, since any tire tracks would have been completely erased— had not, oddly enough, really cleared the air, which was still lowering and electric. Poor Ryland, this was the sort of thing that was always happening to him—he gave dinner parties where people had heart attacks or got kidnapped. Even storms didn't clear the air, but just lingered around, looking ominous. Well, this might give him back his pessimism at least, which Peale had missed so much; with that thought, Peale and Webster left and revved across town to the office.

It surprised Peale, and cheered him somewhat, to find he was coping with this at all. At the office, he got out a large county map and, after marking down Johnson's route in red, started circling all the houses that overlooked it. Then, with the help of his dispatcher, he placed calls to all those houses; a fair number of the people with whom he spoke had seen the van pass, and thus Peale succeeded in narrowing its passage and pinpointing its termination. Incredibly, it seemed that the van had simply vanished on Pond Road: it had entered the south side and never emerged on the north. Come on now, how was that possible?

Several people, returning from work, had passed while Maggie Esterhaczy and Richard Minot and the two Russians had been lounging around the south end of the Pond, throwing rocks into the water and chipping the cliff for samples, but old Mrs. Sizemore, Crane's widowed mother and a woman who spent most of her life these days buttoned to the front window of her house, where she could observe all the small commerce that took place in her part of the world, swore that the Saguanay's van had not emerged from Pond Road. She could not have missed it, she declared, and question her as he would—had she not, perhaps, gone to the bathroom at some point, gone to the kitchen for a drink?—Peale could not shake her firm assertion that the van had never driven by. Why, her oldest son, Crane, was a deputy sheriff, and it was he who had told her about these Reds, and though she couldn't get about much anymore, of course, she had sworn she would see them at least once.

Peale thanked her finally and hung up the phone, feeling well and truly bewildered. If the van had gone into the south side of Pond Road, and had never come out of the north, then there was only one place where the van could be, which was in the Pond itself. And though it made no sense that he should have received an anonymous tip that the Russians had been "spirited away" if what had really happened was that the van had gone into the Pond, at least twelve people *had* really drowned there, and ten of those had been in cars. Making quick calls to the fire department and the rescue squad, he directed them out to Pond Road, then jumped into his own car, with Webster at his heels, and put on a Signal 10. By radio, he directed Tanner's crew back to man the office, and Sizemore's to join him at the site.

But at the Pond itself there was no sign of an accident. Peale and Tom Webster had traversed the length of the road once, slowly and carefully scanning the retaining fence for signs of damage, when a fire engine and the rescue squad arrived, and about ten extra cars behind them. The extra cars were full of those people who, as Peale had discovered since he became sheriff, felt it their sacred right and duty to see any accident that occurred in the county, in all its gore and misery, and they were disappointed, to say the least, when an accident wasn't evident. A number of them started honking their horns, and Peale had a momentary and vicious desire to arrest them all for obstructing a public thoroughfare. Instead, he sent Sizemore out to deal with them, and he himself conferred with the fire chief.

"Listen," said Peale. "This is very mysterious. It looks as if they've vanished into thin air." He explained the circumstances as he had discovered them and the absence of any accident. "Could they have jumped the fence somehow? Lifted in the air?"

"A van? On this winding road?"

"Is it possible?"

"I supposed it's possible, sure. But it'd have to be set up in advance."

"But it could be done."

"If there was a ramp . . . and they wasn't expecting it. I guess it could happen that way."

"But that would be murder."

"Oh, it sure would. I think you should call the state police."

The state police. How sweet that sounded. The state, the state police. But as Peale stood there, staring at the fire chief and trying to imagine what kind of operation it would have taken to set up a ramp on Felicity Pond Road just where the Russians were going to be passing this afternoon, and thinking, too, of the anonymous phone tip, and the business about disappearance and witchcraft, he had a strong conviction that this was all nonsense, and that something else entirely was going on. Granted that Mrs. Sizemore had been right, and the van had never made it to her side of the Pond; granted that it had been seen coming in; still, there must be *some* explanation. Although there wasn't a lot of room to turn around here, could the van by some means have done so? Or perhaps . . . he had the beginnings of an idea, but it stayed, for the

moment, merely that. Still, he decided not to call the state police
except for an APB; asking for more direct help could wait a few
more hours, or so he hoped.

"Not yet," he said. "Let's clear the area, and then search for
anything . . . odd."

"Like what?"

"How do I know? Out of the ordinary. Weird. I'll go west on
Pond Road."

And soon, just short of the Dickensens' pig farm, he found something very strange. A large truck, the kind that was used for light
moving and hauling, and with closed sides—not a cattle truck—
was parked haphazardly by the side of the road, with its left front
tire blown. A jack, with which someone had clearly intended to
change the tire, was lying next to the truck, and the spare, which
turned out to be flat as well, lay just behind the jack. There were
tracks in the dirt, both from the truck and from some other vehicle,
but unfortunately they had been quite eroded by the storm, and
little could be told from them. When Peale and Tom Webster
circled the truck, they found a hole in its side.

"A shotgun blast. It was done from inside."

"Today?"

"I don't know. Let's go see."

They climbed into the truck, being careful not to touch any
surfaces that might have taken prints. Inside they found, alarmingly,
five drops of dried blood, or what looked very much like it. But
certainly if anyone had been shot with a shotgun, a lot more blood
would have been loosed; there seemed to be still a slight powder
smell in the air, though that may have been only from the storm.

While Webster ran a make on the truck's license plate and radioed
for someone to come take fingerprints, Peale walked back along the
road toward the Pond, trying his damnedest to think. The Pond
was a strange place, and stories about it abounded, though they had
never before much impressed him. He had not been a particularly
imaginative child, and though he had learned, at the age of eight,
that it was at the Pond where that necking couple had *almost* been
caught and murdered by the man with the hook instead of a hand,

and that it was at the Pond also that anyone who spent the night went mad—"But I'm not crazy, I'm AAAARRRRGGGGGGHHHHHHH!!!"—these stories had only made the mildest of impressions, generic as they so evidently were.

Other stories, though, not quite so generic, had not troubled him either. If you looked into the Pond for more than an hour, staring deep into its deepest part, a dead body would float to the surface and sink, and then it would surface again. It would surface three times altogether, and the last time, it would come back to life, after which it would be sucked under forever. If you swam in the Pond anytime after the first of October and before the first of March, you would die within a year of that swim—by drowning on dry land. The Pond, the stories went, had been created by visitors from another galaxy, where the lifespan was ten thousand years; a few of these visitors were still hibernating at the Pond, where you wanted to be careful not to disturb them. And finally, perhaps most pervasive, were the stories about the times of the full moon; you could hear voices singing then, and people shouting. You could see figures dancing in the woods. Some of these figures wore stag horns on their heads, and were swathed in animals skins and strings of teeth; some of them, it was said, wore long white robes and linked arms in great circles around the trees. For the first time, Peale understood the lure of these stories—because life really *was* very strange.

Peale turned once more and walked back to his car, where Webster had gotten the truck owner's name.

"It's Howell Bourne, sir. Address in Felicity. I think he's got a farm outside of town."

"Howell *Bourne*?"

"That's right, sir. B-O-U-R-N-E."

"Oh, great. Oh, that's just terrific."

"Why?"

"Because his . . . well, I imagine it was his sister who came in to my office this morning. And then whoever called said *she* was the kidnapper."

"Well, that sure looks like a tie-in."

"Yeah. Listen. Call Tanner. Tell him to get out to the farm and question whoever's there—politely. Find out where Howell Bourne is supposed to be now, why his truck was abandoned, all that. You and I'll go to the sister's, see if we can get her to talk. And we'd better leave somebody here."

"Right."

"How about Sizemore?"

"Right, fine."

These assignments made, they headed back for Felicity. And while they drove, Peale figured out suddenly, in a flash of inspiration that led him absolutely nowhere, that the kidnappers—Howell Bourne, presumably, and whoever he was working with—must have forced the van to drive into the truck, and then unloaded it again after the blowout; that left the shotgun blast still unexplained, as well as the blood on the floor. And though it gave Peale a momentary rush of pleasure to have solved that impossible disappearance, a momentary rush was all he got, because the truth of it was that until the kidnappers called again, he could do nothing but sit around feeling helpless. He might, of course, persuade Bailey to talk; but what if she really was involved? Did he want her to talk so he'd have to arrest her? Oh, this was all the worst stuff yet. For although he didn't doubt that all his conclusions—about the way laws and prisons don't avert crime—were correct, these conclusions seemed of very little practical use when a crime was already in progress. Most men he knew would have been delighted to be investigating it, rushing around at top speed; that he did not feel so, but felt almost sad—well, what did that say about him?

Peale drove quietly down West Walnut Street, looking for 102. After she'd left his office that morning, he had looked up Bailey Bourne's address and committed it to his heart, and now, as he came upon her house this afternoon, he was hardly surprised at what he found. The street maverick, it lacked all the adornment that the other houses on the block felt pleasure in displaying, and though, in this, it contrasted mightily with its first-floor inhabitant— who was adorned up to the hilt every time that Peale had seen her—it seemed strangely fitting that her house should be so plain; it was, to Peale, the more alluring.

With as little fuss as he could, he parked a half a block past it; then he and Tom Webster made their way back—like cows, thought Peale, to a salt lick. And when they had knocked on the door and Bailey had, after a short pause, answered it, Peale could only be glad that Tom was with him to keep him from saying something foolish. Because Bailey looked to him as wonderful as ever; she had changed her clothes yet again, but her face could not, Peale felt, ever change. It would always make him feel the same amazement.

She did not smile at Peale or his deputy. She looked guarded and watchful.

"Hello," she said. "Is there anything wrong?"

"As a matter of fact, there is."

"What?"

"It's been reported that you are a . . . witch. The Russian professors have been kidnapped."

As he said this, Peale looked at his feet, trying to muster up a smile. He felt in anything but a smiley mood, though, and he just couldn't call one up at all. Bailey did not immediately answer; he felt her staring at his face. While he waited, he looked past her through the open door, and then looked again, and sniffed. Incense, she seemed to be burning incense—and the minute he had determined this, and determined, furthermore, that the shades on the living room window were drawn, something he had failed to notice as he approached the house, he was, on the instant, filled with the firm conviction that the woman was, in fact, practicing witchcraft. He had fallen in love, not only with someone who couldn't drive a car without ramming other people's headlights, not only with someone who dressed like an actress on location in the upper Sumali, but also with someone who thought she a witch; all the codicils faded into significance in light of the third, important, clause, which was, to Peale, of an alarming brightness.

"You'd better come in," said Bailey Bourne. "That's terrible."

# 22

TERRIBLE was not precisely the word for it, thought Bailey, as she stepped back to let the sheriff in. Incredible was a lot more like it, or maybe just simply impossible. What a day this had been—and looked still to be—and all because of stupid Howell. He had been, as far as she was concerned, totally out of control for the last month or so, ever since she had refused to sign that ridiculous paper he had brought her from the Dairy Shack, and she had decided in the aftermath of that to ask him for a lien against the farm. She had broached the topic one afternoon when both Charlene and Howell were in the kitchen, and his face had gone all round and red, and he had almost gurgled when he spoke. But she hadn't backed down; she had stuck to her point, though she hadn't done much about it since. When it came right down to it, where would she go? What should she do with her own life?

Still, when Charlene had called her that morning, early, she had thought it was about the lien. It had to be something important, after all, since Charlene never even *answered* the phone if she could help it, and she certainly never placed calls. So when Charlene, not one to waste words, had proceeded to announce that Howell was planning to "kidnap them Russians what was coming," it had taken Bailey a minute to catch on.

His plan, said Charlene, was to get them while they were touring, to put their car into his truck. Then he would take them some-where—Charlene didn't know where—and hold them for ransom until "they burned them mortgages. It's this Federal Reserve situation." Although these words had communicated nothing in particular to Bailey at first, gradually she had extracted from Charlene the information that Howell thought Russia was behind an international conspiracy to defraud all Americans of their farms, and that it was, as usual, simply inconceivable to Howell that people could be at the mercy of forces so complex that they were beyond any individual's control, as they were beyond any individual's understanding; he needed to think that everything had been planned if he was to deal with it at all. Charlene begged Bailey to help her somehow, to go perhaps to the sheriff. But she mustn't tell him what Howell was planning, or Charlene would end up getting blamed.

So Bailey had gone, as requested, to the sheriff, and tried her best to warn him—but he hadn't seemed to care, he'd been quite brusque about it, and he certainly hadn't taken her seriously at all. And now the thing had happened—and Howell was trying to blame *her!* What an ass he was! He deserved whatever he got! But what should she say to the sheriff?

"Just a minute," she said. "Before you come in. Actually, it's true, I'm a witch. Well, not really yet, but I'm *trying* to be."

"You're a witch?" said the sheriff, in an attentive tone.

"Not *quite*. But anyway, come in."

In the living room, the candles were still burning, and the incense cast a heavy pall. Sheriff Guthrie, who had told the other man to wait outside, stood looking dazed and embarrassed.

"A witch," he said. "Well, that explains a lot."

"But I didn't kidnap the Russians!"

"No, no, I imagine not. Your brother did, didn't he?"

"Probably. It's the kind of thing he would do."

"We found your brother's truck, abandoned by the road. Just on the other side of the Pond. And I think that he's taken the two of them to some hideout. You wouldn't have any idea where?"

"No, not really. I wish I did."

"Or any idea what he wants?"

"Well . . . yeah, I do. I think it's the mortgages. He wants to set all the farms free."

"Free?"

"Of debt. He thinks there's a conspiracy. But I'm afraid he's worried about me."

"Worried about you?"

"About what I'll do. I think he got it all mixed up in his mind."

As she said this, Bailey felt for the first time some sympathy for her brother, who lived in a terrible world. To be as paranoid as he was . . . it must be truly awful. She almost wished that she could help him. But the sheriff had now gone over to her altar and picked up the athame and the wand.

"Is this what it looks like?" he said, holding up the wand.

"I guess so. It's a wand, you know, for channeling."

"Channeling what?"

"Channeling energy. I'm not very good at it yet, I'm afraid."

"How do *you* know?" he asked, giving her a strange look.

"Well, I just . . . well, nothing seems to work."

To Bailey's amazement, she felt suddenly drawn to him, felt a rush of something like tenderness. He was really so attractive and somehow so vulnerable; he seemed very young to be the sheriff. She wished she could help him find where her brother was, or at least help him not have this problem. But she couldn't.

"I'm sorry. If I think of something else . . ."

"Yes, please get in touch with my office."

"I will."

"Fine."

"I'll call you right away."

"Good."

"Well, goodbye then, for now."

"Goodbye."

Peale turned—he gave her a last searching look—and then he hurried away. Bailey screwed up her face. Something odd had just happened. Or maybe it was all in her mind.

When the door closed, Bailey turned back to her altar, in front of which Chance was now sitting. Trying to get focused, Bailey stared at Chance, who was chewing on Bailey's Navajo rug—this was really Chance's only bad habit, her fondness for a good chew.

Whoever had owned her before she came to Bailey—and Bailey had long ago decided that that person must have been an old lady, an old lady who had died, leaving Chance without a home—had never sufficiently impressed on Chance that one had to chew selectively. And while Chance's teeth were very small, and her table manners very neat, she could still do a lot of damage to something if she was left with it for any length of time. The edges of kitchen cabinets were an especial delicacy, and anything made of fabric ran woodwork a close second—but Bailey's riding boots were also a real treat, as was all fine leather. Right now, Chance was carefully trying to extract a thread from the corner of the rug, the only valuable thing Bailey owned. "No, Chance," she said, surprising the dog deeply. She looked up in gentle mystification. Her mouth still held the damp thread, suspended, and her ears were cocked to the side. "No chewing rugs!" The dog, though clearly puzzled and unable to see the point, dropped the thread.

All right, so what should Bailey do now? She supposed she should cast a spell. That, indeed, was what she had been about to do when the sheriff arrived, and if there was ever a time when casting a spell was in order, now was certainly the time. But as she had said to the sheriff, she had begun, lately, to have doubts about her own abilities, and had decided that while it was all very well to say that the primary principle of magic is connection, and that what affects one things affects, in some ways, all things, there was no doubt that the discipline of moving energy was tricky and difficult, and that even if you *could* manage to do it, how could you know where it would lead? Since everything was interconnected—every thought, every action—every attempt to channel power could have bad consequences as well as good ones. And since she didn't really know what Howell was up to, what kind of a spell could she cast?

While she was thinking this, she got her book on witchcraft and sat cross-legged in front of her altar, where Chance climbed into her lap. She turned to the section on spells, and together they studied the pages; Bailey's eye went at once to "Binding Spell." This, she knew, was what she wanted. "A person who threatens the safety of others must be stopped," she read. "This is most safely done with a binding spell, focused on the image of preventing him or her from doing harm. The returning energy, then, will be basically protective. If you bind a rapist, you may find yourself prevented from committing rape, but if that interferes with your daily activities, you have no business practicing witchcraft anyway. The spell may work itself out in many different ways; the rapist may be caught and convicted or he could become impotent or even undergo a religious conversion. *How* it works is not your concern, as long as it accomplishes your goal."

The black humor of this passage seemed quite appropriate to her right now. Yes, this was certainly the spell, all right. She had to focus on Howell being stopped. But stopped from what? Well, from hurting anyone. From doing any further harm. But all spells that influenced another person depended largely on a psychic link, and in order for this connection to be made she would have to identify with her brother. She grounded and centered, then raised the cone of power and started to think about her brother. It was a long time since she had done this willingly, but she would have to do it willingly now. She closed her eyes and cast her thoughts back, to her childhood and thus to Howell's.

As a young girl she had naturally been inclined to adore her older brother, and there had been a time when she followed him around and tried to get in on his life. And she remembered now—how could she have forgotten?—that he had loved, just loved, playing dodge ball, which everyone else had absolutely hated; it rewarded both fear and nastiness. In dodge ball, one team would stand in the center of a circle made by the other team, and those in the center would try to dodge two incoming balls. Though Howell was not naturally agile, and, indeed, was poor at most sports, he seemed to have a preternatural awareness of where the balls would be coming from. Now, that seemed to Bailey quite apt, that Howell had been a champion at dodge ball. If there'd been a job that rewarded paranoia, Howell would have shot to its top.

She closed her eyes tighter and thought of Howell now, keeping Sam always on her chain. He thought that he was saving up energy, that life could store it until it was needed. He didn't understand that the more you used, the more you miraculously had; he thought you had to stand there, waiting for the balls, or that someone would hit you in the head. In a way, this thing he was doing, this kidnapping, was an amazing act; instead of waiting to be hit, he was *doing*. But that was what she had to stop. All she had to say to him was "Howell, get *normal*. Stop acting like someone you're not. Get *normal* Howell; brood and muse." But the funny thing was, she could not. Why, she admired her brother, really, for doing something so wildly dramatic. She admired him—and loved him. Yes, that was the truth. She loved him and wanted to help. He was stupid and exasperating, paranoid and slow, but he was her only brother. All hers.

At that point, she once again opened her eyes. The time had come to take action. She couldn't just sit around *here* all evening. Chance licked her—she seemed to agree.

It was now almost seven, close to the twins' bedtime, though in summer they sometimes stayed up later. Tonight, Bailey felt, they would surely be up; for one thing, the weather was still threatening. There was little point in going to sleep if a thunderstorm would just wake you up again. Out here, the remnants of the first storm still lingered; puddles riddled the driveway, and steam was rising off the field. Some branches had been downed, too, from one of the maples. The tires hit a few of them as Bailey drove toward the house.

Bailey parked the car, then called out to Jake, who was howling and bounding at her in greeting. Or perhaps at Chance; the minute the car door opened, Chance sprang out of her nest in Bailey's lap and raced down the driveway, her back feet kicking at the earth like a happy mule's, little explosions of puddle following in her wake. It was only when Chance arrived at the doghouses and was leaping around Jake in greeting that Bailey realized Sam was missing; her chain lay idle in the muddy ground. How very strange; why would Howell take Sam? Or perhaps she was sick or injured? But Charlene's sudden emergence from the house drove the speculation, for the moment, from Bailey's head, as Charlene called out, "The police been here!"

"They came to see me, too. What did you tell them?"

"Nothing," said Charlene. "That they didn't know already."

"We've got to figure out where he would take the Russians."

"He never said. I don't think he knew."

"Shit," said Bailey. "What a stupid thing."

"He's all riled up about the money. I told him the Nazis weren't exactly models, but he gets these things into his head."

"I know," said Bailey, regarding Charlene with some surprise— she had never said so much at once before. "Let me look at this pamphlet that Howell got the idea from. Maybe it'll help us figure out where he went."

In the kitchen, the supper things were unwashed, and the food was still sitting in the pans. The twins were not in evidence— presumably they had been put to bed when the police arrived, and thus gotten out of danger's way—and Charlene, looking around, seemed subtly alarmed, as if already saying goodbye to everything important. She grabbed her apron and pulled it between her hands, then nodded toward a stack of papers.

"That there," she said. "The one with Debts for the People."

"Charlene, did you tell Howell about the witch stuff?"

"No. Of course not."

"Hmm. I didn't think so." Bailey started searching through the papers.

On the top of the pile lay a copy of *Country Woman*, which Howell had given to Charlene as a present. It was just the kind of present he *would* give, Bailey had thought at the time, to someone who didn't much like to read—and it was, moreover, full of tips about "hubby," a kind of slave's manual. Of course, few of the tips were appropriate to Howell, atypical as he was. It was his biggest pride that he was a *thinking* farmer, with more on his mind than just grain yields. Bailey inadvertently flipped the magazine open, and had time to read: "A farm hubby can fix a combine in five minutes, recite the 4-H creed from twenty years ago, and project his fertilizer needs into 1992, but he can't remember his kids' birthdays or hit a towel bar at two feet if his life depended on it." That must have given Howell great satisfaction as he neatly folded the towel after his bath and hung it with exaggerated care on the metal towel bar next to the tub. Oh, he wasn't so bad. At least he *tried*. Unlike most of the louts he called friends.

Here was the pamphlet—published by Green Apple Press. Bailey leafed through it slowly. It seemed slightly more coherent than the usual tract of its kind, and it certainly had a lot more pages. But from what Bailey could see, nowhere did it advise capturing Russian professors and holding them for ransom as a way of solving the problem. It did say that "most of the owners of the largest bank in America are of East European ancestry and connected with the Rothschild European banks" and that "a debt-free America would mean mothers would not have to work." And Howell had bought this stuff. But where could he be? Bailey suddenly remembered Sam or, rather, her empty chain.

"Where's Sam, anyway?" she said.

"She came into heat this week."

"But she's gone. She's not out there."

"Some woman wanted a litter of hounds. I think he took her there today."

"*Today*? In the truck?"

"I think so. Yes, I'm sure."

"Then it's Ada! He took them to Ada's!"

Bailey couldn't have said just why she felt certain, but she knew, absolutely, that she was right. Howell had always been a great one for "killing two birds with one stone," as he insisted on putting it, and this would have struck him as a perfectly efficient action; simultaneously breeding his bitch and kidnapping some Russians. But if he'd taken them to Ada's, that meant Ada was in danger, and what was more, it was really Bailey's fault. If she hadn't suggested Sam as a possible mate for Boonskie, Howell would have taken his victims somewhere else. She had to get out there and talk her brother out of this, and she had to do it right now.

"Charlene, he's at Ada's, Ada Esterhaczy's. But don't tell anyone till you hear from me. I'm going out there."

"Good. Tell him to come home."

"I will. Bye-bye. And thanks."

"For what?"

"For telling me what was going on."

Bailey called Chance, who came charging up to join her, and the two of them climbed back in the car. As Bailey shoved it into gear, settling Chance, as she always did, behind her own seat belt, she thought again of that magazine *Country Woman*. In its bouncy list of things tht every country woman knew, it asserted quite regularly that "nothing takes the curl out of your hair and ruins your day quite like the frightening call 'The cows are out!' "; Bailey would have to submit to the editors' attention sometime the suggestion that something might be even more ruinous, to hair and day alike— the threat of having your farm "hubby" jailed because he had been stupid enough to listen to and take seriously the right-wing prop- aganda of Fascists who were clever enough to say Rothschilds when they meant Jews, knowing that poor saps like Howell didn't know a Jew from a hole in the wall and would probably mistake one for a Russian. For the first time in her life, Bailey started to get angry on Howell's *behalf*: it wasn't that he didn't try to think and under- stand; it was that these Bible-beating bigots were always there with their dubious explanations, their conspiracies and their "wicked- ness," preying on people who just wanted to find some reasons. She shot off down the drive and with a squeal turned west toward the Pond. Howell was her *brother;* he would have to listen to her now.

# 23

HOWELL stood in a corner of the living room, still feeling perversely out of sorts. He watched Ada Esterhaczy fill Mitch's and Billy Bob's glasses to the rim; they were sitting outside the front door, holding down the stoop, and knocking the stuff back like soft drinks. Howell himself was not much of a drinker—oh, he would have the occasional beer, but it didn't sit well on his stomach—so he merely looked at his own glass morosely and shook his head when Ada approached. Obviously, his two colleagues in this venture were getting sloshed to the gills, and Howell, while he would have liked to advise them to slow it down or stop it entirely in the interests of keeping a clear head, felt that he just didn't dare risk his precarious hold on their loyalties and patience. He should never have asked them in on this to begin with—everything that had gone wrong was Billy Bob's fault—and now they were having fun without him. Nothing ever changed. This was just like the circle jerk. He was the only one who ever acted at all *responsible*.

Howell had just realized the flaw in his scheme to blame Bailey for the Russians' "disappearance." While there was no doubt that this had provided a marvelous opportunity for him to get back at her, if the police believed that she had actually done the kidnapping, then where did that leave him? The whole *point* of this project, after all—a point that was apparently eluding Billy Bob at the moment, as his voice rose in a shriek of delight, recounting a dirty story about a bull—the whole *point* was to get all the mortgages in Rock County burned. To get that done, he would have to come forward, to announce his demands and his name; why he hadn't realized this he couldn't say; he felt let down by God.

On top of all that, there was this business about the Russians. Why, Howell hadn't imagined that they would even speak English—he didn't speak Russian, after all—and not only did they speak English, but one of them was a linguist. Right now, they were both talking with the Esterhaczy woman about his only language, Nicolai sitting straight and tall in his chair, Josef winking in that disconcerting way which almost engulfed his whole body.

"They have 'breech-loading' rifles," said Mrs. Esterhaczy indulgently.

"Oh, ho," said Josef, winking.

"But it is more international than any other language. That is why it excites me," said Nicolai.

"Air traffic control is all done in English," said Mrs. Esterhaczy's granddaughter.

"And four fifths of the world's computer data," said Nicolai.

"Russian scientific abstracts must all be published in English," said Josef.

"Well, good. Are you hungry? Shall we cook?" said Mrs. Esterhaczy.

At that, there was a general murmur of pleasure and approval, and the language talk came to an end. And as the women left the living room for the kitchen, where the clatter of pots and pans soon mingled with the sound of their voices, and Josef and Nicolai began conversing in Russian, leaving Howell more alone than ever, he still stood, unmoving, in his corner, wondering what to do next. He, Howell Bourne, had set all this in motion, and of that he could, he hoped, be proud; but unless he, Howell Bourne, brought it to the right conclusion, then he might just as well not have begun. He wished there was someone here he could really talk to—but there was no one, except for Richard Minot.

Well, Richard Minot would be a good person, probably; he was just sitting and reading that book. Howell craned his neck to see what it was. *Concluding Unscientific Postscript.* Getting up the courage, he moved closer to Minot and asked if he could talk with him for a moment.

Minot looked up, as if astonished. He seemed to have forgotten where he was. "Certainly," he said.

"Do you mind if I sit down?"

"Why not? You're running the show."

Howell sat, then stared at a spot on the wall.

"You're a doctor of philosophy, isn't that right?"

"My doctorate's in political science."

"But, I mean . . . you're a professor, an educated man."

"Certainly the first; I sincerely hope the second."

"What I mean is, to me it makes sense, this international conspiracy of bankers. It makes sense, that's all there is to it."

"Yes?"

"Well, but I mean . . . I'd appreciate your opinion."

"A lunatic theory, pure and simple."

Howell was having trouble formulating his thoughts; Dr. Minot was a hard man to talk to.

"So you think that it's not true?"

"I know that it's not true. And you've already signed up for a good long jail term. I don't imagine you want to make it longer."

"A jail term?"

"Of course. What do you *think* happens to criminals?"

"To criminals? Well. But I'm not a criminal."

At this, Dr. Minot just looked at him sardonically, and Howell got heavily to his feet. Somehow, this little talk had made him feel worse. Howell was certainly ready to admit that in the usual course of events people should be punished for their crimes, but this wasn't a *crime*—it seemed different in his case—there were clearly good reasons for what he'd done.

Outside on the stoop—where Mrs. Esterhaczy was even now taking another trip with the newly refilled decanter, like some perverse angel of mercy—Mitch and Billy Bob seemed to be having an altercation; their voices rose loud and strong. "Why do you care? You're not a farmer!"

"Yeah, I'm a lot too smart."

"Boys, boys! No fighting in *my* house!" said Mrs. Esterhaczy in a funny tone of voice.

Howell, however, had no desire to go out and see if he could calm things down. While one part of his mind was presently concerned with his long defense to the jury—"Gentlemen and ladies," he said. "I ask you; what would you have done? Wouldn't you have done just the same thing?"—another part of his mind was thinking about Bailey; he felt strangely ashamed of his recent phone call. She was, after all, his sister, and though almost from the time she had been born she'd been a trial to him, with that little soft spot in her skull, her hair already thick and curly, sticking out all over her head like the external evidence of the crazy ideas inside, there had been moments, he now remembered, when he'd really almost liked her. That time when she was eight and had set that pig loose in the woods—though naturally someone else had just found it. At the time, he hadn't been comfortable with killing yet, himself, and pigs were, well, pigs were very smart. And when she was a Girl Scout, and all excited about tying knots, he had taught her the half-hitch and the bowline. No, he really shouldn't have reported her to the police. Though he didn't quite know what he could do about it.

Mrs. Esterhaczy, returning from her latest trip to the stoop, poked her head back into the living room.

"Well?" she said to Howell. "What do we all do next? Will everyone still be here for dinner?"

"I think so," said Howell. "But don't go to any trouble."

"And the mortgages? When will the bonfire be?"

"I don't know. I haven't told them about the mortgages yet."

"So do. You must make some more phone calls."

"I guess I should."

"You must do it in the kitchen."

Almost wearily, Howell stumped across the floor, following the

rapidly moving Mrs. Esterhaczy. As he passed Nicolai and Josef—
who were leaning toward each other across the space between their
chairs, Josef emphasizing his points, not with winks this time, but
with one extended forefinger, which he slapped from time to time
against his nose—Josef broke off his conversation in Russian to say
to Howell "Good luck. You must tell them we are fine."

"We are getting on swimmingly. Living the life of Riley."

"Yes, that's nice," Howell replied.

With one hand, Howell held the telephone receiver; with the other
he rooted for Guthrie's number. Despite the heat, he had on his
best light jacket, a poplin khaki jacket with a zip, and in the pocket
was a small accumulation of papers, among them something that
felt like a pad. While he knew perfectly well that this, whatever it
was, could not possibly be Guthrie's number—which he had written
down first on the base of his thumb, and later transferred to a paper
scrap—he wanted to delay having to make the phone call, so he
let himself wonder what it was. Upon pulling it out, he discovered
that it was a tract he had picked up at his church about a month
before; on the cover were the words SOMEBODY GOOFED. Oh, yes,
he remembered this now. He had read it after getting home that
day, and had then stuck it back in his pocket, and now he stared
at it, thinking about its contents.

He supposed that it was intended to appeal largely to young
people, since it had a comic book format, and it featured Bill, a
high school student, whose best friend had just died of an over-
dose. Bill, curious about what had happened to his friend after he
died, asked a Christian who was standing nearby, and the Christian naturally told him. He said that Bill's best friend had gone
to Hell, and that he in his turn would go there too, unless he
chose, sometime before he died, to accept Christ as his personal
savior.

But then *another* man—Mike—said all that was nonsense, that
all you had to do in your life was to obey the Golden Rule and the
Ten Commandments, to treat others as you would wish to be treated;

then, everything would be all right. Mike, furthermore, said that there *was* no Hell, that if God was a god at all, He was a god of love, not of punishment and hate, and He would never put anybody into a hell.

Well, this made sense to Bill, who rode around with Mike in Mike's fancy car for a while—Mike was good-looking in a rugged, craggy sort of way—until Mike decided to drive straight in front of a train, and the car was hit and smashed to a pancake. The next frame in the comic book showed a really good rendition of Hell, with lots of flames and pitchforks and so on, and Bill, dazed, asking, "Where am I? Is this *Hell?* Why am I here?" At that, Mike—who looked, as Howell studied him now, a little like Kirk Douglas, actually—said, "You're here because you didn't accept Jesus Christ as your personal lord and savior."

And Bill said, "But that's not fair! I thought all you had to do was be good! Somebody goofed!" Here, the good-looking Mike ripped off his good-looking mask, to reveal that underneath its fair surface he was really the Devil himself, who had been tempting the young man all along. Now, he roared as he jabbed him with a pitchfork, "Yes, indeed! YOU goofed!"

When he had learned that his church was handing this out, Howell thought it a good idea, but now, still holding the phone receiver with one hand, he wondered if that was true. The whole thing seemed just a little *extreme*, a little, well, a little *arbitrary*. Certainly he had always believed that anyone who wasn't a Christian would, necessarily, have to go to Hell—that was just the way it was, it was a simple law of nature, there was nothing that anyone could do about it—but now he wondered about the whole concept of punishment, which he had never really wondered about before. What was the point of it? *Was* there a point to it? It didn't help people to *learn*. And if you had a brain, you could learn from experience, which was better than going to jail or Hell. Actually, there might be more excuse for jail than there was for Hell, when you thought about it seriously, since there were people who were just so dangerous that they couldn't be allowed to wander around the world loose while they were alive, but after they were dead they could hardly pose a threat.

Feeling seriously unnerved, he dialed Guthrie's number. Now he wanted to just get this over with.

The phone rang six times before it was picked up, but then the same voice as before answered it. "Guthrie residence. Ryland speaking. May I help you?"

Ryland? Was that the sheriff? "Yes," said Howell, feeling ill. Could he have somehow called the wrong man?

"Is this the man? The same man I spoke with earlier?"

"Oh, yes," said Howell. "It's Howell Bourne."

Once he got started, he found it fairly easy to explain the whole situation. First, he told the sheriff to lay off his sister Bailey, that she was not really involved. The sheriff said "Hmmm," but nothing else, so Howell went on from there. He gained eloquence as he expounded on the fact that he represented all the farmers in Rock County, and clarified that he had kidnapped the Russians to draw attention to the plight of the American farmer, a plight that was the direct result of a little-known international conspiracy. At this point Guthrie interrupted him to ask why these conspirators wanted the farmland, and it took Howell a moment to remember that it was because they wanted to get as rich as possible, and when Guthrie went on to ask how getting farmland, which was dropping daily in value, was going to make them rich, Howell had to climb over the question in his mind, as if it were a haystack—and finally finished with the business about the mortgages. There. It was finally out.

"I see," said the voice on the other end of the phone. "And where are you holding the hostages?"

"You don't have to know that yet. Just get the deeds together."

At this point, Mrs. Esterhaczy, who had been pouring boiling water into a teapot full of some sweet-smelling herbs that were filling the air with a fragrant steam, came over toward Howell, and said loudly and enthusiastically, "Very well done! Tell them to bring us more sherry!"

Bewildered, Howell stared at her in silence. Then he said "Good-bye" and hung up the phone.

"I am truly impressed," said Mrs. Esterhaczy. "Truly. You are like me, you have missed your calling. A homespun cherry pitter, you and ideas. You should have gone to university!"

Howell had trouble understanding this statement, and the relevance, at the moment, of cherry pitters, since in the distance he was hearing a strange noise that sounded suspiciously like a car turning in the driveway. As the noise grew louder, there was no longer any doubt; a car was certainly coming.

"Excuse me," he said. "I'd better go check," and he nodded and went out. Once there, he felt flabbergasted; the engine was Bailey's, a frequency that he knew well. But never had the sound of its approach brought to him so confusing a mixture of feelings, and as he pushed his way across the porch through air that seemed almost dense, he didn't know why he felt so happy and so frightened all at once. At the kitchen door behind him, Boonskie was pacing back and forth, eager to be let out—*thump thump thump, thump thump thump* was the sound of his paws pacing, then he picked up a handy shoe and dropped it—and on the grass, Sam sat glumly; she made a halfhearted effort to say hello to him with her tail, but her recent deflowering had apparently taken all the heart out of her for the moment, so it was in an eerily barkless silence, and an eerily heavy light, that Howell waited for the arrival of his sister's car. To Mitch and Billy Bob, who had, for the moment, ceased arguing and were now singing snatches of bawdy songs—and who stood up looking threateningly toward the sound of the car, which must have reached their ears long after it had reached Howell's—he called out, "It's OK, I think it's my sister coming," at which point they sat down again and sprawled their legs out in front of them.

Never since Howell, at the age of eight, had awaited Bailey's advent into the world, had he felt so strongly that his future was hanging on what Bailey did or didn't do. He was unusually aware of his own physical body, and the blood that was flowing all through it; that blood seemed to have been galvanized somehow, starting with the little puddles that usually accumulated in his feet when he stood in his "conversational stance" for any length of time, and moving up his arms and legs and into his body core almost like one of those ads on television that demonstrate the way the whole circulatory system works, and the way a particular product can bring "quick relief." Bailey knew he was here, and if she knew, the world knew. But why had they sent *her* upon his trail?

# 24

W H E N   T H E   P H O N E   R A N G for the second time that evening, Ryland had just emerged from the basement. He had stayed there, with Molly, much longer than he intended to—the cool dry air was so calming and the muffling effect of the floors so pleasant. Moreover, Molly had been so flattered by his visit that he couldn't bear to leave her. As he held her to him, sniffing her black and white fur and scratching her rump, while she wiggled with pleasure and his tears gradually dried, it occurred to him that he and she were a lot alike, both master players of Catastrophe.

He remembered one of his recent fantasies now with a shame-faced sense of embarrassment. Driving toward Richmond the other day, he had gotten behind one of those large trailer trucks that transport cars from state to state, and that always, to him, looked shakily loaded, with the cars held on just by chains. In his fantasy, the topmost car, the one on the ramp, had come down right in his path when its chain broke, and he had smashed into it and been completely crippled; he had become a paraplegic. Paralyzed so completely that the only muscle control he had was of his eyelids, he had nonetheless discovered that life, whatever its restrictions, was something he wanted to hang on to, and this had surprised him, but it had been a pleasant surprise; how lucky he was to be alive! One day, however, Maggie—no longer his girlfriend, but still a friend—had asked him if he would prefer to die, and had gone on to say that if he *would*, he should blink twice, but if he *wouldn't*, he should blink once, and naturally he had gotten nervous and all tensed up as she waited compassionately for his answer. So nervous had he been that, after carefully blinking just once, putting into the gradual descent of his eyelids all the attention of his being, he had *accidentally* blinked a second time, and she hadn't asked him again. So as he drove along to Richmond behind the tractor trailer, he was also lying in bed waiting to be murdered; his breath had come fast, his palms had sweated, and his heart had clobbered his chest.

But there in the basement, holding Molly, her friendly, hopeful self for the moment in ascendance over her dark, psychotic self, her mouth open in an apologetic way, as if she were seeking his forgiveness—forgiveness for her own insanity, which was crueler than *he* could ever be—he felt embarrassed at this memory of his own self-torture when there were those who had real reasons for their fears. Why, he had wasted so much of his life engaged in fruitless thoughts of disaster; he vowed again that from now on it would be different, if only he got Maggie back unharmed.

At last he let Molly go and emerged upstairs into the kitchen. As he closed the door behind him, the phone began to ring, and he ran out to pick it up. He knew it would be, again, the kidnappers. And as the man on the other end moved from the initial announcement of his name—Howell Bourne—to his plea that the sheriff lay off his sister Bailey, who was "not really involved," and finally into his weird and almost incomprehensible explanation of the international conspiracy, Ryland felt more and more incredulous and relieved. This guy was too loony to be dangerous. But the sister, on the other hand—he wasn't sure about her. He remembered her as genuinely strange.

"I see," he said. "And where are you holding the hostages?"

"You don't have to know that yet. Just get the deeds together." In the background a voice said, "Very well done! Tell them to bring us more sherry!" The voice that said this was awfully familiar. The voice . . . it sounded like Ada's.

Ryland, who had been standing, suddenly sat down, still clutching the receiver to his ear. How could it have been Ada? How could it have been anyone else? Her accent was probably the only one like it in the entire state of Indiana, and when Howell Bourne, apparently done for the moment with acting as the representative of what now appeared to be a whole consortium, said "Goodbye" and hung up the phone, Ryland did not follow suit. The tone in which Ada had spoken, and the words that she had used, were really not open to any interpretation other than the one Ryland so badly did not want to put on them—that she was one of the driving forces behind the craziness this evening.

And while, of course, Ada *was* Hungarian, and presumably had resented it fiercely when the Soviet Union had invaded her homeland and run it like a puppet state, he would never have imagined that she would do *this!* And Maggie had even less reason. Though if the kidnapped Russians were at Ada's, and Ada was involved, even Ryland could see that there was no reasonable explanation for Maggie's concomitant disappearance in the Saguanay's van other than one that suggested her as prime kidnapper. How *could* she, with her political views, possibly want to do this? Why, it was Maggie who had alerted Ryland to the unbelievable danger of nuclear war, a danger that, in all the dangers of the world, he had somehow failed to grasp properly until she had pointed it out to him. And those BB's and everything. What a noise they had made! His ears were practically still ringing.

And if she had done it, why hadn't she *told* him? Why hadn't she invited him to come along? Oh, it was hard to discover that he had spent the last hour or so grieving for Maggie when she was not only not in danger, but had deceived him from the start, when she had, really, almost gypped him. People were just . . . oh, people were horrible. And *now* what should he do?

The maid came in with some empty serving trays and set them down by the sink.

"Shall I serve dessert, sir? They seem to be ready."

"Oh, sure," said Ryland, but hollowly. Actually, it seemed to him suddenly well-nigh inconceivable that fine as his food and wine undoubtedly were, and hard as he had worked to put his guests at ease this evening, those same guests had not, by now, departed; but the fact remained that they were still here. The near death of one of their number—Ryland had not yet called the hospital to check on the status of Mrs. Wickenden, and he hoped fervently that the near death had become no worse—that terrible accident on the Tree of Life rug, coupled with the complete disappearance of the guests of honor, two citizens of another country, whose vanishing would certainly have consequences well beyond Felicity; why, these had just given them something to talk about, a marvelous boon at a party. Indeed, though Ryland had had many formal parties not unlike this one when he and April had been married, he had trouble remembering any that had been more full of animated, interested people, if the sounds through the closed kitchen door were any guide. Even the lugubrious Russian music that Amanda had, at his request, kept playing, had failed to dampen the enthusiasm; nor had the heat and the lowering weather, which seemed to have something yet in store.

As he sat there watching the maid place petits fours on a silver platter, he still hadn't decided what to do. On the one hand, it seemed clear that he should inform the sheriff that he had deduced the whereabouts of the kidnapped party, and let the sheriff take it from there; on the other hand, since the sheriff was Peale, well, maybe that wasn't the best idea. As the maid went through the door to the hall, pushing it open with her hip, Ryland jumped to his feet and followed her out; at least he would talk to Amanda. When he found her, she was calmly conversing with a very old man with a hearing aid—the sure sign, in Ryland's experience, of an advocate of a world beyond war. But that was, apparently, not the subject at hand now, which appeared to be Friends of the Library.

Ryland had, of course, never much liked Amanda, who shared with his brother Peale a quality of remoteness from the tribulations of everyday life that was even more irritating than it was in Peale, because she took it to greater lengths. But he disliked her even more than usual now as she regarded him with placid interest.

"Listen, Amanda, I've gotten another call. Peale hasn't been back here, has he?"

"No, I haven't seen him. We also have Teas." This last was addressed to the hearing aid.

"Well, thanks," he said, rather sarcastically, and then returned to the phone.

The sheriff's office had not heard from Peale since his partner had called in to ask for data on a license plate, and though for a moment Ryland was tempted to ask them to try to raise him on the radio, and to tell him that his brother had discovered the location of the missing people, he quickly decided against that course, which would broadcast the news to the world. Although he knew that Peale would eventually have to be told that the Russians and their captors were at Ada's house, Ryland certainly didn't want to tell his deputies; they would probably charge out there, guns blazing, like their favorite characters on TV.

Then, for the first time, it occurred to Ryland that he might take care of this himself. Why, who knew the principals better than he did; who could better "talk them down"? If he sent Peale and his compadres out to Ada's house, where the kidnappers were no doubt standing guard with guns, everyone might get excited and upset, and somebody might get shot—but even if they didn't, Peale would have to arrest them. Arrest Maggie and Ada as well. And though Ryland was angry with them for not having involved him, he loved them both too much for that. If Ryland went out there, they certainly wouldn't shoot him, or do anything bad to him at all—and he could take along the sherry Ada had requested. He was sure he had some about. Perhaps he would even take some other gifts, too, for the rest of the conspirators, to placate them; most especially for that Bailey Bourne, who, he had no doubt, was also there. He had some idea that lunatics could be placated with gifts of sufficient size. Perhaps something from the store? A piece of furniture? Well, he would think it out on the way.

All at once, Ryland himself felt animated, quite vibrant and pleased, in fact. Now that he had a straightforward course of action outlined, and one, moreover, that would permit him to get the jump on Peale, not in the privacy of his own lingering fantasies—in which, from time to time he would, for example, replay a particular childhood Christmas so that he got all the presents and Peale got none—but right out in the open, where everyone could see it, he felt actually braced. Though he would have preferred not to let Peale know anything at all about what was going on, he compromised with this feeling by writing him a note and informing him of the present situation. Marking it FOR YOUR EYES ONLY, he sealed it and then took it to Amanda; she was still reviewing fund-raising methods with her hard-of-hearing friend.

"Give it *only* to Peale. Or if he calls, you can tell him about it." She nodded dreamily and put it in her purse. Ryland went back to the kitchen to give the maid some final instructions regarding the coffee maker; then, remembering Ada's request for sherry, he went back into the dining room, where his liquor cabinet was located, and was happy to find there a full bottle of Harvey's Bristol Cream. He also discovered, standing by the sideboard, Dr. Ludgar, of all people, and though the last time he had had anything to do with this man had been when he had kept Ryland waiting in his office for almost forty-five minutes before disappearing into the blue to take care of what he called an emergency, perhaps it was that very word "emergency" that, by a natural association of ideas, made Ryland wonder whether this wasn't a happy encounter. For all he knew someone might be hurt, might be lying in Ada's back bedroom at this moment, and though Ada was the best doctor in the world when it came to health, actual health, when it came to gross abnormalities—wounds—Ludgar and his ilk were in their element. At another time, Ryland would certainly not have asked him, would have let his own distaste for the doctor subsume any feelings of concern for others, but with Maggie involved, he was less cavalier— and was, anyway, extremely excited.

So, roughing in the broadest outlines of the situation, first swearing the doctor to secrecy, he asked Dr. Ludgar to come along with him, to which the doctor agreed at once. He said only that he should get his bag out of his own car first and though it had been so long since Ryland had seen a doctor's bag that he had thought they didn't make them anymore, when Dr. Ludgar met him at his car a few minutes later, there the bag really was. He set it carefully down on the floor in the back, and then climbed into the car, where Ryland was waiting, fully in place, with the engine already running. And while he gunned off down the street, Dr. Ludgar silent beside him, he promised himself that when he next saw Maggie, he would immediately ask her to marry him. He would continue to take risks, he would not measure everything, he would imitate his own son, Clayton. Why, Ada had told him that happiness was an art, that you had to practice and encourage it; you couldn't just expect it to walk up to you in the park, like a tame cow offering you a haunch!

Before heading out to Ada's, Ryland drove to the store, where he could pick up an appropriate gift. The idea that Bailey Bourne—who, though Ryland had met her only once, had made a striking impression—the idea that she, with her seemingly limitless capacity for fraudulence, was at the bottom of this somehow, had taken by now a fixed hold on Ryland's mind. It was a lot easier to believe that *she*, rather than Ada or Maggie, was the mastermind, and as wrought up as he presently was, what might have some other time been merely a passing fancy—that lunatics could be placated by the proper choice of offering—was, right now, an inspiration. The store was closed this evening, and the van was missing at the moment, but as long as he chose something that wasn't too big, he could put it in the trunk of his Mercedes.

Dr. Ludgar, when Ryland explained his thinking, seemed slightly doubtful about the impulse, but he didn't argue. "It's up to you. You know these people best."

So Ryland drove to the store, and as he parked—just across the street from the courthouse thermometer, COURTESY OF SANGU ANAY'S FUNERAL HOME, which, he had no doubt, was still reading exactly seventy-two degrees, a morsel of certainty in an uncertain world—he noticed that the weather, which should have been completely cleared up by the fine fierce storm they had had late that afternoon, was still lowering and strange, with the sky a muddy yellow color. When he parked in front of the store, he looked at his watch. It was only seven-thirty, and the sun, this late in May, would not be setting for a while—but it seemed, right now, almost dusk.

Saguanay's was well lit at all times, and as the light outside was dusky, its windows shone now with the warm orange glow that seemed to Ryland to summarize order. He asked Ludgar to wait, saying he'd be only a minute, and then let himself in the front entrance of the store, where two glass doors with brass tongue latches sparkled invitingly, and where the vestibule—lined with slate and bedecked with a Turkish Dosmealti—welcomed him graciously. He took a deep breath, the smell of leather and fine cotton, silk and brass and wood, wafting toward him in a cloud of consummation.

Now for the witch. What should he take her? Wasn't it country estate they had finally agreed on? So country it would be, some beautiful bit of country. But the armoire was simply too big. The wooden sleigh with the birch logs in it might have been all right had it been autumn, but as it was spring it would seem a little tacky. How about the brass cauldron with the ficus tree? *That* would be more like it—after all, witches had a reputedly inexhaustible need for cauldrons—but as he thought about it, he seemed to recall that she had bought one at the Widau auction that day. Not a gorgeous piece of Yugoslavian craftsmanship like this one, but still, she already had one.

The thought of the auction reminded him of the sword, the Sword of Communism he had bought there. After Clayton had discovered that it was not, in fact, the Sword of Communism, he had lost all interest in it, and he told Ryland that he really didn't want it, so Ryland, having no particular use for a sword in his home, had brought it down to the store, where it now hung boldly on the wall above a leather couch, in a display that had proved so popular in the front window that he had brought it inside, enlarged it, and labeled it A MAN'S PRIVATE DEN. Right next to Thomas Saguanay's breech-loading rifle, which was not for sale, the sword glittered temptingly, above its own tag: *Antique. Early American. $250.00.* He had hoped it would sell immediately, but in the time since, he had grown rather fond of it, and now it occurred to him, with a flash of genius, that probably witches used swords, too. Why, of course! It was perfect! He would bring Bailey Bourne the sword. He hurried to lift it down from the wall.

Then, however, he hefted its weight and balance, and realized that this was actually a weapon. Under the present circumstances, it would probably not do to drive up to Ada's house, park his car at the trellis, and emerge from the driver's seat holding a sword; gift or no gift, it would probably scare them. He would have to take something else. But he had gotten so attached to the idea of the sword as a gift that he was reluctant to let it go; perhaps it would be wise to take two gifts, the one to follow the other. After the first one had paved the way, he could bring out the sword as the second. The first could be anything that came to hand—a lamp, a small table, or a chair. Suddenly aware that time was pressing, and having in any case satisfied his own sense of the appropriate by his magnificent choice of the sword, he looked vaguely around for a chair of some sort, with country estate still on his mind. The first chair that he saw that could in any way have been considered country was large and overstuffed, with a one hundred percent cotton English chintz slipcover. Moving toward this with immediate decision, he bent over and grasped it by the arms. It was heavier than he had anticipated and also somewhat larger, but he bent down the second time a good deal farther and took it around the back. This time, it lifted into the air, and he was able to struggle it out of the store.

Dr. Ludgar was waiting by the side of the car, and he came now to Ryland's assistance. Together they managed to situate the chair in the trunk of the Mercedes, although Dr. Ludgar looked even more doubtful than ever about the efficacy of this whole idea; then

Ryland darted back into the store for the sword, and locked the doors behind him. And while Ryland didn't delude himself into thinking that his presents, chosen with whatever amount of care and consideration, would make everything all right, he thought, well, after all, *everyone* loves to get presents. And he had sherry and a doctor with him, too!

# 25

THIS WAS MORE than bizarre, thought Maggie as she cooked; it was freakish, maybe just plain silly. Since Bailey had arrived twenty minutes earlier, bringing the total number of human bodies at the house to ten—undoubtedly the most people who had ever been here at once since the construction crews had built the place fifty years or so before—she and Howell had been out near the trees, talking, it seemed, quite intently. Howell looked dazed and unhappy, and completely at a loss, the most miserable person present. Mitch and Billy Bob were as drunk now as lords, as drunk as Ada could make them, but they were still, unfortunately, alert enough to stand. To someone of Maggie's temperament, someone who had spent the bulk of her days on this planet waiting for species extinction, there was little reason to be sanguine in the presence of drunken, inept men, and certainly no cause to relax. But she seemed to be the only person present who felt that way; the incompetence and indecision of the kidnappers aside, what made this occassion so genuinely absurd was how gay everyone else seemed to be. Those ridiculous Russians, Ada, and Minot—did they think they had come to a party?

Maggie was still pretty angry with Ada for having scared her so badly. That moment at the Pond, when she had been sure she was going to die—and had even gone so far as to imagine, for a moment, her own simple funeral, with Ada and Ryland standing by, weeping—might have happened anyway, even if Ada hadn't been involved. But since Ada *was*, it seemed logical for Maggie to feel a certain resentment, though logic, as such, was rarely a feature of anything with which Ada was connected. In any case, Maggie was far too worried now *about* Ada to be all that angry *with* her; even if they all got out of this unscathed, Ada could still be arrested. She clearly did not realize this, though, and as she and Maggie stood side by side, pinching noodles off a lump of dough and tossing them into boiling water, Ada was more in her element than Maggie had ever seen her—making a Hungarian meal for ten.

"Isn't this fun?" she said.

"Fun? Are you crazy?"

"Oh, my brat, will you never learn to laugh?"

"I can laugh just fine, thank you, when there's something to laugh at."

"And life? Life does not make you laugh?"

"Listen, Ada, do you know what you've done? You've gotten involved in a *conspiracy*. You could go to jail."

"An old woman like me?"

"Old woman, my foot. You're a terror. Just tell me *why* you thought this was such a good idea."

"Oh, the Russians. I came to hate them when I was only a girl. During the Commune, when Béla Kun and his Bolshevik butchers took over Hungary some soldiers burst into a family's home on the outskirts of Szatymas—a family not of our class, but respectable peasants, after all—and demanded that they be served liquor, at once. The family had no liquor—it had four daughters, no sons— and when the father told them this, the soldiers would not believe it, and they ransacked the house for drink. But there was none— all they could find was a cleaning fluid that had in it—what was it?—wood alcohol. So *this* they mixed with milk from the family's dairy house, and they drank it, and of course they all went crazy. They raped the mother and the four daughters, one by one, and they finished by raping the man. Well, I ask you. Do you blame me if I despised them? But not these, of course. They are gentlemen."

Something about this story made Maggie feel very sick, literally sick to her stomach. She was stirring the chicken paprikash, and the smell of it was suddenly horrid; she had to turn away and cover her face.

"Are you all right?" said Ada.

"Jesus, Ada, how sickening. Do you think we can talk about something else?"

"But you brought it up! You wanted to know why I did this!"

"So now I know, so let's change the subject, all right?"

"All right, Miss Princess. Would you like me to make you some tea?"

"Yes, thanks. That would be very nice."

While Ada put on more hot water, Maggie sat down in a chair, feeling, strangely enough, still rather sick. Well, no wonder that she did, with all that had been happening. She wished that she could just go right to sleep. Under the table, Boonskie was sleeping, and she studied him, trying to distract herself from nausea. Right now, he was dreaming; stretched on his side, with his legs drawn up slightly inward toward his chest, and his chin tucked down in the same direction, his paws were flapping rapidly on their stems, and small shudders swept quivering through his ribcage. It was a bad dream, this time, Maggie could tell—sometimes, when he enjoyed his dreams, there was a manly, assertive quality to his *grrfff*'s, quite unlike any of the sounds he made when he was awake—but often, as now, he was alarmed by his dream events, and his sounds were little yelps of fear. Maggie reached her hand out and gently ran it down his ribs.

"It's all right, kiddo, it's just a dream." His eyes opened blearily, and then wide, and he lumbered to his feet and stuck his nose into her stomach, letting her rub and fondle his ears.

Although Maggie was hardly the fanatic that Ada was, there *was* something special about Boonskie. It was impossible not to attribute to him the generosity one assumes of Fools. The sweetness with which he would immediately sit down when there was a biscuit offered, hoping that it wouldn't be noticed that he was actually still a quarter of an inch from the floor, the whole of his lower body resting in a powerful haunch-sit that was quite illusory; the respect that he accorded all visiting cats, who held a powerful attraction for him that was wholly untinged by aggressiveness, and the astonishment that he manifested when he was again, for the umpteenth time, rebuffed by such cats, who entirely misinterpreted his friendly advances—to see such a large and powerful dog wagging his tail and thrusting his nose out toward a cat in hopeful anticipation, when dogs much smaller would have hustled right in, growling—the enthusiasm with which he would spring into the air, all four paws coming off the ground at once, when a walk or other special excursion was offered; well, he was a very *emotional* dog, with an exaggerated quality to all his feelings. When he was hurt— when he had a small cut in a pad, or had somehow acquired a little limp—he would lie in a corner of the room swathed in a perfect miasma of self-pity, radiating wounded sorrow, as if whoever else was in the room was certainly, though he hated to mention it, responsible for this tragedy, and at such times his lap-sits lost their comical aspect and became desperate attempts to return to the womb, where nothing like this had ever happened.

Maggie assumed that it was this emotionality which made him seem so human, although the truth of it was, he was far *more* emotional than most human beings she had known. He seemed, in a way, to be the essence of the human, the comic and the tragic combined, and he reminded one always of how very special dogs were in the overall scheme of life on earth. They had done, after all, what all other animals since time began had been too sensible, and too cautious, to do; they had decided to become friends with *man*, of all creatures—and only a saint or an idiot would do that.

Now, Boonskie was sitting in his illusory haunch-sit as Ada prepared him a little snack. First, she set down in front of Maggie a mug of the special tea that she had grown fond of, and Maggie took a sip of it, relieved to find that her nausea was now entirely gone. Then she watched while Boonskie inhaled a plateful of Hungarian pinch noodles, and sat back on his air cushion, eager for more, which Ada naturally provided him.

"You've had a hard night, haven't you, darling? Yes, you must have some good nourishment."

Maggie drank down the rest of the tea in one long gulp, and then got up to set the table. She noticed that, outside, the little dog that Bailey Bourne had brought with her was playing with Sam—Raga was still locked in the barn—and she heard from the next room the sounds of hilarity as Josef and Nicolai conversed. Maggie had to get Howell to assert that Ada had known nothing about any of this— and if nothing further happened, she was confident the Russians could be persuaded not to press charges. She poked around in a drawer until she found ten forks, then set ten mismatched plates around the table. Ada had just gone to the bathroom, so she went over to stir the chicken—and once again the smell revolted her. Feeling nauseated, she turned away in disgust. Boonskie looked at her, quite concerned.

Well, this was very strange, strange and highly unpleasant; moreover, it reminded her of something. Some other time in her life, some time when she'd been sick. Or, no, she hadn't been sick, exactly. No, she'd been . . . when was it? Maybe ten years or so before? Well, yes, she'd been sick . . . she'd been pregnant. She'd been pregnant! Oh, my God. And now she was pregnant again. And it hadn't once before occurred to her.

No, no, she couldn't be pregnant. So what if her period was late? She often misssed it altogether. And, except for that first night with Ryland, she had been using her diaphragm quite regularly. And that first night she had certainly been post-ovulatory. Why, if it hadn't been late in her cycle, she would never have done it—even though she was still hysterical about the Beyond War meeting— what was she, some kind of naïve teenager? But all this, she knew, was profoundly beside the point; she was pregnant again, like a fool. She sat down on the floor, too stricken even to stand; Boonskie immediately sat in her lap.

The first time Maggie had gotten pregnant, she had had a terrible time of it, a time that came flooding back to her now. Twenty years old and using an IUD, she had naturally not considered the possibility that she might not be one of the ninety-nine percent of women for whom the IUD was an entirely effective birth control device, but might instead be part of that statistically inconsequential group for whom it wasn't. But she had known, nonetheless, within days of getting pregnant, that that was, in fact, what had happened. To compound her problem, though, her urine test hadn't worked— it repeatedly came up negative—and though she knew for certain she was pregnant, her doctor had not believed her, relying entirely on his science rather than on her. In fact, she had been almost twelve weeks pregnant, and had entirely *recovered* from her morning sickness—which, perversely enough, never occurred in the morning, but always around dinnertime, just as it was occurring now—and her breasts had been swollen as large as melons when his little piece of paper finally turned red. The doctor, with great surprise and little apology, had finally admitted that she might be pregnant after all and not delusional, as he had thought her. Then, sadly, he had told her that she was too close now to the deadline for a legal abortion—and that he really didn't think he could perform one.

Finally, she had found a doctor who would, and had felt like kissing his feet, so grateful was she for his intercession. Being pregnant was far and away the most disturbing thing that had ever happened to her; she felt as if her body had been invaded by a creature from outer space, a kind of Puppet Master or Body Snatcher, and the double coincidence of being one of those women for whom an IUD was a puny defense against the iron grip of a determined zygote and also being one of those women on whom a urine test didn't work had really made her very bitter. The day she got her abortion had been one of the happiest days of her life, and the unembellished fact was that she had never felt one moment's regret about it since; she strongly suspected that all this brouhaha about the great grief that women felt when they were driven by circumstances to have to perform this heinous act was just a hypocritical, but natural, attempt on the part of various women's groups to preserve the right to their *own* lives in the face of the determined and richly financed campaigns of those who would remove it. However that might be, Maggie herself, when she had woken up from the anesthetic—so late had the abortion been performed that she had had to have full anesthesia—had lain between the clean white sheets, sensing the emptiness inside her with a feeling of absolute bliss. She had vowed then that she would never again get pregnant—and now she had broken that vow.

At this point, Ada came back from the bathroom. "What are you doing on the floor?"

"I'm thinking."

"Oh, yes? Thinking of what?"

"I'm thinking that I've somehow gotten pregnant."

"It usually happens in just one way, my pumpkin."

"Well, that's the way it happened."

"So why do you sit on the floor with the dog?"

"Because this is really *all* I needed."

"So I have often told you. Well, what wonderful news!"

"What do you mean? It's the worst news I've had in over a decade!"

"To have a pink-cheeked baby? This is terrible news?"

"I'm not going to *have* a pink-cheeked baby!"

"But why not? They are lovely. They have faces just like little flowers."

"Let's just grow some little flowers instead."

"Now, Maggie, it is just so sudden. You need time to get accustomed."

"No, I don't. I'm not going to have it, and that is that."

Ten minutes later, as she gathered the troops for dinner, she felt just the same way. The human race, as this incident tonight demonstrated so plainly, was simply an aberration of nature, a kind of grotesque collection of psychos and felons, with chaos moving always in its wake—dogs, now, well, if she could have a dog, that might be something worth considering. Standing in the living room door, Maggie found that the party was still going strong; Johnson, who had, the last time she'd seen him, been slumped over the desk in an attitude of despair, had obviously been coaxed by the others to try to drink something bracing, and now was sitting sipping decorously at some sherry. Josef was entertaining him with stories of the KGB and the bungling of many of their spies. Johnson seemed grateful, almost pathetically so.

"Dinner is ready," said Maggie.

Next, Maggie went out to get Howell and Bailey, who were still talking underneath the trees. When she approached them, Bailey, whom Maggie had met once or twice but never to talk to, and who had on those occasions been shy and quiet, now broke into an enormous relieved smile.

"Hi," she said. "Listen, I'm sorry about what happened. We've just been talking about what to do."

"Well, for now you should come and eat. Ada says it will give you strength."

"Yes," said Howell. "All right, we will." He looked much more forlorn than his sister. The little dog lay serenely at his side.

"What's your dog's name?"

"Chance. Chance the Intrepid."

"Did you tell anyone you were coming here?"

"No. That is, only Charlene."

"Would she tell anyone?"

"Charlene? Never."

"Good. We'll need some time to straighten this out. I know the sheriff, which might help."

"That's great. I know him a little, too."

It was rather like sitting down to dinner in a boarding house when they'd all gathered around the table—even Mitch had lurched into the kitchen, leaving Billy Bob on drunken watch. They seemed almost like gamblers while they helped themselves to food. There was a moment of silence before they all started eating, a strange, abashed instant of reserve, and in that silence a buzz was heard in the distance; someone seemed to be coming up the drive. When none of them leaped to their feet, or seemed even surprised at the sound, Maggie felt obliged to go outside herself. Then the others followed, and they gathered on the lawn, waiting to see who would be arriving this time.

Outside, Billy Bob was lying at full length in the grass with his arm slung over his eyes, and though he jerked and gurgled slightly when Maggie called out to him "It's all right. Don't bother to get up," he made no other sign that he had heard her. Since Bailey had been quite firm about having told no one except Howell's wife of her deduction of Howell's location, it was hard to imagine who this might be—but she was not too astonished when it turned out to be Ryland, driving a lot faster than was his wont. Taking the bumps and potholes in the driveway more enthusiastically than was good for his Mercedes, he came roaring up to the other vehicles, and slammed to a stop beside them, revealing that he was carrying a passenger.

Maggie began to wave and call out to him—really, she was so happy to see him that for a moment she forgot that she was pregnant—but though the passenger, who now climbed out and came around the front of the car, carrying a black bag that looked remarkably like a doctor's, though the passenger waved back tentatively, Ryland didn't even notice, so intent was he on unloading something from his trunk. Maggie watched him, perplexed, her pleasure turning to incredulity; he seemed to be delivering an overstuffed chair. Grasping it tightly around its bottom, he hoisted it into the air, then staggered toward the house like chintz with legs.

"Don't shoot!" he called out. "It's all going to be OK!" His voice was muffled in the hand-tied stuffing.

# 26

AT FIRST Ada had trouble determining who was staggering toward them behind that chair. When she saw that it was her sweet friend Ryland, her future grandson-in-law and the father of her coming great-grandchild, she was absolutely delighted though a little bit puzzled; she couldn't remember ordering the chair. Living on the minute pension that her husband Tibor had been entitled to—in a rich country like America, you would think they could have done better by her, really!—she hadn't bought such a thing for years and years, and didn't ever again expect to.

But the few times she had admitted aloud that she didn't remember some small thing that had happened—as if anyone was capable of remembering every trivial detail with which her life was cluttered!—Maggie had treated her with such consideration, had abandoned so completely her usual judgmental attitude toward the whole world, including her grandmother, and replaced it with a deference that was nothing less than sickening, that Ada certainly didn't want to admit that she'd ordered a chair, then forgotten it. If she *had* ordered a chair, she certainly wouldn't have ordered *this* chair, which had none of the dignity of tight upholstery and exposed line that she considered truly artistocratic, but instead was swathed in a bundle of chintz, like a fat peasant woman at the market. But since there was no other conceivable reason that Ryland should be staggering toward the house with this monstrosity in cotton, she decided to meet the situation with grace, and stepped forward to thank and direct him.

As she did so, Boonskie, who had come out with her from the kitchen and who had, until now, been confining his alarm about this thick strange creature on legs to wild barks of outrage and horror, dashed forward, infused, by her presence, with courage, and circled the package, snarling. Bailey's dog, Chance, who had naturally figured out a lot more quickly than darling Boonskie that this, what had appeared so threatening, was merely a man with a chair, leaped in greeting at Ryland's legs, unfortunately covered by the furniture. The ground was still, in spots, muddy from the rain, and so were the paw prints on the chair.

"Get down, get down," said Ryland to Chance, and set the chair on the grass. "Oh, no," he added. "I should have covered it. How could I have been so careless?" But his voice was lively and vibrant.

"Well, never mind, never mind," said Ada comfortingly. "I will get the dirt out later."

"It's for Bailey Bourne," blurted Ryland.

Bailey was, Ada saw, rather taken aback; she herself was relieved. "For me? Why on earth?"

"I just thought you'd like it. You know, that day, by mistake?"

"Ryland," said Maggie, "have you gone completely off your rocker?"

And Howell said solemnly. "I wouldn't take it, Bailey. All *my* trouble started with free furniture."

"But that isn't the main present," said Ryland a little desperately. "The main present is the Sword of Communism. That is, it's a sword. For your rituals and so on."

"Why are you giving presents to me?"

"Well, I thought . . . you know . . . the kidnapping and everything. Somebody did get kidnapped, didn't they?"

"How did you know we were here, anyway?" asked Maggie.

"I heard Ada's voice on the phone."

"The Sword of Communism?" asked Josef with interest, taking the first opportunity. "It's a very sturdy one, don't you think, Nicolai?"

"You thought I was involved with the kidnapping?" asked Bailey.

"Well, your brother said you were a witch."

At this point, Boonskie, who had finally figured out that Ryland was Ryland, and the chair was a chair—by dint of a great deal of snuffling, nose elonated as much as was physically possible, body stretched back and out of the danger zone like something that didn't really belong to him—relaxed, and to greet it, this friendly new chair, leaped gracefully into its lap. As he came down, hitting the stuffing with an audible *whump* and curling into a polite interrogation mark, Ryland dashed forward, protesting, but too late; Boonskie was already quite comfy. Thumping his tail in approval, he cupped his ears back and up. "Do you want something, Ryland?" he seemed to be asking. "Can I get you any little thing?" Ada, while she watched this behavior fondly—now that she had discovered that this was not, in fact, a chair she had ordered, and that she was not, therefore, getting forgetful, she was free to scorn the chair as she had wished—thought she had better intercede.

"Boonskie! Bad doggie! Get down on the ground at once."

And Boonskie slunk reluctantly down.

A little later, Ryland gave Bailey the sword, and almost everyone went back into the kitchen. Ryland had brought a bottle of sherry with him—the dear man had heard her ask for it!—and so, as they gathered once more around the table, they had the proper refreshment with their meal. Mitch, who had decided that he was not hungry after all, had elected to remain outside this time; and his place was taken by this Dr. Ludgar, who had remained in the background during the chair scene. He had, in Ada'a opinion, showed remarkable modesty for a doctor, so she was willing to make him a place at her table, though he protested that he had already eaten. He and the others conversed while she and Maggie reheated the chicken, and though normally Ada liked to have meals proceed without too much interruption, because it was bad for the digestive juices to be interrupted in their task, this time she didn't mind the delay; sometime in the interval between the present and the moment when they had all heard the buzz of Ryland's engine, the whole mood of the assembly had changed. Oh, Howell Bourne and his nincompoop friends were still here, and presumably somewhere out on the streets of Felicity the sheriff and his men were driving up and down in a hearty American way, searching for troublemakers, but to everyone at the table it was clear that the incident was finished, that nothing more would come of it. Howell's thoughts were engrossing him completely now; he would take no further action. While the other two—well! Drunken louts that they were! Contemptible, that was the word for them.

"Oh, Mrs. Esterhaczy," said Josef when she served him, "what a fine display this is. I pay food the strictest attention."

"Yes, he keeps his eye on the ball."

"For God's sake," said Dr. Minot from the other side of the table, "just give it a rest now, can't you?"

"Give it a rest, I will give it a rest," practiced Nicolai, *sotto voce*.

Now that Maggie was safely pregnant, and by a seed that had such a fine track record, Ada could look at Minot with a good deal of repugnance; she had certainly never liked the man. There had been a time when, in desperation, she had wished that Maggie would marry him, but she was glad that Maggie had been sensible enough to hold out till someone better came along. And Ryland! Ryland didn't even know yet that he was to be again a father.

Now that everyone was served, Ada took some chicken for herself; then she sat away from the main table, taking time to consider her own feelings. She was, of course, both happy and upset—happy beyond words that her hopes had borne fruit so soon and that she would, if all went well, be able to hold her great-grandchild in her arms in eight months or so, with every expectation of raising him, or her, to be an Esterhaczy of a caliber to rival the best of them— and upset that Maggie had threatened an abortion, an unexpected hitch in Ada's plan.

She wanted this baby very much, she still was not sure why; she wanted to watch it open its mouth and yawn like a tiny pink O. She was getting goopy in her old age, perhaps—when her own babies had yawned like tiny pink O's she had still been so bruised and shaken from almost dying as they beat their way out of her body like small steam shovels that she had taken very little pleasure in it, and only when they were older had she really enjoyed them at all—but whatever the reason, she felt a little concerned about what was probably merely a threat. She knew Maggie well enough to know that if she had even the slightest doubts about something, she would exaggerate them instead of admitting them; she would blow them up as she blew up the world. So, although it seemed to Ada *possible* that Maggie was serious, and that she would decide to get rid of this sweet little group of cells that Ada had worked so hard to create, it seemed even more possible that she was just making statements, was trying them on for size.

Now, for a while, there was appreciative silence, as everyone concentrated on the food. Ada, despite her bath, still felt a little cold; her joints and muscles ached as if from exercise. Could that little rain have chilled her? She had never been particularly sensitive to cold, having inured herself to it as a child—she had been rather delicate as a girl (lively, of course, but delicate), and she had had to walk four miles every day back and forth to the convent school, where her mother had arranged with the nuns that she should get a glass of wine each day, and this had toughened her— but now she felt just a little tired, and a little cold as well. Outside, the weather still seemed strange, awkward with anticipation, and though there was no wind, it felt as if there should be—or perhaps it was just imagination. At least everyone was hungry, and there was such praise for the food. Well, everyone always loved paprikash!

About fifteen minutes had passed since the company came inside, and now there was a pause in the eating; outside, Ada heard the voices of the louts. They were engaged in some quarrel.

"*I* want it!"

"Forget it!"

"You bastard, I'll get you!"

"Oh, you will, will you?"

Thuds on the wall.

Exasperated, Ada looked around her table again; it was clear that this dinner was to be unfinished. Could no one do what he was supposed to for once? Could these so-called guards not simply guard? But no, they had to fight and disrupt the meal again. Well, most of the food was already eaten.

Agitated, Howell was now clambering to his feet, and everyone else at the table once more followed. Outside, in the strange and unhealthy dusk, the easy chair still sat in the middle of the lawn; it looked eerie and thronelike, in a deserted room that comprised the entire world. The louts were brawling on either side of it.

"Now stop that!" Howell shouted.

Ada was convinced that they hadn't heard him. They certainly didn't pause in their fight.

"Oh, dear," said Ryland. "This didn't even occur to me. I offered to give Billy Bob the chair."

"You *did?*" asked Maggie.

"Well, when Bailey didn't want it."

"They fight over the chair?" asked Ada.

"I think so."

"But how absurd."

The fighters paused for a moment to gasp raggedly and to exchange a few words with each other, words that centered on Mitch's claim that since it was *he* who was losing his whole farm, *he* should get the chair, especially since it looked as if nothing else was going to come out of this. Mitch did not say this in quite those words, but Ada was able to do a kind of simultaneous translation in her head, and it was easy to understand when Billy Bob—ouf, what a name!—responded that he could really not care less. Billy Bob, though he seemed to be the drunker of the two—both his excessively slurred speech and the misdirection of most of his movements argued that Ada had been very successful—seemed to be the angrier of the two, which to some extent counteracted his drunkenness.

Now, as the remaining members of the party gathered to watch the fight, all of them, with one accord, silently agreed to let it proceed—all of them, that is, except Howell, who continued to say "Now, men, now men!" And while Ada watched, the sky strangely yellow above her, the smell of fresh earth in her nostrils, there seemed to be something unreal about it all, the two figures lunging and hitting. God knew, she didn't care if they beat themselves into a pulp, didn't care if they managed to kill each other, but she felt almost as if she were watching a dance, something that had been choreographed. Not only was it in slow motion, not only did it consist of a few nicely stylized moves, but the two men so clearly were working together in order to affect their collisions. If they had suddenly lost their eyesight and wandered away from each other, they would have been lost, they would have been alone and afraid, there would have been nothing left them but despair. Instead, they were supported by the strength of their animosity toward each other, they were two halves of a spherical whole, defined only by opposition. Maybe it was the sky that caused it, or the sense of her own growing chill, but it struck Ada suddenly as very, very sad, the hatred men had for each other. Why, she herself was a hater from way back; she had always been proud of her feelings! But they were not, perhaps, so fine as she had thought them—or even, perhaps so necessary.

"Come, come, that's enough," she found herself calling imperiously. "Come on, now, it is time for this to stop."

But instead of stopping, the men lunged with greater violence, pushed together, now, by something else. And as Ada, too, staggered from the force of the sudden gust of wind, which had struck out of nowhere, and then passed, everyone looked at the sky and then at one another. It was Howell who said, "A tornado." At that word, one that had never, for Ada, held any terrors, but had always still been cause for some caution, it all became plain, this weather and what it meant. Of course, there was going to be a tornado! Maggie and Boonskie—and Sam—must instantly go to the basement, and the others as it could be arranged. "Boonskie!" she shouted. "And Maggie! Into the basement. Boonskie, where are you? Where is Boonskie?"

Even while she shouted, though, the second blast of wind struck, and this one almost knocked her down. All around her, people started running, and the trees seemed almost to be running also; they were twisting and writhing, trying to get away, trying to escape from the mighty grip that held them. Mitch and Billy Bob, whom Ada had thought knocked senseless by their last collision, managed to sway to their knees once more and start leaning into the wind. Maggie shouted, "Raga! He's still locked in the barn," and began running east and away from them; Ryland chased Maggie, saying "Wait, wait, I'll get him."

Ada's shout to them both was lost. When the lawn chairs, which Ada had put out one morning the week before in the happy conviction that summer was surely here at last, started not just to blow, but to rocket away to the east, and one of them hit Nicolai on the leg, any doubts Ada may have had about the gravity of this wind were fully dispelled. Nicolai had no idioms for this occasion; he stood trying to support himself in place against the wind while Johnson, who had suddenly come to life again and who seemed almost pleased to have something he felt he could do, was trying to explain to the Russian about tornadoes. "They're winds that blow in a big, big spiral."

"Yes, yes!" shouted Josef. "Let's get inside!"

Bailey's little dog, Chance, started to blow away, turning end over end, her claws extended rigidly as she tried to catch herself on something, her ears litte tufts of fur helpless in the wind. "Chance!" shouted Bailey, running after her; she caught her and grabbed her in her arms.

"Boonskie, Boonskie, where is Boonskie?" Ada shrieked again, and at last Boonskie appeared.

Sam was not in evidence. Ada hoped that she was safe, but one dog was all she could possibly handle.

It was lucky that the wind was blowing from the west and that the house now stood to their east; that wind helped propel them all, like so many weightless forms, toward the kitchen and the basement beneath it. Maggie and Ryland had a mighty struggle to get back from the barn with Raga, but Ada was having such a struggle of her own that there was nothing at all she could do to help. Boonskie dragged her partway to the house, and then he got confused and stopped; in the end, it was Dr. Ludgar who came and put his arm around her shoulders, to support her. The rain hit just before Ada reached the house, it hit with incredible violence; it made the last storm seem like a pleasant little shower, and this one a flood with a vengeance. They got inside somehow, all of them piling up in front of the door and then popping through it like so many corks out of bottles, and once they were there, the wind's force redoubled. It was as if a huge hand had slapped the house. It trembled to its stones, and the kitchen window exploded. Water started pouring onto the floor.

The speed with which this all happened might have left Ada bewildered had she not had so much to do. "Boonskie, you must go! Maggie, right this instant. You go down and you *stay* in the basement!"

"But, Ada . . ."

"No buts! First Boonskie, then you! Then Ryland, he is the father."

"The what?" said Ryland.

"Never mind, she will tell you. So go now, you go and take care of them!"

By now, the wind was blowing so hard that the rain fell upward—it was like nothing that Ada had ever seen. Although she had lived here now for many years, and had many times prepared herself for this moment, she had never imagined it all all correctly, since, for one thing, the air was yellow, a dense, murky yellow that prevented one from seeing anything more than ten feet from the house; for another, the sound was deafening, it was pure, magnificent *noise*. Somehow, in the confusion, everyone managed to get into the basement; Ada knew that it was her turn, but she was, of a sudden, reluctant to leave this thrilling, thrilling world. Outside, objects continued to shoot by the window at tremendous force, and inside, the floor was flooded with water. Everything was wild, everything was excited, everything was alive. And as Ada, laughing, watched one of her beloved bushes whip by the window, she had the strangest feeling suddenly that she should jump out into the storm, that she should plunge herself right into its path. She was eighty-seven, after all; she had had a happy life, a longer one than most people hoped for. Why not die now, this way? What better way than this? To be caught up in such a violent dance!

But before she had time to do one thing or the other, the yellow murk weakened for an instant. And through its mask, she could see to the edge of her clearing, where the black funnel cloud was revealed. The wind did not cease roaring, objects did not cease flying, the rain did not cease flooding the floor, but to Ada, it was all stilled as her heart leaped, terrified, upward; this was, indeed, a very ugly thing. Now she wished that she *had* run, but now it was too late—the funnel reached down and twisted two of her oak trees. It picked them up in darkness, then flung them before it like lances, then whirled and jerked away to the east. Pushing lightly off the earth, it was galvanized into motion, and it swirled and then shot away through the pastures and fields.

Within seconds, the wind was gone, and a silence descended around her. Ada, shaken, pushed open the door and went outside. It was truly cool now and the sky was rapidly clearing, though only to make way for the true darkness of night. The world looked lovely, and the air smelled sweet as flowers, but it seemed taciturn, mute, unapproachable somehow. And when she noticed that the strangest thing had happened when the twister came across the lawn—that while it had wrenched the stems of the two giant oaks so rudely, grabbing up the trees as if to fling them away, the ugly chair, with its skirts and its fat dimpled legs, had been lifted up by that same twister as politely as a mailman lifts a letter—she felt a little dizzy, trying to take it in, the oddity of these sudden events. Because it had carried this letter—delivered it, perhaps—to the very peak of Ada's roof, where it had set it down, its skirts concealing its legs, exactly on top of the chimney.

Why this disturbed Ada, she could not exactly say, but merely the sight seemed to make her uneasy. And while she tried to tell herself that it was nothing, that the chair and the trees were just accidents, the same kinds of accidents with which one's life was filled—and that one ignored every minute!—she had trouble listening. Was everything, then, accident? Did nothing make, finally, any sense? Behind her, she heard the whole crowd emerging from the house, but she did not turn around to greet them. Howell came up and said something to her, something about a tornado, but though her ears heard it, her mind could not listen. It was so *hard* to live in this world, that was the truth which she had forgotten, this world that was like a tangle of wires; it was all connected somehow, but who could see where the sense was? Who could know how one's own little life was attached? Why, Ada had always felt that *she* was the purpose of the universe, and now—had she missed her most crucial connection? There was a feeling of weakness that started in her knees—those nice knees she had loved so much since childhood.

# 27

WHEN ADA COLLAPSED, she landed on Howell's left foot, which was spread in his conversational stance. He had been about to tell her the story of how Daisy and Darell had been brought into the world, and how tornadoes had, ever since, pleased him; this tornado was the best thing that had happened to him all day. It had really lifted his spirits. But, unfortunately, she had not seemed to be listening—and neither had anyone else—and that had begun to counter his mood and return him to where he'd been before. Oh, no one had paid much attention to him lately—no one, that was, except Bailey—and Howell had been feeling really old, transparent, as if he weren't really here. Now the sudden impact of Ada's body landing on his foot was almost welcome. But what was he thinking? The woman had fainted! She wasn't just visiting his foot.

He pulled his foot back, then was buffeted aside by Maggie and Ryland and Boonskie. Boonskie was actually the first to arrive on the scene, sniffing his mistress anxiously and licking her face with large friendly strokes, and though Maggie firmly asked him to get back, he paid no attention to the request. He seemed particularly anxious about Ada's eyes, and he inserted the tip of his tongue delicately below her eyebrows and swept the eyelids with slightly smaller strokes. While Ryland said aloud, repeatedly, "Where's Dr. Ludgar? Where's Dr. Ludgar?" and Maggie said, "Ada, wake up, wake up now," Boonskie kept up his dextrous ministrations, and Ada moaned lightly and then sneezed.

"Boonskie. You are making me sneeze. Well, thank you, darling, now that is enough."

Ryland and Maggie helped Ada to her feet, and while she resisted their aid in words—"Good Heavens, I can stand by myself, after all"—she seemed to be grateful for it physically, and let herself be urged off toward the house, from which Dr. Ludgar was just emerging. He came forward to her side and asked something Howell couldn't hear; then the four of them disappeared from sight. Looking around for her, Howell found that Bailey was still inside, also, though he felt they had been holding hands just seconds before.

Strangely enough, Mitch and Billy Bob were still angry, despite the tornado they had both just lived through. Now that they were once again outside, they decided to resume their fight where it had broken off, but it was more a chaos of confused movement than anything that could effect harm, with Billy Bob favoring one particular uppercut movement that never seemed to make contact with anything but air, and Mitch pushing his elbows aggressively outward, though again with little real impact. This fight should have astonished Howell, he supposed, but he was well beyond astonishment; he felt that he was swimming under water, but he could somehow still breathe. After the brief relief of the tornado, his veins had once again, it seemed, been injected with some drug, the main effect of which was to render him incapable of feeling certain—certain about anything, even the inarguable, even the absolutely fixed. And since he had always seen it as his duty as a human being to be certain about everything he felt, this was a horror, this doubt that surrounded him; it was dragging him under.

From what seemed like an enormous distance, he heard Nocolai's voice saying, "Oh, yes, like shooting fish in a barrel," and he realized that the Russian was responding to Dr. Minot's suggestion that they go and tie up the two fighters. That both Minot and Nicolai felt quite secure in discussing this plan in Howell's presence proved what had not needed proving, that he had become just a joke.

"Like taking candy from a baby," added Nicolai. "Like falling heavily from a log. These are my favorites, these phrases, so *masculine*. Nothing requires any effort."

"You know, Nicolai, you really should defect. You'd fit right in in America," said Dr. Minot.

"Do you think so, really? How kind of you to say so. Would I not seem very 'green'?"

The conversation faded again, like a bad connection, as Howell wondered where Bailey could be. He had been so unnerved when she first drove up, had felt so strongly that his future somehow hung on her actions, and now she seemed the only thing to cling to in a world that was suddenly so changed. When she had climbed out of her little foreign car, her clothes and her hair as wild as ever, her ideas presumably as infirm, he had felt, instead of irritation, that she was trustworthy and dependable, come to remove him from harm's way. Then, when she had dragged him out under the trees, away from everyone else and into a kind of protected bubble of Bournes, instead of feeling angry, he'd felt humble and subdued, and had listened while she told him what she thought. What was he thinking of, risking a jail term? She'd thought he *cared* about the farm. Well, who would work it when he was in jail? And what was the *point* of this, anyway? Did he imagine for a *second*, for God's sake, that they would really burn the damned mortgages? Or did he just want publicity, his name in the paper? If so, why not raise a prize pig? But she had said all this nicely, almost tenderly, as if she honestly cared; she lost her temper only when she got to the pamphlet that had inspired all this in the first place. Bailey had rarely, if ever, talked to him like this before. She'd always seemed to feel he wasn't worth it.

Now, as the moon began to rise in the east—it would be a full moon tonight, Howell observed—and the small wind that had been gusting since the tornado vanished like a thought, Mitch and Billy Bob ran out of steam, and both sat down, panting and forlorn. For all their talk, Dr. Minot and the Russian had not tried to interfere in the dispute, and now they left, as if they were cold, or bored, or unconcerned. But Bailey at last came out of the house, leading Sam on a makeshift leash.

"She got scared, I think. She was hiding in the crawl space."

"What, in the cellar?" Howell asked.

"Back behind it. I had to crawl in to try to convince her it was all over. She'll be all right now, I think." Bailey released the loop of rope from around Sam's collar, and Sam meandered over to Howell's side. Once there, she stuck her nose into his palm, and he closed it gently around her flews.

"I'm glad you came, Bailey," he said, to his own surprise.

"I'm glad I did, too," she said. "And I think it's time to call the sheriff.

"Oh?"

"So we can all go home."

"Oh."

"There's nothing to worry about. His *brother's* here. We'll just explain it was a kind of misunderstanding."

"Can't we wait a little longer?"

"Howell. Charlene will be worried."

"Oh. Well, let's do it then, and get it done."

Bailey began to lead the way toward the house, and automatically Howell began to follow—but he stopped as a sudden thought struck him: he was sick to death of making phone calls. He didn't want to phone, he didn't want to see the sheriff, he didn't want to be here at all; he wanted to be somewhere else entirely, and he wanted to be there right now. And since the easiest way to get to somewhere else was to walk there on his own two feet, he turned those feet and started for the woods, liking the way this made him feel. Bailey, in the belief that he was following her, continued to walk briskly toward the lights and the voices in the kitchen, but Sam was not so easily fooled. She stuck by his side and followed him into the woods, where he hid behind a large tree. Howell's breathing, stimulated by this maneuver, continued to come hard and fast—it seemed to him deafeningly loud. Surely his sister would hear it.

But when she turned around, she neither saw nor heard him. "Howell? Howell? Where are you?"

Howell didn't answer, just stood stock still.

"Howell, you can't just run away!"

Twenty minutes later, Howell was still walking through the woods, and he was beginning to get a little tired. Active though he was on the farm, and much as he stood on his feet, he wasn't accustomed to going hiking, particularly when it was dark. Of course, the full moon, which had now come up and was shining down into the tree-filled landscape like a benign white face peering at him from the sky—a white face that was somehow, at the moment, more pleasant and reassuring and even friendly than the face of God Himself, which Howell was strangely reluctant to summon, which he really didn't care to see at all—the full moon made it easier, but even so, he had to watch his feet. For someone who had lived all his life in the country—all his life, in fact, quite near here—he had spent relatively little of that life in the woods, especially since he rarely hunted. These woods, he discovered, were very nice; being in them made him happy.

For one thing, the air smelled sweet in the woods, with no fertilizer or manure to make it pungent. For another, there were the trees; as a farmer, concerned with the growing of crops, he had never thought much about these most perennial of plants, so large, so solid, and so enduring. As he hiked on through their clustered ranks, tired and happy both, he discovered that they had personalities, that some were dark and brooding types, given to jealously and spite, and that others were joyous, willing to try anything—they changed and evolved through time. There were those which seemed to resent being rooted, and those which took pleasure in their state. Most of them, he felt, loved to have air on their fresh new leaves, and they often just trembled with elation. Sometimes, two trees had interconnected branches, and of course, beneath the earth their roots met. Altogether, they had a complex and interesting society, which Howell was pleased now to be part of.

Sam, too, seemed pleased as she bounded along at his side, her paws scrabbling occasionally for purchase on a log, her head held low to snuffle at the ground. She had always seemed so gloomy, holding down her job at the end of her chain; now she was jubilant, dashing through the woods and once in a while howling. Perhaps he should have hushed her, but he wanted to let her be gay. He felt gay himself, almost, a most unfamiliar feeling.

Oh, how decorous, how sober-minded he had always been, going through his daily chores; how dutiful he had been to his own heavy-heartedness, which he rarely if ever, had seen. He had thought he could change his life by committing some important act, by extending his responsibilities, but that had made it worse, had made him feel so burdened, wreathed in a self-erasing gloom. He'd thought himself required to oppose and assert—it was wonderful now just to be. He was running away! He was running away! He broke into a small and awkward jog.

He was heading, as near as he could figure it, toward the Dickensens' pig farm on Pond Road. He needed a destination, however illogical, since he couldn't eradicate all in an instant a lifelong conviction that everything he did had to have a purpose—and the pigs were still in his mind from his afternoon visit, when all this had barely begun. Their scrubbed smiling faces, their shavings of tails, their unanimity of purpose as they'd fled; they'd run away from *him*, and now he was running away himself, so it seemed apt that he should go to meet them. With luck, he was climbing the hill that would lead down to their farm—he had certainly started to climb something. Whoof, he was tired. But he still felt light of heart, and as if he was heading in the right direction.

Yes, whatever this was, he liked it. Not knowing for sure what to do. Not knowing for sure where to go from here. When he had turned away from Bailey and gone to hide behind the tree, he had made, he was confident, the right decision; why should he turn himself in, and wait for the sheriff's verdict? He had to stop thinking in terms of verdicts once and for all. That Dr. Minot, with his punishments, had really disturbed Howell deeply, because he had reminded Howell of *himself*. What was this whole thing, anyway, but an attempt on his part to punish, to rule and direct the lives of other men? Well, not anymore, he wouldn't. He felt too good just running and liking the trees and the pigs for what they were.

Oh, rules, rules, rules, he had lived his life by rules and had resented it when other people hadn't. But why had he, really, why had he? Hadn't he just been scared? Well, he wasn't scared now; no, he was marching. He was marching up quite a steep hill, and he had to pause now and then to rest. When he did, he would stop and look around him. The fourth or fifth time he did this, he was hit with the strangest sensation, as if somewhere, not noticing it, he'd lost his way.

Living the highly regulated life he lived, Howell had never had the opportunity to discover whether or not he had a good sense of direction, and he feared now that he hadn't, not even with the help of the moon; surely he should have reached the pig farm by this time. Perhaps—well, could he be lost? As this thought entered him, he felt a touch of panic, and then a touch more after that, and in no time at all his euphoria vanished. He was lost! He would die! Where was Sam?

Sam had taken off on the track of an appealing scent, so Howell was now all alone; since he had never been lost in his life, he had no idea of what to do. He had heard somewhere, he couldn't remember where, that when you were lost you should just sit down and stay put, and that either you would eventually regain your bearings or someone would eventually come to find you; but though he tried to do this, tried very hard, forcing his legs to bend at the knees and lower him, he had not been down on his haunches for more than a second before he was back on his feet again, since from his sitting position the friendly trees seemed suddenly tangled and full of threat. Where had he come from? Had he come from *that* way? But no, what was this vine-covered boulder? Well, perhaps it had been *that* way? No, no, that was a gully. He had never seen the gully before.

So without being able to stop himself, he set off again through the woods, but this time fast and in total dismay. There must be a road somewhere, if only he could find it. Or maybe a light from a house. Something, he prayed, anything. But the trees seemed to go on forever. He breathed hard; he ran twenty feet, then stopped and turned and ran back the way he had come. Under his feet, the sticks broke loudly, and the branches clattered above him, and when he tried to stop and breath some air, he found someone had taken it away. So he started running in earnest, searching for the air, and as he ran, he thought about God. Of course, God! God would know where the air had gone. God could help him now.

But when he closed his eyes to try to summon him, Howell stumbled and fell to the ground; in his confusion, he leaped up and kept running anyway, and closed his eyes once more. Running headlong through the woods at night, with your eyelids clenched tight together and the panic a taste of metal in your mouth—well, this is never a good idea, but right now it was an especially bad one. Howell had come almost to the edge of the Pond, right up over the rise of its cliff, and when he tripped again slightly and his eyelids popped open, he saw he was heading over the rocky wall. Desperately, he tried to stop himself from falling, to call back all the energy he had released, but his legs continued to pump in slow motion, and his arms spread wide like nascent wings. He had time to see the moonlight on the Pond, the stillness of the water in its chalice of soft rock, and then he was delivered from the logic of the earth, he was loose, he was flying, he'd broken free. And while he was, naturally, tugged down by fear, certain he was going to be killed, he was also so relieved to have located himself once again that he felt buoyed up even as he fell. When his legs were stopped by a ledge that rose to meet them, he felt, for an instant, more relieved, but the ledge kept coming—it was very determined—and it shook one of his legs so vigorously that it cracked. The pain was remarkable; it held him on the point of a needle, a needle that was stitching him to the world.

# BETWEEN
# THE WORLDS

# 28

AS DARKNESS FELL, Peale, back in his office, decided that he'd better call the state police. His deputies had, of course, been telling him this all along, and while it seemed to him all very well for *them* to talk, since *they* were not the ones who had been elected by an overwhelming majority of their townsfolk to deal effectively and swiftly with emergency situations like this one, yet he thought now that maybe they were right: the state police were a lot more experienced than he was at all this sort of thing. "All this sort of thing," this evening, had consisted largely of driving up and down the major exits from Pond Road, looking for suspicious signs, abandoned vehicles, walking people, and skid marks, interviewing Crane Sizemore's mother again—no, the van had never *ever* come by her, not even going the other way—and brooding about those five drops of blood and the shotgun hole in the truck. Another call from the kidnappers was certainly in order, but so far none had arrived.

Now that darkness had fallen, there was nothing more Peale could do, so he called the state police. Naturally—he wasn't a *total* incompetent—he had put in a call to them almost immediately to broadcast an APB for the Saguanay's van, but this time he was asking for their best investigators to go over the abandoned truck. As the police headquarters was at least thirty miles away, it would take them some time to arrive, and in the meanwhile, Peale thought, he'd visit his brother and see what had happened with Amanda. It had only just now occurred to him that he should have called her right after the second storm; Peale had been out at the Pond when it hit and a mighty fierce one it had been. Funnel clouds had been reported in at least three locations so far, and though no one had asked for police assistance and presumably there was no major damage, power lines might be down, or who knew what—yes, he should certainly have called her. Well, he would go to see both her and Ryland. Perhaps Ryland, who had taken the original phone call, who had been the only person so far to deal with the kidnappers in person, perhaps he had some ideas, had come up with a new approach.

Certainly Peale had to do *something* to pass the time before the investigative team arrived, because if he sat around in his office alone his thoughts would go back to Bailey. And while that might, at first, seem a pleasant place for them to be, in actual fact it was not at all; it was irritating in the extreme. To find himself having such feelings about a woman, feelings that were outside the range of his prior experience, and were, moreover, inappropriate to a married man, well, that would be bad enough in itself, whoever the woman might be. But to find himself having such feelings about her, a self-proclaimed witch, and therefore, however you tried to explain it, a complete flake, someone who had, for goodness, sake, a cauldron and a wand in her living room, though nothing else to speak of, and who was the sister of a farmer who was proving to be an extremely unwise man to say the least, though to call him a psychotic nut case might meet the situation more completely— well, all this was really horrible and made him feel queer. When he had met and married Amanda, it had been his expectation that being in love would stir things up, would throw his life into pleasant disarray, and when it had done nothing of the kind, he had been mildly disappointed. But only mildly—they were, after all, perfect for one another, toes to hair.

Now, with his life thrown into such disarray—God, how he wanted to have Bailey!—he felt almost furious at her for doing this to him. He felt furious at least, at someone. And since fury, like real lust, was a completely unfamiliar emotion to him—he who had been so orderly all his life—he didn't realize this would probably pass, and thought he was stuck with it forever.

After telling his men he'd be back in thirty minutes, he climbed into his shiny red Corvette. He had noticed when he was at Bailey's house this evening that she, too, had a red car—he must have also noticed it when she had smashed into him, but he hadn't been paying much attention—and the shared color was an unnerving coincidence; Amanda prefered gray or white. When he got to Ryland's house, after roaring through the streets at a speed that was certainly illegal and probably unsafe—not because he had a pressing need to get there quickly, but because shoving his foot down hard on the gas pedal made him feel a little bit better—he found to his amazement that the party was still going on. The house was ablaze with lights.

You would think that these people would have the common decency to go home when it became clear that everything that could possibly go wrong *had* gone wrong, but he supposed that if Ryland wanted to keep on being the good host, that was Ryland's affair, not his. So crowded was the street with cars, though, that he had to park almost a block away and walk to the house, and though he had no gas pedal on his feet the walk did little to calm him down. By the time he pushed open the front door and saw Amanda sitting on the love seat in the vestibule, engaged in conversation with, of all people, the president of Powell College—a man with whom Peale had had several run-ins in his student days, and who had probably, as a result, been one of the few voters in Felicity who had not thrown his confidence behind Peale Guthrie—he was ready for an argument, with anyone, about anything. And Amanda would do fine for a start.

"Where's Ryland?" he asked her, interrupting.

"He left. It was, maybe, an hour ago. He gave me a letter to give you."

"He *left?* His own party?" asked Peale incredulously.

"Well, yes. He got a phone call. I think something came up."

Amanda delivered this second statement with an air of supernatural calm that irritated Peale beyond words; he still retained enough sense of his own reputation, though, not to be rude right in front of Dr. Davidson.

"I see. Do you mind if we talk in the kitchen?"

Once there, he said, "All right, where's the letter? This is an emergency, in case you haven't noticed."

Amanda pulled an envelope from her purse, staring at him with a faintly worried air. He snatched it from her fingers before she had a chance to relinquish it properly, and he tore it open with impatience. The first time he read it through he was so flabbergasted by the business about the mortgages and the bonfire that he got stuck on it and had to read the letter through again; the second time he absorbed the stuff about the sherry and about what Ryland had deduced. But it took three readings for him to grasp fully that Ryland had gone out to the Esterhaczy place, on his own and without reporting to Peale, apparently in the hope that he and he alone could take care of this incident without recourse to the sheriff, and as he absorbed this—his brother had completely usurped his prerogatives as sheriff and seemed to think that Peale would *appreciate* this—his irritation mushroomed into wrath, and he directed it, unfairly, toward Amanda.

"And even this doesn't upset you, I suppose?"

"Even what?"

"Didn't you even read this?"

"Of course not. It's marked 'For Your Eyes Only.'"

"That's typical. You have the curiosity of a rock."

"Peale, what's wrong?"

"Are you really *happy*?"

"Of course I'm happy. Aren't you?"

"I'm utterly miserable. I used to have to write down our dates."

"What do you mean?"

"I'd write them down. You know, so I wouldn't forget them. And I'd see your name there and I'd think, 'Who's Amanda?' Then I'd remember, 'Oh, yes, *her*.'"

"I see."

"And when I come home even now, at night, I sometimes forget that you live there."

"You've never mentioned that."

"Well, maybe I should have."

"Peale, I don't think you're yourself."

At this, Peale stopped; she was certainly right. He was not, not, not himself. He felt no less resentful about the whole situation, but he realized that these few words they had exchanged were wholly inadequate to define the problem, which would have to be tackled some other time. It was, in any case, not very satisfying to yell at Amanda; perhaps it was not very satisfying to yell at anyone, he didn't yet know, but Amanda, since she just stood there, made him feel slightly ridiculous. He might as well go out to the Esterhaczy place and yell at Ryland, who could be counted on at least to do *something*, so he told Amanda he had to go, and he darted out through the swinging door. For just a fraction of a second, it occurred to him that the state police would be arriving at his office in ten minutes or so, and that perhaps he should wait for them to go with him, but he was much too irate to sit around just now, and he ran to get into his car. He was in uniform, he had his gun; in his trunk was a bullhorn and a flasher. He wouldn't even go back to the office; he'd just take his own Corvette.

Driving dangerously fast, he roared down High Street, then turned onto Lesser Pond Road. He had almost had an accident here one night when he was in high school, and a great snowy owl—he had not known that was what it was at the time; he had known only that it was huge and white—had decided to take a sweep across the road, and had soared in front of his car in such a way that it came directly across the moon. The huge shadow, like that of a dream creature, had fallen on the windshield and drawn his eyes inexorably up to the thing that caused it—the bird, its wing span six feet wide, its movement slow beyond measuring. "Watch out, Peale!" his girlfiend had shouted, and he had wrenched the car back onto the road. Ever since, he had been cautious driving here— ever since until now. Now, he just kept going, reveling in his breakneck pace. Mortgages, for God's sake, bonfires, sherry. His tires squealed as he took the curves.

It was strange how strongly he wanted to even the score, to get back at Ryland for his presumption. It was strange, because all his life he had loved his brother easily and had found him a great source of comfort. Ryland had been the other side of the seesaw on which rode Peale's happiness; he had suffered, in a way, for them both. Well, Peale's luck had turned, so why couldn't he be gracious? He just couldn't, that was all; he just couldn't. Tonight, for the first time, he was going to act like a sheriff. He would be a sheriff if it killed him. Another turn, another squeal, and he was on Pond Road proper. He slowed down slightly when he got there.

And then his headlights picked up something in the road, and he hit the brakes as if they were on fire. Ahead of him, on the macadam, two dogs were trotting calmly, side by side, a little to the left of the center line, for all the world as if they were taking a constitutional. He gripped the steering wheel, and the car almost shook as it shuddered to a stop just in time. Peale felt weak with relief and also still angry. He rolled down the window and shouted, "Get out of the road, you stupid dogs! Do you want to get killed, or what?" They looked at him startled, almost aghast. One of them, he saw, was a dachshund.

"Go home!" he added. "Go on, get lost!" The dogs now regarded him doubtfully, then they turned and started, clearly bewildered, to trot back the way they had come.

Peale drove on perhaps a hundred yards and then looked in his rearview mirror; in the light of the moon he could see that the dogs had halted, and then turned and proceeded on their way, percisely as if that strange man with his little idiosyncrasies had never stopped and tried to get them to change their plans. Side by side, one large, the other small, they were, like all good friends, adjusting their gaits to each other, so that, despite the extraordinary difference in their leg length, they moved forward in perfect accord. Now, as he slowed again, they slowed also, and looked at each other in confusion.

This time when Peale stopped, he turned off the engine and

climbed out of the car. He felt embarrassed and ashamed at his recent behavior, and he wanted to make it up somehow; perhaps he could give the dogs a ride to where they were going, since they so clearly knew where that was. Leaving the door on the driver's side invitingly open, he walked back and tried to approach them; for a moment, they didn't know what to do. The dachshund had *very* short legs, which bottomed out in wrinkly little stumps of paws, and as it stood there, its long pointed nose thrust downward with an air of disappointment, it lifted one leg and then set it down again, as if its pads were sore. The other dog, a brindled hound-cross, chocolate brown with speckles of white all over, had nestling ears with a disarming curve, and a look of hopeful acquiescence.

"It's OK now," said Peale. "I'm sorry I scared you. Come here, let me see you, it's OK," and while the brindled hound did not need to be asked twice, deducing that this stranger who had, just moments before, been in a very bad mood, was now recovered— she came trotting happily up and thrust her nose directly into Peale's armpit and snuffled around there for a minute while he ran his hand down her head and flanks, marveling at the delicate soft-ness of her fur—the dachshund was shyer, or less quick to forgive, and he circled Peale just out of reach. The hound smiled at him trustingly in the moonlight, her lips lifted slightly to reveal her canines and her velvety tongue, but the dachshund only once let Peale's hand come close, and then jumped quickly back out of range. It seemed clear that the brindled hound would get into his car if he urged her to, but he doubted seriously that the dachshund would. Still, he could but try it and see.

Peale left them for a moment and walked back toward the door, saying over his shoulder, "You want a ride?" He intended this to be merely the opening gambit in what would no doubt be quite a lengthy conversation, but at the word "ride" both dogs perked up their ears and came hustling up alongside him. Having once reached him, they continued past him, leaping straight into the car, the dachshund as unhesitating and familiar as the hound, both of them wasting no time. They looked, more than anything, relieved to find that their driver had at last arrived, and while they couldn't fathom why he hadn't identified himself earlier, well, everyone had his little quirks.

Within seconds, the two had clambered directly over the driver's seat and the stick shift and emergency brake and were getting settled in the passenger's seat as if they'd spent most of their lives there. The dachshund settled down at once, curling his small body into a ball and stretching that elongated snout out upon those wrinkled paws; he was sound alseep by the time Peale got in, or at least his eyes were closed tight. The hound sat up for a minute or two, sniffing and looking around; she located a day-old crust of sandwich that Peale had left on the floor, and saliva started running freely from her mouth until she had picked it up and eaten it. That done, she licked her lips, lay down, and curled herself over her friend, then went to sleep with her head on his, the two perfectly entwined. Peale reached over to rub their bellies, and found that the dachshund was certainly a male. But he had the smallest set of nuts that Peale had ever imagined, and as he took them between his thumb and forefinger and rolled them around for a second, he discovered that they were no bigger than peas—little, tiny nuts. The dachshund opened his eyes and looked at Peale nastily, then closed them and went to sleep again.

At the turn of the Esterhaczy driveway Peale stopped and tried to work out a plan. Now that he had gotten here he was neither angry nor full of vehement determination, but just plain nervous; before he continued up to the house he loosened his gun in its holster and got out his bullhorn and flasher. He hooked the latter up but didn't turn it on yet—in fact, he decided to turn his headlights off, since the moon was bright enough to see by. The dogs were still asleep on their seat, perfectly trusting and contented, and that might make things more complicated when he got there—he certainly didn't want them to get hurt. The one thing that was clear in the present confusion of his mind was that as soon as he could get to a phone, he should call the local vet; one of the dogs had a rabies tag; maybe the vet would be able to identify both of them. Why, *that* was the kind of thing he'd wanted to do when he ran for sheriff in the first place—save small living things from imminent death, return dogs to their loving owners. Not *this*, which he was presently engaged in—sneaking around in the darkness.

Peale's breath was short when he drove on; the driveway was longer than he'd expected. When he got to the top, it took him almost by surprise, because by then he had decided he'd never reach it, but he stepped on the brakes and turned off the engine and sat for a moment in the dark. At this abrupt cessation of sound and vibration, both of the dogs woke up—they looked around, then looked at Peale questioningly, but they made no move to get out. There were lights on in the house, but Peale could see no one on guard; everything was quiet in the aftermath of a tornado, which had torn two great trees from the ground. The Saguanay's van was parked beside the arbor—the moon was bright enough to reveal the dark blue letters on its side—and Ryland's Mercedes was also there, parked a little way behind it. But it was the small red Honda that immediately captured Peale's attention; although the moonlight turned all colors to shades of gray, unless he was very much mistaken it was the same car that had been parked out in front of Bailey Bourne's house earlier that evening, the same car that had run into and smashed his headlight a month before. It was, in fact, Bailey's car, or he was in bed and dreaming, and that meant that not only was he, as he had already known, in love with a woman who dressed like a Gypsy, not only was he in love with a terrible driver, not only was he in love with a woman who wanted to be a witch, but he was in love with a woman who lied and committed criminal acts.

As he listed these points bitterly in his mind, carefully separating them out for greater ease of reference, it seemed to him that he was in love with four separate women, each of them horrid in the extreme. He climbed out of his car, suddenly all in a rush, hardly caring how much noise he made; he took his bullhorn in his left hand and held his gun in his right; then he flicked the switch that would turn on his flasher, and as soon as it went on, and its red and blue, red and blue knives started slicing the night, he darted back behind the trunk of his car and turned on the bullhorn as well.

"You in the house!" he shouted through it. "Come out with your hands up, now. The house is completely surrounded by police. You don't have a hope of getting out." The moment was sweet, a sweet revenge. But nothing whatever happened.

"I know you're in there! You're holding my brother! Come out at once, all of you."

Again nothing happened. The night was silent. A soft breeze played on Peale's upraised hands.

And then, just as he was starting to feel discouraged, and even worried that nobody was home, the back door opened and somebody stuck a head out.

"Hi, Peale. This is Ryland. Nobody's holding me."

"They aren't?"

"Of course not. The whole thing was a misunderstanding. Why don't you just turn those lights off and come in?"

"Come in?"

"Sure. Most of us are in here. We're just having coffee and dessert."

"Dessert?"

"Just come *in*. And for God's sake, put that gun down, all right? We don't want anybody hurt *now*."

"I'm an expert marksman!" shouted Peale, in sudden outrage. "I don't shoot anything I don't intend to."

"I know that, Peale," said Ryland, quite patiently. "But you don't intend to shoot *any*thing, do you?"

"Oh, I don't know, I don't know. What about that chair? What's that chair doing up on the chimney?"

"It's sitting there, Peale. The tornado took it up there."

"Well, fine. And I'll just take it down." And, to Peale's enormous surprise and everlasting chagrin, he found himself drawing back the hammer on his .357 Magnum and aiming his gun at the air above the chair, squeezing the trigger back toward him. The distance was enormous for a handgun—at least a hundred feet—but by allowing for the trajectory, he managed to hit the chair, which rocked slightly on the chimney but stayed put. It took him four shots to down it, but when it took one right in its gut, it tipped over and slid down the roof, landing out of sight on the other side of the house, with a thud and a smash of breaking wood.

"There," he said. "You see? I'm a terrific shot, Ryland. You don't have to worry about my gun."

Ryland, however, was no longer outside the door; he had closed it behind him at the first shot. Peale holstered his gun and stood in the sudden silence, trembling a little in the hands—that had been the worst yet, that uncontrollable impulse. Inside, they must all think he had gone mad. The dogs were certainly thoroughly excited—the hound was obviously a gun dog—and both of them had climbed to the driver's seat and were trying to squeeze out through the window.

"Hey, guys, it's OK. You just stay put for now. I'll get you home soon, don't you worry."

When they had quieted down, Peale turned off his flasher and put the bullhorn back in the truck; he unslung his holster belt and put it there also. Then he turned and walked toward the house, and when he knocked, Ryland opened the door. Behind it there were more lights, and animated, concerned faces.

"I'm sorry about the gunplay," he said to the faces. "But at least you won't have to get out a ladder."

"I'm glad you got here," said Ryland.

"Hello, Sheriff," said Maggie Esterhaczy.

"This gorgeous young man is your brother? Introduce me, please."

"Mrs. Esterhaczy, my brother, the county sheriff."

"The ex-sheriff," said Peale. "I'm going to resign."

"What? What!" exclaimed most of the faces.

"I never should have run for the job in the first place. My brother should have. In fact, here you go, Ryland." Following a sudden impulse, Peale unpinned his badge, then walked over and pinned it to Ryland's collar.

"Oh, Peale . . ."

"No, it's true. You'd be much better than I am."

"Well, we can talk about that later on. For now, we all want to explain—"

"Yes, where have you located the kidnappers?"

"Mitch and Billy Bob aren't feeling very good right now. They're down on the floor in the living room."

"Mitch Ketchum? And Billy Bob Watson?"

"That's right."

"And Howell Bourne? What about him?"

"My brother took a walk," said Bailey, whom Peale had not yet looked at.

"We were hijacked by American desperadoes. But we have no wish to make charges," said Josef.

"That's good," said Peale. "I'm glad." The whole thing was beginning to seem simply like a dream.

"That's *good?*" said Richard Minot. "Well, I intend to press charges."

"Forget it," said Peale. "I won't let you."

"You won't arrest my brother? He's got a farm he could lose and everything."

"I'm never going to arrest anyone again."

"Well, that's good," said Dr. Ludgar—Dr. Ludgar!? What was *he* doing here?—"because we were just about to play cards."

"Poker," said Ada. "I love to play poker. And the stakes—we will play for and against defection!"

Now everyone started moving about the kitchen again, putting cups and saucers into the sink, arranging chairs, looking for packs of cards, and Peale was left standing, feeling awkward and out of place, the last one to arrive at an excellent party. But when Bailey Bourne came over to him, the rest of the room just faded, and he was there, standing with her alone.

"Sheriff Guthrie," she said, "I don't want you to think I deceived you. I really didn't know where they were when you came."

"You didn't?"

"No, I figured it out after you left. But I can just imagine how you must feel about me now."

"I doubt it," he said. "You clearly have no idea."

"But anyway, Howell was just confused."

"I *said* that I wouldn't arrest him. What else do you want me to say?"

"I don't know. I really don't know. Nothing, I guess." And as Peale stood there glaring at her angrily, she looking at him in astonishment, he knew he had never wanted anything so badly—and that it was the wanting which was new to him, the intense desire that ruled him. He had never imagined that this could bring such pain. Oh, he hated her, he really hated her, and as he stood stock-still in the crowded kitchen, unable to turn away, he felt he was falling out of his own life toward that of some stranger. There was a spiral, a tornado-shaped spiral, moving backward toward this moment from the future, and another spiral, this one gentle, moving foward toward this moment from the past, and this woman, this Bailey, was at the junction of the spirals; her lips were the portal where they met. He saw now, all too well, what he had thought he would never see—why people stole, why they killed, why they kidnapped. They did it, clearly, because once they had loved, and that love had been taken away; they did it because they'd *wanted* something more than life itself, and that want had turned inward, on itself. Oh, yes, this was it, and whether she rejected him and sent him on his way, or whether she returned his feelings, he would never again be able to claim that he didn't know how to be sheriff. People suffered and in their suffering they harmed, and they harmed because of separation; if you were once *of* the world, you would always rub against it, in the wind that whirled both ways.

"Hey, Peale," said Ryland, beside him suddenly. "You'd better take your badge back."

"I guess I'd better," he said.

# 29

RYLAND had been very embarrassed when Peale had given him the badge, and he was glad when his brother took it back without argument, and pinned it once more to his own chest. Oh, it might look, to someone just arriving, as if Ryland had done something quite amazing, but in fact he had misjudged the whole situation, beginning with his assumption about Maggie. She had been, he was afraid, rather exasperated with him when he got here; well, no wonder that she had, seeing that he had thought *her* involved with this. He should certainly have known better than to think that. And then there was that business about the chair, which had *caused* trouble rather than solved it—to compound his error, he had offered the chair to Billy Bob, without realizing that Mitch might want it, too. He had felt slightly better about things, though, after calling the hospital and finding that Mrs. Wickenden had stabilized, and though unfortunately her first word had been "nap"—Ryland was apparently the only one who realized that this must refer to the texture of the rug onto which she had fallen when her heart had gone into spasm, and not to the fact that she had just awakened and would probably go right to sleep again—there was no question that it was good news that she was going to live. With any luck, everything would turn out all right.

Probably the biggest shock of the evening, though, had been the shootout between Peale and the chair. It wasn't like his brother to act that way, at all. So he added, "Are you all right? Would you like some coffee, or something?"

"No. But listen, I just remembered."

"What?"

"I've got two stray dogs in the car. I should probably call the vet and find out who they are."

"Oh," said Ryland, not really understanding. "Well, the phone's there, on the wall."

"I've got to check their tags first."

"Do you want me to help?" asked Bailey.

"That would be very nice," said Peale oddly, and they left.

Their departure was fine with Ryland, who wanted to get back to Maggie; she had been just about to tell him something when Peale arrived. Five times she had started to speak, and five times she had decided not to, just staring at him accusingly instead. To Ryland, this was arresting behavior; it had aroused his curiosity, which he was glad that he could satisfy now. Maggie had started washing dishes, so he went over and took her by the shoulders.

"Come on, Maggie, let's go somewhere else. You had something you wanted to tell me."

"Oh, go away. Leave me alone."

"Have I done something wrong?" he asked.

"Yes," she said, and glared at him. Oh, she was so wonderfully *grumpy;* she simply would not admit that there was anything at all good about being alive, and he found this somehow a never-ending source of satisfaction, as it made him feel less grumpy himself. Why sometimes, compared with Maggie, he felt like a really happy guy— a bold and dashing optimist in the larger scheme of things. Or maybe he just felt that way now—after all, he had gotten her back! And soon he was going to ask her to marry him.

"Well, what? I really love you." It was the first time he'd ever said it, and she took her hands out of the dishwater in response.

"Go on," he added. "You can tell me."

"All right, all right, I'm pregnant. Great news, isn't it? Just what we needed to hear."

To Ryland, who had heard these words—directed to him in this particular way—just once before in his life, there was something awfully novel still about the way they sounded—the way the emphasis fell on the "preg." Preg-nant, it sounded so technical. Pregnant, I'm preg-nant, loaded with extras. He continued to stare at her, expectant, as if there would naturally be *more*—for example, "I've made a breakthrough in mammalian reproduction"—since the truth of it was, he had expected something stronger to follow the long waiting period he had gone through. The sheer pedestrian sound of Maggie's words threw him off balance; indeed, not only did he not fully grasp what she was saying—he remembered this inability, remotely, for the time that April had announced to him that she was pregnant with Clayton, the long time it had taken him to grasp the statement, as if it were a complex mathematical formula that he was expected to solve, one of those quadratic equations, perhaps, that he had never been able to fathom—but he actually wondered why she was telling *him* instead of whoever was involved. As she continued to stare at him accusingly, wiping her hands on her pants, he slowly started to absorb her words. Obviously, she meant she was pregnant by him. Obviously, she wasn't happy.

Though Ryland had spent much of his childhood in a state of premature old age—old age that had been brought on by the birth of his infant brother—he had, since the advent of his own son, Clayton, come to see birth as an exciting event. Although his anticipatory glee over the arrival of Clayton five years before had been muted by a sense that it was unfair that April was the one who got to have the baby—something the universe had typically made impossible for *him* right from the start—after the delivery he had been nothing but happy. Clayton was a wonder of the world. Though this was not news he had been expecting, therefore, and though Maggie still looked pretty peeved, Ryland didn't see that this development was so terrible; it was really rather all right. In fact— and here at last his true feelings were able to catch up with his thought, like a person running alongside a moving street car and managing to grasp the handle, finally, and swing off the ground—

in fact, this was just the most wonderful news! Maggie was pregnant! Hooray!

"But that's *great*," he said. "Come on, let me hug you! We're going to have a baby!"

"*I'm* going to have a baby. Or, rather I'm not. You're going to have nothing to do with it."

"Are you sure you're pregnant? Should we ask Dr. Ludgar?"

"Dr. *Lud*gar," she said. "Hah-hah!" Now she just glared at him, more bitterly than ever, and crossed her hands on her chest.

"What do you mean Dr. *Lud*gar? He's a pretty nice man."

"Doctors!" she said. "I hate them!"

"Oh," said Ryland. Well, he certainly understood that.

"I was pregnant once before, remember? They treated me as if I were a moron."

"Oh," said Ryland. He understood that, too. "But that time was different. You weren't married to *me*, then. Together we can take on the whole system. Oh, *come* on, be happy. Clayton had April for a mother. Just think what ours could be like."

"Clayton's a nice kid," said Maggie grudgingly.

"He certainly is. He's *nice*."

"But anyway, we're not married."

"But I was going to ask you tonight. Anyway, I really hardly have to." And as he said this, it seemed to Ryland that he was already married, had been married since that morning when Ada had introduced them at the auction, and he and she had taken Clayton's hands and walked him between them through the crowd, and he had bid on the Sword of Communism. Maggie hadn't laughed, she'd been so understanding. It was as if she'd already been his wife. Oh, she has such nice red hair, and such a pleasantly peeved expression, and she had theories and attitudes so like his own. Why, really, they had been made for each other; it made him feel almost complacent. Nothing within him felt even slightly gypped.

"And we won't have charts, and we won't worry about anything. And if you want to, we can have the baby at home."

"You're happy?"

"I'm euphoric. I've never been so happy in my life. See?" He danced a little jig.

At that, Maggie laughed, and began at last to relax, and to unwrap her arms from her chest. Ryland went over to her, and twined those arms around him, then hugged her as hard as he could.

Over at the table behind them, the troops had settled down to cards, or, rather, to discussing cards and trying to settle on a game. The voices, which had for some time combined to form merely a low mumble of amiable chatter, now suddenly rose to a crescendo of wild argumentation, very good-natured but very vigorous. Looking over at the players, Ryland saw no poker faces among them—even Dr. Minot had joined in the whooping—and while he was glad that they were all so animated, he wanted a lot more silence and privacy.

"What do you say we go somewhere else and kiss?"

"Like where?"

"We could go outside. It's such a beautiful night."

"OK. But let's take a quilt or something. I'll get it." Maggie pounded upstairs and returned with a quilt and a blanket.

"Have fun, chickens," Ada called after them.

The night really was very lovely, with a sweet warm air and a moon that looked as if it had just been formed. But when Ryland and Maggie emerged through the living room door—they had taken that route rather than the kitchen exit in order to avoid having to circumnavigate the crowded table—Ryland at first had trouble paying attention to the lovely night, since he saw something, right in front of him, a good deal stranger. His brother Peale was kissing someone who looked like Bailey Bourne—in fact, there was no question that it was she—and not just kissing but gripping her to him as if they were both to be shot together from a cannon. Although Ryland had never thought of himself as someone who was easily shocked, he found himself, at this fantastic sight, quite staggered; why, Peale was married, and had always been so correct!

"Do you see what I see?" asked Maggie.

The sound of Maggie's voice penetrated the embrace, and Peale dropped Bailey as if she had just short-circuited.

"Hello," said Peale hoarsely. "We were just out getting the dog-tags. To call the vet and find out where they belong."

"Oh," said Ryland. "That's right, you picked up some dogs."

"I think I know whose they are, anyway," said Bailey.

"You do?" asked Peale.

"Some guy who works out at Grey Rock. Or, rather, I guess they're actually his wife's."

"Oh," said Peale. "Well that should make it simpler."

"Where'd you find them?" asked Maggie.

"On Pond Road."

"Ah," said Ryland. Then, after a longish silence, "Luckily, I left Molly in the tornado cellar."

"Yeah?" said Peale.

"I mean, not because of the tornado. But it was lucky she was there when it came."

"Oh, very lucky."

"Yes, that was fortunate, wasn't it? Molly hates even ordinary storms." Here, Maggie jabbed him in the stomach with her elbow. "But, anyway, we were just going for a walk."

"Well, have a nice walk. I guess we'll go back in the house now."

"They're playing poker in there."

"Yes."

"See you later!"

Five mintues later, Maggie and Ryland were lying on the quilt, which they had spread underneath one of the large black walnuts. As soon as they were safely out of earshot of Peale and Bailey, Ryland had started to laugh in weakness and relief.

"Good God!" he said. "Peale unfaithful! Not that I like Amanda. But it just seems so, well, it just seems so *weird*."

"Poor man," said Maggie.

"Yes. I don't know why he ever got to me. I used to imagine that he had it all."

"Do you think he'll really resign?"

"I don't know. I kind of hope not. Whoever took his place would be bound to be worse."

"Yeah. Law, religion, and authority. What a mess they've made of the world. It'd be nice if we could just go ZAP and they'd all be gone."

"And babies? What about babies? You wouldn't go ZAP to babies?"

"I don't know. We'll see. I need time to decide."

"I know. But I promise I'll help you with things." By this, he meant help her with doctors.

Oh, he knew just what she meant about doctors, of course—the preeminent modern "authority"—and how dreadful it would be to be stuck in their hands for almost nine months and for many months thereafter. Having to be poked and probed, admonished and advised, reprimanded and firmly separated from one's identity—well, it would be enough to make *anyone* stop and wonder whether having a baby could be worth it. For the first time, though, he wondered right now why doctors and modern medicine were so hateful; he could afford to, for once, since he himself was well, and this was, for him, an entirely new condition. Why, just fifty years earlier, people had been *glad* to see their doctors; they had trusted and liked them quite a lot. Of course, doctors then had tried to help people for the love of it, and not, as they did now, for money. Now, they were likely not to care about people, but only about tests and drugs and procedures. But why were they so unfeeling? It couldn't *just* be because of the money. It was as if they felt totally helpless. Since Freud, Ryland thought proudly—Maggie had told him all about Freud—the individual ego had become everything, so physical illness and mortality were probably simply more horrifying than they had ever been before, and the doctor might be consequently more defensive. Because underneath it all, they must realize they could do little, and they were afraid that someone might actually notice.

"Help me?"

"With the doctors. With all of that stuff, you know. And Dr. Ludgar . . . he's really not so bad."

"Dr. *Ludg*ar," said Maggie, just as she had before.

"Oh, well. Let's talk about it later."

They pulled part of the quilt up over them and lay staring at the stars in silence. Ryland felt, somehow, like a very young child; he felt a lot more like a young child than he had ever felt when he *was* a young child, and even though his brother Peale was only three hundred yards away, he did not feel old and bulky and in imminent danger of getting gypped again, he felt young and lithe and like the luckiest person in the world. Poor Peale—he still had so much to go through, learning to sink to the depths of worry and pain—why, a divorce alone . . . and whether to be sheriff . . . it was all going to be quite a handful. But he, Ryland! All that was behind him. He was with Maggie now, his dear friend.

"Oh, Maggie." He held her hand to his heart. "Do you remember when you had hysterics?"

"Beyond War?"

"Yes."

"It was the first time I'd ever had them."

"I could tell. Your nose began to run."

"You know," said Maggie to that, moving over to nuzzle his neck, "this is the way I always thought that it could be."

"It's *better* than I ever thought it could be."

"Really?"

"Uh-huh. Really." Ryland turned slightly and started to kiss her mouth. But at the last minute he changed his mind and moved down to kiss her belly instead; he kissed it over and over again, whispering general remarks of welcome and incoherent salutations to the nubbin inside her uterus that would someday become their child, and he wished, as he kissed, that he could sing it a song, though he'd never been much of a singer. It really did seem, though, that singing was somehow called for, so after mumbling to her belly for a while, while Maggie laughed at him, he drew back, sat up, and placed his hand on her stomach, then stared intently up into the sky, trying to think of a song. He knew a birthday song that went, "Happy birthday, Happy birthday, just for you," but as it went on to say "When you blow out the candles, one light stays aglow," it didn't seem strictly appropriate, as he had no cake; and all the other songs that popped into his head one after another were more for singing around a campfire than for welcoming a new family into the world. But there *was* something; he *knew* there was something; and then he knew what it was.

"Oh, Maggie, Maggie," he said excitedly. "The Jumblies!"

"The Jumblies?" she asked, a little sleepily. "What are those? Some kind of candy?"

"No, no, it's a poem. Clayton's favorite poem." And while, five minutes before, if he had been asked, Ryland would have said politely that he didn't know "The Jumblies" by heart, that he had always read the poem to Clayton from a book, he found now, in his excitement, that along the way he had learned it, and that he could recite it to Maggie. He got through the first verse with just a few hesitations, and then, as the second verse began, surprised himself by remembering it all, and by declaiming it like a pro.

> They sailed away in a Sieve, they did,
>   In a Sieve they sailed so fast,
> With only a beautiful pea-green veil
> Tied with a riband by way of a sail,
>   To a small tobacco-pipe mast . . .

As he went on, his voice gained in power and assurance, so that, moving into the next lines, he found he was belting out the poem as if he were the ringmaster of a circus, and he only wished that Clayton were with them and could join in with his shrieks of joy.

> And every one said, who saw them go,
> "Oh, won't they soon upset, you know!
> For the sky is dark, and the voyage is long,
> And, happen what may, it's extremely wrong
>   In a Sieve to sail so fast!"

And as he finished this verse, still staring up into the night sky above the trees, where the stars were twinkling like glitter and the moon was rising with ponderous grace, there was a flash of light and an arc of motion, and a shooting star fell through the sky, going on and on, so that Ryland gasped, and Maggie sat upright beside him. They watched the tail of the meteor penciling its shining message on the sky, and Ryland, the words of the Jumblies still filling his head, found to his astonishment that he was weeping again; his face was screwing up and his breath was getting short, and his throat was closing in upon itself, so that the only thing to do was sob, the tears streaming down from his eyes. It was so wonderful, it was all so wonderful, life and the stars and the way that things came together, the way that, just as Saguanay's Funeral Parlor had given way, at last, to Saguanay's Furniture Store, so, too, the wake that had been Ryland's own life had turned into a real party. Oh, you never knew, you just never could guess, and though no doubt a time would come when he would once more play Catastrophe, would brood darkly about the tragedy of mortality and the constant threat of loss, for now he could say, "How happy we are / When we live in a Sieve and a crockery-jar! / And all night long, in the moonlight pale, / We sail away with a pea-green sail," could say them aloud, as a matter of fact, or at least could choke them out; they mixed with sobs and the tears that had by now gathered to tickle his upper lip so that he had to arc his lips downward in a perfect snarl of sorrow in order to let them run off.

"Oh, Maggie," he said, "will you marry me, please?"

She laughed and wiped his tears off with her palms.

# 30

BAILEY saw the shooting star, too, as she stood outside waiting
for Sheriff Guthrie. He had gone into the house to call Joel's wife
and see if her dogs were really missing—an unnecessary effort, but
one that Bailey didn't object to, since it gave her a little time to
recover her breath. Sheriff Guthrie's sudden desire to kiss her had
taken her totally by surprise, and she had acquiesced mostly because
she couldn't imagine what to say when he asked her "May I kiss
you?" He had taken her silence for agreement, and had gripped
her to him so tightly that she had found it almost wonderful; it had
certainly taken her breath away, which was very unexpected. Perhaps, she thought, remembering the moment in her apartment
early that evening, it should not have been unexpected, but she
had dismissed that moment as being all in her mind; it was pleasant
to find that it hadn't been. It might have been even more pleasant
if Bailey could have forgotten about Howell, but she was worried
about him—where on earth *was* he? And how were they going to
find him?

When Bailey had realized that Howell was running away, she
had felt immensely discouraged. Although there was a full moon—
and this moon was *really* full, unlike the one on the night the month
before, when she had gathered those women at her house in an
attempt to interest them in forming a coven, thus setting, to some
extent, this whole thing in motion, since if it had not been for
Janet's and Thea's report to Billy Bob and Mitch, Howell would

never have enlisted the help of those two incompetents, who were even now asleep on Ada's floor—she didn't feel she could pursue Howell through the woods. She didn't know what direction he'd taken. She had called him until her voice was almost hoarse, but he had not responded; of course, now that Sheriff Guthrie had promised not to arrest him, it would be quite all right for him to come back. But he didn't know that, and she wondered where he was. She wished that he were still here.

Despite the kiss—or even, perhaps, because of it—she felt lost and lonely, totally out of place, as if things were shifting around her. When she had come out here, all steamed up on her brother's behalf, ready to do battle against him for his own sake, for once, rather than hers, she had felt a flush of love that was really almost frightening, because it was deep and familiar, fundamental. Although it had been years and years since she had allowed herself to feel or to express any of the tenderer emotions toward Howell, there had been a time, as she had finally remembered, when she had really almost adored him. Even then, of course, he had been stiff, with a staid attitude that others might have found laughable, but she hadn't laughed; she had found it enthralling. He was so different from her, so intriguing. Why, as she had played her strange, imaginary games, he had trudged around with the milk hose; it had impressed her, she remembered now, that skill in the physical world. When he had climbed up onto the tractor to plow his neat rows, when he'd taken apart and repaired a motor, those moments had bewitched her with their profound gravity. They showed a world where everything was real. She had loved him, loved him for who he was. Maybe she could love him again.

Behind her, in Sheriff Guthrie's car, the dogs were moving around, and she opened the door to let them out; they probably needed to pee. But instead of leaping to the ground, as most dogs would have, they just shifted over to make room for her; she remembered Joel saying how much they loved cars, and this was certainly the proof of it. She closed the door again after rubbing their ears, and heard Ryland and Maggie laughing in the woods.

The sound of the laugh made her lonelier than ever, and she

decided to go back inside. Sheriff Guthrie had asked her if she wanted to go with him when he returned the dogs to their home, and she had agreed, still dazed by the kiss, but she really didn't think she should go. If Howell came back and she wasn't here, he might decide to run away again.

In the kitchen, Mitch and Billy Bob were still missing, but the others were sitting around the table—Dr. Ludgar at one end, Dr. Minot at the other, with Nicolai, Josef, Johnson, and Ada in between. They had chips and a pack of cards lying in front of them on the table, though at the moment they were not playing; instead they were wrangling about the rules.

"We will play for defection," said Ada firmly. "Two teams, for and against."

"I don't like playing poker in teams," said Dr. Minot.

"Will we ever get started?" asked Josef.

"Yes, yes, let us start. Five-card stud. Bailey, will you be playing?"

"I don't think so."

At this point, Sheriff Guthrie got off the phone. "Yes, they're her dogs all right," he said to Bailey. "We may as well go."

"You go," she said. "I think I should wait here for Howell."

"Oh. Oh. All right. I'll see you in twenty minutes. When I get back, maybe we can go look for him."

"That would be nice."

"Is Ryland still outside?"

"I heard them laughing. They're back in the trees."

"Well, if he comes in, tell him I'll be back."

"All right."

Sheriff Guthrie turned and left.

Immediately, Bailey was overtaken by the feeling that she should have gone with him after all, but it was too late now, so she might as well make the best of it. Maybe she would go look a bit for Howell.

"You are sure you will not play?" asked Ada energetically.

"No, you go on. I'm going back outside."

"Now don't you get lost in the woods like your brother!"

"I won't."

"Good. Everyone has a good time. Even my little pumpkin, off with her fine young man. She has forgotten, I imagine, about Doomsday."

"He seemed insane," said Dr. Minot dryly. "That sword and that chair—very strange."

"He is not insane!" said Ada, full of indignation. "Indeed he is not. He brings gifts. He is thoughtful, as should be others—who eat with no thank you!"

"Dinner was very good," said Dr. Minot, shamefaced.

Leaving the six of them settled around the table, Bailey wandered back outside. In the recent excitement, she had forgotten about the sword, but now she started to look for it, and found it leaning against a tree, where she had set it after Ryland presented it to her. The tree was, serendipitously, an oak tree—one of those which had been untouched by the tornado. The sword's sheath gleamed faintly in the light of the moon, and as Bailey bent to lift it she felt a moment of strangeness, as if the wind had suddenly gusted warm. She unsheathed the sword and held it up in the moonlight. Really, it was lovely, so tempered, so thin, like a stalactite formed by dripping steel, or like the visible embodiment of an energy that swirled and had been caught and arrested by this art.

Slowly, without thinking about what she was doing, she lifted the sword above her head; then she brought it down, raised it again, and moved it sideways through the air. At every shift of direction, she felt a slight resistance, not as if the sword itself were heavy, but as if the air it moved through was heavy, and was sluggishly dancing with the sword. The tip of the sword seemed to argue with the air, or to tug it, like a kite, behind it, and Bailey imagined that it bore a bead of light, a sphere impaled on its point. Above the sword, the trees had an immensity in the moonlight; they were to other trees as thunderclouds are to small clouds, although with no threat of a storm. With a great deliberation of movement that seemed natural and unforced, Bailey moved farther away from the house; she felt suddenly intoxicated, by the moon and the sword and the air—which smelled bright, like a color, like silver. And then, at the edge of the clearing, the sword extended full above her head and the moon riding on its tip like a top, spinning against all logic, she started to talk softly aloud.

"Oh, moon maiden, goddess, queen of all worlds," she said. "You are me, and I am you, and we speak of the old beliefs. Of the days that dawn with brightness, and the nights that set with sorrow, of the time that comes from nowhere, and rides us like a storm. Oh, moon maiden, goddess, lover, let us speak of the creation, let us thrill to the song of the two worlds, let us learn the language of love. Oh, moon maiden, goddess, hunter, take me now into your orbit, let me spin like the sound of the thunder, let me cry like the blade of a sword." And as Bailey spoke these words aloud, words that came not from a book, but from somewhere deep inside her, somewhere so deep that she had never known it was there at all, lying like a crocodile coiled in the mud of a river, waiting for the right prey to happen by so that it could open its hinged jaws and let fall two sweet round tears, she felt for the first time since she had started to practice witchcraft that she *was* practicing witchcraft, that she was alive with a force that possessed her, and that was linked to all things beyond. The sense of power filled her, and as she moved around the clearing, not trying to mimic any ritual she had ever read or thought about, but simply overcome with the desire to dance beneath that moon, to let her body bend and sway in the glory of its light, a light more tender and caressing than any other light the world can know—the light of reflection, the light of response, the light that has been taken and then changed—she felt that her flesh was truly one with the spirit and with the spirit of the universe that had formed her. Why, she herself was a stalactite, a dripping blade of steel that had been captured for a moment, arrested in its whirling dance and poured into a vessel that would contain it, and she embodied all things, *was* all things; She was herself, and her self was all around her. This was, indeed, the greater magic, not the casting of spells, not the moving of energy, but the worship that was the worship of creation. That there was no creator just made it the more glorious, just made it the more important to be you. It was simply a matter of seeing behind the veil, of embodying that which lay around you—to attract love, you had to become love; to arrest harm, you had to perceive it.

"A wand, a wand, I will be a wand, a witch, a witch, I'll bewitch you. A sea, a sea, I will summon the sea, I will ride on the ocean, I'll touch you." Again, the words came from herself, and if they seemed meaningless, yet Bailey felt, as she danced, still carrying the sword as if it were a child she had plucked from the reedy edge of a lake, wet, but alive and crowing, that these words had power beyond meaning. Indeed, what was language itself but a form of magic, a ritual invocation of things that were, apparently, beyond the reach of sound, and yet that offered themselves up to the mind through the intercession of the ear, that were reincarnated in the realm of thought like seeds that exploded in the springtime? That funny Russian, Nicolai, who seemed to be studying idioms—well, he understood that, the wonder of meaning and the lasting wonder of language. The words that you used to describe things could forever change what was being described, because those words were connected to the spirit itself, which could actually bring things into being. Men were all gods—the world they described became the world they lived in. Or rather, you lived somewhere between the two worlds—the true one and the one you invented.

Bailey stopped with a sigh and lowered the sword, then closed her eyes and tilted her head back. She almost imagined that she could feel heat from the moonlight that fell on her face, but perhaps she was flushed with the dance; she opened her eyes again when she felt small paws suddenly propped up on her legs. Chance, who had been lying patiently at the edge of the clearing, watching her as she danced, had come forward and jumped on her shins, looking earnest and hopeful and kind. Bailey set her sword once more against a tree, then leaned over and scooped Chance into her arms. "Are you my familiar? My little familiar?" Chance sank back against her in bliss.

Bailey was tired and a bit dizzy, and she looked around for somewhere to sit. Just at the corner of the house, she noticed the chintz chair, which had, when Sheriff Guthrie shot it off the roof, crashed onto its side and was now looking crumpled, and which would, no doubt, be wet. But still possessed of a strange, intuitive certainty, she went over the chair and, picking it up, righted it, then sank back into the depths of the cotton. Yes, it was damp, but not as wet as she'd have thought, and the bullets hadn't done that much damage. Chance nestled up to her in tensile delight, and Bailey gripped her with total affirmation.

When Sheriff Guthrie returned, ten minutes later, Bailey was almost asleep, and at first the small muttering of his car in the trees seemed just a pleasant backdrop to her dreams. Only when it topped the rise with a funny snuffling noise did she come awake and realize who it was and that she had nearly fallen asleep. Still holding Chance, she got to her feet and walked over to the arbor to say hello.

"Hello, Sheriff Guthrie. Did you find the house?"

"Please—please—call me Peale."

"All right. Peale. Were the dogs glad to get home?"

"I hope so. They didn't want to get out of the car."

"Oh, they both love cars. They'd live in one if they could."

"Yes, that's what Mrs. Messner said."

"It was nice of you to do that."

"Oh, well, I really liked them. In fact, I didn't want to give them back. The dachshund bit me on the thumb with those tiny little teeth when I tried to get him to move off the stick shift."

"I know just how you feel. It's so easy to love dogs."

"Yes."

"Do you want to hold Chance? Your brother found her for me."

"Ryland?"

"Well, in a way."

"OK."

Bailey handed him the dog, and Chance immediately pushed her head against his chin. And as he stood there in the light of the full moon, holding her familiar against his chest, she had, of a sudden, a strange and vivid vision; she saw him dancing with her on the night of the summer solstice. He was naked and lovely, his body a shining beacon that she worshipped as she had tonight worshipped the moon. Right now, he was gentle and transcendent, quiet and utterly beautiful—far beyond anything that she had ever hoped for.

"Why did you kiss me?" she asked him.

"Because I think I'm in love with you," he said. Chance shifted, and looked at her very alertly.

And as he said these words, it was as if a channel had opened, a channel between Bailey's head and her heart. To say that it had never occurred to her that when she cast her spell for love, she might actually find some, well, that was fairly close to the truth. Oh, she had hoped she would find love all right, but sometime way in the future, when she'd figured out what she was doing on the earth. So reluctant had she been to truly contemplate being in love with someone—despite the "spell" that she had cast when she had known no more about what a spell should really feel like than she had known what it would feel like to be with the KGB—that she had never even let herself *think* about this man who was staring at her now, almost in torment. Yet the truth of it was that from the very first moment she had met him at the auction—he rather sweetly blurting out that he was the sheriff, she mortified beyond words at the damage she had done to his car—she had thought he was exquisite, touched with grace, with a profound innocence of face and soul. But she hadn't let herself feel it; she had kept herself closed, ignoring the feelings she might even then have had. And today, when she had gone to see him at his office, although she had felt nervous in his presence, she had put it down to anxiety about her mission; he had been more acute, more in touch with his inner self. Now that there seemed to be something that was really torturing him—he was suffering, actually suffering, she could sense that—she felt that she was responsible, that her stupidity had done this. She had made him carry the vision all alone.

"It's all right," she whispered. "Here." He paused only long enough to set Chance on the ground and then he moved into her arms, and this time the kiss eradicated space and discovered to Bailey her union. Why, she didn't have to go anywhere, after all— she could figure out what to do with her life right here, right in Felicity—since, as the moon continued its journey across the sky, she was mirrored in the clarity of Peale's face, and there was a consonance between them like that between a horse and a fine rider. The difference between *this* and whatever she had known before was like the difference between swimming and standing in the rain. For the first time in her life Bailey could believe tonight that people as well as the other animals had souls; she felt freed from an ignorance to which she'd been wed, and she parted from it with relief and gladness. Oh, their souls were nothing like the marketable commodities the Bible beaters tried to promote; they weren't goods to be auctioned to the highest bidder, no, they were more like shreds of a fabric of being—they were *already* one with all things. It was true, it was really true, desire was an infinite and eternal piece of cloth that clothed the whole of creation, and that you couldn't cut to fit you, any more than you could cut time. You could only feel its warmth as it wrapped itself around you, as an electron was drawn to a proton, as a planet encircled a sun.

# 31

INSIDE THE HOUSE Ada was still playing poker, and her team, happily, was winning. One of her teammates was Nicolai, who turned out to have a profound understanding of the art of bluff, which she would never have anticipated in such a seemingly humorless man. He also had a wide knowledge of various forms of poker that Ada would have thought had never been exported from America at all, and they had just concluded another stunning victory with something called High Low Chicago, a game so complicated that Ada admitted quite freely she hadn't understood what they were doing for a minute. It was a form of seven-card stud but that was the only thing that was clear to her.

"How about a round of Indian poker?" Dr. Ludgar asked now. "It would be better if we had even more people."

"Indian poker!" said Josef. "I have played that! You stick the cards on your forehead."

Nicolai, Ada, and Dr. Ludgar were gambling for defection, and the other three men against it. They had arrived at this arrangement with some difficulty, in part because Dr. Minot at first absolutely refused to play poker as a team game—saying that it would take away the point of it for him, and that the idea of giving everyone points for hands won was nothing less than ridiculous—and in part because both Nicolai and Josef wanted to play for defection; they seemed to think it would be quite a lark. Ada, however, had refused to take the other side, and in the end she had gotten her way. To her, it was the principle of the thing that counted; she found gambling for a principle quite exciting.

When they had started playing, she had still been a little woozy from her unexpected faint—really, she had never fainted before in her life, not even when she was a young girl and it was still fashionable in some circles to do so—but now she felt completely recovered. Well, not *completely* recovered, but she had had a good strong cup of coffee and had been sitting down for a while now— and seeing Ryland and Maggie go off together had been a fine tonic in itself. She wished that Boonskie were still inside—his high spirits were always infectious—but Maggie had locked him and Raga in the barn again to lessen the general confusion. In any case, this Indian poker sounded like fun, and she was ready to try a few rounds, although most of the people who had been there earlier in the evening had now disappeared into various quarters of the globe, and if they needed more players they were going to have to go outside to find Maggie and her young man or—heaven forbid— enlist the aid of the lummoxes. They had managed to stagger in from the living room a short time before, and were now sitting in a corner of the kitchen, their faces dirty, their aspect very grumpy; one of them had gotten sick in the bathroom, she couldn't remember which one. They certainly weren't good for much anymore, but perhaps they would do for a few rounds. Josef seemed to have the same idea, as he called out now, "Will you join us?"

"Yes, you must play," said Ada firmly. "It will be better for you than brooding."

In the end, though, it was Dr. Minot who persuaded them to join the game; he did so by arguing that it would show civic spirit and that their sentence might be reduced as a result. This was, of course, a fabrication, particularly since there would be no sentences, but as it persuaded them to play, Ada just let it be. When they had settled themselves at the kitchen table, and decided that Mitch was to join the team for defection and Billy Bob the team against it, Josef explained the rules of the new games, which involved only one card.

"Everyone is dealt a card," he said, "and, without looking at it, whips it quickly up to his forehead like a feather. Everyone can then see everyone else's card, but no one can see the card he wears himself. You bet on your own card, based on what you see. It is rather like life itself."

"Sounds stupid to me," said Billy Bob indistinctly.

"Yes, it is stupid, *like* you,. You must watch those prepositions," said Nicolai of the poker face. Josef winked at the assembled company.

When everyone had a card held to his forehead with a finger, Ada could not help but laugh. What a silly bunch they looked, these men, each with his forefinger gluing his card in place; she looked silly, too, no doubt, but at least she could not see herself. The bidding began with a high bid from Minot, who had, happily, just a three.

As they played, it struck Ada that Josef was right. This was a lot like life itself; she could merely hope that she held a high card, and proceed as if that were true. Right after the tornado, when she had stood on the lawn looking around her at the world, which seemed suddenly so taciturn, and, with a feeling of sickness in her stomach, at the great oaks twisted on the lawn, she had felt that she, too, was trembling at the roots—they had grown so long, did they not deserve more?—and that most of life was simply accident, beyond control or counsel. But you could not indulge that, that feeling of doubt, you had to forget it and bid high, with your head up; yes, it was accident, but you had to learn to use it, to get it to work to your advantage. And you had to direct it, so that if there was a *chance* of order, that order would reveal itself to you. Maggie didn't know that yet—that was why she had threatened an abortion—because she worked with the abstract instead of the real. But an abortion would not make her happy, not this time—she was in love. And she was, as all were, at the mercy of facts. So she would, in all likelihood, keep threatening to not have the baby, at least until she couldn't fit sideways through a door.

Oh, God knew, Ada thought, moving from accidents to mammalian reproduction, women had reason enough to wish they weren't pregnant when they were; why, the whole experience was quite ludicrous. Ada remembered still, all too clearly, the way her ankles had swollen up like puffballs, and whenever she had lain down to take the weight off her feet, the pain had scurried up to her sacrum. It had been like a sick joke on the part of the universe, and not funny even when it was all over. But that was not the point; the point was that while Maggie, brat that she was, would no doubt complain bitterly from now until the time the young one went to university, in the year—Ada did a quick calculation in her head— in approximately the year 2007—with both Ryland and Ada encouraging her to have it, she would have trouble doing anything else. Even now, judging from her prolonged absence outside, Ada thought Ryland had no doubt made some progress; and when it was all over, Maggie, too, would have learned about accidents and about how one must make the best of them.

"I raise you five," said Billy Bob belligerently, his whole face one enormous scowl. "What the hell is defection, anyway?"

"We would be your closest neighbors," said Josef. "You wish us for your neighbors, do you not?"

"Wait! Change that to ten," said Billy Bob quickly. Billy Bob had a deuce, and Ada could hardly restrain her laughter. Oh, she knew that she had just recently, while watching the two lunks fight, wondered whether her scorn for them was something to be proud of, but she had come to consider that it was. After all, being able to hate—it was necessary in order to also love. So long as you did not try to harm those you hated, and so long as you could always change your mind. She had changed her mind about the Russians in a second when she had seen them for the gentlemen they were— but why should she change her mind about *these* two fools? She could not imagine how Howell had gotten involved with them, as they were different sorts altogether. Why, Howell had a certain dignity; he was a fine man with a slightly weak brain. As she thought of Howell, she had a sudden intuition; he hadn't returned because he was hurt.

Although Ada's intuitions were not always correct, she remembered only those which were, and since her successes were so prominently filed in her brain, she was convinced that this one was true. Now, therefore, as she waited for the hand to end, she wondered what to do about Howell; there was no doubt that he was hurt, or sick, or even dying, somewhere in the reaches of the woods. And while this may have been precisely what he deserved if he had actually succeeded in doing something, since he had not, it seemed very harsh—and, then, he was Bailey's brother. Moreover, he had introduced her to these men, Nicolai and Josef, and she had not had so much fun in ages; if she could, she really should try to help him, though it was hard to see just how.

Now the bidding stopped and the cards were laid on the table. Ada's team won by thirty points, which set them strongly ahead. Just as Nicolai was gravely entering this fact on his scorecard—Mitch, on the winning team, looked vaguely pleased, though they could hardly thank him for his help—Sheriff Guthrie and Bailey Bourne came through the kitchen door, both of them looking flushed and disheveled. Bailey carried that little dog, the only one who looked quite calm; what had they been doing, out there in the night? And wasn't the sheriff married?

"Still playing poker?" the sheriff asked.

"Perhaps we should end the game," said Josef. "It is getting late, and we have a big day tomorrow."

"Oh, *no*," said Sheriff Guthrie. "Mrs. Wick!"

"We were just talking about Howell," said Bailey. "We think we should get up a search party."

"I think the same thing," said Ada. "Well, we have won."

At this the players rose, and they all shook hands, quite gravely, as if a principle had been upheld.

"Mrs. Wick?" asked Bailey.

"How do you search the woods at night?" asked Minot.

"They are my woods," said Ada. "I will think of something." She did not mention her intuition that Howell was hurt; there would be time enough for that later on. But though she had spoken out so strongly about her woods, she couldn't think of what would help. She wished again that Boonskie were with her; he always inspired her best thinking about things. Darling Boonskie, always so eager, always wanting to do his bit to help, but always so alarmed by everything that, really, he could rarely accomplish a great deal. Boonskie . . . Boonskie . . . something about Boonskie. Oh, goodness, where *was* her mind tonight? And Sam, where was Sam? Perhaps she had gone with Howell? Already carrying Boonskie's sweet puppies. But still smelly, of course—why, that was it! She was brilliant! Boonskie would find him! Boonskie would rescue the cherry pitter!

In the time that he was gone delivering the dogs—and quite a long while it had taken him—Sheriff Guthrie had decided, Ada was glad to see, that the louts should be sent home. Now he ordered his man Johnson to drive them back to their houses in the Saguanay's van, which he was then to return to the store. After this was set in motion, and the van was driven away, Ada was able to secure some attention for her intuition, or at least for her idea. Bailey called Charlene, that sad stiff wife of Howell's, to make sure that he had not gotten home on his own somehow, but, of course, he had not. How would he?

"We must search the woods," said Ada. "With Boonskie's help, we will turn him up in no time," and although there was, at first, a lot of dissatisfaction with this suggestion—Dr. Minot pointed out that, from what he had seen, Boonskie would be more likely to turn up a dead skunk than any more subtle smell (really, the man was so annoying, she wished she could box his ears!), and then Maggie and Ryland emerged from the woods just in time so that Maggie could, to Ada's complete indignation, half agree with him—but eventually, when no one had a better idea, they all went off to the barn. Maggie first collected a rope and a thermos of coffee, in case, she said, "they actually found him"; Ada, of course, was not about to tell anyone that Boonskie would follow only Sam.

When Ada unlatched the door to the barn and both Boonskie and Raga came bounding forth, Raga was indignant, but Boonskie was simply scared—it was scary, alone in the dark! He tried to climb into her lap, and although she was, as always, flattered, she managed to disengage his front paws from her shoulders and urge him back down to the ground. Then, with a very serious demeanor, she explained to him carefully that he must follow *this* smell, and she held under his chin while she spoke the jacket that Howell had luckily left behind. And though at first he appeared to be taking it all in, as he stared at the jacket with wild hope in his eyes, when she was done with her address, he elongated his nose toward the jacket, not to sniff it, but to take it delicately between his teeth and then trot off with it to a discreet distance, at which he could more effectively whip it violently from side to side in an attempt to break its neck.

"No, no," said Ada, but Boonskie, once the idea of doing violence to the jacket was implanted in his head, did not want to relinquish it without a struggle—he had few ideas, after all, so every one of them was precious—and eventually Ada had to ask Maggie's help in getting Howell's jacket back.

"Maggie, darling brat, you are young and strong—go and get that jacket from my idiot dog. We will set him on the right track afterward."

Maggie shouted at Boonskie, who froze in place, in the midst of one of his more wholehearted attacks on the jacket yet, his ears flat back on his head and his eyes wide with uneasy anticipation. After prying his jaws apart with her hands, Maggie disengaged the jacket and brought it back to Ada, who received the now slightly damp and mangled item with a certain amount of discouragement. She *knew* that Boonskie could follow a bitch in heat, after all—it was just a matter of securing his attention first.

"Why don't I get his collar and leash?" asked Maggie. "Then we can at least get him over to where Howell was last seen."

"Yes, yes," Ada agreed. "A fine idea." So Maggie went into the barn, but when she emerged with the leash and collar and fastened them to Boonskie in the usual way, he immediately took a loose section of leash in his mouth and started to prance happily from side to side with it.

"I'm not sure this is going to work," said Ryland.

"I must agree, I fear," said Nicolai.

Everyone else seemed to agree as well, and Ada felt momentarily discouraged. But Maggie made one last try, hauling Boonskie bodily to the edge of the woods where Howell had probably entered them, and there—perhaps because Sam had sat patiently in one place for a long time waiting for Howell to make up his mind to go—Boonskie looked alert from his nose to his tail, and stared off into the night. While the others gathered around him, and Ada, with a firm clap on his shoulders, encouraged him onward, his tail quivered, his nose quivered, and he suddenly started to move.

"He smells something," said Minot, with grudging admiration.

"He smells Howell," said Ada firmly.

And then they were off, the whole troop of them, Boonskie in the lead, putting his nose to the ground like a small bulldozer, Maggie second, hauling away on his leash until Ryland came up and took it from her, the rest keeping pace as best they could as they all made their way through the woods. It was a beautiful night, cool and calm now, with the wind whispering through the trees and the moon a shining beacon, and as Ada fell behind the group and found herself alone, she was taken back to a night in Szatymas long ago.

The family had been at the vineyard for the summer, and the vineyard was the best place in the world, since there Ada's mother, dearest Mimpli, had let Ada run barefoot with the peasants. This particular summer she had had her first romance—she had been a child and a woman both at once—but the war by then had started in Europe, and there were all kinds of epidemics raging. From the typhus, babies were dying by the thousands, and some serums were shipped to Szatymas; the peasants generally came to Mimpli with all their ills, and she healed them by using only her herbs. This new thing, this serum, they wouldn't go near—they refused to have their babies injected with poison—so Mimpli had stood in line first and been inoculated, and then they also had stood in line with their babies.

Something had been wrong with the shipment of serum, and many of the babies had died. Ada's mother had also died, after much suffering; it had been a dark, a terrible time. The night before Mimpli's death, Ada had gone out into the woods with the dogs, and one of the dogs, her mother's favorite, had howled and howled at the moon, as Ada, bundled in her good summer coat, had sat on an iron bench and wept. The world had been so beautiful, it had broken her heart in two, this loveliness that her mother was soon to lose; Ada had been only fifteen, and yet it seemed to her now that only an instant had since passed. She was the very same girl that she had been then, the same person she had been all her life— wayward and fickle, selfish and strong, with the same clear perceptions of the world. The very same eyes, the very same nose, the very same heart and mind—time was a cruel master, but so far she had tricked him, though others lay cut down like corn.

And things still grew, that was the wonder of it, just as they had grown at the vineyard in her youth. Apples still blushed and reddened, oaks still dropped their acorns, wheat still stood limber in the sun. Oh, she had nothing to complain of; life had treated her gently, it had always given her living things to love. Even Indiana, to which she had come with such reluctance, even Indiana had proved a bountiful home. Those squares she had feared had not come to rule her; why, look at her now, running around in circles! Raga had stayed with her, and he frisked around her feet as she stopped to try to catch her breath—but this time, instead of weeping, she took in the air and laughed. The soft echo of her laughter was all around her. Oh, she was a wily one; she had prevailed! What fun life was, after all!

# 32

HOWELL was lying in a pile of pain, staring unblinkingly at the moon. When he had first fallen, and heard the bone in his leg snap so loudly it seemed to drown out all the other sounds of the moment—the abrasion of his body against the rock behind him, the strangled cry that he had not been able to contain—he had tried, torturously to crawl back up the cliff, but it was, quite simply, impossible. With only his hands and one leg to use, it might have been possible in and of itself, but with the other leg dangling in such excruciation, it would have taken jthe will of Lot. And Howell had felt, as he thankfully gave up the effort, easing his body back down onto the narrow ledge that had stopped his precipitous plunge to the lake below it, that not only did he not have the will of Lot— as evidenced by the alacrity with which he had decided to stay where he was—but he did not even think, anymore, that he *wanted* to have it. Will power or resolutions or ideas. If it hadn't been for will power and resolutions, he would never have landed where he was now. Landed, he thought, and smiled weakly.

He had, he suspected, lost track of time as the moon rose steadily through the sky, but several hours must have passed, at least, since he had plunged down so suddenly to this ledge. He had certainly had the occasion, while he lay here, once again to review the mistakes he had made—the first had been taking that couch from Richard Minot, the couch he had had the Idea on. Oh, trouble

always came of fancy furniture, there was no saying no to that. Look
what had happened with Mitch and Billy Bob this evening, the way
they had almost killed each other about that chair. Once he had
taken the couch, though, he should certainly never have sat on it,
or if he had had to sit on it sometimes, it should never have been
when he was alone. He had been so *pleased*, reading that mystery,
not able to look ahead into the future; well, more fool him, to think
that the Bankers would burn all the mortgages. Why in tarnation
should the Bankers burn all the mortgages to get back two Russian
professors, when, for all Their protestations to the contrary, they
probably didn't even like Russians to begin with? Howell couldn't
say just when it had happened, but he had, at some point, started
to see Them—all the people he had ever mistrusted—as pairs of
Siamese twins who, instead of wearing large fur fortresses on top
of their heads and a kind of glowering look on their faces, like the
one they had worn when they were Russians, instead smiled slyly
at the camera, in Howell's mind, wearing flashy and colorful suits.
They looked like the kind of folks who would always tell you one
thing and mean another; They didn't look nice at all. And They
thought Howell's pitiful efforts were funny; yes, They were still the
conspirators.

By now, Howell was shivering hard, his good leg bent at the
knee. He had placed his hands, palms down, beneath his buttocks,
so at least they were somewhat warm. Despite the shivering, despite the pain, the world looked somehow wonderful—more wonderful than he could ever remember it—from his crumpled pile on
the ledge. The moonlight glimmered on the smooth surface of the
Pond except when, from time to time, a swift breeze would slap
that surface and the light would be broken into a thousand small
striations, running fleetingly across the depths below them; the
breeze blew, the leaves on the tree above his head would suddenly
jerk straight out on their stems. Then the wind would die, and all
would be calm, except for the tiny noises from the floor of the forest
and the wings of the birds passing back and forth looking for prey.
Once, Howell thought he glimpsed across the Pond, near its eastern

edge, a huge bird, whose wings spread wide to almost cover the moon, but he saw it only from the corner of his eye, and when he turned his head, wings and shadow were gone.

Howell wondered when he would be found. He knew that he should be worried—he seemed to remember from the Boy Scouts, before he had dropped out to join the FFA, that if your system got a great shock, like a bone being broken, and you were also exposed to dampness or chill, then for no reason anyone could really put a finger on, you might just end up dead. But as time had passed he found himself getting less and less worried, more and more relaxed and calm. Oh, the chances were good, actually they were excellent, that no one would even come looking for him tonight. Why *should* they come look for him, come to that? He had caused them nothing but trouble. In the morning, of course, the sheriff, in a kind of cleanup operation, would no doubt send his men through the woods to locate Howell so that he could put him in jail, but by then he would probably be dead.

Howell wasn't actually sure how he felt about dying, and he started to consider it now. He had always thought that if a man did his job on earth right, setting goals and organizing everything—if he was a take-charge kind of person—then dying would be just another job. A man would lie in bed, surrounded by family and friends, who respected him anyway for all the tasks he had already accomplished, and he would address a few calm words to each of them, urging them on in much the same way that a retiring ball player would urge on the guys who were staying on the team, and then he would take a few deep breaths and, with enormous dignity, proceed up to Heaven on his own two feet. It struck him as strange, now, that it looked as if he would not only not be surrounded by family and friends when it happened, he would not only not have the opportunity to tell anyone his final thoughts about the big job he had taken on, but he wouldn't even have the time to finish the job itself—and he had never been one who thought there was much point in taking on a job you wouldn't be able to finish.

Why should God have put him on the earth at all if He wasn't going to let him Do the Job? Why would God, for that matter, put *anyone* on earth if He wasn't going to let him reside on it for the promised seventy years? You couldn't very well be expected to *organize* things properly if at any moment the whole undertaking might just be grabbed out of your hands, given to somebody else for no good reason. Why, look at what had happened to his parents! They had died *long* before they had reached the proverbial three score years and ten, and no wonder that they hadn't had their wills made out all properly. It really wasn't fair of God at all. Why, when he thought about it in this new way, he could see there was no point in being mad at *Bailey*. It was God who was responsible for the mess that things were in. It was God who was so disorganized.

Up to now, Howell had always believed that even if he couldn't see it, there must be a good reason for all these kinds of things happening, but suddenly it was anything but clear. Oh, sure, he had made a mistake in what he had done today, maybe even a big mistake, but his intentions had been good; he had really wanted to help—his fellow farmers and all of America. He had *meant* to be doing something helpful, and if God was going to make him die just because he hadn't known for sure how to do that, well, God had a pretty strange angle on everything. Here God, who had been extremely noticeable by His absence from Howell's head all evening long, appeared at last, for the first time, and to Howell's surprise, seemed to resemble, not Kirk Douglas in one of his most manly roles, but a flashy song-and-dance man with a shiny suit, not unlike the ones They wore. He winked evilly at Howell and then said, quite audibly, "SOMEBODY GOOFED!" After which He vanished again, with a flippant wave of His right hand.

Well, Howell liked that! He had tried to make sense of things, he had tried to act correctly, and here was God announcing to him that somebody—meaning Howell!—had goofed! He had never much liked the word "goofed" anyway, and though, at the moment, he could not exactly remember where he had last heard it used, in what context, he was fairly certain that it hadn't been a nice one, and it irritated him a lot. He tried to sit up straighter, so that he could think things out once again, but the pain that shot through his leg and his brain was devastating, and he sank weakly back.

Sure, maybe he *had* goofed, but They didn't have to say it in that nasty tone of voice, as if They hadn't ever goofed, as if They were so all-fired perfect. Who were They, anyway? And why did God seem suddenly like one of Them?

They, They, thought Howell to himself, Who were They, who were They, who were They? In his peculiar state of mind, brought on, no doubt, by the excruciating pain and the shock, as well as by the prolonged loneliness and the glory of the night around him, this seemed to him a reasonable question, and one he should really try to answer. Were THEY the Russians, as he had thought so long? No, it appeared that THEY weren't. Anyone with two eyes could see that those fellows he had shanghaied this afternoon had nothing to do with THEY; why they couldn't have been less THEY if they'd tried! He couldn't say that he had actually liked them—they were too weird to actually like—but yes, yes, he was forced to admit it. They hadn't seemed at all like terrible guys. If Russia was sending out Nicolais and Josefs, instead of locking them up, then someone along the line had told him something wrong. No, they were certainly not THEY. All right, was THEY his sister Bailey, and other people who were like her? Atheists and so on, people with no respect? Well, of course not. That was even more absurd. It was silly to be afraid of her.

Worn out with thinking, he let his mind empty, and stared some more at the moon. So clear was the sky tonight, after the storm, that he could easily see, with his naked eye, the craters and mountains that made dark patches on its surface. He couldn't remember ever in his life having stared at the moon like this, with nothing else to do and nowhere to go—oh, he had looked at it, from time to time, but usually in relation to some task. But just lying on the ground and staring up at it? No, he'd never done that. It amazed him how good it made him feel to let his thoughts go and stare at the sky; it made him feel that the sky was all his, and that he was a part of the sky. The stars, naturally, were not as visible tonight as they would have been had there been no moon at all, but they, too, were present, and they kept him company, clustered as if to say hello. There might be no people present at his deathbed, but these stars, these suns, these huge chunks of matter; they would be, for now, his friends. "Hi, friends," he said aloud, waving his work-hardened right hand slightly. "Hi, friends, you want some coffee?" That sounded so silly that he almost giggled, but he stopped himself in time.

More time passed, and Howell thought less and less. He smelled and he felt and he heard. The water, he could smell, was actually wet, and the leaves of the trees smelled green, and he could hear what he was certain were mice, running around just under the earth. There were coons in these woods, and possums, and they made a fine racket as they went about their business, and sometimes Howell heard what he thought must be a rabbit, a springy, squishy hop. No large animals came by, but Howell thought that he saw that bird again, a huge owl, maybe, snowy white, and he was sure that the pain in his leg was growing less. He was growing sleepy. Die or not die, die or not die? Well, he guessed he would see. Even now, it was kind of fun not being in charge, just being one of the gang. Maybe no one was in charge, not ever, not anywhere. Maybe there *was* no THEY. Them and us, them and us, he thought. Them and us. Us, us, usss . . . and then he was asleep.

Howell woke to the sound of a hound howling and another hound howling back. He had been having a wonderful dream, he discovered upon awakening, a dream in which he and Bailey were little children again, and they had run away from their parents for the day and had a picnic in the woods. Although it was a warm spring day, and they had not needed to light a fire—after all, the food they had had with them, fried chicken, jo jo's, cole slaw, and macaroni salad, hadn't needed any cooking; it had just lain there in its beautiful basket lined with checkered cotton—they had lit one anyway, a perfect fire, and had sat around it while they ate. The sun was the color of fire, and the chicken was the color of the sun; everything important was warm and golden, even the color of their skin. And he had felt, well, happy, so happy it was impossible to describe—just filled with wonder and joy at everything, the way things looked and taste and smelled. It had seemed to him, in the dream, that there was nothing in the world to do more important than what he was then doing, eating, stretched out on the ground, happy; and his sister was happy, too; their dog, a young pup, had lain on the ground and panted. Only at the end had it howled.

Now, the howling broke for a moment, and Howell heard human voices. Human voices! Why they'd come for him, after all! And one of them, he was sure, was Bailey. Although it sounded older and deeper than it had in his dream, the voice had a lot of the same inflections, but she didn't sound happy, the way she had then; she sounded worried. She was calling "Howell!" As the hound began howling again—it must be Boonskie that was howling, since Sam couldn't have achieved such volume—Howell tried to call, but he had to swallow first. He was so thrilled that his mouth was dry. For a moment he feared he was still asleep and that this was an extension of his dream, and then he was trying to shout above the howls to let them know that he was here. "Hello, hello!" he called out, more strongly than he would have thought possible. "I'm here! It's my leg! I broke it!" Up above him, the howling shut down for a minute, and there was a shout back from Bailey. "Howell, is that you? Are you all right?"

"I broke my leg. I can't get up the cliff."

"OK, Howell. Just hold on a little longer. Some of us'll come down and carry you."

At that, a confused babble broke out as more voices joined in with hers; Howell could distinquish Ada's and Minot's, and at least one of the Russians'—he thought Josef's. He wasn't sure who else was there, but *that* voice was probably the sheriff's; he just lay quietly, however, waiting, still feeling half in a dream.

"I told you he would find him," said Ada triumphantly.

"I wouldn't have believed it if I hadn't seen it," said Minot.

"Is it possible," asked Ryland. "that he was just following Sam?"

"Now you be quiet," said Ada, "or I will bop you."

"How are we going to get down to him?" asked Dr. Ludgar.

"I'll climb down," said the sheriff.

"I'll come with you." This last seemed to be Bailey, and for a moment Howell was worried, but then he relaxed and lay quietly.

It took a while for anyone to reach him—he heard scrabbling on the rock and discussion—and then Sheriff Guthrie was lowered down on a rope. Very formally, Howell began to give himself up to the law, trying to raise himself slightly on his hands, and saying, "Sheriff Guthrie, I realize that it is your duty as an officer of the county to—" but here Sheriff Guthrie interrupted him very firmly, saying, "Oh, forget, it, forget it, we're all just going to forget it. Just don't do it again, all right?"

Well, that was amazing, but Howell was beyond amazement, so he nodded his thanks and shut his mouth. Dr. Ludgar appeared next, to splint Howell's leg—he did this, Howell was interested to see, with two large sticks and Howell's own jacket, mangled and torn but fastened to the sticks with a lot of men's belts—and although there was one moment, when Dr. Ludgar tightened the splint, during which the pain blew through Howell like a wind through wheat, effortlessly blowing everything before it, on the whole it felt good to have those hands on his legs, to have someone taking care of him, touching him. After the leg was secure, Sheriff Guthrie and the doctor tied a rope around his chest, and he was half hauled, half carried up the cliff; the pain of *that* was so intense that he thought he was going to faint, but he was conscious when they laid him down on the duff. And as he lay there, staring up at the faces of the vast horde of people who had come to find him, he felt that things weren't really in such a mess—no thanks to Them and their conspiracies. Maybe you didn't really have to work for everything—maybe some things could just be given to you. And maybe central control by God wasn't so vital as he had once thought it.

# 33

MAGGIE found herself walking with Ada as they carried Howell toward the house. The men had decided to take turns carrying him on their backs, and though nobody seemed able to manage this for more than about a minute at the most, it was amazing the distance you could walk in a minute; so far the system was working. At first, Dr. Ludgar had suggested that they leave Howell in the woods and go call an ambulance, which could bring a proper stretcher, but Howell hadn't wanted to be left. He seemed to think it would be bad luck. Personally, Maggie had trouble getting up a whole lot of sympathy for him—as far as she could see, he deserved a little bad luck—but Dr. Ludgar had given him some painkillers from his bag, and they were sharing the task of the piggyback.

Right now, Howell was on Ryland's back, and Peale and Nicolai were supporting him on the sides. Maggie still felt a little flummoxed by the totality of Ryland's approval of her sudden announcement that she was pregnant, but though at first she had felt an instinctive desire to resent his approbation—what did he think she was, after all, a baby machine?—by the time he started crying, she had quite forgiven him his approval. His recitation of that nonsensical poem followed by a long bout of sobbing had, in fact, quite disarmed her, and though even, as he'd sobbed, she'd had twinges of doubt about the wisdom of her own happiness, she had not been able to help letting down her guard and feeling almost thoroughly hopeful. She had missed him so much this afternoon, and had loved him so much this morning, and even now he was still euphoric, happier than she'd ever seen him. After he staggered to a stop and Howell was transferred to Nicolai's back, the first thing he did was to hook his arm through hers, and though he was immediately called back to Howell's side as a steadier, he didn't give up, but kept reaching out to touch her every time they came near enough to touch, even planting a kiss once on her ear.

"He is sweet," said Ada. "That young man of yours."

"He's pretty sweet, all right. Are you OK?"

"What do you mean?"

"Well, all the excitement, all the exertion."

"Do not worry about me, worry about yourself. From now on, you must take it easy."

"Oh, good grief, Ada, that's just a lot of bullshit. How do you think four billion people ever got born?"

"Oh, you always know so much. It is true you must take it easy. Though you must also, of course, remain lively and vigorous."

"God, that's so typical. It's a total contradiction. Besides, I told you I'm not going to have it."

"Yes, yes, I know. So fine, don't take it easy. You will do, as always, just what you want."

But what did she want? That was the question. What on earth did she want? Maggie looked down at her stomach inquisitively, not responding to Ada's last remark. Having children was always selfish; there were just no two ways about it. It was the thrusting of consciousness, as she had often reflected, on somone who had never requested it. And while that might be all very well if there was a reasonable expectation that the person on whom you had thrust consciousness would be happy at least half the time, that was not a reasonable expectation, since in the world Maggie had known, suffering beat happiness hands down. For all the gooey hoo-hah that surrounded the delivery of the human animal into the world, most people did it for one or two reasons, both of them pretty damned bad. They did it either because the biological imperative of their genes was so strong that they just couldn't help themselves—and this irritated Maggie mightily, the sense that she was nothing but a vehicle devised by her own cellular structure to preserve its genetic material—or because they wanted guaranteed love, a guaranteed connection. The first reason was certainly more forgivable than the second, since hormones and mitochrondria operated at a level far below reason, but it made the second reason even more poor, more blind in its pathological hopefulness. How could you reasonably expect to receive love from a creature you had thrust, unasked, into this world; how could all the love you could find or create make up for that first scurvy trick? Naturally, and despite all the astonishment of parents at the incredible perspicacity of their own offspring, those offspring inevitably figured out the nature of this trick, and they generally figured it out in record time, and by the year they started school, they had begun to formulate a still-vague but certainly a powerful resentment toward the folks who had *done* this to them. The torments of simple arithmetic, the bane of spelling and penmanship, the distressing harassments of their fellow fiends—all these need never have *been*. And later, when confronted with their own mortality, with the entirely inexplicable mysteries of existence—with the great big WHY that could never be answered—oh, later, it got even worse. It had been one thing, perhaps, in the days before birth control, when sex just caught everyone in its threads—but these days, children were always a choice, and they always figured that out. Why, if Maggie had the kid, he would hate her, that was all, there were no two ways about it. She'd have maybe six good years before he caught on, and then *bammo*, it was enemies for life.

Behind her, there was another shift of carriers; Nicolai now came to a stop. Then Peale and Ryland transferred Howell to Josef while Josef hunched forward like a great bear.

"Come on, Mr. Bourne," he said. "Shall we go? You should really learn to spelunk!"

"He needs that like he needs a hole in the head," said Nicolai, now moving to the side. Oh, people could be nice, there was no doubt about it. But they could also build hundred-megaton bombs. Where had things gone wrong? Why was the species such a mess? She suspected it all went back to a belief in God.

Yes, the threat of nuclear annihilation was the natural end result of a society that had reified its own institutions—so that they'd *all* congealed like warheads, so that everything was separate, particularly power and responsibility, which should have been inseparable. And people were convinced of the inevitability of this position by their own fairy tales about a God. "God," after all, never explained the suffering he inflicted; no, he demanded a blind faith that he had good reasons—and the pretense that without a Big Daddy, meting out commands and punishments, everyone would be somehow very naughty, was the very same pretense that supported law and authority. So people got to make decisions who didn't have to live with them, and that was the horror of most modern cultures; the doctor who forced the premature infant onto the hospital's expensive toys didn't have to care for the blind retarded creature that was the result. Oh, and you saw it absolutely everywhere, the separation of power from responsibility—there was nothing that hadn't been tainted with it. The genetic engineer didn't have to *love* the life forms he created, the priest who counseled the pregnant teenager wasn't there when the girl beat her infant until it died. The judge who sentenced that girl to prison had never been inside one, the manufacturer who made electric chairs never sat in one or saw it used. And certainly the politician who supported a nuclear buildup would not be there as the earth itself expired, and humanity dragged down with it two or three million other forms of life. People thought they had the *right* to run the lives of other creatures, because "God," they purported, had the right to act on them. It was a terrible historic tragedy, the ascendance of Western culture, which believed that the whole could be separated from its parts. And for an anarchist like Maggie to bring a child into this world, it would be simply an immoral act.

Behind her, she heard Peale and Ryland talking. Neither of them was assisting Howell at the moment—indeed, they were only five minutes now from home, and soon this would all be behind them.

"But why did you *call* the state police?"

"I hadn't gotten your note yet."

"They're going to think you've been kidnapped, too."

"I know. I just don't know what to tell them."

"Why don't you tell them you had a flat? You brought your Corvette, not your squad car—and your Corvette doesn't have a radio."

"That's true. But what do I tell them about *this?*"

"Tell them it was all a computer error."

"A computer error? They'll think I'm crazy."

"They'll think you're crazy anyway."

Now Ryland came up beside her again and put his arm around her waist.

"How are you feeling?" he asked, "We're almost back. It's just a few more minutes." At his question Maggie, who had, up until then, been feeling physically all right, suddenly realized she was breathless—she remembered that this was one of the early symptoms, feeling breathless practically all the time. All at once, she simply stopped in her tracks and moved out of the path of the others. Then she sat on a handy rock while Ryland followed her, looking concerned. Oh, she remembered this, all right, among the other unpleasantnesses of pregnancy, and it was yet another argument against having a baby, the sheer discomfort of it all. It seemed typical that those genes which wanted so badly to replicate themselves had not been able to find a more charitable way of doing it. Why did they care how much she suffered, as long as they managed to endure?

"It's all right," she said, in response to Ryland's question. "It's just sucking the breath from my lungs."

"It?"

"The cell clump. The little divider. Endlessly splitting in two."

"You mean the baby?"

"It's not a baby yet."

"Oh, April was very crabby, too. But that didn't last long—then she turned into a powerhouse. But for now, you should really be in bed."

"What are you, my trainer? Worried about the game?"

"What?" he said.

"Why don't *you* have it?"

"I'd love to, I would. But please don't rub it in. I told you I wouldn't be jealous."

"Never mind, never mind. Just let me breathe for a minute." Ryland sat down beside her on the rock.

Immediately, Maggie felt physically better; she probably *should* be in bed. What with getting hijacked on the highway at gunpoint, riding in the back of a closed truck like a refugee, and getting delivered to her own home as a hostage, it had been quite a strenuous evening—it would have been enough to exhaust her even if she *hadn't* found out she was pregnant and hadn't had to try to decide what to do about it. Although, really, no decision was necessary; the verdict was already in. It was too bad, but that was just the way it was. Strangely enough, having realized this fact, Maggie felt worse instead of better, particularly with her beloved Ryland sitting beside her. Usually, when she thought something out as carefully as she had just thought all this out, and came to a decision on the evidence, she felt a sense of relief and a clarity of purpose, but now she felt just the opposite—she felt hurt and depressed, almost bossed around, and consequently quite resentful. It was crazy, but like a defense attorney about to make her closing remarks to the jury, she wanted to find a chink in the armor of the other side, and right at the moment she couldn't.

"If you're rested," said Ryland presently, "we should probably go. Do you think you can go on?" He squeezed her hand.

"Oh, I guess so. This is all your fault."

"That's OK," said Ryland. "I don't mind."

Back at the house, an ambulance was called; it was now a little after midnight. It took fifteen minutes for the ambulance to arrive, and during that time Maggie found herself with Bailey, whom she had never talked to much before. But now the two of them had something large in common—"the Guthrie brothers," Maggie thought, amused—and though Bailey was more than a decade younger than Maggie, that should give them something to talk about. Bailey's little dog Chance came over and stood at their feet, her two ears cocked forward, with their superimposed layer of tufted fur cocked even farther so that the two ears formed perfect inverted triangles, which, nestled neatly along the line of her triangular face, created one large triangle of attention, with two serene eyes in its middle. Boonskie and Raga were now in the house, and Sam had been put in the barn, so Chance was the only dog still running around, and she stayed close to Bailey, as if leashed.

"That's a very smart dog you've got there," said Maggie.

"Ryland gave her to me, you know."

"He did?"

"That time he came to my apartment. He thought Chance was already my dog."

"Well, where was she really from?"

"I have no idea, In witchcraft, you'd say she was a gift of the Goddess."

"Yeah?" asked Maggie. "What's all this witchcraft stuff, anyway?"

"Actually, it's just common sense. It sounds weird, but it isn't."

"So who's the Goddess?"

"She's just a metaphor they use for the earth. The idea that the earth is a creature, and that everything alive is a part of it."

"That sounds like the Gaia hypothesis," said Maggie.

"The what?"

"There's this British scientist. He says the planet itself is the core of a living organism, a unified, self-controlling system."

"Yes, that's exactly like witchcraft; it's just a pagan religion."

"The American Indians. The pre-Hellenic Greeks. You know, it's funny, but I was just thinking about this."

"You were?"

"Well, about Western culture—as a horrible historic mistake, you know. A kind of epic disaster."

"But if that hypothesis thing, that Gaia, is true—if the earth is really self-controlling . . ."

"Then human beings would have to be part of it, too?"

"You'd think so."

"You'd hope so. I don't know."

At this point in their talk, the ambulance arrived and Howell was helped onto a gurney, then loaded into the van. Bailey climbed in with him, and Chance hopped up to join her; the attendants didn't object to this, but simply closed up the doors.

When the ambulance was safely off, Peale said to Josef and Nicolai, "I guess we'd better go. Mrs. Wick will be mad enough as it is, and there's no point in putting it off."

"We will ride in your Corvette?" asked Nicolai reverently.

"Yes. I'll drop you off, too, Dr. Minot."

"Goodbye, Mrs. Esterhaczy," said Josef, climbing in. "We will hope we may see you tomorrow."

"Perhaps. But don't forget. You have promised to defect!" The Russians laughed, as did Ada and Dr. Ludgar.

"That poker game was certainly like nothing else on earth." This, of course, from Richard Minot.

"Red," said Nicolai, as a kind of postscript. "I have always wanted to ride in a Corvette." Josef merely winked, and then everybody waved as the car shot off down the driveway.

"Now," said Ada, "You two, go! You must have something to celebrate?"

"Oh, yes," said Ryland. "You're going to be a great-grand-mother!"

"I know," said Ada complacently.

"We'll see," said Maggie. "But what about you? Are you going to be all right here?"

"I am eighty-seven, I think. I shall certainly be fine. I don't need to be cared for by infants!"

"Well, I'll see you in the morning before I go to school."

"Yes, all right. Just go now, have fun."

Dr. Ludgar got into the back seat of the Mercedes, first saying goodbye to Ada; while they drove home, Ryland talked a bit with the doctor, but Maggie was getting sleepy and didn't listen. The lights were on in the house when they got there, but, although Ryland had expressed the fear some of his guests might not yet have left, there were no cars on the street except for Dr. Ludgar's, and he climbed into it now, and took off.

The party was finally over. And while it had been a rather different party from the one that Maggie had expected, it hadn't been

a bad one, all things considered. It hadn't been a bad one at all.
The house tonight looked even lovelier than it had the first time
Maggie had seen it, its delicate and inviting porch wrapped halfway
around it like a ribbon, its tall windows shining with clarity and
sense, with an aspect of comfort and calm, and she felt as depleted
with emotion now as then, though her hysterics had been more
dramatic and physical. The earth itself might be one big organism,
but a lot of its emotions were in its humans; probably the one thing
that people could always do well was to wear themselves weary
with their feelings. Oh, and talk about them, too—they were excellent at talking—but right now she just wanted restoration.

The door was locked, so Ryland unlocked it, and then hurried
immediately to the kitchen.

"I left Molly in the basement," he said. "I hope she's still all
right. I'll be right up; I just have to get her." But Maggie followed
him as he went rapidly down the stairs, calling "Molly, Molly, are
you all right?" as he did so, and she was reminded again of her
extraordinary luck in finding him, this man whom she seemed always to have known. Molly came, yawning, out of the tornado cellar,
and wagged herself into Ryland's arms. He lifted her up and carried
her into the living room, then set her down carefully on one of his
rugs. He stroked her from head to tail, murmuring queries and
hellos.

"What a pretty, *pretty* girl. You want to go outside? You missed
the big tornado, you lucky dog." At the word "outside," Molly
looked very alert, so they all went back again to the porch. Molly
ran out to the yard, and Ryland and Maggie sat down in the chairs,
from which, in silence and holding hands, they watched her. When
she was done, she ran back and settled herself at their feet, tucking
her head on her tail with a sigh. Maggie untied her shoes and kicked
them across the porch, then put her bare feet on Molly's silky fur.

Then, as they sat there on the porch, staring out at the sky,
through which the moon had begun to sink again, satisfied, for the
moment, with its brilliant upward climb, another shooting star sizzled through the night, dragging its fiery tail behind it across their
sight. Ryland said, "Oh, another one! That's very good luck,"

squeezing her hand in joy, and Maggie found that her contentment, which had, in any case, been growing stronger by the minute, as they sat, the three of them, in sleepy silence, suddenly swelled to perfect happiness; they had seen two shooting stars tonight. Two audacious wanderers had made it through, where the uncounted others burned away. Though they, too, had burned, what a journey they had made before succumbing to that final fatal friction.

Maggie had always loved to consider the night sky, particularly while she was waiting for the End—she'd found it useful to remind herself that it really wouldn't matter much if the earth and everything on it were to blink out one day. Why, the Milky Way alone contained a hundred billion stars, and it was only one of billions of galaxies in the cosmos; and all those galaxies were expanding all the time, moving outward at just the speed of light. Now, almost despite herself, she found herself considering for once not her own insignificance, and the insignificance of the earth, in this great scheme of things, but rather the sheer unlikeliness of her being here at all; she was a fact in the face of enormous odds. When you saw a shooting star, you were seeing the earth at work, protecting the life it had somehow created—and that life was so improbable that it simply shouldn't be. She, Maggie, was practically statistically impossible. And so, of course, was the fetus that had come to life inside her. They were like the few shooting stars that made it through the ozone, like the meteor that had conjured up the Pond.

Oh, she was fooling no one, least of all herself; of course she would have this baby if she could manage it. It was obvious now that she wasn't going to die young, as she had always thought, and her long-standing assumption that it didn't matter if she didn't accomplish anything meaningful in her life—and that it was almost her duty to take a stand, against the attempt—no longer had much going for it. It seemed clear that she was a failure at underachievement, since without even trying she had been a success at every job she had ever had, and it also seemed clear that her fascination with the future was probably not going to go away. Its political edge might be broadened, of course, to include the more personal and close to home, but all this stuff that was opening up to her—it was just too interesting to forget. And although she had moved to Felicity in the first place in part because she thought that here, if anywhere, the continuity of her life would be effectively destroyed, her luck, always pretty good, had been better here than ever; she had a good job, a great man, and she had just lived through an attack. Yes, it was possible that if she had this kid, if she let the cell divider turn into a fetus, which in turn emerged as a baby, the baby would live just long enough to die, to go up in a puff of nuclear smoke. It was possible. But it was also possible, seriously possible, that not only would that child not go up in a puff of nuclear smoke, not only would that child not become one of the Stumblers, with no ability to feel or to speak, but that instead it would live and grow and flourish, and perceive with an amazing seeing mind.

Why someday her child might sit on this porch, staring up, like her, at the night sky; someday her child might gasp aloud in wonder as a shooting star vanquished the night. The missiles that Maggie had spent her life fearing might just stay forever in their cradles; if the earth was truly a self-controlling system, they should never nose through the night. Humans could stop them, humans like her, and humans, perhaps, like her baby—the very same species could somehow demolish what it first had wished into being.

Of course, there was a lot to be done for that to happen, a lot of things to change in people's minds, but if it *did* happen, well, it changed everything, didn't it? There was a future for the earth and what was on it. And the future was forever, it was as big as the cosmos itself, not as small as the planet from which she now tried to regard it—and almost all of the evolution of humanity might lie before it. The real stuff, the stuff of the mind. People already passed their thoughts from one brain to another with great speed and a fair amount of accuracy, and when the Beyond War folks talked about a new way of thinking, they were focusing on what people already did best. If they kept communicating for centuries, for eons, who knew what might happen then? Billions of minds, all working together; *that* was much stronger than a bomb.

Thinking of it that way made it seem exciting to be alive, not a sad process of waiting for coming death; everyone was part of this,

this giant creative endeavor, the evolution of the biota and of the brain. Even deeper than the need to describe how things worked lay the knowledge that they all worked together—*that* was the genetic encoding that mattered, to hell with that endless DNA. And that was where misery came from, too, from not being able to feel it; but sometimes you could, and you could live for those moments, and put your life in the service of that cause. As the man with the cauliflower ears had put it, everything was "cinched together"—the Palace of Knossos, the shellfish in the sea, Peace Links, a new breakfast sausage . . . and maybe man, the infant species, could someday grow to childhood and really feel the world that lay around him.

Good grief, thought Maggie suddenly, with amusement. Was this what it was like to be pregnant?

"Come on, guys," she said. "I'd better go to sleep." Molly leaped up and backed rapidly away.

# EARTHING:
## AN EPILOGUE

# 34

THE NEXT DAY, Ada woke up with a bad cold and a sense of ache in all her joints. One of her joints in particular, the hip on which she had fallen when she fainted so embarrassingly the night before, hurt very much, and she found, to her chagrin, that she could not easily climb out of bed alone. Only when Maggie got home at eight o'clock—nine o'clock on Ada Time—was she able to get up, with assistance, and hobble to the bathroom so that she could do her morning exercises in the tub. But even those were painful and slow, and when she accepted Maggie's assistance back to her bed, she decided she'd better stay there for a while.

Four days later, the cold took a turn for the worse, and she was alternately hot and freezing; for all the teas she had Maggie brew, at her direction, nothing at all seemed to help. Oh, well, she was dying, that was all there was to it, and while death was not something that had ever held any terrors for her, as she simply refused to consider it, there was the little baby to come, whom she wanted to see—or perhaps she could be reincarnated? But no, she refused to be one of those pitiful old people who suddenly converted to all sorts of weird principles at the last minute, and as the days in bed stretched to weeks, boredom was more pressing than fear. Sometimes, Boonskie would come to visit her, and when he lay at her side stretched to his full length, he would often raise his top rear leg to expose his stomach for her scratch; then she would lift and juggle his testicles, which were firm in their cool, shiny sack. Then Boonskie would go away again, and Ada would be left with her clock, which she took to studying with a certain fascination, watching the hands go round and round the face. At times, she was certain that she could see its hands move, and once, for a long stretch of what might, of course, have been a dream, she could have sworn that she was actually watching the hands spin round furiously, the hours following their minutes in an absurdly speeded-up progress forward. While this did not precisely make her doubt her own sanity—why should you not be able to see the hands move if you simply concentrated very hard?—it did make her doubt her own wisdom and sense in condemning these anti–Daylight Saving types out of hand. So when, to her own astonishment, she got better and was able to clamber out of bed mid-June, she decided that perhaps she wouldn't live on Ada Time after all, and set all her clocks back with satisfaction. A letter from Russia arrived that week—the Russians had not, after all, defected—and Ada felt pleased to have gotten it one hour sooner. Oh, Ada knew the time of day!

Maggie was feeling more and more moody as her pregnancy inexorably advanced. After three decades of peaceful indifference to a future that she had been convinced would never get here at all, she was now, by her ill-considered accession to the possibility of life in the next century, caught up in a sequence of events that certainly guaranteed that her *own* future was going to be a nightmare, an endless struggle against insuperable odds. When she had believed that the human race was going to extinguish itself quite soon, there had been a clarity to the way she had lived her life, and she missed that clarity, that conclusiveness of vision, so much that it sometimes made her weep. Or maybe she was weeping at something else—who knew, when one was swimming in a sea of hormones? Who knew, when a zygote was using one's brain?

When Ada got better, Maggie was immensely relieved, not only because she loved her, but also because her latest plan was to have the baby and then stick it firmly into Ada's arms. Ada and Ryland both seemed to relish the prospect of caring for an infant—the former probably because she was going senile, the latter because he'd mostly done it from afar—and it seemed like another grim trick of nature's that the people who were most enthusiastic about babies were not capable of actually having them. But to Maggie's horror, when she was at work, meeting in a string of hour-long sessions with summer students whose troubles, whatever their origins, she was paid to give the strictest attention to, she would find herself drifting complacently off in thought, losing sight of the child at hand. She thought of all the ways in which she, with her deep understanding of the mechanism of cognitive development, would be, of course, a superior mother, with a highly superior child. *Her* child would never be the mess that these kids were; *her* child would be, simply, perfect. When it was throwing its plate of food on the floor for the tenth time that evening, she would patiently pick it up and place it back on the tray of the high chair—calm, because she knew, as most poor mothers didn't, how crucial would be this developmental stage.

She would jerk herself back from these daydreams with disgust, and try to pay more attention to the slack-jawled youth sitting slumped in his chair in front of her. He wore an earring shaped like a skeleton in one ear, and his pupils were huge with drugs. But it was a losing battle, and though she didn't grow less moody until she was well into the third month of her pregnancy, she could see even before that the writing was on the wall; she was afraid she had a ferocious maternal instinct.

At the Bourne farm, Howell was in a cast, one that stretched from his hip to his ankle. For the first time in his life he was unable to work, and he sat all day on the living room couch, with the hound Jake beside him for company. Jake liked to rest his chin on Howell's plaster cast; occasionally he would lick it and screw up his face. Sam was still living at the Esterhaczy's, or Howell would have had her in, too. He saw no need, anymore, to chain hounds up. Hounds, after all, had found him when he'd been lying all alone in the dark.

If they'd been chained, they could hardly have done that, now, could they?

While Howell was laid up, Charlene took over the farm, and to his amazement seemed to relish doing it; she got almost bossy, coming in from running the tractor, and he rather liked this new attitude she exhibited. Sometimes his leg itched, and she gave him a knitting needle which he could poke down underneath his plaster and scratch his thigh, but since the itch was almost always farther down, there were times when he was in agony. The strange thing was, the itch always went away, whether he was able to scratch it or not, and in his present leisured life this small fact about the way his body worked was absolutely wonderful, and he tried repeatedly to make something of it: if you *didn't* scratch it, the itch went away; if you *did* scratch it, the itch went away also. Try as he might, he just couldn't quite get it, so he turned his attention to other things.

His sister Bailey had brought him an economics textbook, and he was laboriously making his way through it. Most of it he didn't understand at all, but one thing was pretty unmistakable: whoever had written this book had believed what he was saying. There was just too many graphs to think otherwise. But while the economics textbook had difficulty holding his attention, the people he conversed with did not. He had a regular stream of visitors, from his church and the surrounding farms, and he entertained them while watching the corn grow. And though most of these visitors seemed intent on having him recap, for their benefit, the events of the night of the kidnapping, what Howell wanted to talk about was something different. He wanted to discuss his ideas. But when he proposed, for example, that maybe man's job on earth wasn't to follow a list of rules that someone else had come up with, but simply to contribute to the overall happiness, most of them thought he had lost his mind.

Richard Minot, however, who visited him one day when he would otherwise have had no visitor at all, proved to be a fine conversationalist, and told Howell that he was grappling with the age-old theological dispute about faith versus works, and when Howell—upon understanding what he meant by this—said that no, that wasn't really it, Minot proposed that perhaps what he was concerned with was the absolute nature of the deity. That sounded a little more like it, and Howell, after getting from Charlene a pad of paper and a pen, started to make some notes to himself about what he really thought. Perhaps he would write an article that could be printed in his church newsletter. "Why We're Doing God a Favor" was the tentative title he came up with. Minot, returning one day the next week with a book he thought Howell might be interested in, found him hard at work on this article—engaged in orginal thought.

Peale had moved out of his house on Vine Street and was living for the time with Ryland. He knew that this arrangment couldn't go on forever—for one thing, Maggie would be moving there herself as soon as Ada was well enough to be left alone—but he still felt almost shellshocked from the recent dire events, and he needed someplace where he could recover. It turned out, luckily enough, that Amanda was hardly upset at all when he suggested they'd better break up; she admitted that she, too, had always felt surprised when she remembered that the two of them were married, and she was now making plans to move back to her home town, where she could avoid such surprises in the future.

Until she left, though, Peale was with his brother, whose hospitality was almost alarming. In the morning, before work, Ryland would make them both a big breakfast in the kitchen; in the evening, if he was with Maggie, he always called to say hello and to find out how Peale's day had gone. While Peale was used to going to his brother for fraternal advice and reassurance, he was also used to a level of reluctance, but now everything seemed to be changing. It would have been easier to deal with if this relationship with Bailey had brought him the same kind of peace and tranquility that Ryland's relationship with Maggie seemed to bring him, but far from being peaceful or tranquil, his feelings for Bailey were still volcanic. When he was away from her, he missed her like crazy, so that he felt a physical pain in his heart; when he was with her, he often wanted to hurt her rather than to be loving or kind. Sex, which had always had for him about the same emotional content as a nice workout on a sunny day, now became something tortured and confusing, and subject to amazing caprice. He had no idea where this was leading him, but he thought about sex all the time, just as if he had never grown up at all. The only part of his life that seemed truly satisfying was his work. He now *loved* to arrest all lawbreakers.

Her relationship with Peale made Bailey uncomfortable, too, since it seemed, quite frankly, impossible. She was used to relationships with a different type of man, and Peale's intelligence and charm often dismayed her; they made her feel even more of a misfit than she was used to, whereas the misfits had made her feel normal. What was worse, she had an odd desire to want to wait on him hand and foot, to do literally anything he asked her—and this threw her off balance, as if she had vertigo, or had been awakened, disoriented, in the night.

His job also troubled her, and the pleasure he seemed to take in it. As far as she could see, he lacked discrimination. On the night of the summer solstice, two women were arrested for performing Indian ceremonies on an Indian mound at Indian Creek Preserve, and instead of dissuading the park ranger who had arrested them, Peale essentially did nothing at all to help. The women were charged with digging a small hole in the mound and leaving flowers and feathers there, and when the case came to court they were found "guilty as charged," to Bailey's complete incredulity.

She had discovered, however, a new technique for dealing with the foibles of humanity; she simply imagined that all people were beavers, and she found it, thus, easier to like them. When she was in a supermarket, for example, surrounded by crowds of distracted shoppers, she visualized them all as huge beavers, their flat tails held high in the air. They were pushing their carts, their beaver feet slapping; they were reading the labels on cans. They were clacking their teeth as they got their totals and reluctantly wrote out their checks. Or if she passed the Pond when teenagers were swimming, as the hot days of summer came on, she saw them simply as happy beavers sunning and doing cannonballs into the air. So here were two beavers leaving flowers on a mound, and some sticks, with pointy chewed ends; and here was the police beaver, switching his tail like a billy club, and forcing them to cease and desist. Oh, she was a witch, all right, she'd always been a witch. She could turn people into beavers with a wink.

Ryland was contentedly at work in his store, only rarely now feeling gypped. When he did, it was generally because it had once again occurred to him how unfair it was that Maggie, just because she was a woman, got to have babies right in her stomach while all *he* got there was a stomachache. But most of the time he was pretty busy, too busy to dwell on inequalities; there was so much to do before the baby was born that he didn't know whether he could manage it. In the first place, he wanted to win his custody suit by the time that Clayton's sibling came along so that Clayton could be there right from the start, sharing in the joy of it all. He had, tentatively, broached the idea to Maggie of allowing Clayton to be present at the birth, but Maggie had snarled at him, "Are you crazy? *I* don't plan to be there myself!" Well, she was still crabby, he understood that; in a month or so he'd approach her again. He had such a vision, Peale and Bailey, too. The whole family, standing around and watching the miracle. It was such an exciting concept that he wondered why, the first time, he had simply stayed out in the hall, and then had seen the afterbirth before he'd even seen the baby.

Ryland didn't much like Saguanay's Egyptian tomb atmosphere now, and he was working on ideas to change it; one day he thought of the concept of Living Furniture Displays, people *using* furniture, running around and laughing. But while this was, as far as it went, a perfectly good idea, who would the people be? Felicity had no homeless. And actors would defeat the whole point. For the time, the idea stayed on the back burner while Ryland concentrated on other things. One of those things was avoiding Mrs. Wickenden, to whom he had given his Tree of Life rug. He had found, after her collapse on it, that just looking at it gave him a pain in his heart, but now, unfortunately, she dropped by all the time to thank him again for the gift.

It was with pleasure that Ryland had returned to a low-grade hypochrondria, although Ada was keeping him very healthy. He had toyed for a while with the idea of mental illness—it seemed natural, as he was marrying a psychologist—but that, too, Maggie had quickly moved to squash, and that, too, he thought, could wait. So, much of the time he researched baby furniture while he pretended to be working for the store. Baby furniture was more complicated than you'd think—it offered a great many options. Here was a cradle that could turn into a carriage, which in turn could be made into a stroller—why, furniture these days was becoming like life itself, malleable and subject to improvement.

Several weeks later, as the synapses of her brain misfired, Molly had her first major seizure; for some time now she had had a small brain tumor, which was rapidly growing larger. One day when Ryland was away at work, and she was lying in the sun of the back yard, feeling the breeze on her face and the warmth of her fur and dreaming of a fountain of water riffling, she suddenly grew rigid and started shaking all over. Even the muscles around her eyelids were convulsed. She drew her legs up to her chest in absolute consternation, and opened her mouth as wide as the bone would go—she let foam coat her tongue and her muzzle as well, and she lay as still as she could. From the inside, it felt as if her house and yard had vanished, and she was slipping on a tiny raft toward the sea. The raft was too small, and there was water all around her, and the motion felt exactly as if she were falling. Still, for all the danger, she felt somehow as if she were returning to a place from which she had come, long ago. Then the raft she was riding on stopped and moved to shore, and she looked once again at a familiar world.

After the seizure, she felt totally exhausted, as if she'd been running for fourteen years, and she wandered around the yard, her legs sometimes giving way under her, and tremors running through her still, like aftershocks. She wanted to be with Ryland, who she finally believed loved her, and she wanted something else, but she couldn't remember what it was. Was there a thunderstorm coming? Was that thunder charging the air? She panted and looked up, her eyes oddly bright. She'd always tried to be a good dog. She wanted to do the right thing—it was so worrisome not to know just what that was.

Chance adored Bailey, who she felt she had always known and who seemed, in fact, like an extension of herself. It was hard to remember that not long before, she had lived with a woman who had rarely left her house, and Chance had been required to sit mostly on this woman's lap, which she had done with good nature, though it got dull. When the woman had died, her son had scooped Chance from her basket, had driven her to another town, and had dumped her abruptly on the street, and while this had surprised her at the time, now she was glad it had happened, since it had turned out there was lots to life besides lap-sits. There was tearing around like a streak of lightning, making neat figure eights with your body, until your feet almost singed the earth and your wet nose made the air ring; there was picking up wood that was heavier than you were and transporting it to some other place. There was digging bad animals like moles from the earth and then whipping them in your mouth till they went limp; there was catching bees on pleasant afternoons and laying their furry bodies at your feet. Oh, now that Chance was free to roam, she discovered how much she liked to *do* things—she felt so productive, ripping covers from books, chewing holes in pieces of cloth. Yes, it was important to have work in your life, and not to live simply in leisure.

Of course, she still loved to sit upon humans, whom she thought of as personal role models. They had even more activities than she had herself, and you had to admire them for that. And she still liked their smell, and cuddling in their armpits, from which vantage point you could stare into their eyes. She found human eyes curious, very determined sometimes, but sometimes irresolute. In that last, they were different from her own.

And Boonskie continued to love the earth, and to live on it with great zest; he chased it and he caught it, he worried it and he lost it, and when he wasn't actually playing with it, it was still nice to know it was there. He was sometimes frightened and sometimes bold, he sometimes liked to be told what to do—but more often he preferred to figure things out all by himself, and not come, for a while, when he was called. In general, he suspected that he was the purpose of life, and that all things were just other parts of him, but occasionally he wondered whether there was something he should do, whether he should, as other dogs did, work. Outside this concern, however, everything was marvelous, the sights and the smells and his friends—oh, he had the occasional itch, and once in a while bad dreams, but mostly, each day was very satisfying. Sleeping felt snuggly, and waking up was exciting, and food, for the most part, made him drool. He was trying to learn English, also, so that he could share his feelings with people—already he could say more words than any other dog he knew. His vowels were excellent. It was the consonants that were difficult, and that made his remarks, so far, a little blurred. But he was going to keep trying—it was just a matter of time. Nothing else had proved insurmountable yet.

When his children were born, and Boonskie finally got in to see them, he was perfectly entranced by their smell and their taste. He would lie nearly still for hours while they sat on him and chewed his ears, and attacked his rump with their razorlike teeth until he knew for sure it was there. Then he could roll them over with one enormous paw and clean their bellies from their genitals to their chins while they wiggled and squirmed ecstatically beneath him, wiping the ground with their still-little tails. He liked to sleep with Sam, the puppies nestled around them, their snouts so soft and blunt; oh, this was the life, the only life, and he'd live it forever and ever. But then one day Ryland and Maggie took him for a car ride, with his biggest and best pup beside him, and he saw for the first time that the world was even larger and existence even more wondrous than he had known. The sun rode on the fields of winter wheat, the day lilies trumpeted on their stalks, small rivers and streams dashed, sniffing, through gullies, and the finches were like flashes of light. And Boonskie, who thought of himself as a person, and didn't understand the concept of dog, for a moment, just a moment, felt the awesome dimensions of the universe and held his breath, like a secret, in his mouth.

# ACKNOWLEDGMENTS

I owe a large debt to Starhawk's book *The Spiral Dance: A Rebirth of the Ancient Religion of the Great Goddess* (Harper and Row, 1979) for the information about witchcraft—its history and its contemporary expression—that is integrated into this novel. There are direct quotes from *The Spiral Dance* (the book Bailey is studying) on pages 13–14, 23, and 231, and general information from it incorporated into pages 89–93 and 162–163. In addition, many of the spells and rituals described prior to Chapter 30 were inspired by *The Spiral Dance*. I recommend the book to anyone interested in the subject of neo-paganism.

I would like to thank Jonathan Schell for writing *The Fate of the Earth*, which forced me to understand that it is not just the future of the human species that is at stake in the nuclear arms threat, but the future of all species—the sea otter, the barn swallow, the moose, the wolf, the humpback whale, the horse, the hound—and the British producers of the movie *Threads* for having the courage to trace a postwar world to its logical, imaginable conclusion.

To Tom Lee, a deputy sheriff for the Hendrix County Sheriff's Department, my thanks for his lucid explanations about sheriffing in Indiana. Any errors, of course, are mine.

I am grateful to William Plater and to the English Department of Indiana University/Purdue University of Indianapolis for giving me a teaching schedule that allows me the time to write, and for supporting this book, in particular, with two summer research grants.

I want to take this opportunity to thank, as well, Jean Naggar,

ACKNOWLEDGMENTS

not only for her work in relation to this novel, but for the faith and enthusiasm that she has, for nine years, consistently shown me.

My abiding thanks to my maternal grandmother, Cunci—Johanna Swoboda—who was born in Hungary in 1882 and who died in America in 1978. Not only was she the model for Ada in this book; she continues to be a model to me when other such models are lacking.

And finally, to my husband, Steven Bauer, my thanks for everything—for the patience with which he has listened to me complain, for the numerous good ideas that he gave me, freely, and that have been incorporated into this book, for the tangential stuff of life that he has taken off my hands since we have been together, for his expertise and care as an editor and critic, and, most of all, for the happiness he has brought me—which is, in the end, what truly made this book possible.

# ABOUT THE AUTHOR

Elizabeth Arthur was born in New York City, grew up in New England, and has lived in Wyoming and western Canada. She was educated at the University of Michigan and at the University of Victoria, British Columbia; her first book, *Island Sojourn*, was a memoir of her years in the Canadian wilderness. She is the author of three novels, *Binding Spell*, *Beyond the Mountain*, and *Bad Guys*; her nonfiction articles have been published in *Outside*, *Backpacker*, and *The New York Times*. The recipient of fellowships from the Vermont Council on the Arts and the National Endowment for the Arts, Ms. Arthur now lives with her husband and their dogs in a farmhouse in rural Indiana. She is currently working on a fifth book.